If
You
Follow
Me

HARPER PERENNIAL

NEW YORK • LONDON • TORONTO • SYDNEY • NEW DELHI • AUCKLAND

If You Follow Me

A Novel

Malena Watrous

HARPER ● PERENNIAL

HarperCollins books may be purchased for educational, business, or sales promotional use. For information, please write: Special Markets Department, Harper-Collins Publishers, 10 East 53rd Street, New York, NY 10022.

FIRST EDITION

Designed by Betty Lew

Library of Congress Cataloging-in-Publication data is available upon request.

ISBN 978-0-06-173285-0

10 11 12 13 14   OV/RRD   10 9 8 7 6 5 4 3 2 1

For my parents

PART I

Gomi

AUTUMN

Deep Autumn—
my neighbor,
how does he live, I wonder?

—BASHO

CHAPTER ONE

semai: (ADJ.) *narrow; confined; small*

Dear Miss Marina how are you? I'm fine thank you. A reason for this letter is: recently you attempt to throw away battery and jar and some kind of mushroom spaghetti and so forth, all together in one bin. Please don't try "it wasn't me." We Japanese seldom eat Gorgonzola cheese!

Now I prepare this sheet so you could learn target Japanese words and gomi law in one simple occasion. I hope it's so convenient for you. It's kind of so rude if you "can't remember" about gomi law. Your neighbors feel some stress about you, and they must be so busy. They can't talk to you every time you make a gomi mistake. I think they want to know you so much. First learn gomi law, second Japanese language, and third you can enjoy international friendship. This is like holding hands across a sea!

Let's begin with gomi law for Monday. Getsu-yobi means Monday in English. Kanji for Getsu comes from the moon. On a moon-day, you can throw soft plastic bottles, for example from Evian water, in blue bin by stone temple. Please save hard plastic bottle tops. On second and fourth Monday of a month, you can throw clear glass bottles in orange bin by #71 bus stop. But not bottle tops! You should take all bottle tops, together with brown or green glass bottles (for example from French wine you enjoy often), to red bin outside Caves de la Matsumoto sake store. Before you throw a bottle, please clean (very clean!) and remove paper from outside. You should save this paper for Tuesday's burnable collection, to put in a bin by Mister Donuts. I think you eat a donuts every day. Maybe you know Mister Donuts location well.

Please share this letter with your special friend. Your neighbor, Mister Ogawa, reports that she became angry when he tried so gently to explain gomi rules. "Kowai," he say. He feels frighten. He is very old man. He only wants to help two young ladies sharing traditional Japanese house. You know some saying: when in Rome, please become Roman? When in Japan, please obey gomi law.

That's all for now.

See you,
Hiroshi Miyoshi

My supervisor gives me the first letter on a Monday afternoon in late November.

I am sitting at my steel desk in the buzzing, empty faculty room, reading a novel I should hate more than I do as I wait for the dismissal bell to ring. Since coming to rural Japan, I read only the books that my mom sends in her care packages, mostly comedies of manners. These novels are formulaic, but at least I understand them. People play by and break the rules of love and social conduct, and the right twosomes always find each other at the very end. At least I know when to cringe and when to cheer, who to be charmed by and who to be wary of. There are rules here too, governing my days and shaping my weeks, but four months into a one-year teaching contract, I still don't have them down.

As the after-school cleaning music starts to play—a Muzak rendition of "Whistle While You Work"— Miyoshi-sensei enters the faculty room, shuffling in flan-colored plastic slippers with the high school logo calligraphed on each toe. They make his feet look like hooves. As he nears my desk, rubbing a palm over his blow-dried hair, I hide my novel in the pleats of my skirt. "Mari-chan," he says, and the female diminutive, *chan*, lets me know that I'm about to be reprimanded for something. "Would you care for a cuppa'?"

The idiom is one he learned from Joe Pope, the British expat who taught English here until I took his place last August. Before his teaching contract expired, Joe was plucked off the streets of Kanazawa City by a scout from the *gaijin* modeling agency with the unfortunate name, "Creamy Talent," which places foreigners in local print and TV ads. But he still makes the two-hour drive up to Shika every few weeks to join our teaching team, strumming his guitar and leading sing-alongs to which only Miyoshi-sensei sings along. Rumor has it that my supervisor pays for Joe's visits out of his own pocket, and I believe it. On my first day here, Miyoshi-sensei informed me that English is only his number two hobby, his number one being karaoke. Usually, when he asks me to join him in a "cuppa'," he has a new English CD and wants help translating the lyrics. But today he has no CD.

"I'd love a cuppa'," I say, waiting for him to leave so I can stash my novel in the drawer. Instead he leans over my shoulder, studying the photo trapped under my clear plastic desk cover.

"Miss Marina's friend is very . . . *hansamu*," he says.

"Thank you," I say, wondering if the word "handsome" often applies to women here. With her short hair and lanky frame, Carolyn sometimes used to pass for a boy, and you can't see her face very well in this picture, which was taken at the Halloween party we threw at Shika's recreation center. Carolyn cut ribs, pelvises, and femurs from white contact paper and we stuck them to black turtlenecks and jeans, smearing black shoe polish in the hollows of our eyes, across our cheekbones and lips. We tried explaining to the quivering senior citizens that Halloween costumes are *supposed* to be scary, but they preferred Joe's Elvis costume, touching his sparkly gold jumpsuit as if it were something truly precious.

"Do you enjoy putting on a costume?" Miyoshi-sensei asks me.

"Yes," I say cautiously. "Sometimes."

"I thought so," he says. "Me too."

I follow him to the *soshiaru kona* or "social corner" at the back of the faculty room, where he pumps green tea from an electric carafe into two cups. As we sit side by side on the couch, my body sinks lower than his on the cushions. Our hips touch briefly and he pulls away, crossing his legs. He pulls a pack of Mild Seven menthols from his jacket pocket, clamps a cigarette between his lips, and lights it with his Zippo, the silver engraved with his favorite song title: "Imagine." Usually he offers me a smoke, but today he puts the pack back into his pocket.

"It's good you stopped smoking," he says, tapping his ash in an abalone shell piled with butts. "Woman teachers who smoke set a bad example, *ne?*" I'm about to point out that male teachers who smoke set an equally bad example when it occurs to me that I never told him I was trying to quit. I haven't even told Carolyn, in case I fail again. "Recently," he says, "your neighbor Ogawa-san discovered a box of Nicorette chewing gum in soft plastics recycling bin. Product description is in English. Also, we don't have this gum in Japan. So we know it must be yours." He reaches into his pocket and pulls out a folded piece of paper. The first thing I notice is that the page is covered in a strange cursive; faint swashes of lead joining not just the letters, but also the words. He tells me to study it well, then ask him any questions afterward.

I chew my lower lip as I read his letter twice, just to delay looking up. When I do, he is also biting his lip. His right eye flickers, the way it does whenever he's embarrassed and trying not to show it. He dislikes confrontation, and I feel worse for putting him in this position than I do for having thrown a box in the wrong garbage can.

"*Gomen nasai*," I say: forgive me. "*Shitsureishimashita*." This translates literally: I have committed a rude. After four months in Japan, I'm fluent only in apologies.

"*Daijoubu*," he says. "It's okay. I know there are so many *gomi* rules here in Shika. And you can't read the Japanese signs above the bins. So I promised Ogawa-san that I would teach you better. After you read the rules in English, then you couldn't make any more huge mistakes, *ne*?"

"Miyoshi-sensei, I am sorry to cause so much work for you," I say, slipping into Japlish like I do whenever I'm in trouble. "It's true, Shika's *gomi* system is so complicated. I have tried to follow the rules but . . . so difficult. In America, we can throw away all together. Thank you for your help. From now on I will do better for you."

When I first arrived here, Miyoshi-sensei told me that I needed to space my words more clearly, so that the students at this vocational high school would stand a chance of understanding my English. "Americans talk like cats," he complained. "All sounds blend together. Mrowmrowmrow." Now I pronounce English, "En-gu-ree-shu." I drop contractions and speak like a record played at half its speed. By making myself as easy as possible to understand, I try to compensate for reading novels when I should be planning lessons, sneaking out of school early, and throwing unsorted garbage in the wrong bins. But the senior citizens who police our neighborhood garbage cans understand neither my glacial English, nor my stammering Japanese. They are not charmed into overlooking my negligence. Neither is Carolyn, who teaches at a rival vocational high school in Hakui, ten kilometers south of Shika. She gets up before me to ride the bus to work, so she is the one who usually answers the door when Mr. Ogawa turns up at dawn to return our garbage while the rest of the neighbors gather round to watch.

"Mari-chan," Miyoshi-sensei says, "I think for you, Japan must be so . . . " His eye twitches as he searches for a word. "*Semai*. Can you catch my meaning?"

"Crowded?" I guess.

"Nooo . . . Maybe yes, crowded, but also . . . *semai*. You know what I mean?"

"Narrow?"

"Yes! So narrow." He claps my shoulder with the hand that holds his cigarette. Ash snows on my legs, but in his excitement over finding the right word, he doesn't notice. Speaking in English animates Miyoshi-sensei. In English he talks loudly, emphatically, coming up with inventive, spot-on similes as strange as they are apt. At thirty-two, Miyoshi-sensei is ten years older than me, but he is the youngest Japanese teacher at this school and the only one who doesn't yet have a family of his own. He is also the only son of the mayor of Shika. He alone has the time and money to spend his vacations abroad, in New York, Los Angeles, and San Francisco. On these trips, he likes to slip into high schools, snapping pictures to shock his students back here. His desk is barricaded by a row of photo albums, filled with shots of cafeteria lunch trays, kids framed by metal detectors, and Dumpsters spewing trash. Miyoshi-sensei likes me, but he also likes to be an expert, especially on the paradoxes of the West. My presence makes this an interesting challenge.

He stuffs the cigarette into the abalone shell, where a finger of smoke rises from the heap. It looks like a tiny volcano about to blow. I wish I could pluck it out and take a drag. Instead, I thank him again for his help.

"It's okay," he replies. "You are my job. If you need help with something else, please ask me."

"Actually, we do need help getting rid of something," I say. "Our refrigerator is broken. Joe offered to help us drive it to the dump, but we don't know where the dump is."

"What is 'dump' meaning?" he says.

"The place where you take big trash," I begin. "Where you throw away furniture, cars, large appliances, that kind of thing."

"Oh no," he says, shaking his head vigorously. "Japan is much too *semai* for some kind of dump system. You had better call refrigerator manufacturer, to come to your home and collect broken one from you."

"The refrigerator is an Amana," I tell him. "I think the missionaries who lived in the house before us had it shipped from Iowa."

"Ah," he says. "Probably Iowa manufacturer could not come to your home."

"Probably not," I agree.

"I have one unusual idea," he says. "How about using refrigerator for another purpose, for example to hold all your books or souvenir?"

"That's an interesting suggestion," I say, "but the fridge is huge and it smells bad and we'd really like to throw it away and get a new one."

"You had better not attempt to throw away some huge and smelly refrigerator," he says, clapping his knees and standing up. "Please obey *gomi* law!" He taps his index finger against the page of *gomi* instructions before walking away. "Ask before you throw!"

To: Miss Marina. How goeth thy day? Mine sucketh royally. In front of our first period class, my supe said, "Kyaroryn becomes so womanly

lately in pretty dress and longer hairs. Maybe she has some secret new
boyfriend, don't you agree?" The drowsy studentia roused themselves
to vote unanimously that yes, I indeed possess a shi-ko-re-tto ra-ba,
hidden in the depths of my closet. If they only knew what's really in
there! Then, during lunch, my supe announced that I was showing
great strides wielding my chopsticks. She said, "Don't use chopsticks
<u>too</u> well. If you eat too much, your bosom will become so big you
couldn't see your feet anymore."

  AVESAY EMAY!

  Plz pick me up in front of school asap. I'll be waiting outside.

  XOXO C.

As paper inches from the fax machine on the vice-principal's
desk, I recognize the handwriting instantly. As always, Carolyn wrote
in code to frustrate roving eyes. Whenever she faxes me at work, I
imagine her sitting in a faculty room just like this one, having a day
almost identical to mine, and I wonder if she might be feeling the
exact same way as me.

I wait until Miyoshi-sensei has gone to the bathroom before leaving school ten minutes early. The wind whips a dust of new snowflakes across the driveway and the air feels tight with cold. Ever since
the start of November, it has been snowing on and off. The cherry
trees that line the school driveway are bald, each branch encased in
a dripping sleeve of ice. But even though it was freezing this morning, I had to walk to work instead of driving, so that Miyoshi-sensei
wouldn't see the car he helped me buy three months ago.

"Temporary people probably shouldn't drive," he warned me at
the used-car dealership, having accompanied me there with reluctance to translate the epic sheaf of paperwork. "The rules here are
different, the roads are *semai*, and how could you communicate in
case of accident?" I assured him that I was a good driver, and that

since the only vehicle I could afford was so small—a Honda Today! with a two-cylinder engine and Big Wheel-sized tires—Shika's narrow roads wouldn't be a problem. This did not turn out to be true. A week after buying the car, I scraped the left side against a telephone pole, knocking off the handle and side-view mirror. A month later I skidded on an ice patch, crashing the other side against the Dumpster in front of Mister Donuts. Now the car looks like it was squeezed by a giant pair of tongs. Neither door opens anymore, and we have to leave both windows down at all times, so we can crawl in and out like thieves.

The upholstery is dusted with snow, which soaks through my tights and sears the backs of my legs. The heater activates the smell of mildew and cat piss. Keeping both windows down, I drive to the end of our block, turning onto Shika's commercial strip. I pass a shop with a window display of dusty trophies, sporting goods, and knitting supplies, a store selling tofu in buckets of cloudy water and mountain yams still packed in dirt, a police station that doubles as a post office, and a liquor store with a wall of bootleg videos and a cooler of imported cheese. This is downtown Shika, the town where the Japanese Ministry of Education placed us, despite our request to live in a major Japanese city.

I turn onto the coastal highway, a narrow ribbon of a road at the edge of the cliffs, high above the Sea of Japan, which stretches blue as a bruise all the way to Korea. Steering with my knees, I open the glove compartment and grope among the crumpled rice ball wrappers for the pack of cigarettes I forgot to throw away when I decided to quit. I light one and stick my head out the window to exhale. Harvested rice fields stretch to the bottoms of distant hills, and water surrounds the cropped brown stalks, reflecting the silver-bellied clouds. When the wind blows, the earth shimmers. Every quarter mile or so, a blocky apartment building sprouts from these rice fields, deserted-looking except for the occasional futon flung over a chipping red fire escape. "Always air your futons," Miyoshi-sensei told me when we got here, "so your neighbors will see you are clean."

Carolyn is standing on the curb in front of Hakui High School, a three-story beige stucco edifice that looks like a carbon copy of Shika High School, down to the round analog clock set in the second story grille. She's shivering in a pink miniskirt, which she borrowed from me, a black cardigan, green argyle knee socks, and her ancient army boots. Her hair is growing out from its old buzz cut, the cherry dye faded to a more conservative auburn, and she looks almost girly. She glances around before lifting one leg into the passenger-side window and then the other, arching her back and lowering herself onto the seat like someone doing the limbo. White circles of chalk dust her breasts, where she must have rubbed against the blackboard while teaching. I reach out to brush off the front of her sweater, and she seizes my fingers as a pair of high school girls skip in front of our car, pausing to wave and yell, "Bye-bye Miss Kyarorin!"

"Be careful," she says.

"Sorry," I say, squeezing her knee instead.

"It reeks of cigarettes in here," she says as she opens the glove compartment and fishes out the pack. Carolyn claims to hate everything about smoking—the smell, the taste, the look she describes as my "craving face." She claims never to have been addicted to anything, only to smoke the occasional cigarette to make me feel guilty for corrupting her, but I think she wants a vice of her own, something to tether her. The matchbook is limp and she tears through a half-dozen matches before I take the cigarette and light it for her. She smokes like a kid: fingers stiff, cigarette close to her palm, lips pursed. I ask how her day was and she says that it was crappy.

"Didn't you read my fax? My supervisor kept insisting that I have a secret lover."

"Do you think she knows about us?" My pulse jump-starts at the thought.

"She has no clue. She thinks I'm dating Joe."

"Joe Pope?" I laugh. "What gave her that idea?"

"I don't know," she shrugs. "Because we're both foreign, I guess. I couldn't possibly be with a Japanese guy, let alone another woman."

"Maybe you were right about being open with people from the start," I say. "They would've had to deal with it. Now it seems too late to tell them, like they'll think we were lying to them or something."

"We were," she says. "We are."

Carolyn came out in high school. She has been with a thirty-year-old biker chick, a homeless busker, a divorced lawyer with two kids. We met in college, where we lived in the same dorm, our rooms stacked one over the other, and I sometimes think our relationship bored her in its simplicity. We had to make our own complications.

"I'm actually glad no one knows," she says, throwing her cigarette out the window.

"You are?" I say. This is a first. "Why?"

"It's been hard enough. I don't want to stand out more than we already do." She pulls off her boots, plants her heels on the edge of her seat and wraps her arms around her knees, looking out at the rice fields. I look out my own window, at the ocean pounding the cliffs. There is no guardrail here. It would be so easy to miss a turn, tumble over the rocks and into the water below. All you'd have to do is close your eyes. I don't want to think these thoughts. These are not my thoughts. But I can't help but see the world as full of traps. Tempting, if you lean that way.

"Just look at this place." Carolyn shudders as I park in front of our house. A slumped and rusting storage area made of corrugated aluminum surrounds it, blocking all of the windows on the ground floor. This storage area is filled with the possessions left behind by decades of tenants, in boxes stacked from floor to ceiling. When she's bored, Carolyn likes to go shopping in storage. She has rescued a poster of the human skeleton with every bone labeled in Japanese, a set of lacquered nesting bowls, and two china bulldogs joined at the throat by a chain. She has a great eye for finding treasures in trash. She always gets to these things first, and then I wonder why I didn't notice them.

The cat climbs out of the drainage ditch, greeting us with a meow that sounds like a newborn baby's cry. Carolyn scoops her up, burying her face in the scruff of her neck. From the beginning, loyalties have been clear. We both love Amana but she belongs to Carolyn, who knows just how to pet her, how to play with her, when to pick her up, and when to leave her alone. She honors her feline whims and is rewarded with canine loyalty. Amana follows us whenever we go on walks, running in the bushes and then stalling until we catch up. Once we came out of the supermarket and found her waiting in the basket of a stranger's bicycle. She likes to sleep right in between us, the middle spoon.

"The *gomi* froze," Carolyn says, as she sets the cat down and peers into the garbage can in front of our house. Sure enough, water has dripped from the roof and filled the can, melted and frozen solid, forming a giant cube of ice sealing in the garbage. She pushes the can onto its side and the cube slides heavily to the pavement. The setting sun, faint as a headlight pushing through fog, illuminates the cylinder of yellow-veined ice. Like scraps of insects trapped in amber, I see a wine bottle, a milk carton, kibble, and cigarette butts.

"It's a trashsicle," I say.

"An unsorted trashsicle," she says, looking at me from beneath one arched brow.

"At least Ogawa-san won't be able to get at it with his tongs," I point out.

"We can't let him see it," she says, looking around almost furtively. "Bring it inside and put it in the bathtub. After it thaws, you can sort through the melted trash."

"Why is this my job?" I ask. "We both ate that stuff."

"But you didn't sort the trash before you threw it away. You never sort the trash." She's right. She bought a special sectioned garbage can, but it's hard to remember what goes in what compartment. There are so many rules to keep straight. When I make this argument, she rolls her eyes and says, "It's really not that hard. You just have to listen."

"I listen," I protest.

"Well we wouldn't be stuck in this house, dealing with the *gomi* police every day, if you'd listened to me in the first place."

I can't argue with that.

gomi: (N.) *garbage; trash; waste*

The original *gomi* sin was not my fault.

Four months ago, we arrived in Shika on a hot and moonless night, after having spent five days at a training seminar in Tokyo with three thousand other English teachers on their way to every corner of Japan. We traveled twelve hours by bus from Tokyo to Kanazawa, then two hours by train to Hakui, then completed the final leg of the journey by taxi. By the time the white-gloved driver reached our new address, the only light came from his headlights, which shone off the aluminum siding, two yellow tunnels attracting a flurry of insects. The back doors of the cab opened automatically. The driver handed us our luggage, bowed and sped off. In the darkness, I fumbled to find the key that Miyoshi-sensei had sent to New York, along with a letter apologizing for the fact that his vacation coincided with our arrival, so he couldn't come to the station to meet us. I'd barely opened the door when the stench hit us, a physical blow.

"Something must have died in there," Carolyn said, gagging as she backed away.

She wasn't that far off.

The refrigerator loomed inside the *genkan*, the Japanese entryway traditionally reserved for taking off shoes, putting on slippers, and displaying a floral arrangement. It was a hulking vintage Amana with rounded corners and a cherry red handle, the enamel yellowing like old teeth and splotched with the pale ghosts of lost alphabet magnets, the words "jesussaves" arced at eye level. Pinned behind one remaining magnet was a receipt from a slaughterhouse in Nebraska. The previous tenants, a pair of Mennonite missionaries, had ordered half a cow to be shipped on dry ice to Japan. But in the month of July that elapsed between their departure and our arrival, the house electricity was cut. The stench of rotten meat had seeped out of the refrigerator and into the walls, which are made of a plaster that holds odor like an old sponge. We pinched our noses, but the smell was so foul that we could taste it.

"I told you we should've seen the house before signing a lease," Carolyn said, pressing her face to the inside of her elbow. "I don't know why you were in such a big fucking hurry." It didn't seem like the moment to admit the truth. In Miyoshi-sensei's welcome letter, he'd told me that aside from this house, "a traditional Japanese house built in the Showa period," the only local apartments for rent were six tatami mat studios, "too small for two Americans to share." Carolyn had brought up the idea of renting separate apartments of our own. She thought that living together for the first time in Japan could put too much pressure on our relationship, that we risked becoming overly dependent on each other. But I persuaded her that we shouldn't pass up the chance to live in a traditional Japanese house. I also convinced her to use the tips she'd saved waiting tables all year to cover the "key money," six months' rent up front, which was nonrefundable.

"I'm sure the rest of the house is nice," I said, crossing my fingers that this was true.

To get past the fridge, we had to turn sideways and squeeze

through the gap between the wall, which crumbled at the slightest contact, bits of plaster and twigs falling to the Smurf-blue carpet. A narrow hallway led to a room dwarfed by a ripped vinyl couch the color of root beer, which faced a big TV propped on a sagging cardboard box. In the bathroom, the toilet was a porcelain-lined hole set right into the floor. This "Japanese drop toilet" was something else Miyoshi-sensei had warned me of in his letter, something else I'd failed to mention to Carolyn, since it didn't sound like a selling point.

The kitchen at the back of the house was smaller than an airplane galley, smaller than the refrigerator itself. It had no oven, just a single electric burner lined with scorched aluminum foil. Carolyn loves to cook and had been looking forward to having her first real kitchen. Her face was blotchy, she kept retching, and I felt terribly guilty.

"I'm so sorry, Caro," I said. "It's not what I pictured either."

"It's just so dark and seedy," she said. "It feels like an abandoned storage unit."

"We can make it better," I said. "You're good at that." It was true. Her dorm room had been identical to mine, a shoebox with institutional furniture and zero charm. But with just a few yards of fabric, some plants and random thrift store finds, she had turned it into an oasis of calm. "But the smell . . . " She clapped her hand over her mouth and I was afraid she might throw up. Her nose is sharper than mine, and I was gagging too. The house smelled like death. I said that it would fade as soon as we took out the trash and she agreed, visibly steeling herself.

Carolyn is great in a crisis. She doesn't shirk from a mess, just cleans it up. Luckily, the cupboard under the sink was stocked with garbage bags and cleaning supplies. She had the good idea to smear toothpaste mustaches across our upper lips, and we laughed at how ridiculous we looked as we set to work. Into a trash bag I dumped parcels labeled "ribs," and "ground round," and a disgustingly soft triangle marked "heart," trying not to visualize its sloshing contents. She attacked the inside of the freezer with bleach while I carried the bag of trash down the street, holding it away from my body. I hoped that once the smell did fade, the episode would become a funny anecdote. I hoped we could still make a fresh start on our new life together.

When I got back, Carolyn was seated on the floor in the entry-way, hunched forward, her back to the fridge and her hair falling in her eyes. I heard a rumble and at first I thought she was crying, but when she straightened I saw that there was a cat curled up on her lap. She told me the cat had been hiding behind the Amana, that she'd lured her out with a can of tuna she found in the cupboard. "Poor kitty," she said. "Did they just abandon you here? You must be starving!" Someone had obviously been feeding her. She had the dark mask of a Siamese but the body of an overweight sheep, a belly that bulged over spindly legs that ended in ridiculously tiny paws. She looked like one of those old claw-foot bathtubs. Her stomach hit the stairs as she climbed them, leading us to the second floor room with its pitched roof, tomato red walls, silk-edged tatami mats, and large window—the only one in the whole house with a view.

"This is more like what I thought a traditional Japanese house would look like," Carolyn said, sounding as relieved as I felt. She opened the window while I found two futons folded in a cupboard and unfurled them on the tatami. Too tired to undress, we lay side by side, listening to the cicadas chirp. They all kept the same rhythmic beat, and the sound reminded me of a car alarm. If I closed my eyes, I might have still been in New York.

The stench of rotten beef wasn't gone, but it had faded enough that I could smell other things: the slightly fishy scent of the woven straw mats, the powdery old cotton of the futons, the bleach on

Carolyn's hands, and the tang of sweat dried on her skin. We were alone for the first time in our new bedroom, but we didn't touch. In her stiffness and silence I read a copy of my nervousness. It was as if we'd gotten ourselves this far on a dare and now there was no turning back. Not that I wanted to. I just didn't know what came next. Then the cat crawled into the gap between our bodies. She stretched long, rolled onto her back, and started to purr like a diesel engine. Carolyn suggested that we call her Amana, after the refrigerator she'd been hiding behind. "Amana," I repeated, and the cat actually meowed. She acted like she knew us already, like she'd been waiting for us to come home and there we were.

The next morning, at dawn, I awoke to *The Four Seasons.* Staticky and loud, the music seemed to come from all sides, as if everyone in the neighborhood had simultaneously turned their radios to the same classical station. I joined Carolyn at the window, taking in my first daylit glimpse of Shika. The road was so narrow that I could have reached out and grabbed the boughs of the pine tree across the street. Planted in front of every house were telephone poles, topped with large speakers blasting Vivaldi.

"What is this?" I said groggily, "some evil alarm clock?"

"I've been up for ages," Carolyn said. "I can't believe you slept through it."

"Through what?"

"The smell," she said, making a face. "I kept waking up gagging."

"Poor Caro." Now that I was awake I could smell it too, the sweet and putrid smell of decay. The circles under her eyes looked like thumbprints. She asked how far away the trash can was where I'd thrown the beef away and I pointed to the end of the block, where concrete stairs led to a grassy path bordering a river that looked as green as Scope mouthwash. On the riverbank, a group of senior citizens was performing calisthenics to the sounds of Vivaldi. Following the lead of a lean, gray-haired man in a red jumpsuit, they all rose on their toes and then crouched down again, swinging their arms in unison. Carolyn said that since she couldn't sleep, she wanted to ask the neighbors if she could join them, but she didn't want to impose herself.

"I'm sure they wouldn't mind," I said. "You want me to come with you?"

"That's okay," she said. "I'd be too self-conscious if you were there. Besides, we should really try to make our own friends right away. I don't want people to think we're joined at the hip, just because we're living together. First impressions are so important here. They're almost impossible to undo."

Carolyn, always a perfectionist, was determined to do everything right. For months she'd been studying Japanese, reading up on the culture in every spare moment. When we found out that we'd both been assigned to teach at schools on the Noto Peninsula, a region so remote and conservative that our Japanese teacher in New York likened it to rural Georgia, she was actually excited. As the only foreigners in the area, she said, we wouldn't be able to hide in a *gaijin* enclave. We'd have a rare opportunity to see the real Japan.

Before she left the house, she made me promise not to watch her exercise, saying that she'd be too self-conscious if she knew that I was looking. Carolyn hates to put herself on display, to make a spectacle of herself. But I couldn't resist stealing a peek. She bowed deeply, and our new neighbors stopped in mid-jumping jack to stare back at her. She's not a large person, maybe five foot five, with a delicate bone structure and a small face, yet she suddenly seemed enormous. She was taller than the tallest man in the group, and her cherry-red hair stuck up like a Kewpie doll. She was wearing voluminous baby blue basketball shorts and a pink sports bra under a green tank top, and from a distance the pumpkin-colored freckles on her shoulders and thighs blended together. She looked Technicolor bright compared to the senior citizens in their earth tone tracksuits, as if she'd been painted into a black-and-white picture. They didn't seem to grasp what she was doing there, so to demonstrate she started doing jumping jacks, scissoring the air with her arms, her breasts bouncing. Watching them watch her, I felt embarrassed but also proud. She was so brave. After a moment, the old man who'd been leading the class either got it or gave in. He took over again, bending down to touch his toes, and the other old people smiled when Carolyn followed his example.

As *The Four Seasons* continued to play, I lay back down and thought about the last time I really paid attention to that piece of music. I must have been nine or ten, home alone with a cold, when I found the record in my father's hutch, its jacket printed with Botticelli's *Autumn*. I wasn't allowed to play his records, but I figured that if I was careful and covered my tracks, he'd never know. I'd heard the piece before—it was one of my dad's favorites—but for some reason, on that particular day, it matched my mood perfectly. I turned the stereo up as loud as it could go and bounced the needle back again and again to hear the best parts, twirling around the living room in the hazy golden sunlight, so entranced in my private rapture that I didn't notice my father standing in his hospital scrubs until the record started skipping where I must have scratched it. He didn't say a word. He just walked across the room and picked the record up, cupped in one large hand, and then he sailed it out the apartment window like a Frisbee, where it shattered on the sidewalk below. My mom swept up the shards from the sidewalk when she got home, but for weeks I'd find slivers of vinyl kicked against the curb, like splinters that only gradually work their way to the surface of your skin.

Carolyn returned home sweaty, red-faced, and grinning. She told me that the neighbors had been patient and welcoming, that she felt like she'd already participated in a real Japanese experience. "Participated instead of just observing," she stressed. She was vowing to keep going every morning for the rest of the year when our doorbell rang. There stood the old man who'd taught the class. Still dressed in his red jumpsuit, holding a black plastic bag over one shoulder, he looked like a gaunt and angry Japanese Santa. He used a pair of long tongs to pull the parcels of rotten beef from the garbage bag, stacking them at our doorstep while he lectured us in Japanese, somehow managing to smile as he scolded us.

"I think that means 'today we don't burn,'" Carolyn attempted to translate what he was saying. "Did you throw our trash in his garbage can?"

"I don't think so," I said. "The can was at the end of the block, and it was empty."

"Maybe that should've told you something."

"What?"

"I don't know, but this sucks. We've been here less than twenty-four hours, and already the neighbors hate us."

"Say something in Japanese," I pleaded with her. "Tell him it wasn't our fault."

"I didn't get that far," she hissed.

The old man bowed before retreating to the house across the street. In front of it, an old woman wearing a Hello Kitty apron over purple sweats was feeding the fish in a barrel, reaching into her apron pocket to scatter rice and table scraps into the water. After the door closed behind the old man, she held out her hand and said, "*Chotto machinasai.*" Wait a minute. Then she too disappeared into the same house, returning a moment later with a boy who must have weighed three hundred pounds. His sweatpants hugged his thighs, his stomach hung over his waistband in a broad flap, and the flesh of his face almost swallowed his eyes, only a fingernail paring of black indicating that they were open at all.

"Haruki," the woman said as she lifted the boy's wrist and wagged his hand at us. Carolyn and I waved back and introduced ourselves in rudimentary Japanese, awkwardly trying to explain that we'd just moved from New York to teach English. "*Sensei*," the woman echoed reverentially. She prodded the boy's back, and he crossed the street so slowly it looked like he hoped to get hit by a car midway. When he reached our stoop, he picked up the parcels of rotten beef. "You don't have to do that," I said. "If you could just tell me where to throw it away . . . " But he walked off as I was speaking, vanishing around the corner with our trash.

There were two weeks before school started. Carolyn's new super-visor expected her to come to work every day and sit in the faculty room, just in case any students wanted to stop by to meet her, so I was left on my own to explore Shika. I managed to get lost every time I left our front door. The streets here aren't named and the houses look almost identical, sided in beige or gray plaster with dark wooden support beams, only their roof tiles varying from blue to black to persimmon orange. I dropped things on purpose to mark a trail back home, and just like in the fairy tale, they always vanished before I could retrace my steps.

It was a few days before I managed to find my way down to the sea, even though I could hear the raspy breathing of the surf from almost every part of town. But finally I spotted a vending machine stocked with cigarettes, beer, and cream of corn soup, at the top of a flight of stairs padded with sand. The stairs led down to the beach, where a very long bench stretched on and on like a train. I learned later that this was the second-longest bench in Japan. It had once been the longest, until an even longer bench in Hokkaido was built, and Shika lost its claim to fame.

The beach was empty, but the sand was littered with cans and Styrofoam trays, so it felt deserted, like an off-season fairground. Close to the water, birds jabbed their beaks into the yellow foam, scattering as I approached and huddling in a cluster, each perching on one leg and eyeing me warily. The waves seemed fidgety, indecisive, barely rolling in and out. But the water was a beautiful shade of blue, dark and clear like a bottle. I stripped off my shorts and T-shirt and ran into the water. The ocean stayed shallow for a long time, barely surpassing my knees, until the sand suddenly dropped out from under me. I closed my eyes, plunged under and swam as far as I could, wondering what was down there with me, alert to my intrusion. When I broke the surface, gulping for air, the salt kept me afloat and I lay on my back, drifting for a while.

Three teenaged boys were sitting on the bench when the current bumped me into the sand. They were all smoking and staring straight ahead, watching me with expressions that were almost identical, almost neutral, as if I were some less than interesting TV show. I wanted to hide underwater until they left, but it was ridiculously shallow. The waves kept pushing me into the sand. I yanked on my T-shirt and shorts and then I faced the boys, trying to conceal my embarrassment. "*Ohayogozaimasu*," I managed. Good morning. In Tokyo, we'd learned the importance of proper greetings. The boys didn't answer. Nor did they laugh or jeer, as American teenagers would have. In some ways their silence was more intimidating. Finally, one of them stuck his cigarette in his mouth and mock-saluted me. He had a big, bushy Afro that I assumed was a perm, because it was so tight and perfect, and because his face, while tan, looked characteristically Japanese.

"Good-o morningu, Miss Marina," he said.

"How do you know my name?" I asked, but he didn't answer. He wasn't the first person in town who had greeted me by name. I remembered from Miyoshi-sensei's welcome letter that there was only one high school here. I guessed that I had just met my new students.

But I was wrong. Shika High School is split into two tracks: secretarial and technical, and I was only going to be teaching the secretarial students. While no law segregates these tracks by gender, no girls were enrolled in the technical track, and only one boy—Haruki Ogawa—was in the secretarial course. On my first day, I was surprised to walk into the freshman secretarial class and see him, the one boy in a room full of girls, squeezed into his desk like a snail in its shell.

"Hi," I said, glad to recognize someone. "Haruki, right?"

He flinched at the sound of his name and the girl to his right snickered.

"*Anoko wa dare?*" she said. Who is that?

"*Wakannai yo,*" he mumbled. I don't know.

"I told you my name," I reminded him. "It's—"

"Wait!" Miyoshi-sensei said, ushering me to join him at the front of the classroom. "You shouldn't reveal the answer to the first question on your self-introduction test!"

In his welcome letter, Miyoshi-sensei had told me the date upon which to show up at Shika High School, "only to introduce yourself." So I assumed I'd be meeting my new colleagues and getting a tour of the school and explanation of my duties. On my walk that morning I got lost as usual. "Where is Shika High School?" I asked an old woman pushing a wheelbarrow full of melons, but I couldn't understand her reply. This, I was learning, is the problem with memorizing questions in a new language. No matter how simple the question, there are always more answers than you can know.

By the time I found the school I was dripping with sweat, eager to get my introductions out of the way and return home for a shower and nap. Outside the door stood a slim young man in a well-cut black suit and Converse sneakers. As I neared him, I noticed that his yellow shoelaces matched his yellow tie. His hair was blow-dried back from his face, styled into a kind of pompadour, so that he looked vaguely rockabilly. He had a dimple in his chin, eyes that turned down slightly when he smiled, and a firm handshake.

"I'm Hiro," he introduced himself. "Like superhero, you know? But alas I have no superpower. I am only your supervisor."

"Nice to meet you, Hiro," I said.

"Most people call me Miyoshi-sensei," he said.

I apologized for being late, explaining that I'd gotten lost, and he apologized for having drawn a faulty map. I told him that his map was fine, that I have a rotten sense of direction, and then he apologized for not having been in Shika when I arrived. Just when I thought the volley of apologies would never end, he told me that we should probably go inside, so that I could make my self-introduction test before first period began.

"What self-introduction test?" I asked.

"A test about you," he said. "To make our students listen when you speak."

I told him that I'd rather not test the students on my first day, that I didn't want to make them afraid of me. "This is a vocational school," he said, smiling sadly. "Our students have no fear of teachers. Maybe the only way to make them listen is to give a test." So I made the quiz as easy as possible, with multiple-choice questions and pictures for clues.

The girls in the freshman secretarial class squinted at me and guessed most of the answers correctly. Only Haruki's page remained blank, his UFO-patterned pencil case zipped shut, his hands wadded on his desk. I crouched beside him, wanting to help him as he'd helped us. "You know my name," I reminded him, unzipping his pencil case, "and I told you I moved here from New York." I pulled out a mechanical pencil, clicked out the lead and wedged it between his fingers. When he still didn't budge, I placed my hand on top of his and made him circle the correct answers. His hand was moist and heavy like dough; I wiped my palm on my skirt before returning to the front of the room.

The boy was practically catatonic. Only once in the whole period did I see him move. When I read the correct answers aloud and Miyoshi-sensei told the students to grade themselves, he turned his pencil upside down and erased every mark on the page before drawing a large "0" at the top. Then he resumed the act of sitting as still as a statue. It looked like hard work, curbing his body's every desire to twitch, swivel, and flex. It was difficult to look at. That seemed to be the point.

"What's the matter with Haruki?" I asked Miyoshi-sensei at the end of the day as we shared our first "cuppa'" in the faculty room.

"Matter?" he repeated.

"What's wrong with him?"

"Ah," he paused, "until recently, Ogawa-san was a . . . I don't know how to say in English . . . *hikikomori*? This means hiding in cave. Like a bear in winter?"

"He was hibernating?"

"He was a school refuser."

"A shut-in?" I said, and he nodded. I had heard of such cases in Japan.

"In junior high, some older boys subjected him to *ijime*. Bullying. It's not so unusual. But he could not tolerate. For three years, he refused to leave his room. Naturally, he became kind of fat and nervous."

"Poor kid," I said. "What did he do in his room for three years?"

"I don't know," Miyoshi-sensei said. "I only met him last April, when he joined my homeroom. Usually only girls choose secretarial course. I guess it's his happy place now."

"He seems sort of depressed," I ventured.

"Depressed?" Miyoshi-sensei echoed.

"So sad," I tried. "Upset."

"Ah," he nodded. "Maybe he's upset because he had to throw your *gomi*."

"My what?" I asked.

"Your garbage," he said. "Beef is burnable *gomi*, collected on Tuesdays in your neighborhood."

"That garbage wasn't ours," I protested, glad for the chance to vent at last. "It was there when we moved in."

"Hmm . . . " Miyoshi-sensei turned his lighter around so that sunlight winked off the silver. "Before you arrived, I inspected this house. I even looked inside garbage cans. They were all empty, *ne*?"

"That's because the beef was in the freezer," I explained.

"So why did you throw it away? Don't you like beef?"

"Not really, but that's beside the point. The beef was rotten," I said, increasingly frustrated. "It smelled terrible. We had to throw it away immediately."

"Ah," he said again, "well, in that case, you had better take it to the nuclear power plant, like Haruki did for you. They burn *gomi* every day."

"What nuclear power plant?" I asked, hoping I'd misunderstood.

"Don't you hear the music every morning?" he asked, and I nodded. "In case of emergency evacuation, such a smoothly operating PA system could be quite useful, *ne?*" He opened the bottom drawer of my desk and pulled out a baggie filled with pills, explaining that it was iodine. "Only take in case of radiation sickness," he said. "Don't eat like candy." I asked how far the plant was from our house, wondering why he'd failed to mention it in his welcome letter, which listed the English songs on catalogue at the local karaoke parlor and the flavors of rice balls at the town's two convenience stores. He said, "not far at all," as if this would be reassuring. "Would you like a tour?"

"We can tour the power plant?" I asked.

"Not exactly," he said. "But almost. Come with me. I'll be your guide."

Miyoshi-sensei drove a silver sports car. Before I got in, he pleated the cardboard shade that had been blocking the windshield, and turned on the air-conditioning. Then he got out his cigarettes and a special screw-top ashtray, explaining that it was against the law to drop butts on the street. I wanted one too, but he didn't offer and I was too shy to ask.

We drove on a road that ran parallel to the river. The water that day looked pink, as if it were reflecting a vivid sunset, but the sky was a faded denim blue. I'd noticed that the river seemed to change color from day to day. Sometimes it was fluorescent green, other times a deep indigo, and most often it looked olive drab, like water in a jar holding dirty paintbrushes.

"Why is the water pink?" I asked, turning to look at him.

"Ah," he exhaled. "Maybe, Shika is downstream from a textile mill."

"Maybe?" I repeated. I was getting used to his speech patterns.

"Mmm," he grunted. "Maybe they pour dye into the river."

As we crossed a bridge, I noticed rainbow stripes ascending the cement banks. A man in thigh-high rubber boots stood in the middle of the river, flicking his rod into the rosy current. "What happens to the fish?"

"I don't know," he said. "Maybe they become salmon?"

His delivery was so dry that it took a moment before I realized that he was joking. When I laughed, he laughed too. I noticed that as long as I kept laughing, his hands kept tightening and relaxing on the steering wheel, like a cat kneading its paws in pleasure. He turned away from the river, onto a road that veered up a steep hillside covered in thick bamboo, which ruffled and clacked as we drove past. At the precipice, an empty parking lot faced a brick building. Pointing the way inside was a pasteboard sign cut in the shape of a blond, blue-eyed girl wearing a white pinafore over a blue dress.

"Welcome to Arisu in Shikaland," he said.

"This is the nuclear power plant?" By that point, little would have surprised me.

"Plant is higher up the hill." He gestured at a fence looped with double rungs of barbed wire, beyond which I could see a cement tower purging smoke into the sky. "Arisu in Shikaland is museum. To explain how nuclear energy works."

"It's based on *Alice in Wonderland*?" I guessed, wondering if he got the irony.

"That's right," he said. "Arisu fell down a hole. Into new world she could not understand. Rules were so confusing. To break them was kind of dangerous. Off with their heads, *ne*? People here in Shika felt the same when this nuclear plant was built. So the plant created this museum, to make us more comfortable."

Inside the front doors, a Japanese woman wearing the same blue dress and pinafore handed me an English brochure. "Count Rabbit explains about the benefits of radiation," the cover promised. But instead of an explanation, inside was a poem.

> 'Twas brillig and the slithy toves
> Did gyre and gimble in the wabe;
> All mimsy were the borogoves
> And the mome raths outgrabe.

Curiouser and curiouser, I thought, remembering when I read *Alice in Wonderland* in elementary school, how I couldn't stop thinking about the cake that made her so large that her tears filled a room and almost drowned everyone in it. I was the Cheshire cat that year for Halloween. My dad made my mask out of surgical fiberglass, laying the wet strips across my face while I held a grin until my cheeks burned. The funny thing was, I hadn't really liked the book, the way Alice was always getting in trouble without understanding what she'd done wrong. It was arbitrary, there was no clear cause and effect, and this bothered me.

I followed Miyoshi-sensei into a small movie theater where the burgundy velvet curtain parted as soon as we sat down. We watched a man in a white rabbit costume guide a Japanese girl, in yet another blue dress and pinafore, through the control room of the nuclear power plant. "Count Rabbit was played by Mister Joe," Miyoshi-sensei whispered, even though we were alone. "Arisu was Shika High School freshman, Ritsuko Ueno. Narrator is head of nuclear power plant. Now he explains how nuclear power works."

"I wish I could understand it," I said.

"Me too," he said.

At the end of the short film, he led me to a picnic area outside, where a vending machine stood next to the building. He banged a button twice, sending two cans of iced chrysanthemum tea down the chute. "You don't need money here," he pointed out. "Everything is *sabisu*. Meaning free. Including *gomi* collection." He showed me a mesh bin heaped with trash bags and explained that this was where Haruki brought our trash.

"He had to walk all the way up here?" I asked.

"It's okay," he said. "Haruki should move more. He has . . . how to say . . . spare tire?"

I laughed, resisting the urge to joke that Haruki looked like the Michelin man. "But you are English teacher, not exercise teacher," he went on soberly. "Everyone follows the *gomi* rules. If you make a mistake, your neighbors will know it's you every time."

After leaving the museum, he took me to Shika's "Beach Driveway," a tunnel that ended on a stretch of sand rutted with tire tracks, littered with half-buried cans and bottles.

"There's a lot of trash on this beach," I pointed out.

"Mmm," he agreed, "but it's not Japanese."

"What do you mean?" I said. "How can it not be Japanese?"

"Because it floats from Russian and Korean ships."

"Come on," I scoffed, no longer able to maintain a polite veneer. "I'm sure not all litter in Shika is foreign. That's kind of racist, don't you think?"

"It's fact," he replied coolly. "You can see for yourself."

I rolled down my window and leaned out, trying to read the labels on the trash as we passed, but he was driving too fast, gunning the engine and making sand spray behind us. "Woo!" he yelled, taking his hands off the steering wheel as we sped toward the surf. He braked to a screeching halt, so close to the waves that they spat on his windshield. I could feel the wet sand sliding and shifting beneath the tires. Suddenly queasy, I pushed the door open and lunged out of the car, bending over to grip my knees and take a few ragged breaths. I felt upset and a little humiliated by my reaction to what had obviously been a harmless prank. What had I thought—that he was going to drive straight into the ocean? As a wave swept over my feet, soaking my shoes, I noticed an old Coca-Cola bottle. The writing on the glass was etched away, faded but still legible, printed in Cyrillic.

"You were right," I said, getting back into the car. "The trash is foreign."

I waited for him to say "I told you so," or some Japanese equivalent, but instead he apologized. "I'm sorry if I frighten you," he said. "I was only goofing about."

"I know," I said. "I wasn't scared."

He pulled out a pack of Mild Sevens and held it out to me before helping himself. As he lit a cigarette, I noticed that he had long narrow fingers, perfectly articulated, and that they were trembling slightly. My own hands always shake, so that people are constantly asking me if I'm okay when I feel perfectly fine. I wondered if he had the same problem, or if he was upset. I don't know how he guessed that I wanted a smoke, but it was a relief not to have to ask. I took one and he lit it with his Zippo. Then he rolled down both car windows and we smoked in companionable silence, our arms extending into the sunlight, still facing the sea.

At the end of my first week of teaching, Miyoshi-sensei offered to take me grocery shopping. "I had better teach you how to shop," he said, which made Carolyn laugh. I've never had a hard time figuring out how to spend money. But the truth was we did need help decoding the Japanese supermarket, which still left us stumped after a month in Shika. We'd buy corn oil only to find out it was corn syrup, bring home fresh bamboo tips that remained woody after an hour of boiling, purchase a melon without doing the yen conversion and figure out too late that we'd spent twenty dollars on showpiece fruit.

Carolyn was especially frustrated. When I told her about Miyoshi-sensei's offer, naturally she assumed she'd be coming along. "Don't do anything to give us away," I said as the doorbell rang. She frowned and I shrugged. I sensed that Miyoshi-sensei and I were on the verge of becoming friends—we noticed the same things and found the same things funny—and I wanted this to happen. But I also wanted to keep my home and work life separate. He was perceptive, and I worried that he'd guess Carolyn and I were a couple.

"It's great to meet you," she said. "I've heard so much about you."

"Ah," he said, blushing slightly. "I hope it's good things."

"Of course," she said. "M is always talking about what a fun young supervisor she got. I'm jealous!" Carolyn's supervisor was a grandmotherly type with a subscription to Britain's *Royalty* magazine, who couldn't understand how Carolyn failed to share her single-minded fascination with the landed gentry of the world.

"Ah," he said. "Sorry, but you are . . . ?"

"This is Carolyn," I said. "We both moved here from New York, remember?"

"Of course," he said. "That's why you needed a house big enough to share."

"Thank you so much for helping us find this place," Carolyn said, "and for offering to teach us how to grocery shop. I do most of the cooking, so I'm the one who needs help."

"Ah," he said again, looking back and forth between us.

In the car he offered me a cigarette and I asked Carolyn if it would bother her if I smoked. "Do whatever you want," she said, sounding annoyed. More than the smell of smoke, she hates to police me, to come across as uptight. When I turned around, trying to catch her eye and share a private smile, she was staring out at the apartment buildings rising incongruously from the rice fields.

"Who lives there?" she asked Miyoshi-sensei.

"No one," he replied. "They are vacancy."

"Vacant," she corrected him. "I thought there were no apartments for rent."

I held my breath, waiting for him to blow my cover. *No apartments big enough to share*, is what he'd said. But instead he explained that these buildings had been erected during the real estate boom of the eighties, then abandoned when the investors went bankrupt.

"It's kind of a ghost town," he said.

"This whole place is," Carolyn pronounced with characteristic bluntness. She is compulsively honest, almost physically incapable of bullshitting. I worried that he'd be offended, but instead he agreed. He told us that the Noto Peninsula was depopulating rapidly as companies shut down their small town branches and young people left for the cities in Central Honshu where all the jobs were. In the past, kids had attended their neighborhood high schools—he himself had gone to Shika *Koko* before it became a vocational school—but now, those with entrance exam scores high enough to qualify traveled as far as two hours by bus to attend prestigious schools in Kanazawa City.

"Shika is *inaka*," he said. "Meaning hick town." We laughed and he went on. "When I saw you were living on Manhattan's Broadway before this, I worried for you. It's true, there is not much here for tourists. But this is the real Japan, *ne*?"

"That's what I keep telling M," Carolyn said, touching the back of my neck, pushing her fingers under my hair. And even though he could've seen in his rearview mirror, I leaned back for just a moment.

As we entered the supermarket, Carolyn was almost giddy with excitement. She admires produce the way other people do flowers or jewelry. Inspired by an ingredient, she'll create an ordinary weekday dinner for just the two of us to rival the finest restaurant meal. But Miyoshi-sensei was pushing the cart, and every time she wanted to buy something, he had a good reason why we "had better not." The enoki mushrooms were too expensive; the fresh tofu was not a good bargain; peaches had gone out of season, so we "had better" buy apple pears instead.

In Tokyo, we'd been required to sit through a culture shock panel led by an ex-marine turned EFL teacher, who told us that the expression "you had better" was a direct translation of a Japanese idiom that didn't have the same patronizing tone. "If my Japanese wife tells me that I '*had better not*' go drinking with my buddies after work," he said, "she's not trying to be bossy, she's just looking out for my best interests." He winked. "And I don't have to do what she says." Every time Miyoshi-sensei rejected something that Carolyn chose, she looked at me expectantly and I felt trapped. He was only trying to help us, and we could always come back later. She picked out a package of fresh ramen noodles and he took it out of her hand, adding a dusty stack of Cup Noodles to the cart instead.

"Let me guess," she said flatly, "It's a better bargain?"

"*Sodesune*," he agreed. "Also, I think Americans prefer this kind of ramen. Maybe real Japanese noodles are kind of so difficult to cook correctly."

"I used to work at a Japanese restaurant," she said.

"Ah," he said. "But American Japanese food is so different. When I spent a summer in California, I could never find real Japanese food like home."

"Well you weren't going to the right places then," she said under her breath.

He took us for lunch at Coco's California Café, a family restaurant off the highway that we had already been to several times. There were color pictures of everything on the menu, but he proceeded to describe the specials in detail. The Japanese *hambagu*, he explained, was different from the American *hambaga*, because the patty came without buns, heaped with grated daikon. "You had better try it," he said, and when the waitress came to our table he began to order three *hambagu setto*. A *setto*, or "set," was a prix-fixe meal, with an appetizer, main dish, and dessert. Unlike at home, there weren't different choices in each category, and substitutions were unheard of. You couldn't even ask for mustard instead of mayonnaise on the chicken sandwich, when the photo quite clearly showed a white and not a yellow stripe. The menu was nonnegotiable, with no exceptions.

"Actually," Carolyn spoke up, "I'd like an omelet and a salad." She waited for him to translate, but instead he inspected the menu. "Maybe you should order *hambagu setto*," he said at last. "It's a better value, *ne*? We always order *setto*."

"There is no omelet *setto*," she said.

"Exactly," he said. "Don't worry. *Hambagu* is not so different from *hambaga*."

Carolyn kicked me under the table. She hadn't eaten meat since the fifth grade, when her class took a field trip to a farm. Sometimes her discipline impressed me, and sometimes I found it exhausting. I'd stopped eating meat—at least red meat, at least most of the time—when she told me that she could taste it on my breath when we kissed. But secretly I was looking forward to my *hambagu*.

"*Hambagu* is a Japanese variation on an American theme," Miyoshi-sensei said, "just like Miss Marina's American variation on a Japanese theme. Midwest-o sushi."

This was a sore spot. On the application to teach in Japan, we had to answer the questions, "How does Japanese culture influence or inspire you?" and "How are you preparing for life in Japan?" At the time, I happened to be interning for a short-lived magazine called *Midwestern Palate*. My job was to come up with recipes to showcase the products of our advertisers. I wasn't a very good cook, and most of my best ideas—including Midwest sushi—came from Carolyn. I'd stapled a copy of the recipe onto my application, to go with an essay about how I'd been trying to bring my love of Japanese cuisine to small town America.

Carolyn and I were both enrolled in a Japanese crash course, but only she did the homework regularly. She wrote the Japanese words for every object in her dorm room on strips of paper that she taped to the things they named, while I only learned the words that sounded like English: *foku*, *naifu*, *supoon*, for fork, knife and spoon, *waishiatsu*, for white shirt, *tabako*, for cigarette and (my personal favorite) *sukinshippu* or "skinship," for close physical contact. When I teased her for being such a nerd, she said that I'd be sorry when I didn't know anything about the country, couldn't utter a word except "skinship," and didn't have any money saved.

"I'll have you," I said.

So we were both upset when I got in on the first round and she was wait-listed. I told her that I didn't want to come here without her, which made her even angrier. She said that I was putting too much pressure on her, that she didn't want to be responsible for my happiness, that I shouldn't make her the focus of my life. We were just twenty-two, after all. What were the odds of this lasting? I knew she was right, but I hated her honesty. When she did get in off the waiting list, just a few weeks later, it wasn't quite the celebratory moment that it might have been.

"I translated your sushi recipe for Shika's newspaper," Miyoshi-sensei said to me. "I called it 'Miss Marina's Sushi.' I think so many people smeared Philadelphia on ham, arranged a pickle, and cut into pieces like a maki. Even I attempted, and I never cook!"

"It was actually Carolyn's recipe," I said.

"Did you like it?" she asked.

"Well," he said, "sushi means rice with vinegar. Your sushi had only meat and cheese. We couldn't recognize. However, your photograph appeared next to the recipe, Miss Marina. So probably many people recognize you!"

No wonder those boys at the beach had known my name. I was embarrassed, thinking of the picture that must have appeared in the newspaper, the passport photo I had taken on the day I cut off all my hair last spring. Carolyn swore that she liked my long hair, which was golden and streaky and almost as thick as my wrist when I wore it pulled back. But I wanted to look fierce and androgynous too, so I went to her barber down at Astor Place and paid five dollars to have it shorn off in less than five minutes. I had my picture taken that afternoon to document the change. But what I saw disappointed me. I didn't look like Carolyn or her ex-girlfriends. My face was too round, my nose too prominent, my mouth too big. The blond scruff almost disappeared against my scalp and I looked naked and vulnerable. I looked like a big baby. I started to grow it out right away and suffered through months of puffy, feathered awkwardness, less fierce and androgynous from week to week and more like a suburban mom with a mushroom cut.

"I really appreciate all that you've done for us," Carolyn said, leaving her *hambagu* untouched. 'But do you know if there are any other places for rent here?"

"What?" I said. I knew our house had its share of problems, but she'd never mentioned wanting to move, with or without me. This felt like an ambush.

"I kind of doubt it," he said, looking at us both. "Like I told Miss Marina in my letter, the only apartments for rent are too small to share."

"You told her that," Carolyn repeated, looking at me squarely.

"I'm sorry," I said quietly.

"We could've rented studios in the same building," she said. "We could still."

"Actually, now that you paid your key money, you couldn't get it back again . . . " He trailed off, his eye twitching slightly. "I think you had better stay where you are. Anyhow, Japanese landlords are sort of reluctant to rent to a foreigner. It's not racism exactly, only land-lords want to rent to long-term tenant, not temporary person."

"We both signed contracts for a year," Carolyn said.

"But a year is kind of short," he said. "You'll see. It will pass quickly."

Once we were alone at home, she wasn't as upset as I feared. She said that she understood why I'd hidden this detail from her, that it was sweet in a way, how much I wanted to live together, even if she did wish I'd been more honest.

"Miyoshi-sensei seemed uncomfortable around me," she said. "He obviously wished I wasn't there so that you two could have a blast as usual."

"That's not true," I said. "And we don't always have a blast."

"You're always talking about how funny he is, what a good time you have joking around, and I'm sorry, but I just didn't see it."

"I think you put him on edge," I said.

"He put me on edge! Talk about bossy. Why does he care about what we eat?"

"He was just trying to be helpful."

"It's weird how you're still defending him."

"I'm sorry," I said. "You're right. He was being annoying."

"You could've stood up for me."

"Defended your honor?" I said, but she didn't laugh. I apologized again. "I felt caught between the two of you," I tried to explain. "He was being annoying, but you were acting kind of aggressive. I didn't know what I was supposed to do."

"I felt like a third wheel on a bicycle."

"Isn't that a tricycle?"

"Ha ha," she deadpanned. "He's a good-looking guy."

"You think so?" I asked. I did too, in a way, although I was dying to mess up his hair, untuck his shirt, rough him up a little around the edges. Buttoned-up people have that effect on me. Carolyn was buttoned up too, in her own punk way. For all her body piercings and Manic Panic hair dye, she polished her boots on schedule, ironed her shirts, and never wore dirty underwear.

"What I don't get," she said, "is why it's so important for you that we live together, but you don't want anyone to know that we're a couple." I shrugged and told her that I didn't want to scare people away before they had a chance to get to know us. "Then you had better not do that," she said in Miyoshi-sensei's accent when I kissed her in front of our bedroom window. Our window upstairs looked directly into the bedroom window of Haruki Ogawa, and several times we'd caught the boy peering out at us, obviously spying. It was creepy. I didn't know what he'd seen, but I figured that since he never spoke, our secret was safe with him at least.

A few days later, I was walking home from school when I caught sight of a bulky figure on the road ahead of me, moving at a snail's pace, so slowly that I couldn't help but catch up. "*Konnichiwa*," I said to Haruki.

"*Gomi . . . arigato.*" Garbage, thank you? I hoped he'd get the point. I was about to pass when he reached out and grabbed my wrist. I laughed out of shock and nervousness.

"Dontotesutome," he growled.

"I'm sorry," I stammered. "I don't speak much Japanese yet."

"Don't. Test. Me." He let go of my wrist and took off. Watching him run was like watching a cow sprint. It looked unnatural, like he was being chased, but I was the only other person on the street.

moeru: (v.) *to burn; to get fired up; to have a crush*

It's late November, technically still fall, but it feels like we skipped straight from summer to winter. Last month the leaves turned color and then dropped in a matter of days, like flares that ignited briefly before extinguishing, swept into piles and incinerated before they had time to settle on the ground. In Snow Country, the days start late and end early this time of year. By four in the afternoon, when I leave school, the sky is already darkening. At eight in the morning, the stars still faintly twinkle as our students straggle down the path that cuts between two rice fields, walking their bicycles to delay getting here until the last possible second.

This morning I have first period free. I stand with Noriko Kaie, the high school librarian, warming our hands over the kerosene stove as we stare out the window, which is cracked to let out the toxic kerosene fumes. We watch the girls lock their bikes up, then roll the waistbands of their uniform skirts to make them even shorter, exposing thighs mottled fuscia from the cold. Their *rusu sokusu* or "loose socks" puddle over their platform shoes. Clomping along, they look like Clydesdale ponies.

"Brrr," I say, rubbing my palms together.

"You cold?" Noriko asks. I nod, and she turns up the dial on the kerosene stove. Behind the grille, the sputtering blue collar of flame ruffles and expands.

"Thanks," I say.

"No problem," she replies with a grin, lifting a hand to cover a mouth of teeth more jumbled than a Tokyo city block. Last week, I taught Noriko to say "no problem," "P.U.," and "shit." The librarian is a tiny woman who wears an endless rotation of T-shirts printed with the names of foreign cities she has yet to visit because she has never left Japan. Between my fledgling Japanese and her limited English, our shared vocabulary is barely kindergarten level, but we put it to good use. I enjoy our abbreviated interactions, although it seems like we should be better friends by now. Noriko is twenty-seven, just five years older than me. We've gone to Shika's Friendly Tea Parlor twice on half-days, both ordering the pasta *setto* lunch. But no matter how hard we try, we can't seem to get past acquaintance level. When we run out of things to talk about, we often sit side by side, flipping through the library's book of dog breeds. "Too human," Noriko always says about the big, grinning dogs.

Staring out the window, I notice a strange vehicle moving slowly down the road. It's made almost entirely of glass, as if the windshield wrapped around all four sides. A woman is kneeling in the back, dressed in a white kimono, her face chalky with powder. Surrounded by kitchen appliances, furniture, and lamps, she looks like a ghost that got trapped in a moving van. "What is that?" I ask.

"New bride," Noriko explains. "It's *hajimete* . . . first time . . . to new husband's home. She has *okurimono* for his family. She must show everyone."

Okurimono. I divide the word in half: offered things. "You mean presents?"

"Yes," Noriko says. "And own thing. All she has."

"Do all new brides have to do this?"

"No." Noriko shakes her head. "Only . . . " She pauses to look up a word in the library's large English/Japanese dictionary. "Only *habitual* new husband wants."

"Traditional?" I guess, and she nods.

Rumor has it that Noriko used to date my predecessor, Joe Pope, until her father put an end to it by setting up a meeting with the local matchmaker. Now the librarian is engaged to marry a dentist, a man in his late forties, their wedding date set for early next summer. "Maybe you could not imagine such a thing," Miyoshi-sensei said when he was informed of Noriko's arranged marriage as we shared a cuppa' in the faculty room one afternoon, "marrying someone you hardly knew." I sensed that he was trying to get me to express the shock or disapproval that he could not as a member of this culture. Miyoshi-sensei's own singleness is a subject of endless speculation. Several teachers have started conversations with me by saying, "Did you know that Miyoshi-sensei is not married?" or, "Probably he works so hard, he doesn't have time to find a wife outside of school . . . " It's how you gossip, an endless game of fill in the blanks. I can only guess how they try to fill in mine.

"Will you ride in a glass van after your wedding?" I ask Noriko, hoping that I'm not overstepping my bounds.

"Yes," she says after a pause.

"*Kowai?*" I venture. Are you scared?

"No problem," she says, but she's not smiling anymore.

As I lean forward to get a closer look at the bride, I press against the kerosene stove and a searing pain shoots up my leg. "*Itai!*" I cry out, momentarily distracted from the burn by the fact that I spontaneously recalled the Japanese word for "ouch." Noriko drops to the floor and begins patting and blowing on my smoking tights. "Shit," I say and she grins, recognizing the word she recently learned. I step out of my slippers, peel off my tights and pitch them into the trash. "*Risaikuru,*" she corrects me softly, moving them to the recycling bin. She opens her desk drawer and hands me a pair of pantyhose, still in their flat package. "Too small!" I protest. Noriko is bird-boned, narrow as a pencil. If I were hollow, both of her legs could fit inside one of mine. She looks up something in the dictionary. "Stretch!" she says. "Stretch!" It sounds like a suggestion. She watches me pull the waistband over my kneecaps, tugging so hard that they rip.

"I'm so sorry!" I exclaim, mortified.

"No problem," she says, adding another ruined pair of stockings to the recycling bin.

As Miyoshi-sensei and I walk down the hall to our first class of the day, he keeps glancing at my bare thigh. The burn is dark purple now, striped with grille marks. My leg looks like a roasted wiener. I'm grateful he doesn't ask what happened.

"So Miss Marina," he says, "what shall we do today?"

"Well," I say, "I prepared a special worksheet about gender."

"Gender?" he repeats.

"It means sex," I explain. "Like, boys and girls."

"I know what sex means," he cuts me off. "Is this appropriate for school?"

"It's very appropriate for this school."

At Shika High School, the female secretarial students study typing, word processing, and how to prepare the perfect cup of green tea to serve their future bosses, while the technical boys study basic engineering, computer programming, and machinery. Three years ago, the boys in the technical class sexually harassed their homeroom teacher, a young woman who resigned in shame after less than a month. The vice-principal's solution? Keep women teachers out of their classroom. "You're so lucky," Miyoshi-sensei told me back in August. "Girl students are much easier to control." When I asked him what the girls like, hoping to tailor my lessons to their interests, he said, "make." I assumed this meant they like to make things. "No," he corrected me. "Make. For example, lipstick, mascara . . . They are kind of standard girls."

But I believe that there is more to these future secretaries than meets the eye. I believe that nestled inside pigtailed heads are incendiary minds, that they just need the right person to expose them to the right ideas. Unfortunately, their English vocabulary is seriously limited, and so is my ability to think of simple ways to discuss complicated issues. They have barely mastered a few sentence structures:

I am/am not. I do/don't like. I have(n't). I can('t). I feel.

Fill in the blanks, I wrote at the top of this worksheet.

I like to be a girl because:_____   I would like to be a boy because:_____

In Japan, only girls can:_____   In Japan, only boys can:_____

I am not fooling myself. I don't expect to spark a feminist revolution. My tools are crude. It would be like trying to start a fire by rubbing two soggy toothpicks together. Still, I'm excited to hear their answers, to spark a discussion at least.

Miyoshi-sensei reaches for the stack of pictures that I tore from the Japanese magazines *Cutie* and *Fruits*, of grown women clutching stuffed animals, standing pigeon-toed and sucking their thumbs. I explain that for a warm-up, I thought that we could show the students these pictures and discuss how the women are giving up their power by acting cute.

"Just look at that," I say, as he flips to a picture of a woman bending over to show off ruffled underpants. "She's posing like a two-year-old."

"Don't you like girls?" he asks, eyeing me sideways.

"Yes," I say carefully, "but not grown women pretending to be girls."

"But our students are not grown women."

"Well they're not children either. Whenever I try to speak to them, they giggle or answer in baby talk. It makes me so nervous."

"Don't be nervous," he says. "Students are like crows on a wire. Always chattering about nothing with flashing dark eyes. They are mischievous, but not dangerous."

"Haruki doesn't act like a crow," I point out.

"No," he agrees. "He acts like a rice cooker. Outside he looks like nothing happening. But inside becomes more and more hot."

As we enter the freshman secretarial classroom, I'm sure the girls can smell my feet, which are clammy in my plastic hoof slippers. I'm sure they are ogling the grille marks on my thigh, wondering why I chose to put my big bare legs on display. "Hello," I call out and they giggle as usual. I start to pass out my gender worksheet and Miyoshi-sensei says, "Maybe we had better use the textbook to discuss cultural issues."

"But I didn't plan my lesson using the textbook," I protest.

"Don't worry," he says. "I will steer the discussion."

New Horizons teaches English through a serialized comic strip. International pals Yumi, Ken, and Pablo get in and out of trouble, all the while conversing in "the new global language: English!" Yumi's uncle is a rogue scientist. In the last chapter, the three friends boarded his unfinished time machine. Rascally Ken pushed "the big red button," and off they soared into the dark night sky, landing on the moon one text box later.

"Repeat after Miss Marina," Miyoshi-sensei says. "From the moon, the earth looks like a blue and white ball." Only the most earnest girls mumble after me. The rest stare out the window or glance at the compact mirrors propped open on their desks. "Let's go home," says Yumi, and the friends climb back into the spaceship. They streak through the sky, but something goes terribly wrong and the time machine touches down on a smoking trashscape. A banner declares the year 2030.

"Oh Ken, look at all this trash!" I read for Yumi.

"Look at Pablo," Miyoshi-sensei reads for Ken. "He looks sad!"

"Of course he's sad. The earth looks like a trash bin!"

Looks like, Miyoshi-sensei writes on the board. *Look at. He/she looks...*

"Miss Marina," he says, "I think now is good time to discuss American culture."

"Great," I say, gathering the stack of magazine pictures from the podium.

"Actually," he says, "I think maybe students are more interested to learn about American *gomi* situation. Could you please tell about the dump? Maybe we couldn't imagine such a place."

In our team-teaching Miyoshi-sensei likes me to expose the problems of the Western world. I have learned that it doesn't pay to get defensive, or to admit to how much I don't know. I've begun improvising, making things up.

"America is a big country," I say, opening my arms wide. "We have so much space, we don't need to separate *gomi* into a million categories. We don't burn trash, or dig through our neighbors' garbage cans. We put our trash in big black bags that we leave on the street at night, and early in the morning a professional takes everything to the dump and we never have to see it again."

"I'm afraid dump sounds so ugly," Miyoshi-sensei says. "Like *New Horizons* picture of 2030. If I go to USA, can I be dump tourist?"

"You can't see the trash," I say. "It gets buried in giant holes called landfills." This actually sounds true.

"You are from San Francisco," he says. "You have many earthquake there. When the earth is unstable, you can't dig a hole for trash."

"We just throw it in the middle of the ocean."

He turns to the board and draws an astonishingly accurate map of the United States. Next to it he draws a Japan that's almost the same size. Between the two he sketches wavy blue lines. "One sea," he says. "Same sea."

"And here in Shika, the mill pours dye into the river. What's the difference?"

"Only liquid in liquid," he says. "Never something hard or floating sadly forever." He pauses. "How about recycling? Don't you think it's important?"

"Of course recycling is important," I say.

"Don't you like a tree growing tall, offering some shady or apple?"

"Of course I like a tree."

"Well then, please explain about Christmastime. We can see, in a movie like *Home Alone*, how every American family cuts down a tree only to hang some balls. It's kind of so strange and wasteful, don't you agree?"

"Some people chop them up for firewood after Christmas."

He crosses his arms. "And when human being become dead, you put in a wooden box. Isn't it true? Then you put wooden box in the earth. Same like dump-style?"

"In my family we burn," I say.

"Excuse me?" He blinks rapidly, running a hand over his blow-dried hair.

"My father was cremated," I say. "*Moeru ni narimashita*." This, I believe, translates: "he became burnable."

"I'm sorry," he says. "He must have been so young."

"He was forty-eight." I smile with difficulty, wondering why I started this.

"It's too young," he says.

I brace myself for the inevitable follow-up question. Before moving to Shika, I researched suicide in Japan and learned that it has reached epidemic proportions here. There is a forest at the base of Mount Fuji where so many people have hung themselves that park rangers sawed the lowest branches from the trees and nailed signs to their trunks reading, "Turn around!" and "Don't give up!" Mount Mihara became a tourist destination after a nineteen-year-old jumped to her death in the crater and so many people followed her example that tour buses were prohibited from stopping there. Strangers form suicide pacts over the Internet, meeting at designated locations to gas themselves as a group. I learned that in the Japanese language there are different words for different kinds of suicides: suicide over a broken heart; suicide over bankruptcy; the suicide of a mother and child. But I still don't know how to say that my father killed himself in Japanese. To my relief, no one here has ever asked me how he died.

The bell rings, a shrill jangle. Before Miyoshi-sensei claps his hands to dismiss class, I pass my gender worksheet down each row.

"Please tell the students to do these for homework," I say.

"Okay," he says, "but I think it's so difficult. Don't expect too much."

At the end of the school day, when I return to the library to get my jacket, I hear a male voice with a thick British accent. The longer Joe Pope spends in Japan, the more exaggerated his accent becomes. Even when he's reciting one of the five sentences he knows in Japanese, he still sounds like he's speaking English. Through the window I see him sitting on the edge of Noriko's desk, his long legs sprawled in front of him, his toes visible through his sandals. As a special guest here——a special guest who stands six-four and dwarfs the vice-principal—Joe alone is exempt from wearing the uniform hooves.

"Hallo pet," he says to me. "I was hoping I'd get to see you today."

"I've been sitting in the faculty room for an hour," I inform him.

"Roight." He chuckles. "I try to avoid that place. A bit toxic, innit? Spent so much time in there last year, I actually developed an allergy to my desk."

"Are you teaching with us this week?" I ask.

"Moight be," he says. "We'll see if Miyoshi-sensei wants to pay for one of me special visits. I just popped in for a chat with Noriko-kun."

"Noriko-*chan*," she corrects him. "*Kun* for little boy. I'm *girl*!"

"Are you sure?" he says. "Shall I check?" He flicks the hem of her T-shirt, she punches him in the shoulder, and he groans, doubling over in pretend pain. She eyes him with real concern before he laughs and straightens again, wrapping his arm around her shoulder and tickling her. She giggles and squirms closer to him.

"Is that ad for jewelry or soup?" I point to a picture thumbtacked to the library bulletin board. He's wearing an apron, serving a bowl of ramen to a pretty Japanese woman. Their matching gold wedding bands gleam like cartoon stars.

"Neither," he says. "It's for life insurance."

We both laugh and Noriko looks at us, trying to figure out what's funny. I should explain, but I don't really know how.

"Looks like you've had a lot of work lately," I say.

"Nothing to brag about," he shrugs. Joe dismisses his commercial work as a lark, pretending to be annoyed by his celebrity status here in Shika, but he's the one who brings copies of his ads whenever he returns for Noriko to hang on the Joe Pope wall of fame. "I did one commercial for a car dealership that was fun. I had to pretend to steal a mini-Jeep while the fuzz chased after me."

"It figures they hired a foreigner to play the car thief," I say, rolling my eyes.

"We're a bunch of shady characters," he agrees. "I'm up for the part of an English teacher on a soap opera. If I get it, I'll have to move to Osaka."

"Osaka?" Noriko echoes faintly. "*Toi desu.*"

"Not that far," I say. "It's only four hours by train."

"So what's new with you lot?" Joe asks. "How's Caro?"

"She's great," I say. "We're great."

"You two doing anything later on?"

"Not that I know of," I say. "Want to come over for dinner?" Even though Joe drives us nuts with his endless preening and his procession of Japanese girlfriend-du-jour, he is also mildly entertaining. He doesn't mind being made fun of. He hardly seems to notice. Plus, he's the only person here who knows about our relationship, meaning we can relax for a change, be ourselves around him. Whenever he comes over, we inevitably make a vat of pasta, drink one bottle too many of cheap red wine, and then go for a walk on the beach, where we build a bonfire, sing cheesy folk songs in bad harmony, and make fun of Joe's questions, which grow progressively sillier and more obscene the drunker he gets. He has asked if we turn ourselves on when we look in the mirror. He has asked for pointers. He has even asked if he can watch, "just for educational purposes." Rejection only seems to excite him, perhaps because it's so rare in his charmed life.

"I wish I could," he says, making a sorry-looking face, "but I told Miyoshi that I'd go out with him. I'm taking him to a new hostess bar, if you care to come along. Should be right up your alley," he whispers playfully.

"Nice," I say, "but I think I'll pass."

"I'm just taking the piss," he says, laughing. I don't get this expression. Does he mean that he's not really going to a hostess bar, or that we couldn't come along because we're women? The library door swings open and Miyoshi-sensei walks in. Joe tells him that he's looking forward to their lads' night out and then leaves without saying good-bye to Noriko, who watches him disappear down the hall, looking dejected.

"Mari-chan," Miyoshi-sensei says, "I have something important to share with you. I'm too timid to say aloud. Please read this . . ." My chest constricts as he hands me another piece of paper covered in his oddly linked cursive.

Dear Miss Marina how are you?

I'm so-so, and you?

Now I continue Japanese / gomi lesson. Ka-yobi meaning is Tuesday in English. Ka kanji is fire. This is so convenient to remember, because ka-yobi is also "moeru" or burnable garbage day. For example, you can burn some paper from outside your wine bottle. This morning I borrowed Miss Noriko's jumbo size English dictionary from library. I learned that English word for bottle paper is "label." I'm sorry my English is so poor. Maybe you couldn't catch my meaning before. Mister Ogawa reported that he saw your wine bottle in bin outside sake store, still wearing a "label" on it. He is so kind, he cleaned for you in his own home. Next time you had better clean in your own home, ne?

Another moeru gomi item include woman thing (please forgive my shy), cheese, beef, and so forth. You should put all moeru gomi in clear plastic bag, so everyone can see what you throw, and put this bag in bin in front of Mister Donuts on a Tuesday.

That's all for now.

See you,

Hiroshi Miyoshi

"Ogawa-san called you again to complain about our trash?" I ask, and he nods. "Just because we didn't wash the label off one wine bottle?"

"No . . ." he says. "Not just for that. Maybe also because of . . . woman thing?"

"Gender?" I ask, mystified.

"Not gender." He bites his lip and speaks quickly, without looking at me. "Woman thing happens every month . . . You threw evidence in recycling bin. But this can't be recycled, for obvious reason of sanitation. Next month, please throw on a Tuesday, together with another burnable *gomi*, so Ogawa-san won't have to handle your . . . personal waste."

"Oh my god," I say. "Mister Ogawa had to handle our . . ."

"Not Mister Ogawa," he cuts me off. "Haruki."

The door to our house is wide open. Carolyn is standing in front of the refrigerator, slam-dunking its contents into the garbage can.

"The fridge shut off again," she says. "Everything went bad."

Lately the Amana has been turning on and off at random intervals. The coils at the back of the ancient fridge are so hot that when it turns off it actually heats up, and the food inside spoils like groceries in a hot car, filling the entryway with a sour milk stench.

"I'm sorry," I say, "but why are you mad at me?"

"Because you left the trashsicle in the bathtub this morning. I told you to take it out when it thawed, but you didn't listen. Now the whole house reeks. I'll bet the neighbors can smell it from across the street. No wonder they hate us."

"Are you on your period?" I ask.

"Excuse me?" Her eyes narrow to slits.

"Ogawa-san found tampons in our recyclables. Used tampons. I don't have my period, so I figured they had to be yours. Miyoshi-sensei told me that next time, we—I mean you—should throw them out with the burnables."

Tears flood her eyes, and for a moment I regret telling her, but when I place my hand on her shoulder she shrugs it off and runs upstairs, slamming our bedroom door and yelling at me to leave her alone.

CHAPTER FOUR

nami: (N.) *a wave (ocean)*

I first met Carolyn in our university bereavement group, at the beginning of our senior year of college. Every meeting started the same way, all of us going around the circle like alcoholics, saying our names and explaining who we'd lost, for the benefit of newcomers and also to get used to saying the words, "living with the grief," as our group leader liked to say. Carolyn had been in the group for four years. Unlike the rest of us, who stammered through our introductions, she spoke openly and eloquently about her loss and how it still affected her. Carolyn intimidated me.

At the end of my first meeting, the group leader—a twitchy, prematurely gray graduate student in clinical psychology—gave me a pamphlet listing the warning signs of depression: feelings of hopelessness or worthlessness; the inability to concentrate or experience pleasure; a decline in sexual appetite; rapid weight loss or gain, and insomnia. I viewed the list as a challenge, figured that without the symptoms I couldn't have the disease. I made myself attend every class and turn in every paper, I went to the movies and attempted to read novels and listen to music, and generally acted as if my life were on course, my father's suicide a detour, not a derailing. The only symptom I couldn't shake was insomnia. The moment I lay down, my eyes would spring open, my spine would grow rigid with alertness, and the words, *your father killed himself*, would pass like closed captioning across the screen of my mind.

My father had been an insomniac too, especially after he left medicine to be an inventor. "A surgeon is just a highly skilled mechanic," he justified his decision. He was burning with creative energy. He could hardly sit still, he had so many ideas. He told me that the best inventions were things that people needed without knowing it, things they wanted but couldn't name, holes they felt but didn't know how to fill. The key was to invent something so elemental that people would forget it hadn't always existed. But his designs were elaborate, intricate, and incomprehensible, at least to me, and he couldn't sell any of them. It wasn't long before he started spending most of his time lying on the living room couch, staring at the ceiling with eyes so bloodshot they looked shattered and glued back together.

Carolyn couldn't sleep either. Her room was next to the only TV lounge in our dorm and we often met there in the middle of the night, watching infomercials from either end of the same orange foam couch. Secretly I thought about things she'd admitted to in bereavement group. She wondered whether she slept with women out of real desire or because she craved maternal comfort. She wanted to be taken care of but felt suffocated whenever anyone tried. She always left her lovers before they could leave her. In our late night collisions, she never alluded to the group or asked how I was doing. I guess the answer was obvious. But she started bringing an extra mug of cocoa, and offering me perfect triangles of cinnamon toast from a blue china plate.

At first I didn't recognize my attraction to Carolyn. I'd never slept with a girl before, and she was so tough and spiky, with a rod in her tongue and buzzed hair that moved through a Kool-Aid spectrum. But if she was in the room, I couldn't focus on anything else. And I began not just noticing her but anticipating her, as if I had some sixth sense that picked up on her nearness alone. I'd anticipate her in the cafeteria and there she'd be, head bent over a yogurt and a book. Walking through one of the basement tunnels, my heart would start racing and I'd turn a corner to find her lifting weights in the underground gym.

One Sunday morning I opened the door to the TV lounge and felt my pulse accelerate before I spotted her, lying on the couch, her body pressed beneath that of a woman with short gray hair and hands that looked ruddy against her white breasts. Even after I recognized our bereavement group leader, I couldn't turn away. I stood there, transfixed, until Carolyn opened her eyes and looked right at me, and then I fled, afraid of what she'd seen on my face, lust or confusion or something else, something beginning to stretch out of a long crouch.

All week I avoided the lounge. When I closed my eyes at night, the image of her with her shirt pushed up returned to me, the way her pale skin seemed lit from within, the spatter of freckles pooled in her cleavage. I assumed she would never look twice at a girl like me, a big-boned blonde with a patina of wholesomeness that nothing—not smoking, not four years in New York, not even my father's death—had managed to tarnish. Still, it was a relief to have something new to think about in the dead hours. Also, "decline in sexual appetite" was one item on the list of depression warning signs, one more symptom I'd managed to beat.

The following Saturday, I almost skipped bereavement group but decided to go at the last minute. That morning, a new girl was present whose father had also died. "He had a heart attack," she said, looking at me with watery eyes. "How about yours?" I hated every answer to this question. "He committed suicide," sounded so clinical, "he killed himself," so violent, "he took his life," so vague and euphemistic. Took it where exactly? I also hated the look of pity and regret that inevitably popped up on the face of whoever asked the question. And I didn't know what to do with my own face when I answered it. If I smiled to try and put the person at ease, I felt creepy and robotic. But I refused to break down in bereavement group. I had only joined it because my advisor insisted, as a condition of returning to college just a week after my father's death.

"Um," I said to the new girl, "he put himself to sleep?" Immediately I regretted this phrasing. I'd heard my mom say something similar. *He was sick*, she always stressed, *he hadn't slept in almost a year and he refused to get help. He literally put himself to sleep.* "I mean he was depressed," I backtracked, "and, well, you know . . ."

"How old are you?" Carolyn asked me, cutting off my stammering.

"Twenty-one," I said. It was the first time she'd asked me a personal question.

"I thought so," she said. "Your dad waited until you were an adult to kill himself."

As her words sank in, I felt punched in the stomach. This coincidence, if it was one, hadn't occurred to me. How long had he been waiting, counting off days until he could stop counting off days? Until I was no longer his responsibility?

"My mom died when I was twelve," she said.

"Are you saying I'm lucky?" I asked. "I should be grateful?"

"No," she said. "But I do wish I'd had those extra years with her."

"Your mom died of cancer," I said.

"Brain cancer is a terrible way to die."

"At least it's a normal way."

"What does that mean?" she asked me.

"It means she didn't choose to leave you. She had to die."

"Every loss is different," the group leader intervened, "and everyone handles loss differently. There isn't one right way to grieve."

"Then why do we all go through the same stages?" I asked, and I noticed that Carolyn smirked. According to our trusty leader, I was stuck on "denial," the starting square on the game board of grief. I only seemed to prove her point by denying this, week after week. She liked to say that grief was like a wave. You could be minding your own business, riding the subway, say, when that wave would come out of nowhere and wash right over you. And when it did, you had no choice but to submit. You could no more resist the wave of grief than you could hold an ocean wave at bay. I'd developed an irrational fear of the subway. But I also wanted the wave to hit, so that I could move on to the next stage already. Also, I felt like I owed my dad that much. What was I doing, still standing?

"Everyone goes through the same stages," the group leader explained yet again with obviously frayed patience, "but we all experience them in different ways. For you, denial might mean that you think you could have prevented your father's suicide, if you'd said or done the right thing."

"Maybe I could have," I said. "Why is that denial and not realism?"

"Because it's easier to feel guilty," Carolyn answered.

"Easier than what?"

"Than feeling sad."

I sought her out late that night. She was curled up on the couch, painting her toenails blue while she watched Dionne Warwick pretend to be a psychic on-screen. "I'm afraid of the wave," I said, standing in

front of the TV. "I'm afraid it will wash me away. My dad drowned. I
don't want the same thing to happen to me." For a long time, Carolyn
didn't speak. When she finally said, "I'm here," I didn't know if she
meant "here" as in she hadn't washed away, or "here" as in available to
comfort me. I started to cry, shielding my face with my hands, and she
stood up and wrapped her arms around me. She held me close. She
held me without hesitation. She held me until I stopped crying, and
then she took my hand and led me down the hall to her room.

"I'm sorry I broke down on you like that," I said, shy to find myself alone with her.

"Don't apologize," she said.

Her room was crowded with objects, but everything seemed to
have its place, there were so many plants that it smelled like a green-
house, and one wall was entirely covered in pencil drawings. "You
barely know me," I said. "You shouldn't have to take care of me."

"I don't have to," she said, sitting cross-legged on her bed.

"Of course not. I'm sorry." I sat on the edge of the mattress.
"I mean thank you." I laughed nervously and looked around at the
drawings, which were mostly portraits. When I complimented her
skill as an artist, she brushed off my praise, telling me that she only
drew to procrastinate, so she wouldn't have to figure out what to do
after graduation. "Oh my god," I said, suddenly recognizing one of
the faces. "Is that . . . "

"Yeah," she said, apparently unembarrassed. "I drew you this
morning during group. I hope you don't mind. You just looked
so . . . "

"Angry?" I guessed.

"Tough," she said. "And beautiful."

"What?" I said, because I'd never thought of myself as either one,
and because I wanted to hear her say it again.

"You hold everything in so tightly," she said. "You're always in control. It's almost scary. I've never even seen you cry before."

"I'm sorry," I said. "I can't believe I did that to you."

"Stop apologizing," she said. "You shouldn't apologize for feeling things. And you didn't *do* anything to me. Yet." Before I could ask what she meant or apologize for that too, she stroked my cheek with the back of her hand and I swear I felt a tiny shock from each of her knuckles. I turned to face her in the room, which suddenly seemed even smaller, barely big enough for the two of us, and we kissed for the first time. When I had imagined kissing her, I thought that it would be soft and gentle, a velvet brush of lips. But there was nothing gentle about the way she bit my lower lip and pulled it into her mouth, then pushed me backward onto the bed, wedged her knee between my legs and ripped off my tank top. I tore her clothes off too, desperate to get her naked, then sorry when there was nothing else to take off, nothing between us but skin. I wanted to keep stripping off layer after layer.

"Don't worry," she said. "Just let yourself go for once."

When I came against her hand, I started to cry again, harder this time, unable to stop even as I was afraid that she would stop what she was doing. But she knew not to stop and not to ask what was wrong, that the answer was everything and nothing. I felt like I was sprinting away from one place and toward another, a place I wanted already to have reached.

My dad killed himself in September, Carolyn and I started sleeping together in October, and in November a girl in our dorm overdosed. The girl lived on my floor but I didn't know her name, didn't even recognize her face when it was printed on the cover of the campus daily. Her body wasn't found for three days, while the smell seeped from room to room and students speculated about its source. Carolyn even cleaned out her mini-fridge one night while I urged her to come back to bed. For three days no one reported the girl missing. On the morning they finally broke down her door, while an ambulance siren reverberated uselessly in front of the building, I already knew what must have happened. I ran to the bathroom and threw up in the sink, and the next thing I knew Carolyn was standing behind me, holding my hair and telling me to let go, just let it out.

"It's everywhere," I gasped. "I can't get away from it. I can't even breathe."

"I know," she said. "Let's get out of here."

Within an hour, we'd boarded a bus to southern New Jersey, to the small town where she grew up. The turnpike stench was almost welcome as it infiltrated our nostrils, scouring them out. Her father met us at the station. I could tell that she had told him everything—that we were girlfriends, and about my dad, and what had happened at school—because he was careful not to bring up the reason for our sudden visit, and his smile didn't falter when she held my hand. He brought our bags to his bedroom, dropped them on the king-sized bed with its blue and green quilt, and told us he'd be in the guest room, that we should help ourselves to whatever we needed.

"Your dad's amazing," I said to Carolyn. "I can't believe how accepting he is."

"Why wouldn't he be?" she asked.

"Well," I said, "a lot of dads might have a problem if their daughter . . . "

"Was a big dyke?" She laughed and accused me of not being able to say the word.

"My dad hates conflict more than anything," she said, "including the fact that I like to have sex with women. When my mom died, he thought it was his job to make everything okay again, and I thought it was my job to pretend that he could."

"At least you both tried," I said.

"But pretending just makes it worse."

That night she fixed the three of us a special dinner of poached salmon, roasted potatoes and asparagus with a garlicky aioli. Like everything that Carolyn makes, it was perfect, but I was having a hard time swallowing, my throat still raw and tight from throwing up. When she noticed that I wasn't eating, she got up on a chair and reached to the top of a kitchen cupboard, pulling down a shoebox containing Hostess cupcakes, Twinkies, and Little Debbie cakes.

"You can't hide a thing from this one," her dad said. "She catches every trick."

"I've noticed," I said. I liked this about her. Everyone else was so easy to fool. Her vigilance made me feel safe. As the three of us sat side by side in his study, tucked under an afghan, watching old black-and-white movies and working through his stash of junk food, I almost managed to forget why we were there. I almost didn't envy their closeness.

Lying in his bed that night, looking at the photos on the wall, I noticed one of Carolyn and her mother at the beach. Their hair was the same shade of red, their front teeth overlapped in the same way, and they wore identical grins, only Carolyn was looking at the camera and her mother was looking at her. When I said that I liked this picture, Carolyn told me that it had been taken right before they found out that her mom was sick.

"I think it was the last time we were really happy," she said. "No-holds-barred."

"Do you still miss her?" I asked.

"Of course," she said. "I always will." She said this in such a straightforward way that I envied what seemed like a simpler grief. "I was thinking about what you said before," I told her. "About how my father waited until I was an adult to kill himself? If you're right, I almost wish he hadn't. He was so depressed at the end of his life, it's like he was a different person. Now that's how I remember him, instead of the way he was before." She didn't answer for a while, which was another thing I liked about her. She didn't just blurt out the first thing that came to mind.

"I can see why you feel that way now," she said at last, tracing my eyebrow with her fingertip, "but I'll bet someday you'll be glad you got that time with him. When my mom got sick, I didn't really know her yet. I mean she was my mom, and I loved her, but I didn't get to go through that adolescent phase where your parents turn into real people and you hate them for their weaknesses, and then you get older and appreciate them for the same reasons. Right now, all you can focus on are your dad's weaknesses, but later you'll remember more."

"When?" I asked.

"I don't know," she said.

The next morning at breakfast, Carolyn asked her dad if he would take her shopping for a suit. She had decided to apply to a teaching program sponsored by the Japanese Ministry of Education, and she needed something to wear to the embassy interview. We were graduating in six months, and we often talked about how we had no idea what to do next. This was the first I'd heard of her plan to teach in Japan. I had to remind myself that we hadn't made any promises to each other. She didn't owe me anything. I had no right to feel hurt.

Her dad wanted to buy her a skirt suit with a blazer, but she insisted on shopping in the men's department, selecting a single-breasted charcoal suit made of wool so fine it felt like silk, a white shirt and a blue tie. Her father remained silent as she disappeared into the changing room, avoiding the salesman's eye, but when she emerged in that suit, looking proud and shy and lovely as ever, he got down on his knees to turn her cuffs, and then he taught her how to knot the tie, and I had to look away.

After he paid for the suit, he was oddly quiet. He told us that he had some errands to run, that he'd see us at dinner, and he dropped us off downtown.

"He's upset," she said.

"Because you wanted a men's suit?" I guessed.

"Because he doesn't want me to move to Japan."

"I don't want you to move to Japan either," I said.

Instead of responding, she stopped in front of a tattoo parlor, grabbed my hand and said, "Let's do it. Do you want to?"

"Right now?" I asked. "Without thinking about it?"

"If you think too hard about every decision, you end up never doing anything."

"But a tattoo," I said, laughing. "It's so permanent."

"Come on," she said. "Even if you end up regretting it, you'll have a good story."

She frowned as she flipped through a binder filled with Celtic crosses, prowling tigers, and big black Chinese characters. "This guy's good with a needle but his taste sucks." She picked up a pencil and sketched on the back of a flyer. Within minutes she had drawn a dragon with a long, pensive snout and a lean body that tapered into a wind-whipped kite, explaining that both she and her mother had been born in the year of the dragon. She asked if I knew what I wanted, and suddenly I did. When I told her, she didn't ask why, didn't insinuate that my desire was dark or ominous. She just nodded and proceeded to sketch. "That's perfect," I said when she put her pencil down. But she shook her head and picked it up again, drawing a rope knotted to the top of the anchor.

"So someone can pull you back up," she said. "When you're ready."

"I'm ready," I said.

Lying in her father's bed, our fresh tattoos protected under thick pads of gauze, she told me why she'd decided to move to Japan. She'd gone to college near home because she didn't want to leave her dad, but now it was time. Japan was the most foreign place she could think of, the money was good for English teachers, and she didn't know what else to do with her life. "It seems like an interesting way to delay figuring that out," she said.

I thought about the Japanese exchange student that my family had hosted when I was in junior high. Her name was Takae, which she told me meant "expensive" or "tall," although she was short and introverted to the point of invisibility. On Christmas morning, after unwrapping the presents my mom had put under the tree for her, she wrapped them all back up and then left them on her dresser for the rest of the year. Before she left, she packed them still wrapped in her suitcase. In the car on the way to the airport, she cried and told my mother that she didn't want to go back to Japan, where she'd always felt like a disappointment to her parents, who'd wanted a son. She said that she had never felt so at home before, which made me feel guilty since I'd barely noticed she was there.

When I thought of Japan, I also thought of a picture I'd seen of a Tokyo subway platform so crowded that a man was using a long stick to prod commuters onto the train. People talked about going abroad to find yourself. Japan seemed like a place where you could get lost.

That night, I had the same nightmare that plagued me every time I managed to fall asleep. In it, I was up there with my father on the ledge of the bridge, gazing down at the city lights reflected in the dark gloss of the bay. Right before he jumped, he turned to me with his eyebrows raised, a wordless invitation to keep him company. And even though I did, I waited just a second too late and he never looked up. I hit the water hard, right after him, slipped into its cold depths, and fought my way back up to the surface, amazed to find that I was still alive, unhurt. I treaded water for a long time, waiting for my dad to surface beside me, and when this didn't happen it dawned on me that he hadn't made it. He was gone. And he never even knew that I had tried to follow him. I woke in a cold sweat, relieved to realize that it was just a dream until I remembered that it wasn't really. He was still gone and I was still here. But I had no idea where I was. My mouth was dry and my heart threw itself against my rib cage. Then my eyes landed on Carolyn's sleeping face. She was snoring softly, her lips parted over her crooked front teeth, her skin luminous even in the darkness. I pulled her close, whispering, "Don't leave me," knowing that I could never say something this needy if she were awake, but hoping the message would infiltrate her dreams.

On the bus ride back to New York the next day, when she asked if I'd consider moving to Japan with her, I didn't hesitate before saying yes. I had no idea how to make a life for myself in New York, and I couldn't go back to San Francisco.

San Francisco was that bridge.

A few hours after our fight, I come upstairs carrying a giant bowl of egg noodles slathered in butter and ketchup. This is Carolyn's kryptonite, the dish her mom used to fix for her when she was little and sick or upset about something. She is reading the novel that my mom sent me, and I can tell that she's deciding whether to stay mad. I crawl under the covers next to her, and when I hold out the fork, twirled with noodles, she opens her mouth to take a bite.

"How's that book?" I ask.

"Surprisingly, not that bad," she says. "Of course the woman is obsessed with her weight, and of course she's blind to the fact that the guy she should be with is right under her nose, but at least it's funny. It's a good escape." Carolyn never used to enjoy escapist fiction. She only read serious literature, books she could learn from. I must be a bad influence. "Read to me?" I say, lying with my head on her lap. Carolyn claims that she's a terrible performer, but when it's just the two of us, no one else around, she'll slip into each of the different voices, pausing in just the right places to draw out suspense; it's way better than watching a movie. It's like being able to share the same good dream.

At the end of a chapter, she closes the book. I open the window and line up a carton of milk, a dozen eggs and a stick of butter on the ledge—groceries I bought to replace the ones that went bad—hoping they won't freeze before morning. She turns off the lights and joins me at the window. It's snowing lightly. The moon looks like a dented melon in a graphite sky. Its light reflects off every sparkling surface. Across the street, Mrs. Ogawa is standing in her front yard, wearing a flannel nightgown, scattering rice for her koi. The fish form a tangled mass at the surface of the water, their gummy mouths opening and closing. We watch the old lady croon a lullaby to the fish, rocking on her feet, her eyes shut.

"Poor thing," Carolyn whispers. "She's not all there, is she?"

"It's probably for the best," I say. "Can you imagine being married to the *gomi* police? I'll bet he never lets her throw anything away."

"The horror, the horror," Carolyn jokes. She doesn't like to throw anything away either. The attic at her dad's house is officially called "The Carolyn Museum," complete with placards to go with various artifacts, like the depleted tube of Looney Tunes toothpaste she carried everywhere as a toddler. Carolyn is incredibly loyal to objects. I've given her things of mine that I didn't want to have around but couldn't bring myself to part with, like the boomerang my dad used as a paperweight. But whatever she takes, she keeps. I'll never get that boomerang back.

"Oh shit," I say, watching as Amana leaps onto the edge of the barrel where Mrs. Ogawa is feeding her fish and swipes a paw across the water. Carolyn gasps as we watch the cat dart into the shadows, a wriggling carp caught in her jaws.

"It's not funny," she says, burying her face in my neck to avoid looking at the old woman's wrinkled face, twisted in confusion.

"I know," I say, swallowing my laughter, "but isn't there some saying? Like catching fish in a barrel? Now we know why Amana was so fat when we got here."

"I don't want to give the neighbors anything else to hold against us!"

I wrap my arms around her waist and pull her closer, telling her not to worry, that the old lady is senile enough that she won't remember any of this in the morning.

"Come to bed," I say. "I mean, come to futon."

"I have my period," she reminds me, pulling away for a moment but keeping her hands on my waist in a way that gives me hope.

Usually she's the top, the spark that gets things burning, but lately there always seems to be some good reason why it's not a good time. Behind her back I see something move in the upstairs window across the street, a gap in the Venetian blinds framing a face as round and pale as the moon itself. I don't mention this to Carolyn. Instead I push her backward onto the futons and press my full weight on top of her. She can take it.

kawaii: (ADJ.) *cute; adorable; tiny*

Amana likes to come and go through the bedroom window, using the pine tree as a ladder to climb up and down. In her nocturnal prowling, she must have knocked our groceries from the windowsill to the street below. By the time I got downstairs this morning, Mrs. Ogawa was already outside cleaning up the mess, maneuvering her broom around the cat, who was lapping up milk streaming between the shattered eggs.

"*Gomen nasai,*" I apologize. "*Reizoku wa kowareta. Neko wa itazurako.*" I'm sorry. The refrigerator broke. The cat is naughty. It sounds like a haiku. I hope she gets it. The old woman nods and continues to sweep around Amana, who weaves between her rickety ankles. I lunge at the cat, but she leaps onto a table covered with bonsai trees and overturns a pot that falls onto the ground, cracking and exposing the plant's hair-thin roots. I apologize again as Mrs. Ogawa picks up the shards, dropping them in a bag filled with our *gomi*.

By the time I return upstairs, Carolyn is showered and ready for work, wearing a green sweater dress of mine that skims her body instead of clutching it. I'm still not used to seeing her in my clothes, or in clothes that show off her curves. Before we came here, she always wore pants, layered sports bras to flatten her breasts, and baggy hooded sweatshirts. She walked without swinging her hips and kept her head bent slightly as if pushing against a strong wind. She was more chivalrous and more aggressive than any of the guys I'd gone out with before her, opening taxi doors for me and engaging in shouting matches with guys who leered at us on the street. Back then, she liked me to wear the skirts. "You have great legs," she said. "R. Crumb legs. You look like you could kick over a horse."

She sits on the floor with her legs under the *kotatsu*, the heated table that Miyoshi-sensei loaned us when it got cold. It has an electric coil bolted to its underside and a quilted tablecloth to tent in the heat. She is reading *The Daily Yomiyuri* and eating peanut butter from the jar. This is her personal jar of peanut butter. We both ordered jars from a catalogue of international imports, and when they arrived by mail she wrote her name on the lid of one, with a Sharpie. "I just want it to last," she said when I complained that she was treating me like a roommate. Sure enough, I polished off my own jar long ago while she continues to enjoy the daily-recommended portion size.

"Amana broke the eggs," I say. "There's nothing for breakfast."

"You have to go by Mister Donuts to throw out the trashsicle," she reminds me.

"We need a new refrigerator," I say. "We can't keep throwing out our groceries."

"First we have to go to the dump and get rid of the old one."

I'm about to tell her that there is no dump when she informs me that she and Joe are going this afternoon. "When did you talk to Joe?" I ask, trying not to sound too interested.

"I didn't," she says, sucking the peanut butter off her spoon. "He faxed me."

"He faxed you?" I repeat. "Out of the blue? That's weird."

"We fax sometimes," she says. "It's no big deal."

"When did all this start?"

"All nothing. I don't know." She pauses. "I guess he faxed me for the first time on the anniversary of my mom's death, just to say he was thinking of me."

"You told him about your mom?"

"It came up last month when we visited the junior high. The English teacher wanted us to talk about our families. She told us to draw all of our family members on the board, and Joe drew like eight people, but I only drew a picture of my dad. The kids asked what happened to my mom, and when I told them that she died I started crying. I hadn't even thought about her for so long. I guess it just hit me . . . "

"The wave?" I ask, oddly jealous.

"What?" She looks confused. "No, the fact that those kids were already three years older than I was when my mom died. They were so tiny. It made me realize how much I'd missed out on. Anyways, Joe was great. He took the attention off me by telling the kids how his parents split up when he was six, how his dad is about to get married for the third time, how he has three brothers by different moms. We started this excellent discussion about nontraditional families. Not exactly what that teacher had in mind!"

"That's funny," I say. "Yesterday, I told my class that my dad died."

"You did?" She sounds surprised. Carolyn thinks that I'm still in denial. She would probably laugh if I told her about my awkward attempt to translate the word "cremated" into Japanese. *He became burnable.* But the subject came up because we were talking about garbage: specifically about my inability to follow *gomi* rules. I don't want to give her any more reason to think that I'm careless. I pick up the newspaper and she goes downstairs to put away her personal jar of peanut butter.

Once again The Curry Lady of Wakayama has made the front page. Earlier this year, a woman named Masumi Hayashi slipped arsenic into a pot of curry at a neighborhood festival, putting sixty people in the hospital and killing four. While lab results determined that the arsenic in the curry matched a box of rat poison in the Hayashi garage, she has yet to issue a formal apology or explain why she did it. "Hayashi Won't Break Silence!" reads today's headline. Criminals here are always asked to explain themselves, as if there were logical reasons behind the most impulsive and violent crimes. Speculation has it that the poisoning was an act of revenge against her neighbors, who frequently criticized her for not doing her share of chores and for showing up late to neighborhood functions.

I go downstairs to read the story to Carolyn. We both get a kick out of these Curry Lady stories. She is in the bathroom, standing an inch from the mirror, styling her eyebrows. First she brushes her right eyebrow with clear mascara, then she fills it in with brown pencil. Catching sight of me behind her, she startles and scrawls a diagonal line up onto her forehead, so that she looks theatrically mad.

"Do you mind?" she says. "Don't watch me. I know I look stupid when I do this."

"You don't look stupid," I say. "But you don't need to do that. I like the way you look without makeup. You really don't need it."

"Well maybe I want to look different," she says. "Is that okay with you?"

"Of course," I say. "I'm sorry. Let's not fight."

I stand behind her, wrap my arms around her waist and kiss the nape of her neck. I want her to turn around and kiss me back, for it to be hard and close like the first time. She pivots and presses her lips to mine and my breath catches. It's not quite the kiss I coveted, not rash or urgent or new, but it feels as familiar as any home, and I'm sorry when she breaks away.

"Don't forget to take out the trashsicle," she says. "And sort through it first!"

As I put on my shoes in the entryway, I notice that a picture has slid to the bottom of the refrigerator. One weekend in late September, Carolyn and I took the train down to Osaka. We went to the Panasonic Museum of Technology, where everyone's favorite attraction was the baby maker. A computer took a picture of me, then it took one of Carolyn. It averaged our bone structures, added a few dollops of fat, and created the image of our genetically impossible daughter, posed between us on a park bench. She looks about five, dressed in an awful purple dress with puffy sleeves. She has Carolyn's blue eyes and sharp nose, my heart-shaped face and full lips, and an ironic little smile. On the train ride back to Shika, we kept passing the picture back and forth.

"I know I'm biased," Carolyn kept saying, "but she really is cute."

"She's totally cute," I agreed, "and she looks smart too. She looks like a great little kid, like she'd have all these strange, interesting things to say. I wish—"

"We could really have her," Carolyn finished my thought.

We stuck our digital daughter's picture to the refrigerator, where she greets us every time we enter or exit the house. But lately I've been averting my eyes from her ironic little smile, and I've noticed Carolyn doing the same.

Mrs. Ogawa is still outside, raking weeds from the cracks in the black-top between our houses. I wait until her back is turned before I set the trashsicle on the roof of my car—I don't want it to ooze onto the already smelly upholstery—and crawl in through the window. As I drive down the block, an empty bottle of soy sauce blows out of the trash bag and careens into the ditch. In my rearview mirror, before I have time to brake, I see the old woman rush to pick it up. At a cross-walk, a group of elementary school kids stops and points and laughs at me, as if I were some kind of circus freak instead of a tired blonde driving a car with a bag of trash on its roof. In front of Mister Donuts, two old ladies wearing aprons and galoshes guard the trash bin. As I approach, they make the X-sign with their arms and say, "*dame*."

"What's forbidden?" I ask, leaning out my window.

"*Zenbu*," they say, smiling. Everything.

I drive past the convalescent home, the post office, the liquor shop, the persimmon grove, where the fruit has been picked and is now hanging to dry from the branches. The orange globes look like Christmas ornaments, which reminds me of Miyoshi-sensei's recent criticism. *In your country, you cut down a tree only to hang some balls. It's kind of strange and wasteful.* I could drive up to the nuclear power station, where they burn *gomi* every day, but I'd never get back in time for first period. I haven't even sorted the trash, I realize with a sinking feeling. I am driving past the conveyor belt sushi restaurant when I notice an unattended metal Dumpster in the otherwise empty lot. It's larger than the one in front of Mister Donuts, so tall that I can no longer see my bag after I toss it in.

I will not let Miyoshi-sensei steer another class toward garbage.

I am taking matters into my own hands.

Before first period, I sneak into the secretarial classroom, my pocket heavy with magnets. On one side of the blackboard, I stick pictures from the Japanese magazines *Cutie* and *Fruits*, of models posing like little girls. On the other I hang pictures of female politicians and sports stars from *Time* and *Newsweek*. The bell rings and the students file into the room, trailed by Miyoshi-sensei. Like a school of fish, they cluster around the pictures from Japanese fashion magazines.

"*Kawaii*! Cute-o! Cute-o!" they chirp. This is one English word they all know.

"*So* cute," one girl says, reaching a finger to trace the ruffled panties of the model bending over. The right half of this student's face is puckered with a pink burn scar. I try to remember her name. It's either Junko or Chiemi. A dozen common names get recycled over and over here, and since I don't know what they mean, I can't keep them straight.

"Look at her," I say, pointing at Venus Williams, smashing a serve at Wimbledon. "Doesn't she look strong and powerful?"

"So big!" she says. "Like man!"

"She's an athlete," I say. "She's not trying to look like a little girl."

"Who is that?" asks Ritsuko Ueno, as she points at a picture of Hillary Clinton.

"That's Hillary Clinton," I reply.

"Bill's wife?"

"Yes, but she's a politician too. She's a smart and independent woman, just like you." I don't even know how much I like Hillary Clinton, but I put her up so I have to defend her.

"Maybe *too* independent?" Ritsuko says.

"No way," I say. "You can't be too independent!"

Ritsuko says something in Japanese, and Miyoshi-sensei laughs before translating. "When Bill was president, Hillary was never in the white home. She made it so easy for Monica-chan, *ne*?" I laugh too, in spite of myself.

Ritsuko is funny, playful with her words in both English and Japanese. She's a head taller than most of her classmates, but she doesn't seem to mind sticking out. "Same size," she always says, standing beside me and grinning without covering her less than perfectly straight teeth. She has, as she likes to say, "a very Japanese face," a porcelain oval with long narrow eyes and a pink bud of a mouth.

She looks like a girl in a traditional woodcut, or the model for a Noh mask. But there is nothing old-fashioned or demure about her. In the future, Ritsuko wants to work as a tour guide in San Francisco or New York. She got a copy of the questions for one company's certification test, and she often visits me in the faculty room so I can quiz her. She knows more about the places I've lived in than I do.

Once, she happened to be hanging out at my desk when her mom dropped by. Sakura Ueno is the matchmaker here in Shika, the force behind Noriko's engagement, but she also manages the local bank, and she comes to Shika High School at the end of every month to distribute the faculty salaries in cash. She brings a metal box filled with money and bank books belonging to each faculty member, and she goes from desk to desk, subtracting whatever each person owes for gas and electricity, rent or mortgage payments, helping to determine what portion of their remaining salary should go into savings, then distributing the rest as pocket money. She knows everyone's debt patterns and spending habits, information she puts to use as a matchmaker. When she approached us with her metal box that day and asked me a question, Ritsuko shook her head before translating.

"She wants to know, are you *singuru*? You don't have to tell. She is very noisy."

"Nosy?" I guessed, avoiding the question of whether I was single.

"That also," Ritsuko said, which is what I love about her. She is so quick.

Now the girls sit down and get out their gender worksheets. I read the first question and ask Miyoshi-sensei to choose a student to read her answer aloud.

"I like to be a girl because . . . "

"Chiemi," Miyoshi-sensei says, and the girl with the burned face stands up.

"Because I like cute skirt," she recites in a rush.

"Okay," I say. "Great." I try not to feel disappointed when the next student he calls on reads the exact same response. I ask if anyone has a different answer. "Because I like make," replies a third girl. I write the word "makeup" on the board, and most of the girls pick up their pencils to adjust their answers.

"Question two," I say, "I would like to be a boy because . . ."

I'm optimistic when Miyoshi-sensei calls on Mai Murata, the volleyball team captain, who wears sweatpants bunched up under her skirt, swaggering like a cowboy. She gnaws on a hangnail, then reads her answer in Japanese. The class snickers and Miyoshi-sensei presses a fist to his mouth to conceal a grin.

"What did she say?" I ask.

"It's kind of so rude . . ."

"That's fine," I say. "Girls don't have to be polite or ladylike."

"Okay," he says with a shrug. "Mai would like to be a boy so she could . . . how to say . . . make yellow water standing up?"

"Pee," I translate.

"It's more convenient," he says. I have to laugh. They're funny, these girls. They will not be manipulated or even led. It's a kind of strength.

"Question three," I say. "In Japan, only girls can . . ." Without looking to Miyoshi-sensei, I call on Haruki Ogawa. The boy has been sitting like a stone throughout this discussion. At the sound of his name, he jerks back in his seat as if whiplashed. He braces both palms on his desk and pushes himself slowly to his feet. The first time he opens his mouth, nothing comes out. "It's okay," Miyoshi-sensei says, but the boy opens his mouth again, and this time, a tiny, raspy sound escapes, like an insect he's been holding on his tongue, barely alive.

"In Japan," he whispers, "only girls can stay home forever."

At the end of the day, as I climb the stairs to the faculty room, I hear the thumping background track of The Carpenters' "Close to You." Miyoshi-sensei often plays karaoke CD's after school, keeping the faculty windows open to attract students to his after-school club. But no one ever shows up. I sit at my desk and he turns off the machine before approaching me, hands in his pockets. "Congratulations," he says.

"Thanks for translating," I say. "I enjoyed hearing what the girls had to say."

"So did I," he says, "I did not think they could answer such questions."

"Questions about gender?"

"Questions without multiple choice. Without one correct answer. But this is not why I said congratulations before. Reason is because Ogawa-san did not have to sort your *gomi* yesterday. Maybe you didn't make any more *gomi* mistakes . . . "

"Great." I force a smile. We didn't throw anything away yesterday. But I decide to take advantage of his good mood, telling him that our groceries all went bad again, that we really need a new refrigerator.

"But new refrigerator costs much money," he says, "and you couldn't take it home to America. It's also a waste, *ne?*"

"We could buy a little one," I suggest. "Or we could rent one."

"Shika does not even have video rental store," he reminds me. "But I have one unusual suggestion. . . . . . . How about buying groceries such as bread and noodles and fruit? Food that does not live in refrigerator . . . "

"That's a temporary solution," I say.

"Exactly," he says. "A temporary solution for a temporary person." He claps his hands as if the matter were resolved and offers to take me grocery shopping. "I think you are kind of helpless," he says.

"I am not helpless," I snap.

"I'm sorry," he says. "I only meant that you need help. How should I say? You are needy? Is this better?"

At the supermarket, I feel like a contestant on *The Price Is Right* as I chase after Miyoshi-sensei while he weaves the cart down the aisles. Apparently we're in a big hurry.

"Do you eat rice or bread for breakfast?" he asks me.

"I eat both," I say.

"But how about for breakfast?" he presses. "Rice or bread?"

This is a trick question, one I've been asked many times, a way to gauge whether a foreigner is resisting or adapting to Japanese life.

"I usually have cereal," I say.

"Okay," he says, "but you need milk, I think, to swallow cereal, and milk needs refrigeration, *ne*?" From the cooler he pulls out a package of steak, sliced ribbon thin. He tells me that he's buying it for his own dinner. Stuck to the plastic wrapper is a sticker printed with a photograph of a man's face, his nose engorged and ruddy, his eyes bugging out.

"Is that guy some wanted criminal?" I ask.

"Oh no," he says, laughing. "This is Yamagawa-san. Manager of Jade Plaza."

"Why is his picture on every piece of meat?"

"Recently," he says, "in another town, a supermarket manager faked expiration dates on old meat, resulting in a small E. coli epidemic. So supermarket managers put their own face on every package. It's personal guarantee of freshness. Do you want to try tonight?"

"I don't think so," I say.

"Right," he says. "I remember now. You don't eat meat. This is

why you threw so much beef in your neighborhood soft plastics recycling bin."

I follow him to the produce section at the front of the store,
where every apple is cradled in a nest of foam, every melon swad-
dled in tissue, clusters of grapes polished and shining in open boxes.
One corner has been sectioned off with padded rope, the floor covered in foam squares. Inside, two old women and a little boy are
seated on folding chairs, their eyes closed and their hands resting
on their knees. Pressed to the insides of their wrists, plastic suction
cups connect them by wires to a buzzing machine.

"Konnichiwa, Miyoshi-sensei," says a man in a white lab coat with
shaggy bleached hair.

"That's my former student," Miyoshi-sensei says. "He is entre-
preneur now."

"What's going on in there?" I ask.

"Maybe they're receiving a kind of *shokku* treatment."

"A shock treatment?" I interpret, and he nods. "Like for depression?"

"Mmm," he says. "Or another problem. People come for many
reasons. Hoping to cure a disease, to lose weight, to replenish
energy . . . even to restore hair to a bald head."

"Those people don't look shocked," I say.

"But current is inside them. You don't believe? Come. I can prove
to you."

He approaches the man in the lab coat and says something in
Japanese. Then he pushes up his jacket sleeve and the man presses a
suction cup to the inside of his wrist. For a moment we stand facing
each other, close enough that I can smell green onions on his breath
and the pomade in his hair. I feel like a couple at a junior high dance,
waiting for the music to start. "Now shock is inside me," he says. "But
I can't feel anything until . . . " He reaches out for my shoulder and
the current springs from his fingertips, forks down my arm and into

my hand, which buzzes like I slipped it into a glove full of bees. "*Itai!*" I cry out, jumping backward and shaking my hand in front of me. My palm is mottled red and white. It looks like raw hamburger.

"I'm sorry," he says, biting his lip. "That was more powerful than I expected." He takes my hand and rubs it between his palms.

"Have you done this before?" I ask, my flesh still tingling.

"Maybe," he says. "Once or twice."

"So did it work?" I venture, wanting to know why he would sit in a grocery store shock booth, where anyone could see him.

"What?" he says, only now letting go of my hand.

"The shock. Did it fix all your problems? Your hair is awfully thick." I keep my tone light, so that he can crack a joke if he wants.

"I came with my father," he says. "He has *gan*. . . . . . . you know, cancer?"

"Oh god," I say, wishing I could fall down a hole. "I'm so sorry."

I met Miyoshi-sensei's father once, at my welcome banquet at a Chinese restaurant. The mayor presented me with my *hanko*, a narrow bamboo cylinder carved with the characters for my name. He showed me how to press the stamp into a red inkpot to sign my contract. He was stockier and shorter than his son, dressed in a double-breasted suit with a sheen that matched his silver hair. He didn't seem sick. But when he introduced himself, he pressed what looked like a beeper to his throat. His lips moved, but the sound came out of the device. I laughed obligingly, thinking it was some kind of zany Japanese invention, an automatic translator, and wishing that I had one too. The rest of the night, Miyoshi-sensei did the talking. Only now do I realize my mistake.

"It's okay," he says, smiling in an embarrassed way that I recognize, trying to put me at ease.

As he pulls onto our street, we pass Haruki Ogawa trudging home from school. His grandfather is outside, tinkering with his miniature forklift, and as he catches sight of my supervisor he sets down his tools, clamps his hand around the back of Haruki's neck, and steers him toward us. More than twice his size, the boy could easily over-power his grandfather, but instead he trembles like an overripe fruit at the end of a gnarled branch.

"Recently," Miyoshi-sensei translates for the old man, "Ogawa-san was sorting the *gomi* in Haruki's room when he found your failed test."

"What failed test?" I ask.

"Your self-introduction test. Haruki scored zero percent."

"That wasn't a real test," I say, glad that for once I'm not the one in trouble. "It was just a worksheet." Miyoshi-sensei translates this for Ogawa-san, who still doesn't release his grandson's neck. "Ogawa-san says if it's not a real test, you should not call it a test." I remind him that he told me to call it that, that he said the students wouldn't listen otherwise. "It's true," he says with a sigh, "but Haruki is not like other students. He did not attend junior high school. He only studied English alone in his room with a book. So of course he lacks confidence in his voice. His grandfather is concerned that if he fails, he will return to his room once more."

Then maybe the old man shouldn't shame him, I think, or root through his trash.

I don't say this. Instead I tell Ogawa-san that Haruki did a great job in English class today. "*Sodesune*," Miyoshi-sensei agrees, reaching into his briefcase and pulling out the boy's worksheet. He passes it to Ogawa-san, who scowls and turns it around and around like an indecipherable map to a place he'd rather not go.

"What was his score?" he asks at last.

"*Hyaku pacento*," I say.

"One hundred percent?" the old man repeats, sounding grudgingly impressed. "I can't believe it. All he ever does is sit in his room, listening to noise."

"Haruki loves American music," Miyoshi-sensei tells me. "He introduced me to his favorite band called Smashed Pumpkins."

"Smashing Pumpkins," Haruki and I correct him in unison.

Today is the greatest day I've ever known . . . " I sing, then stop abruptly. "Sorry," I say. "I have a terrible voice."

"I have one unusual idea," Miyoshi-sensei says, "for how Haruki could improve English and confidence in one convenient method. He could join karaoke club. In karaoke, correct words appear on screen. You couldn't make a mistake. There's nothing to fear, *ne?*"

It is easier for me to picture the boy flapping his arms and lifting into the sky than crooning into a microphone. But Miyoshi-sensei seems excited. "Have you asked him?" I say. "He already said yes." He grins. "Belonging to a club is mandatory for all students. He has to join one. How about you?"

"How about me?" I repeat.

"Would you like to try? A club needs more than one member."

"But I can't sing," I protest.

"You can sing," he insists. "You must simply change gear. Like a bicycle."

"I think I'm a one-speed."

"You are not a one-speed," he says. "I can tell."

After hitting Play on his karaoke machine, Miyoshi-sensei launches into song. It's "Close to You," by The Carpenters, a horrible song but his voice is good, a steady tenor, and he nails every syllable perfectly, just as it darkens on screen. I'm sorry when he stops singing and hands me the microphone, hitting Rewind. "Why do birds suddenly appear . . . " I come in too late and rush to the end of the verse, my voice quavering on the high notes.

"I told you," I say. "I can't sing."

"Don't be afraid," he says. "Have you heard a baby learn to speak? Baby begins with singing. Speech comes second. When we learn fear, we forget how to sing." He pauses and I reflect upon this. "When you are afraid you breathe like this." He bounces his shoulders up and down. "Baby breathes from the belly. Like this." He pulls his shirt close to his torso and I watch it expand and flatten when he exhales. He gives Haruki the same instructions. "You have much room for air," he says. He hands him the microphone and hits Rewind again, but when the music starts the boy doesn't make a sound, sitting frozen in place as usual. "Just like me," Miyoshi-sensei prompts him, "they long to be . . . "

"Close to you," Haruki finally joins in, his voice a helium whisper.

"Don't be afraid," Miyoshi-sensei says. "There is nothing to be afraid of."

He tells us both to stand up and then wraps handkerchiefs around our eyes, explaining that he wants us to sing blindfolded while we walk around the faculty room, listening to our voices reflect off different surfaces. This is a new Miyoshi-sensei, a man with a plan, no one to say no to. We put our trust in him, and before long it starts to pay off. As Haruki and I take turns on the verse, I manage to hit the high notes and he starts to sing for real. I realize that I've never heard his voice before. It's fine, remarkably unexceptional. The way he keeps quiet, you'd think he had something to hide.

I am leaning against the wall, listening to him take his turn singing, when I hear something else: the crunch of suppressed laughter. I strip off my blindfold and see three boys in the doorway, their fingers pressed to the underside of their noses. I've seen these boys. They are members of the technical class, the ones who sexually harassed their last female teacher. Two of them are Goth, with bleached hair in sculpted disarray and gobs of eyeliner, while the third is a *ganguro*, or "blackface" with a huge Afro-perm. To me they look more goofy than scary, but Haruki is obviously petrified. His shoulders are bouncing up and down, and his blindfold is pushed up on his brow. When he rips it off and throws it to the ground, the boys laugh harder. He pushes through them and bolts down the stairs.

"Are those the boys who bullied Haruki?" I ask Miyoshi-sensei, who has collapsed on the couch, his head in his hands.

"Maybe," he says.

"Does that mean yes?" I press.

"I don't know," he says. "Probably. He never told."

On my way out of school, I pass the open door to a classroom in which a woman wearing a kimono is distributing flowers to a group of girls seated in a circle. The daylight is fading and the room glows with two kerosene stoves and I linger at the threshold until the woman turns around and sees me.

"Miss Marina?" she says.

"Yes," I say, wondering if we've met. She has a striking face, triangular like a cat's, with high cheekbones and eyes that are gray rather than black. Her hair is more gray than black too, short and messy, alive with cowlicks. I think I'd remember her.

"My name is Keiko," she says. "I teach elementary school art. Also I coach *ikebana*." She gestures at an arrangement on the floor, an asymmetrical spray of purple cosmos with chocolate brown centers, puffy marigolds and pussy willows. "Do you want to try?"

"Wah!" the girls exclaim. "Your English is so good, Ishii-sensei!"

"Thank you," she says. "English is my favorite subject, in my student time."

"What a coincidence," I say. "Art was my favorite subject."

"Coincidence?" she echoes, tucking her short hair behind her ear.

"A coincidence is like fate," I try to explain, but this isn't quite right. "It's when two people have something unexpected in common, or two strangers meet for a reason."

"Like destiny?" she asks, and I nod. "Sorry, but I don't believe in this."

"Me neither," I say, laughing. "Life feels too random."

"It's all accidents," she agrees. "But," she holds up a finger, "if there's no destiny, then a . . . coincidence is even more lucky, *ne?*"

"That's true," I say. "I never thought about it that way."

"It's lucky to meet you," she says. She hands me my own newspaper cone filled with blooms and grasses, a shallow ceramic bowl and a pronged metal disc, and the girls make room for me in their circle. I ask if I should copy the arrangement on the floor.

"Not copy," Keiko says. "Inspire. *Ikebana* should look wild. Like nature put it there."

My dad would've liked this wild style of floral arrangement. He used to keep garbage bags and a trowel in the back of his car, and when we drove through state parks on our family road trips, if a flower or plant caught his eye, he'd leave his engine idling while he got out and uprooted it to replant in our own yard. He called this, "liberating the natives." My job was to keep a lookout for state troopers. My mom told him that he was setting a bad example, but he said that he was like Robin Hood. And it was true. When our garden was in full bloom, he made lavish bouquets, filling jelly jars with flowers to give to the nurses at the hospital, his favorite patients, the guys who ran the coffee shop on the corner, the dry cleaner. At his memorial service, people I didn't know kept coming up to me to say how much they'd appreciated receiving his bouquets, what a special man he was, so full of life; the unspoken question lingering in the air.

I've just finished placing the final stem in the metal brush when Keiko pauses in front of my desk, tilts her head to one side and says, "*Ikebana* is so difficult, *ne?*" I feel deflated, assuming I messed up somehow. I must not have cut the stems short enough. The flowers are flopping to the side, weighted by their blossoms. Still, it doesn't look so different from her arrangement and I wish I could see what I did differently, what I did wrong. "*Ikebana* is so difficult," she repeats, "so I can't believe this is your first time!" After a moment, I realize that for once I've done something right.

"*Kawaii*," a few girls say, but Keiko shakes her head. "It's not cute. It's *wabi sabi*." She explains that the character for *wabi* means stillness or loneliness, while *sabi* means old or broken.

"That doesn't sound very pretty," I say.

"No," she agrees. "It's not pretty. It lasts."

When I get home, there's a note on the refrigerator.

M.: Joe and I went to get some sushi for dinner. C.

It's barely five, but the sky is almost black by the time I reach the sushi restaurant. From outside I can see Joe and Carolyn still sitting at a window booth, empty plates stacked between them. Laughing, Carolyn lifts a hand to cover her crooked front teeth. This is a new gesture, one she must have picked up from her students. Joe raises his chin as I enter the restaurant and Carolyn swivels to face me, her expression hard to read. "Sorry I'm late," I say, as if the three of us had planned to meet here. I slide into the seat beside her. When I kiss her, she turns her face so my lips find the hollow behind her jaw. The sushi chef in the middle of the conveyor belt looks at us, his knife poised in midair. I reach for a plate of egg sushi as it passes by and trickle it with a stream of soy sauce, watching the yellow darken.

"Sorry we finished eating," Carolyn says.

"That's okay," I say. "Do you mind hanging out for a while? I'm starving."

"We've got five minutes," Joe says, raising his Sapporo bottle to request another.

"You two have somewhere important to be?" I ask.

"We're meeting some of the lads from the power plant for a pint," Joe says. "Caro hasn't met many people on her own. It's been rough on her."

"I know," I say, wishing that he wouldn't speak for her, and that she wouldn't let him. "It's been hard for me too."

"But you teach in Shika," Carolyn says. "Everyone knows you."

"They know my name," I say.

"You should come," she says, but she doesn't sound like she means it.

"I'm pretty tired," I say. "I had a long day." I wait for her to press, to try and coax me into joining them, but instead she asks what happened and I tell her about the karaoke club incident, how Haruki got laughed at by the boys who bullied him.

"That the shut-in?" Joe asks, and I nod. "I remember how hard Hiro worked to get him to join his homeroom last spring. He was at that boy's house every afternoon for a month, listening to music with him, talking to him, forcing him out of hiding."

"Really?" I say. "He never mentioned that."

"It was like a personal mission. The teachers placed bets on whether the kid would stay in school once he started coming."

"It's still tenuous," I say.

"I reckon it doesn't make much difference," he says. "Waste of space, innit? The way he just sits there doing fuck all."

"That's harsh," I say, even though I've thought the exact same thing.

"We're going to be late," Carolyn says, reaching across the table to pick up Joe's wrist and look at his watch. "I'm sorry to leave while you're still eating," she says to me.

"No problem," I say. "Have fun."

She reaches for her wallet but Joe says, "Allow me," slapping down a thousand yen bill, which comes five hundred yen short of their total.

At first I think that someone must have broken in. The ikebana arrangement is strewn across the floor in the entryway, the leaves ripped to shreds, the flowers torn from the trampled stems. I hold my breath, listen for the sound of an intruder still lurking, but all is quiet and still. Even the refrigerator's engine is silent, the enamel warm as I squeeze past to investigate the living room, kitchen, bathroom, and storage area. Aside from the ruined floral arrangement, nothing is out of place. The house is just as I left it an hour ago, down to the sour milk stench.

I go upstairs with a pot of tea and turn on the *kotatsu*. Sliding my legs under the heated table, my feet collide with something soft and I hear what sounds like a newborn cry. "Come here, Amana," I say, rubbing my thumb and fingers together, eager for the cat's small warm comfort on my lap. She crawls out on unsteady legs, her face stained a dark ochre, her eyes glazed and filmy. "Kitty?" I say. "What's wrong?" She jumps up onto the table and retches, throwing up the chewed head of a flower. When I try to pick her up she recoils, leaping onto the window ledge where she teeters for a moment, then topples out. By the time I get downstairs she is gone, which I take to be a good sign. If she can run away then she must be okay.

Animals like to be alone when they're sick, to lick their wounds in private.

Carolyn comes home just before midnight, smelling like whiskey and cigarette smoke, with her eyebrow pencil and lipstick worn off. I ask if she had fun and she shrugs, says it was okay. She doesn't offer any details. When Carolyn has a crush on someone, she stops talking about them, at least to me. She says I make it impossible for her to be honest.

A few weeks before we left for Japan, Carolyn and I were at the Union Square Barnes & Noble reading guide books, when she put hers down and said that she might like to sleep with someone else. Not hypothetically. "We have an open relationship," she reminded me. "So I wanted to let you know." Carolyn always said that desire shouldn't be pinned down; that lies ruined relationships, not infidelity, and monogamy was a heterosexist construction. So I was shocked when she told me that she wanted to sleep with a guy, a line cook at the restaurant where she worked, who gave her rides back to the dorm on his Vespa. I knew the rules. There were none. We just had to be honest. I'd agreed to these terms because I sensed that they were nonnegotiable, because I wanted to be as cool and unconventional as Carolyn, and because I hoped that I would change her mind. When I said that I had no idea she was even attracted to guys, she told me that she wanted something fun and easy for a change. "Everything is out in the open with guys," she said. "They don't crowd you. You can keep certain things private." I tried to stay calm. I took a sip of my cappuccino and dabbed the foam from my lip. "Fine," I said, "but if you do sleep with him then I won't go to Japan with you." If she did, she kept it hidden. She didn't want to come here alone.

CHAPTER SIX

reizoku: (N.) *refrigerator*

Amana never came home last night.

All morning Carolyn has been searching for the cat, convinced that something horrible must have happened to her. "Don't worry," I say, pulling her by the hand out of the storage area, where Amana sometimes curls up in boxes to sleep. "She'll come home again when she's hungry." Carolyn grabs the box of Grape-Nuts from the cupboard, buries her hand in it, and crams a handful into her mouth. I ask if I can have some and she turns her back on me, hugs the box of cereal to her chest. "Just one handful," I coax her, sliding a palm under her arm, accidentally brushing her breast. As she raises her arm to ward me off, the box of cereal gets knocked to the floor. Grape-Nuts skitter everywhere and Carolyn drops to her knees. Within seconds she's not just crying, she's sobbing, like a car shifting directly from neutral to fourth gear.

"Hey," I say, offering her a hand up. "They're just Grape-Nuts."

"That's not the point," she says, crying harder. "Nothing is mine here."

"I'll buy you a new box," I say. "You can write your name on it with a Sharpie."

She shuts herself in the bathroom and when she finally comes back out, twenty minutes later, her makeup reapplied, she's missed the bus to Hakui.

"I can give you a ride to school if you want," I say.

"It's not like I have a choice," she says.

It's a dreary morning, gray and bone-chillingly cold. When Carolyn climbs through the passenger-side window, the peg that locks the door catches on the back pocket of her favorite pants. Ripping, the wool makes a sound like tires driving through slush. I wait for her to start crying again, but her face just turns red while her nostrils whiten and flare. It's a scary new expression on a face I thought I knew by heart. I turn the key in the ignition, but the engine refuses to turn over. Sputtering, it seems to be laughing at us.

"What's wrong?" she asks. "Why won't it start?"

"I don't know," I say. "I guess the battery must be dead." My bewilderment is an act. I know exactly what's wrong. The needle on the gas gauge is aiming straight at empty.

"I'll call Joe," she says, going back inside to change.

Enter Joe, a knight in a miniature Toyota "YO" truck, the other letters painstakingly scratched off the fender. His acoustic guitar rides shotgun, its hourglass torso covered with a patchwork of stickers, some politically correct (*Arms Are for Hugging*; *Recycle, The Earth's On Loan From Our Children*), some band names (*The Clash, Nick Cave and the Bad Seeds*), but mostly photo booth shots of Joe himself, a tall blond man in the center of group after group of black-haired girls, tucked around him like petals around a stamen. He jumps out of his truck, kisses both of us, and apologizes for being a bit damp, explaining that he just came from a morning *shorinji kempo* practice.

"I didn't know you did martial arts," Carolyn says. She's all blinky and peach now, one of the only people I know who looks better after a big cry.

"I've got the darkest belt in my *dojo*."

"If you do say so yourself," I mutter.

"Well, pet," he says, "since the other members of my *dojo* are a dozen elementary schoolgirls, the competition's not too stiff."

"You do martial arts with little girls?" Carolyn asks.

"Oh Caro, it's fantastic. Those girls don't understand about race or nationalism yet. It's a shame they can't stay that way forever."

"Yeah," I say. "Too bad they have to go and become real women."

"Someone woke up on the wrong side of the futon," he says, tweaking my nose. Who does that? And why is he always touching us?

"Aren't you worried about hurting them?" I ask.

"I'm more worried about them hurting me," he says. "*Shorinji kempo* is all about sizing up your opponent, figuring out their weaknesses and using them to your advantage. A little girl is going to be quick and light on her feet, even if she can't match my strength."

"Just how strong are you?" I ask. I feel light on my own feet, as if the blood in my veins were carbonated. I could punch someone out. I could kick over a horse. I could lift my car off the ground and spin it around on the tip of one finger.

"Why, pet? You want to arm wrestle? What's the prize?"

"Save your strength," Carolyn says. "You're going to need it this afternoon, when we take the refrigerator to the dump."

"You can't," I say. "There is no dump."

"What are you talking about?" Carolyn says. "How can there be no dump?"

"Because," I say, "in this microscopic crowded country, nothing really gets thrown away. It's all burned or recycled." Only as I say these words do I realize their truth. "You tell her," I say to Joe. "I'm sure when you lived in Shika, Miyoshi-sensei must have gotten on your case about the *gomi* rules."

"Not really," he says, raking his hair out of his eyes.

"Because he followed them," Carolyn says.

"I didn't make much trash," Joe says. "My students—well, their mothers—took pity on the young foreign lad living alone. I don't think I fixed one dinner all year."

But then he remembers how he had an old stereo he wanted to get rid of, and Miyoshi-sensei told him to put it in the wire cage by the river. Carolyn runs up the flight of stairs and returns grinning, reporting that it already holds a rice cooker, an old microwave and a pair of headphones. Joe says that it must be the day when electronic goods are picked up, that if we hurry we can move the refrigerator out right now.

"You'll never have to see it again," he tells Carolyn.

"Or smell it," she adds.

"Will you take the blame?" I ask Joe.

"Take the blame?" he repeats, laughing. "We're not committing a felony."

"Fine," I say, "so when Miyoshi-sensei gets upset, you'll tell him it was your idea."

"No worries," he says. "Hiro never gets upset with me."

Carolyn opens the front door wide, and Joe slides between the wall and the fridge. He tries to push it forward but it won't budge, so he turns around and uses the back of his shoulders, groaning softly until the fridge advances a few inches. He straightens, shakes his head and shoulders in a Rocky impersonation. Carolyn laughs, covering her mouth. The three of us each take a corner. We all open our arms wide and it's like a group hug, the refrigerator coming between us. On the count of three we lift the fridge and carry it a few feet before the enamel slides down our palms and it lands with a thunderous clatter.

"Let's tip it," Joe proposes. "Think martial arts. This thing is bigger than we are. We have to bring it down sideways." Carolyn comes downstairs with the *kotatsu*, the heated table that Miyoshi-sensei loaned us. Joe and I tilt the fridge, walk it out the door one corner at a time, and hoist it up onto the squat table, which sags under the weight. Joe backs his truck up to the building, leaves the engine idling and jumps up into the bed with a goatlike agility. "Push gently," he says. "I'll get out of the way at the last second."

"You're going to hurt yourself," Carolyn says.

"I'll be fine," he assures her. "Just watch your own fingers."

I make it look like I'm pushing gently as he requested. I put a lot of muscle into that push. As metal hits metal, I expect every door on the block to fly open, every neighbor to pop out to see what's happening. But the street remains empty.

The river this morning is yellow, not the golden yellow of sun reflecting on water, but hamburger mustard yellow, a jaundiced soup. Carolyn and I stand on the riverbank while Joe slides the refrigerator out of the truck bed. Miraculously, it lands standing up, right next to the wire cage. Joe places a heavy boulder in front of the refrigerator, explaining that you're supposed to take the door off its hinges, but this should keep any little kids from getting trapped inside. Carolyn walks around the Amana, tracing it with her finger.

"Don't tell me you're going to miss it," I say.

"Of course not," she says, but I can tell she's lying. "Look at what we almost forgot." She holds up the picture of our digital daughter, half her and half me.

"Cute kid," Joe says. "Who is she?"

"She's ours," I say, glad when Carolyn doesn't correct me or explain.

"Can I keep it?" she asks, and I say sure. Part of me wishes I'd gotten to it first, but a bigger part is glad that she still wants it.

Joe and I are in the library, chatting with Noriko before first period, when Miyoshi-sensei enters, karaoke machine in hand. I'm about to tell him how we took the refrigerator out this morning—I want Joe to take the blame as promised—but before I can speak, he hands me a letter. Noriko and Joe both stop talking and stare, and I'm grateful when Miyoshi-sensei pops his CD into the machine and asks Joe's help to decipher the lyrics.

Dear Miss Marina how are you?

I'm not so great. Yesterday, Ogawa-san called me again. Maybe you tried new gomi technique. This time you throw gomi in sushi restaurant bin. Oh no! I think. Restaurant need own gomi space. They have much fish and rice and chopstick and so forth, to dispose every day. I know my English is so bad. Maybe you couldn't understand my gomi letters well enough. So let me be more clear. When you throw gomi in anotherbody's bin, even restaurant bin, this is like throwing gomi on anotherbody's futon.

Thursday is Moku-yobi. On a Thursday you can throw electronic goods such as radio, clock, blender, and so forth, in wire cage by the river. It's close to your home, so you don't have to carry far. Some manufacturer will come to collect electronic goods on Thursday afternoon, to break open for good parts.

Speaking of good parts: good part of Thursday is: Mister Joe is teaching with us today. So you shouldn't prepare any lesson on girl thing. I think students enjoy Mister Joe's lessons so much. He is very talented, don't you agree? Tonight we have "enkai." This means

faculty party. Enkai fee is 5,000 yen. This includes dinner, all you
can drink beer and sake, and Japanese "onsen" bath. Please come to
Royal Hotel at 6 pm to take a bath. It's Japanese bath, meaning
all together in one water. Of course only man with man, woman
with woman. So I can't see you. After dinner, we can enjoy singing
karaoke. I hope Mister Joe will duet with me. He has voice like sweet
melon. He sings like professional.

That's all for now.

See you,
Hiroshi Miyoshi

"Thank you," I say. "I'm sorry."

And while I am sorry that I got into trouble, and that he had to write me yet another *gomi* letter, I can't help but think that people here spend way too much time rooting through the garbage. I'm sure the sushi restaurant really has that many chopsticks! At least he didn't say anything to shame me in front of Noriko and Joe. I remind myself that he doesn't want to give me these letters any more than I want to receive them. He hits Rewind and we listen to a song called "Jambalaya," which sounds like it's being sung by chipmunks.

"Pole the pirogue," he reads off the lyric sheet. "I can't catch the meaning of this."

"I think it's Cajun," I say. "Or Creole. Whatever they speak in the Bayou."

"The Bayou," Miyoshi-sensei repeats. "Now I plan my next vacation. Travel agent recommends Gulf Coast. He says I could hear great music and enjoy barbecue Longhorn."

"Sounds deelish," Joe says, and I laugh in spite of myself.

"Have you ever been to the Bayou?" Miyoshi-sensei asks me.

"Once," I say. "But I was really little and I don't remember much."

I was with my parents on that trip. I must have been seven or eight. We went on a swamp tour, and the captain of the boat had a cooler that was full of beer and a live baby alligator, its jaw held shut by a rubber band. After lunch, he passed it around like show-and-tell and my dad slipped the rubber band off. When it clamped down on his finger, he flung it off the side of the boat. The captain kicked us off too, miles from our rental car. This is all that I remember—this, and the way my mother cried as we trudged through swamp grass.

"How about you?" Miyoshi-sensei asks Joe. "Have you been to the Bayou?"

"Love, this is my first time out of England," Joe says.

"You're kidding, right?" I say. "I mean you've been to other parts of Europe."

"Roight," he says, but the way he avoids my eye makes me think that he's lying. He stares at the bulletin board covered in pictures of himself and I notice for the first time how cheap they look, grainy and pixelated, like the kind of flyers that get stuck under your windshield back home, advertizing tire sales and cut-rate electronics.

Miyoshi-sensei lights a cigarette, watching Joe get up to flirt with Noriko.

"I should warn you about tomorrow's *ensoku*," he says to me.

"What does *ensoku* mean?" I ask.

"Outing," he says. "Tomorrow is long-walking day. To observe the end of autumn, the whole school will take a long walk up the river, to the sea. We will pass by your home. It's convenient, if you forget something."

"Great," I say. "I'm looking forward to it."

"Looking forward?"

"A long walk sounds like fun."

"Hmm," he purses his lips and blows a ribbon of smoke that curls toward the ceiling. "Maybe *fun* is incorrect usage. We will walk all day, in one long line of bodies. By the end, we come to feel like Japanese imperial prisoner of war." I laugh, and he smiles at the success of his joke.

It's raining this afternoon and Carolyn faxes to ask for a ride home, addressing her fax to Joe and me both, so I go with him to pick her up. She sits in the middle, the three of us pressed hip to hip in his truck's tiny cab. Every time he shifts, his fist rubs against her knee and I feel the friction. He suggests that we all drive up to Wajima, a fishing town at the tip of the peninsula, and I remind him that we have to go to the faculty party.

"I think I might skip it," he says. "Things are a bit dodgy with Noriko."

"You seem pretty comfortable together," I argue.

"Do you know she didn't even bother telling me she got engaged? I had to learn about it from Hiro."

"That's terrible," Carolyn says.

"The worst part is what he said. He explained to me that at the ripe age of twenty-seven, Noriko is getting up there. If she doesn't marry soon, she might miss her chance. 'If you don't have this intention in your mind,' he said, 'you had better step to the side.'"

"Unbelievable," Carolyn says. "That is so sexist."

"Maybe he's just looking out for her," I argue.

"Come on," Carolyn scoffs. "She's old enough to be an old maid but she can't make her own dating decisions?"

"I reckon it's for the best," Joe says. "Noriko is a sweet girl and all, but I need someone who can stand up for herself. A partner."

I try to catch Carolyn's eye. When we got together, she made me promise never to call her my partner. Partners were in business together. We were lovers. It really bothered Carolyn when straight people used this term "partner," to seem hip and inconventional.

"I'll go for a drive with you," she says. "I don't want to go home."

"Miyoshi-sensei is going to be disappointed," I tell Joe. "He was counting on singing a duet with you."

"I'm sure he'd rather duet with you," Joe says.

"What do you mean?"

"You should hear what the other teachers have been saying."

"What have they been saying?" Carolyn asks.

"Miyoshi-sensei is always passing her secret notes. Everyone thinks they're love notes. They keep asking me whether the feeling is mutual."

"That's ridiculous," I scoff.

"Don't lie, pet," Joe says. "I was right there when he gave you one this morning. You read it all quiet like, blushing even . . . "

"That was no love note," I say.

"So what was it?" Carolyn asks, looking at me for the first time all afternoon.

"It was nothing," I say.

Let her be the jealous one for a change.

taoreru: (v.) *to fall; to collapse*

Inside the lobby of Shika's Royal Hotel, a carpet patterned with purple and gold diamonds stretches from wall to wall. Chandeliers throw puzzles of light on the black lacquer bar, and Japanese women in French maid costumes pad in eyelet lace slippers, balancing trays of beer bottles and sake. One of them approaches me and bows.

"Miss Marina?" she says.

"*Hai.*"

She reaches into the pocket of her apron and hands me a note written on hotel letterhead in Miyoshi-sensei's too familiar linked cursive.

Dear Miss Marina,

This become final gomi message. This method, I learn today, is no good for sharing some important rule with you. Of course Ogawa-san called me about refrigerator situation. To tell the truth, I was kind of so disappointed. To tell the truth, I couldn't believe the phone. To stand a huge refrigerator by river walking path is illegal and dangerous. "Itsu taoreru," Ogawa-san say. When will it fall? "Itsu

*taoreru, Itsu taoreru?"he repeat, and I repeat after him.When, Miss
Marina, when will it fall?*

*Do you consider another person? Me? Mister Ogawa? Some
kindergarten child playing by the river? I consider Mister Ogawa. I
have no choice, when he calls me every day. You have become huge
responsibility for me. You are my job, but recently my job become
heavy like your refrigerator. Mister Ogawa is old man. He can't move
huge refrigerator alone. So you and I must "brainstorm" together.
This is how I feel honestly. A storm is moving in my brain. Can Miss
Marina hear my words?*

*For tonight we had better forget our troubles. Everyone is taking
a bath. Let's not talk about refrigerator tonight. Tonight we become
clean, and tomorrow is Long Walking Day. Then we had better figure
out how to move a refrigerator back inside.*

See you very soon,
Hiroshi Miyoshi

I am naked with my colleagues. We sit on pink plastic stools at the
low showers that surround the black slate tub. One by one, the other
women finish rinsing off, stand up and ease into the bath. For the third
time, I pump soap into my hands and fleece my body with suds until
I'm almost decent. I am trying not to think of the tattoo of an anchor
on my breast, or how large my ass feels sticking out behind me on
this stool. I am trying not to think about dusk falling over town, or
the refrigerator about to fall by the river. I wonder if Miyoshi-sensei
told the other teachers what I did, whether he complains in Japanese
about my inability to follow the rules, his heavy burden.

I hesitate at the edge of the tub, cowering behind a tiny towel
smaller than most dish cloths. My colleagues look up and smile in-

vitingly. The elderly history teacher pats the surface of the steaming water. The school secretary makes a satisfied *mmm* sound. Rub-a-dub-dub, twelve ladies in a tub. I drop my towel and plunge into the scalding bath, but my breasts bob to the surface, two pink buoys.

Noriko, who has been soaking in the cold tub on the deck, walks in through the sliding glass doors and toward the bath on the pads of her toes. Steam rises off her skin. She is slightly, charmingly, bow-legged, so thin that her pelvis is visible beneath her skin, jutting out like the top of a heart. I remember the new bride on display in her glass van, surrounded by possessions. That woman seemed so vulnerable, whereas Noriko looks perfectly at ease. She slides into the bath next to me, points at my anchor tattoo and says, "*sekushii.*" Sexy. When my nipple stiffens (only reflexively!) I start to apologize but she says "*sekushii*" again and all of the teachers let out ripples of laughter. Tension melts in the steam. "*Ookiisugi,*" I say, cupping my breasts in both hands. Too big. She shakes her head and says, "*sekushi-sugi.*" Too sexy.

The sound of water rushing into water is nice. I slide forward, slip under the surface and let the bath fill my ears, push against my eyelids. I open my mouth and taste a sip. It's a little salty, this water we're all steeping in, this broth of us. After a while, my fingertips start to feel like rubber, wrinkly and numb. When I touch my own skin, I have the gorgeous illusion of someone else, someone new, touching me for the first time. I don't want to get out. I don't want to face Miyoshi-sensei, to have to apologize yet again. But eventually the other women stand up, towel off and get dressed in the hotel *yukata*, cotton kimonos patterned with exploding, hot pink fireworks. Noriko calls my name, tells me that it's time for the banquet. To my surprise, the *yukata* fits me. Noriko ties my sash in a pretty bow and the other female teachers tell me that I look very beautiful, very

Japanese, that I'm sure to break hearts. At least I think that's what they're saying. All I know is they're softening up to me, and I have to say, it feels good.

There are no tables or chairs in the hotel banquet hall, just two rows of cushions in front of lacquer trays spaced far enough apart to make conversation awkward. Most of the teachers are already kneeling and eating. The sound of chopsticks scraping dishes and glasses clinking fills the room. I am trying to figure out where I should sit when Miyoshi-sensei beckons me over.

"Mari-chan," he says, "I know you don't like beef, so I ordered tofu for you."

"Miyoshi-sensei," I say, "I got your note. *Gomen nasai. Shitsure-ishimashita. Sumimasen.*" I'm sorry. I have committed a rude. Forgive me.

"Not tonight." He holds up a hand. "This is *enkai*. A party is no time to sing the *gomi* blues." I laugh and he fills my glass with beer. "Japanese *enkai* is a rare and precious chance to take off the *tatamae*. The work face. And show the *honmae*."

"The *honmae*?" I repeat.

"The true face. For tonight, I am not Miyoshi-sensei. I am just Hiro."

"Hiro," I say. "My superhero." We both laugh.

"When you drink," he says, "you become red face."

"You should talk," I say.

"I should talk about what?"

"Nothing." I laugh again. "'You should talk' is just an expression. It means that whatever you say about me is also true of you."

"Yes," he says. "We are alike in many ways."

"Really?" I say. "You think so? Like what?"

"We both want to fit," he says, "but we also want to be *yuniku*. Unique. We want to be liked. We want things to be smooth. But we don't like to follow rules."

"*You* don't like to follow rules?" I can't help teasing him.

"I know," he says, "to you I probably seem like typical Japanese. But to most people here I seem . . . oppositional. I don't like to do a thing only because everyone else does this thing. I don't enjoy hostess bar or package tour of Hawaii. I don't give fifty dollar melon present, or buy designer label goods. I can take a compliment and I can speak directly. Well, sometimes." I'm about to tell him that he's right when he grabs my wrist, right before I refill my glass with beer. "You should not pour your own drink," he says, and then he grins. "Maybe I am not a *typical* Japanese, but I am still Japanese, *ne?*"

He winks as he fills my glass. I've never noticed his dimples before. They're not pinpricks but slits, vertical lines that could hold dimes. There's something different about him tonight. He looks so much more relaxed. At ease. It's the *yukata*, I think. The men's robe is identical to the one I'm wearing only patterned with blue fireworks. It suits him, accentuates the width of his shoulders, shows off his narrow hips. The triangle of golden, hairless skin at his chest is faintly shining with sweat. Instead of being styled back in its usual pompadour, his hair is damp and falling in his eyes, making him look younger, roughed up around the edges. He taps a cigarette out of his pack and lights it with his Zippo.

"Imagine," I say, pointing at the word engraved on the silver.

"It was university graduation gift from my father."

"Is he a Beatles fan?"

"No. He only listens to Japanese music. *Enka*, you know? It's like country. He used to sing it. He would perform at festivals all over Japan. He had a wonderful voice."

"Is he doing any better?" I ask.

"Not really. He is receiving radiation treatment, but odds of recovery are not good."

"I'm so sorry," I say. "That must be really hard for you."

"Thank you." He pauses, then says, "When did your father die?"

"A little over a year ago." I hold my breath, again waiting for him to ask how.

"You must still feel a great lack," he says.

"Yeah," I say. "Sometimes I still forget." I stop myself from finishing the sentence. Forget that he's dead? Forget to miss him?

"I understand," he says. "Sometimes I forget that my father lost his voice. I ask him a question and then I remember. He does not like mechanical voice box. He feels shame to sound like a robot. He prefers to write on a notepad. Sometimes I write back to him instead of speaking. It feels more natural. Maybe this is why I write letters to you."

"That makes sense," I say, eyeing his cigarette.

"Probably you wonder why I smoke when my father has cancer."

"No," I say. "I was wondering if you had an extra."

"Sorry, but this was my last one." He crumples up his pack. "I smoke too much. I want to quit, but it's hard to give up bad manners."

"Tell me about it," I say.

"Well," he begins, "I began smoking when I was eighteen—"

"It's another expression," I say, laughing. "It means I know exactly how you feel."

"Ah." He takes a drag, and then holds his half-smoked cigarette out to me. The filter is damp, moist from his lips. Other teachers watch as I inhale, then pass it back to him. He takes another drag and passes it back to me. A waitress moves from tray to tray, pouring shots of whiskey, and I accept this too. I am saying yes to everything tonight. Another waitress wheels in a karaoke machine and dims the lights.

"Hiro!" someone calls, and before long everyone is chanting his name.

"Mari-chan," he says, grinning at me, "Shall we duet?"

I get up and follow him to the stage, struggling to walk in a straight line. He types in the number for an Elvis song. The video shows a line of Samoan men in grass skirts dancing a hula. "How inappropriate," he says, and we both laugh. I barely know this song, but Hiro leads with his velvety tenor and is easy to follow. In the first verse we stand stiffly, side by side, shoulders touching, peering at the screen. But as we launch into the chorus we loosen up. The teachers are whistling, fingers in their mouths. On the second verse we pivot and gaze into each other's eyes.

Tell me dear, are you lonesome tonight?

He improvises a harmony, I manage to hold the tune, and the teachers cheer wildly. We are good and we know it. We are Ike and Tina, Sonny and Cher. We own the room. At the end of the song we turn back to back, shoulders pressed together. As the backs of our heads touch, I realize that we are exactly the same height. Only when the music cuts off, when I suddenly feel a little silly gripping my microphone with dramatically pale knuckles, do I realize that the entire faculty is not just smiling at us but smiling knowingly. On-screen, a rollerblading couple spins around and around, then collapses into each other's arms.

"*Sekushii!*" Noriko calls out, wolf-whistling.

"I need some air," I say.

"You are not so strong for beer," he says. "I had better drive you home."

"That's okay," I say. "I can walk."

"You are my job," he says.

"I am not your job," I say.

"No," he says. "You are my friend."

I'm still wearing the Royal Hotel *yukata* as I follow him across the parking lot. Cold air fills the cotton and the sleeves billow like sails. When he starts his car, the same Elvis Presley song pumps at top volume from the speakers. *Tell me dear, are you lonesome tonight?* He must have been practicing, getting ready for tonight. For how long? He cracks the windows and the icy wind whistles through the car. He drives fast, like the boys I used to date, as if driving were a competitive sport, a race to be won. He speeds past the conveyor belt sushi restaurant, the 7–Eleven, the Mister Donuts, turns onto the road leading up to our house, and drives past it, braking in front of the stairs that lead up to the riverbank.

"Now I see for myself," he says.

And there it is, the refrigerator, illuminated by his headlights, standing like the lone surviving relic of the house that once contained it. I get ready to launch into another round of apologies, but before I can start he says, "Mari-chan, do you think we can see this refrigerator from the moon?" He laughs, and I laugh too. "From the moon," he says. "From the moon!" For some reason, these words get funnier with each repetition. Soon I am begging him to stop so I can catch my breath. At last he does, and in the silence I hear geese bark at each other from either side of the river. I shift in my seat, uncross my legs and feel the night air fill me up. I turn to study his profile: one dimple, half a smile.

On impulse, I reach out and touch his cheek. My hand follows the curve of his jaw, slides beneath his *yukata* and settles on his chest. I had forgotten how hard a man's chest is, how unyielding. I feel his heart down there, barred by his ribs, sprinting forward, matching mine stride for stride. I rub his skin, caress his nipple with my thumb. He turns to face me and I kiss him. His lips are cool. He keeps his tongue to himself and his eyes open. We both do, looking at each other like tourists from different countries, both visiting the same place for the first time. When we blink, our lashes brush. When we breathe, we breathe into each other. We hold that kiss—pure pressure and breath—for a full minute, maybe more. Then he pulls back, presses a fist to his lips, returns his hands to the steering wheel. "I guess I should go," I say, and he nods. I fumble for the latch, turning around to look at him once more. He stays there, parked in front of our house with his engine running, long after I've climbed upstairs and under the covers, waiting for his headlights to sweep past.

The next morning, I mistake the knocking at the door for the knocking in my skull. On the alarm clock, the red numerals swim into focus. 6:15. I groan and clutch my head, failing to muffle the rhythmic pounding. "Will you get that?" Carolyn asks, burrowing deeper under the covers. When I stand up, I realize that I am still wearing the Royal Hotel *yukata*. I tighten the sash and pull a sweater over my head. With every step down the stairs, scenes from the night before flash in my mind. The bath. The karaoke duet. The kiss. I open the door to find Mrs. Ogawa standing next to Haruki. The boy is wearing his blue gym suit and his head is bowed forward at an almost ninety-degree angle. I can see the buzzed hairs at the back of his head, which are already turning gray.

"*Irashite kudasai*," she says. Come with me. Her voice is as shaky as I feel.

"I'm. Sorry. About. The. Refrigerator." I speak slowly, emphatically.

"*Shitsureishimashita*," Haruki whispers. "I am . . . I feel . . . I have . . . I can't . . . "

Carolyn appears by my side, looking groggy. Mrs. Ogawa takes her hand and pulls her out of the house. I follow them up the stairs and onto the riverbank, the frosty grass crunching under my feet. The senior citizens are standing in a semicircle around the fridge. "They probably need us to move it so they can do their calisthenics," Carolyn says. Mrs. Ogawa marches up to the fridge and then calls Haruki's name. He walks forward, head still hanging as he opens the door. There is a collective gasp from the senior citizens. I stand on tiptoe to look over their heads.

Carolyn sees, before I do, the cold curl of the cat on the bottom shelf. She runs to the refrigerator, sinks onto her knees on the grass, reaches into the fridge, and then jerks her hand back. Mrs. Ogawa and Haruki also get down on their knees. Mrs. Ogawa says something in Japanese and the two of them lean forward until their foreheads touch the earth. They right themselves and bow again, apologizing in a chant.

"*Shitsureishimashita.*"

"Stop it!" Carolyn sobs. "Why did you do this?"

"*Haruki wa mondaji,*" Mrs. Ogawa says. Haruki is a problem child.

I take off my sweater and make a little woolly bed for Amana, who is stiff and doesn't change position when I take her out of the fridge. Her chin is tucked between her front paws. Her fur feels silky and cold. She is cold and stiff but she still looks like herself. The boy is still apologizing. But I know that she was already sick. She must have been easy to catch, so easy to trap. Carolyn can't stop sobbing. She holds the cat's paws in one hand and strokes them with her other hand and I wrap an arm around her shoulders, holding her close, not caring what the neighbors see or think. We stay like that for a long time, a little tableau of grief. When I finally look up, the river is cobalt blue and everyone—Mrs. Ogawa, Haruki, the other senior citizens—has left us alone for once.

"Amana died in the Amana," Carolyn says.

It's not funny. Of course it's not funny. But still we both start laughing. Tears drip from Carolyn's chin onto the cat's fur, splotching it.

"What are we going to do?" she asks me.

"We have to bury her," I say.

Mrs. Ogawa is outside as usual, pruning her bonsai trees. I point to her trowel, ask if I can borrow it, and when Haruki emerges from the house she thrusts the trowel in his hands and he follows me to the riverbank, where he crouches down and begins digging.

"What the fuck is he doing here?" Carolyn says.

"I don't know," I say. "He followed me."

"Leave!" she yells at him. "Go away!" But he ignores her and just keeps digging. The earth is half-frozen. It glitters with ice crystals as he excavates a grave for the cat.

When the hole is deep enough he finally backs off. Carolyn lowers the cat's body down into it, and then she hands me the trowel, but I can't do it either. I can't drop dirt on Amana's face. She may be cold and dead but she still looks like herself. She still has her face. So I take off my sweater and place it on top of her and then Carolyn and I take turns filling in the hole, covering her with earth until she's gone.

We are still squatting by the little grave when the students file by on the path, a long line of girls wearing their pink gym uniforms trailed by a clump of boys in blue. It's Long Walking Day. I completely forgot. I'm supposed to be there. I'm not supposed to be here. We duck lower in the reeds, but the students aren't looking in our direction. They are marching two at a time, their footfalls evenly matched. Leading the procession of future secretaries is Miyoshi-sensei, who walks backward, calling "*ganbatte!*" or "do your best for me," tipping a large Evian bottle into the girls' cupped hands, encouraging the frail, the tired, and the cute.

PART II
Mo Ichi Do

WINTER

Don't imitate me;
it's as boring
as the two halves of a melon.

—BASHO

jikoshoukai: (N.) *self-introduction*

1. My name is:

a) Miss Marina   b) Alice in Shikaland   c) Leonardo DiCaprio

2. I am:

a) **12** years old   b) **52** years old   c) **22** years old

3. I'm from:

a) London, England   b) New York, USA

c) Seoul, Korea

4. I speak:

a) Korean   b) English   c) Japanese

5. I can eat:

a) pickled plums   b) fermented soybeans   c) jellyfish

6. My favorite character is:

a) Flat Panda   b) Afro-ken   c) Kitty-chan

At Shika's elementary school, the children wear miniature versions of the same uniforms worn by the high school students. The boys wear tiny blue jackets, with stiff mandarin collars and big brass buttons, and shorts year-round. The girls wear double-breasted blazers over blue pleated skirts held up by suspenders. They are not allowed to wear tights or leggings, so their knees are as flushed as their cheeks when they enter the classroom on mornings frigid as this one. Nor are they allowed to wear scarves or knitted hats. Both boys and girls must wear a bright yellow cap with a long bill, to stand out against traffic. These hats are allowed to come off only once they pass through their homeroom doors, at which point they become their homeroom teacher's responsibility.

"Hurry up," says Kobayashi-sensei as his second-grade students hang their caps from pegs on the wall. "Today we have a visitor from abroad." The word he uses, *mukou*, translates to "overseas," or "the other side." Kobayashi-sensei doesn't seem to know where I'm from. He may not know my name, although I've been coming to this elementary school for the past six weeks now. The second grade teacher is a former sumo wrestler, an athlete turned soft, built like an overstuffed sofa. He wears aloha shirts under a brown leather jacket so tight that it creaks when he moves.

He waves his arms, conducting the kids in a song to welcome me. It's "Silent Night" in Japanese. Their voices are high and sweetly off-key. *All is calm, all is bright*, I translate the lyrics in my head. But all is not calm, not with me. I've had a toothache for the past month, a pain that travels from tooth to tooth, coming in and out like a radio station with bad reception. This morning I'm getting a loud and clear signal. When the kids finish singing, I smile and clap and Kobayashi-sensei invites me to sing a song in return. I don't feel like soloing. Instead I boom out, "Hello!"

"Hello," the group echoes faintly.

"*Mo ichi do*," Kobayashi-sensei prompts them. "One more time."

"Hello!" they repeat with increased confidence.

"How's it going?" I ask them.

"Howsitgoing?" they ask me right back.

I draw a smiley face on the board and point to it as I say, "I'm great!" Then I draw a sad face and say, "I'm not so hot." I no longer teach students to say, "How are you?" "I'm fine" is the only answer anyone ever gives, and I don't like questions with only one answer.

"Hot?" Kobayashi-sensei repeats dubiously. "*Samui desu ne?*" It's cold, isn't it? This is a standard winter greeting here, another question with only one possible answer. "It is cold," I agree. In Japanese, I explain that "hot" means *atsui*, a hot temperature, while "not so hot" means not fine. "How's it going?" I ask the class once more. A little boy raises his hand. He's wearing a giant, padded ski glove held in place by an elastic band looped around his wrist. It looks like an oven mitt at the end of his scrawny arm. This boy is smaller than the rest of the kids, so pale that I can see the veins marbling the skin at his temples, with wide-set eyes that are gray rather than black and hypnotizing, utterly focused on me.

"*Byouki*," he says.

"You're sick," I translate.

"You're sick," Kobayashi-sensei says. "*Mo ichi do*."

"Youresick," the child mumbles.

"Actually," I turn to the second-grade teacher, "he should say '*I'm* sick.'" Pronouns often get dropped in Japanese. *Watashi* means "I," but only foreigners place themselves in front of everything they say. *Anata*, or "you," is used so infrequently that it also means darling, beloved, always spoken by a woman to a man.

"I'm sick!" Kobayashi-sensei prompts the child. "*Mo ichi do*."

But instead of repeating, the boy just closes his eyes, massaging the bridge of his nose in a parody of adult weariness. The teacher ruffles his hair, which is so fine that it immediately falls back into place, parting around his ears. "*Byouki jya nai*," he chides the boy. You're not really sick. "Koji lying," he tells me. "Koji not sick. Koji want to leave class to see his mama." This is the second time I've heard this man speak English. The first time was when he said, "big size," while looking at my feet. True, my heels stick out a good inch beyond the elementary school slippers—everything here is miniature—but he should talk.

We hand out my self-introduction worksheet and I explain to the kids that I'll be saying three things about myself in English, only one of which is true, that they should listen, look at the pictures, and raise their hand when they think they can guess the right answer.

"One," I say, "My name is . . . a) Miss Marina . . . "

"Is Miss Marina's name Miss Marina?" Kobayashi-sensei translates the question into Japanese before I finish listing the options.

"*Hai!*" the children yell in a self-assured chorus.

"That's right," I say. "My name is Miss Marina."

"My name is Miss Marina," the second graders repeat unprompted.

"No, *my* name is Miss Marina," I say. "Your name is . . . " I look around the room, but I can't read the characters on their nametags. "Your name is Koji," I say, pointing to the gray-eyed little boy wearing the giant ski gloves.

"Your name is Koji," Kobayashi-sensei says. "*Mo ichi do.*"

"Your name is Koji," the boy repeats, looking out the window. Following his gaze, I expect to see something special, but find only the anemic sky of early February.

"Is Miss Marina twelve years old?" Kobayashi-sensei translates the next question before I can even ask it in English.

"*Hai*," Koji replies.

"Come on," his teacher says. "Your brother is twelve. Could Fumiya be a teacher?" The other kids laugh and the boy scowls, glaring down at his desk. When the teacher asks the kids if I'm fifty-two, every hand in the room shoots up.

"It's because of your eyes," Kobayashi-sensei says in a conspiratorial whisper.

"I have old eyes?" I whisper back.

"You have foreign eyes," he says. "Foreign eyes have more folds."

"I'm twenty-two," I say, writing the number on the board.

"I'm twenty-two," the class repeats after me, getting into the game of it.

I'm surprised when every student guesses that I'm from Seoul, Korea, even though I'm holding up a dollar bill and a picture of the Empire State Building. Then they all guess that I speak Korean. "No," I say. "I speak English."

"What's English?" lisps a little girl with a jack-o'-lantern grin.

"This is English," I say, wondering if it's possible she really doesn't know.

"This is English," they repeat.

"You will all have to learn English," Kobayashi-sensei informs them.

"Why?" asks Koji.

"Because it's required," he says wearily.

"If you learn to speak English," I say, "then you can go abroad and talk to people from all over the world!" This is a direct quote from *New Horizons*. I look to Kobayashi-sensei to translate.

"If you learn to speak English," he says, "then you can talk to Miss Marina."

The kids finish the worksheet in just fifteen minutes. Since I have nothing else planned, Kobayashi-sensei rewards them with an early recess.

The two of us sit on the ledge of the empty swimming pool behind the school. A crusty layer of snow lines the cement basin, porous and hard as coral. In the pool, dry leaves chase each other around and around, while the kids do the same on the field. Only one child doesn't join in the fun. A tall thin girl with two long braids and a voluminous uniform skirt hanging almost to her ankles stands an arm's reach away from us, kicking up clods of dirt. In Japanese, Kobayashi-sensei explains that this girl's name is Kim, that she moved to Shika from Pusan, Korea five months ago, and that she can't speak Japanese yet.

"Probably that's why the students thought you were Korean," he says, and then he quickly corrects himself. "Of course, you speak Japanese very well. You are fluent, *ne?*"

I ask why the girl moved to Japan and he tells me that her father was hired by Shika's nuclear power station, to ship *gomi* back to Pusan.

"Garbage?" I translate.

"Waste," he says.

"You send nuclear waste to Korea?"

"Not me," he says brusquely. "Mister Kim."

In Japanese, he tells me that the girl's mother died when she was a baby, that her father works long hours and the teachers take turns visiting her at home, checking in to see if she needs anything, but since she can't speak Japanese, they don't really know.

"Are the other kids nice to her?" I ask.

"*Yappari,*" he says. Naturally. "Why do you ask this?"

"Because she's Korean," I say. The problem with speaking such rudimentary Japanese is that it all comes out so blunt. I'm not trying to accuse him or anyone else of racism, but Miyoshi-sensei once told me that the descendants of Korean immigrants, people born here in Japan, are required by law to carry identification cards labeling them as foreign. He told me that once a year, the newspapers report the number of crimes committed by foreigners. "Koreans commit the most crimes," he said. "Then Chinese. Americans don't commit so many. But there are not so many Americans in Japan." When I suggested that most of these "crimes" were probably simple failures to follow the rules, he agreed. "But for the Japanese," he said, "there is little difference."

Kobayashi-sensei stuffs his hand into the pocket of his leather jacket and pulls out a pack of Dunhill's, walking away from me to light up. Cigarette dangling from his lips, he jogs down the slope to break up a scuffle between two boys. I approach the little girl from behind. Her center part is jagged, one of her braids fatter than the other. A father's work. Her eyebrows are downy, her nostrils pink, her lips chapped. To me, she doesn't look noticeably different from the other children, and I wonder if they can see something in her face that I can't, something ineffably foreign, something she and I might have in common without being able to see it ourselves.

"Hello," I say. She paws the ground with her toe and exhales noisily and I realize that she is pretending to be a horse. Her solitary play seems brave to me, like she wants to make it clear that she's not to be pitied. "Neigh," I say, blowing air between loose lips.

"Kim can't speak," says Koji, the gray-eyed boy wearing the ski gloves who has materialized beside us, out of breath from running.

"She can speak," I say. "Just not Japanese. I was talking to her in English."

"Kim-san speaks English?"

"No," I say. "She speaks Korean."

"She can't speak," he insists.

"*Shai desu,*" I say.

"Why is she shy?"

I don't know how to say "homesick," although it's a word I should have learned by now. I don't know the verb "to miss," either. "*Uchi no byouki,*" I improvise.

"Her *house* is sick?"

"Her house is far away."

"Not *that* far," he says. "Her house is near the power station. My mom and I take her home every day after school."

"But she has another home," I say, "and that other home is far away."

"Who lives in the other home?"

"No one."

"Maybe that's why she can't speak," he muses. "She has no one to talk to."

"That's right," I say. "You should talk to her."

Throughout this exchange, Kim has remained motionless, looking down at her painfully white sneakers. While I feel guilty for putting words in her mouth, it's thrilling that this boy understands my Japanese with so little effort. Our conversation feels as fluid and choppy as any conversation between children.

"I want to show you something," he says.

"What?" I ask him.

"It's over there." He gestures toward the side of the school. I glance at Kobayashi-sensei, who is once more sitting on the ledge of the empty swimming pool, lighting another cigarette off the first. The little boy slips his gloved mitt around my hand. With my free hand I take the little girl's. Her palm is so dry that I can practically feel the whorl of each fingerprint. Linked like a line of paper dolls, we disappear around the corner.

A sectioned hutch holds a pair of ducks on one side and two rabbits on the other. The ducks squawk as we pass by, shimmying like wet dogs. The kids lead the way into the cage and I stoop to follow, feeling like Alice after she ate the cake that made her bigger. Alarmed by our intrusion, the rabbits shuffle to opposite corners of their hutch, noses pulsing, ears pressed flat against their backs. One of the bunnies is fat and white and glossy, with a black jellybean splotch on its haunch, while the other is gray and skeletal, its fur as dingy as a sewer rat's. Koji scoops up the gray one, ignoring its frantic hind leg kicks.

"What do you think rabbits dream about?" he asks. My first guess, carrots, meets with serious disapproval. He picks a flaccid carrot up off the ground and wags it at me. "They get carrots every day," he says. "Why would they dream about them?" I remember that the pet rabbit I had as a child was eaten by the neighbor's dog. "Maybe," I say, "rabbits have nightmares about dogs." He considers this for a moment, then shakes his head. "These rabbits are in a cage," he says. "They've never seen dogs. How could they dream about them?" "What do you think they dream about?" I ask, and he closes his eyes for a moment. "*Mukou*," he finally says. Abroad. The other side. It's the same word Kobayashi-sensei used to explain where I'm from. I don't think he means that the rabbit dreams of going overseas. I think he means that it wants to get out of this cage.

"This rabbit is sick," he says, thrusting the gray bunny at me. Up close, I can see that its two front teeth are so long that they're propping its lower jaw open. It's a horrifying sight. I ask what's wrong with the rabbit and he explains that its teeth won't stop growing, that they get longer every day, that it can't eat anymore, and soon it will die. At least I think that's what he says. His delivery is so matter-of-fact that I'm not sure.

"*Kawaisou usagi*," he says. Poor rabbit. *Kawaisou*, the word for poor, pathetic, pitiful, sounds so much like *kawaii*, the word for cute, that I sometimes have trouble remembering the difference.

"*Kawaisou usagi*," says Kim in a surprisingly deep and gravelly little voice.

"Don't repeat," Koji says, his tone sharp.

"Repeating is how we learn to speak," I tell him gently.

"*Usou desu*," he says.

"I wouldn't lie to you," I say. "I'm an English teacher."

"My mom is an art teacher," he says. "*Kim-san no okaasan wa mukou desu.*"

Kim's mom is . . . abroad? On the other side? I remember what Kobayashi-sensei told me earlier, that Kim's mother died when she was a baby. If *mukou* is also a euphemism for dead, or for wherever it is people go after they die, then how confusing for this child, who is from abroad. I can't tell if she has understood any of this. She strokes the rabbit's ears, which are parchment thin, threaded with red veins that match its alien eyes.

"*Otosan mo mukou desu*," I say. My father is also on the other side.

"*Honto ni?*" Koji asks me. Really? Then he asks how he got there.

"He jumped off a bridge," I say in English.

"*Janpu?*" the boy repeats, jumping up and down in place.

"No," I say, amazed that he understood. I arc one hand, balance two fingers from my other hand on top of it, then showing them diving down, into the hay lining the hutch.

"Did it hurt?" he asks.

"No," I say, although I really don't know the answer to this question.

"Where is he now?"

"*Mukou*," I say again, fighting back tears. I'm afraid that if I start to cry I won't be able to stop, that I'll fill the hutch like giant Alice and drown my tiny companions. Kim looks at me with eyes so dark that her pupils blend into her irises. She has old eyes too. Foreign eyes. Older than any seven-year-old should have. Maybe that's why we look alike. She takes my hand and we walk out of the cage together, into the white sunlight.

We sit at the bottom of the stairs leading up to the front doors of the school. The children are on either side of me, leaning against

my shins, propping me up. Kim strokes my ankle, tracing the out-
line of an American flag. My mom sent these tights to me after I
told her that I was visiting the elementary school. She has been an
elementary school teacher for thirty years, and she knows what kids
like. Koji jingles the charms on my bracelet and I tell him that I have
one from every foreign country I've ever visited. "This one's from
Japan," I say, pointing out a tiny silver rice bowl linked to whisker-
thin chopsticks.

"Japan's not a foreign country," he scoffs.

"It is to me," I say, "and to Kim too. We're both from abroad."

Now the little girl shifts so that we're no longer touching. One
of the reasons the Ministry of Education places native English teachers across rural Japan is to help Japanese people become more comfortable around foreigners. I signed up for this job. She did not.

Behind us I hear a door slam. "I caught them!" yells a gruff male
voice. I turn around to see Kobayashi-sensei barreling down the
stairs, fists balled, sweat trickling down his heavy jaw. "Why did you
run off on your own again?" he says to the little boy, seizing his shoulders and shaking him hard. When I try to protest that the boy wasn't
alone, he says something in Japanese without looking at me. All I
catch is, "*abunai*."

"What's dangerous?" I ask.

"You," he says.

A woman runs downstairs, her face blotchy. "*Okaasan!*" the little
boy cries. Mama! I recognize Keiko Ishii, the art teacher and ikebana
coach. She's wearing faded blue jeans and a baggy yellow sweater,
her hair is short and messy, and her eyes are the same shade of gray
as her little boy's. Koji wraps his arms around her thighs, and when
she reaches down to unpeel his hands he starts to sob.

"Why did you run away again?" she asks him. "You promised you
wouldn't."

"I didn't run away," he chokes. "I was with my new teacher."

"That is not your new teacher," she says.

"Then who is she?" he asks, and they all turn to look at me, the two adults and the two kids, as if trying to figure out who I am, where I'm from, what I'm doing here.

"Did you enjoy . . . *praying* . . . with the children?" asks Ooka-sensei, the elementary school vice-principal. He asks this every time I return to the faculty room. Usually it gets on my nerves. Only today I was playing with the children, and two of them were believed to be lost on my watch. I don't know if he was alerted to their disappearance, if I'm in trouble or need to apologize.

"Little kids learn English so quickly," I say.

"Hmm," he agrees. "But by my age they forget everything. My English is so poor. I need to practice so much. Too bad Shika does not have any English conversation school."

Ooka-sensei is a petite man who rarely gets up from behind his desk, which he is constantly polishing with a citrus-scented oil. On my first day here, he asked me how to make "l" and "r" sounds, scrutinizing my mouth as he drew diagrams of tongues touching teeth on butcher paper. They still hang on the wall beside his desk like huge screams. But the more we practice, the more confused he becomes. His dream is to buy an Airstream and drive across North America with his wife, taking photographs of barns, rodeos, and other "evidence of real USA." He pronounces it as one word, oosa, to rhyme with his name. Ooka-sensei is an *eikaiwa* or English conversation addict. After six months here, I have come to recognize the type by the way that they look at me, as a means to their fix.

"You speak English well," I compliment him for what must be the third time today.

"Oh no," he says. "My English is so . . . *lusty*."

I shouldn't still find this funny.

"I'll practice speaking English with you," I offer as always.

"But you are so busy," he says. "Probably you don't have much free time . . . "

He knows how much free time I have, since he makes my daily teaching schedule. I glance at the grid on my desk, the whole afternoon labeled FREE in his block lettering.

"How about the weather?" he asks me, his usual opening gambit.

"It's cold," I say, thinking *just like it was when you asked me this morning. Just like it was yesterday, and just like it will be tomorrow.*

"It *is* cold," he agrees. "I love snowy weather. For tomorrow much snow is predicted. So I feel very . . . jazzed."

"I might not be able to drive here if it snows that much," I warn him. The elementary school is twenty minutes from our house, accessible by a particularly treacherous stretch of the coastal highway.

"Don't worry," he says, "Road gets . . . empty?"

"Plowed," I correct him.

"Proud," he says.

I ask if he knows how many self-introduction lessons I have left to teach and he says that he's not sure, gesturing at the mountain of papers he has moved to his chair in order to polish his desk yet again. He tells me that the count is in there somewhere.

"I'm supposed to return to the high school after I finish giving that lesson," I say.

"Don't worry," he says. "Miyoshi-sensei will call if he wants to take you back. For now, please continue . . . *praying* . . . with the children."

On the Monday morning after the high school faculty *enkai*, I climbed the stairs with trepidation. Every faculty member at that party had watched Miyoshi-sensei and me sing our drunken duet and stumble out of the hotel together, dressed in matching *yukata*, naked and freshly bathed underneath, our skin smelling of the same soap, our breath of the same cigarette and whiskey. I wondered how he would treat me. Would he act embarrassed? Crack a Japanese joke? Present me with a letter detailing my latest failure to follow the rules? Would he want it to happen again?

By the time I reached the faculty room, the door was closed and I could hear the vice-principal droning on about something, which meant the morning meeting had already begun, which meant I was late. The secretary slipped out with the faculty attendance sheet. She made a tardy mark beside my name, then popped her head back in the room and called out in a shrill voice, "Miss Marina just arrived. May she enter?"

"Yes, but tell her to hurry up," the vice-principal said.

As I walked into the room, my eyes locked with those of Miyoshi-sensei and I could tell that he felt as nervous as I did. He stared down into his tea, blowing into it and fogging his reading glasses, and I sat at my desk chair, my back to him. I'd expected a little teasing from the other teachers, some lifted eyebrows or elbow nudges, but they all went about their business as usual, making copies, gathering supplies, hurrying off to teach their classes. I sat there with my pulse racing, my hands clammy, and my mouth dry, waiting for Miyoshi-sensei to approach me so that we could plan our lessons. But the minutes ticked by and when I finally swiveled around I saw that his desk was deserted. I found him standing by the windows in the freshman secretarial classroom, gazing out at the depressing brown stubble of the rice fields. He registered my arrival with a slight nod, still avoiding my eyes.

"How are you?" I asked.

"Fine," he said. "And you?"

"Fine," I said.

"Fine," he repeated, loosening his necktie with one finger. I didn't want to think about kissing him, but I couldn't stop looking at his mouth, remembering its pressure on mine. "I should warn you about something," he said. "According to vice-principal's command, all oral communication must stop from now."

"You mean we're not supposed to talk about what happened?" I whispered.

"No," he said, blushing and reaching a finger in his shirt collar to loosen it. "It means that until the prefectural exam, our oral communication classes must stop."

"Oh," I said, feeling the blood rush up to my own face. "Okay."

He explained that last year, on these same exams, Shika High School came in number fifty-nine out of the sixty schools in the prefecture, ranked only above the fishing and cannery high school in Wajima. "To avoid a humiliating repeat," he said, "vice-principal wants students to use English class time to study."

"Okay," I said again. "How can I help?"

"Just answer questions," he said, hurrying to the assistance of a girl whose hand was in the air before I could ask any more questions of my own.

And that was it.

In the days and weeks that followed, Miyoshi-sensei no longer waited for me to walk to class with him. He no longer approached my desk after school to ask if I wanted a "cuppa'," or reprimanded me for throwing the wrong trash away. I was surprised to find that I missed his *gomi* letters, not the corrections, but the personal stuff that seeped through the cracks. The school days suddenly seemed very long and boring. I missed things about him that I hadn't even realized I liked: his vivid gestures, his way of prefacing difficult statements with "maybe," his odd English metaphors and funny translations of Japanese idioms. One of the idioms he taught me early on is "*hiru andon*," which means "daytime lamp" and refers to people who take up space in a room with no vitality or purpose. Sitting on the faculty room couch, Miyoshi-sensei and I had pointed out the daytime lamps burning weakly around us, uninspired teachers, civil servants nearing retirement. "I really don't want to be like that," he confided in me once while we shared a smoke between periods. "I became English teacher because I love English, and I want to share this. Shika High School students are poor. They feel they have no use for English. So it's good you came here, *ne?*" I nodded, assuming that he meant that I gave the students a reason to practice their English. "At least I can share my love with you," he said.

But suddenly Miyoshi-sensei had become a daytime lamp. And I felt like one too, at the end of a month of team-teaching without teaching. Maybe I had been the one to kiss him, but he had kissed me back. We were two adults. It was only a big deal because he was making it into one. Still, I kept replaying the moment, the feel of his heart beating beneath my palm, the way we'd breathed into each other and kept our eyes open the whole time. Had I forced myself on him? I didn't think so. I couldn't shake the feeling that the misunderstanding was cultural, that if he could only explain to me what exactly I'd done wrong, what line I'd crossed, then we could move past it.

On the Friday before winter break, at the end of our semester's final English class, I followed him out of the classroom calling, "Miyoshi-sensei! Miyoshi-sensei!" as he sped ahead. Students poured into the hallway and I slalomed through the obstacle course. "Hiro!" I yelled, just as he was about to duck into the men's room. At the sound of his first name, the one he gave me permission to use for the first time on the night that we kissed, he finally wheeled around and said, "What?" I crossed my arms so that he wouldn't see them shaking. You would think that after all that time, I could have planned out what I wanted to say to him, but I found myself at a stupid loss for words.

"How are you?" I said.

"I'm fine, thank you," he replied, sticking his own hands in his pockets.

"You don't seem fine," I said, as students continued to stream past us, as oblivious to our little drama as a river splitting around a boulder. "I think we should talk."

"About what?"

"About what happened," I prompted him. "After the *enkai?*"

"Miss Marina," he cut me off. "A Japanese *enkai* is a kind of . . . parallel planet. What happens on this planet has no consequence on earth."

"But you seem upset," I protested. "You've been avoiding me for weeks."

"How do you mean, avoiding you? Every day we teach side by side like *futago*. Like a twins. I could not avoid you, even if I wanted to."

"I'm sorry if I crossed a line," I said. "I felt close to you. I thought you did too."

"A Japanese *enkai* is a parallel planet," he said again, leaning backward so that he pushed open the door to the men's room, exposing a row of urinals. "Working together in narrow space, pressure builds. So we need *enkai* to release steam. To release steam, we couldn't worry about . . . how to say . . . risky behavior."

"Risky behavior," I repeated.

"Exactly," he said. "Therefore, at Japanese *enkai*, there is no risky behavior. Do you catch my meaning? Do you understand how this is possible?"

"Not really."

"Because we never talk about what happened there."

hazukashii: (ADJ.) *shy; ashamed; embarrassed*

This morning, at the elementary school, I'm scheduled to teach two sixth-grade classes in a row. In the first, I sleepwalk through the greetings and recite the questions on my self-introduction test by rote. When I was a kid, I used to repeat the same word over and over until it became meaningless, an empty bag of sound. After repeating this lesson so many times, the same thing has happened to these facts about myself. Even my name sounds funny, like a foreign word that can't quite sink in.

In the second class I am paired with a young and attractive female teacher. Literally paired. We happen to be wearing the same pink chenille sweater, purchased from a sale pile at Jade Plaza, and while her gray pencil skirt bears little resemblance to my gray thrift store corduroy, the girls keep exclaiming, "*pe-a-sutairu!*"—pair style—a term reserved for best friends who dress identically. As the teacher tells them to quiet down, I walk around to put distance between us and the unflattering comparison.

"Is my name Miss Marina?" I ask the class.

"Yes!" they shout as a group.

"Am I . . ."

"You're twenty-two years old!"

I return to the front of the room and ask the teacher if I've already taught this lesson to her class. She nods and my face heats up with shame, not only for repeating myself but also for having managed to forget this whole group of people.

"What am I doing here?"

"*Wakarimasen*," she says, which can mean "I don't know" or "I don't understand."

"Why am I here?" I try, "*mo ichi do?*"

"To . . . pray . . . with the children?" she says, shrugging helplessly.

In the faculty room, the vice-principal sits with his hands clasped on his large wooden desk, which has a patent leather shine. The air is redolent with citrus oil, and the smell turns my stomach.

"I already gave my self-introduction lesson to that class," I say.

"Yes," he says, smiling. "I know."

"I wish you'd told me," I say. "I felt foolish repeating myself."

"Foolish?" he repeats.

"*Hazukashii.*"

"Fool-ish," he says, writing the word down on his special *eikaiwa* notepad. "Repeating is best way to learn new language. You always say so. Don't be fool-ish."

To calm myself down, I picture him behind the wheel of an Airstream, sitting on a phone book to better see the horizon, coasting through Nebraska with his wife by his side. He didn't mean to humiliate me. He doesn't know what to do with me either. He and Miyoshi-sensei agreed that I should stay here until I have given my self-introduction lesson to every class. Surely I'm close to that point. I ask if he found "the count" and he nods.

"Mmm," he says. "Good job. You finished already."

I feel like a character in a fairy tale who just completed some mythically tedious task. Like if I had spun a room full of straw into fool's gold, fooling no one. "Then I guess I'd better go back to the high school?" I say hopefully.

"Maybe," he says. "But I should speak to Miyoshi-sensei before I release you." He claps his hands. "So . . . how about today's weather?"

"It's cold," I say.

"It *is* cold," he agrees. Ding-ding-ding. And we enter the ring for another round.

My teeth are killing me. My whole jaw aches like I got punched. The pain gets worse when I chew, so I only eat soft foods, things I can swallow whole.

"Can't you eat fish?"

It takes a moment before I realize that Kobayashi-sensei is speaking in English and looking at me. I've been using my chopsticks to scrape the flesh from a fried sardine, its desiccated head emerging from a golden turtleneck of batter. The second-grade teacher sits at a diagonal from my assigned desk in the elementary school faculty room. I can see the framed pictures of him and his university sumo team, two rows of fat guys in loincloths. Keiko Ishii's desk is next to his, directly across from mine, as covered in piles of drawings and baskets of art supplies as mine is bare. In the six weeks that I've been coming here, Keiko hasn't been very warm to me. Back in November, Miyoshi-sensei told me that I offended her when I didn't return to her ikebana club a second time. "In Japan," he said, "you shouldn't attend a club you don't wish to join. Otherwise the teacher will lose face." But how could you know whether or not you wanted to join a club without first trying it out? "Be careful what you start," he warned me.

"In Japan we eat fish like this," Kobayashi-sensei says, popping a whole sardine into his mouth. I smile dutifully, trying to tune out the crunch of tiny bones being ground to a paste. He turns his chopsticks around, pinches his pickled plum between their ends, and then reaches across our desks to drop it on my bowl of rice. "I remember from your self-introduction lesson," he says. "Miss Marina can eat *umeboshi*." I only included that item on my worksheet because it annoyed me how often I was being asked whether I "can" eat Japanese foods. I don't have a four-chambered stomach. When I tell people that I've been eating Japanese food since I was a kid, they always say, "But American Japanese food is so different . . ."

"Dame!" Kobayashi-sensei suddenly calls out. It's forbidden!

"What?" I ask, before realizing that he's looking not at me but over my shoulder. I spin around, coming face-to-face with Koji, who is making bunny ears behind my head. He is still wearing those ski gloves. I wink and grin back at him.

"Go back to class," his mother tells him.

"I already finished my lunch," he says. "I'm bored." He tries to climb onto her lap but she swivels out from under him, reminding him that they're at school, where he has to act like a student, not a baby. "Why don't you practice your characters," Kobayashi-sensei says to the little boy, uncapping a pen and drawing a vertical rectangle with a horizontal swish through its center. I recognize the *kanji* for day.

"I don't like to copy," the boy says.

"This is a problem," Kobayashi-sensei says to Keiko.

"Can you show me?" I ask Koji. "I don't know how to write in Japanese." He squints at me for a moment, trying to decide if I'm pulling a dirty trick, before he takes the pen. "Like this?" I ask, copying his character, and he nods. Keiko smiles at me over the bent head of the little boy, who is now showing me all of the other characters he knows, one after another.

When the bell rings at the end of the lunch period, two sixth-grade girls return to collect our trays. One is tall, her new breasts pushing at her uniform blazer, while the other is as thin as a straw and needs her suspenders to hold up her skirt. The larger girl points to my untouched seaweed jello, studded with purple adzuki beans, and tells me that it's delicious, the best part of the lunch.

"Dozo," I say. "You can have it."

Kobayashi-sensei clears his throat and tells the girl that perhaps she shouldn't eat so many sweets. "You are already so . . . big size," he says in English. "So are you," Keiko says, and I laugh. She tells the girls that they may share my jello, but to eat quickly. The bigger girl cuts it in two and they lean over my desk as they chew. I notice that the littler girl is wearing a "Kitty-chan" barrette in her hair and I tell her that it's cute. "Kitty-chan is your favorite *karakuta*," she says, and I feel happy that she remembered this, even though I only put it down on my worksheet to have something in common with 99 percent of the girls here. The bigger girl says that she loves Kitty-chan too.

"No way!" I pretend to be blown away. "What a coincidence!"

"Coincidence . . . " Keiko repeats. "A lucky accident."

"Wow," I say. "You have a great memory."

"Thank you," she says. Her ability to take a compliment is refreshing. It's nice not to follow the script for once. She picks up a pencil and begins sketching a cat head with two far-spaced ovals for eyes and another oval turned on its side for a nose. A thin circle loops through the right side of this nose, a nose ring like my own. "Wah! Marina-kitty!" The girls clap their hands. The bigger one picks up the pencil and begins copying this drawing, but the art teacher tells her to draw her own picture, to try to draw what's really in front of her. The girl bites her lip and shakes her head.

"It's too difficult," she says.

"What do you mean?" Keiko says. "You're an excellent artist."

"But her face is too 3-D."

"Too 3-D?" I repeat, laughing.

"You have a tall nose," Keiko says. "Folded eyes. It's new experience."

She calls out to the vice-principal, who makes a rare appearance from behind his desk, rocking slightly on his feet as he listens to her with his head cocked to one side. "Miss Marina," he says, "you have next period free. You could stay here with me, or you could join Ishii-sensei's art class." It's not a difficult decision. I'd love to spend a period sketching with a bunch of kids instead of having yet another conversation about the weather.

"Thank you so much," I say to Keiko.

"Thank *you* so much," she repeats after me, bowing deeply.

Instead of desks, the art room holds three long sawhorse tables. I lower myself onto a stool between two sixth-grade boys. The table is so low that when I try to cross my legs, I bump my knee on the rough plywood and snag my tights. Otherwise, it feels strangely normal to be back on this side of the classroom, waiting for things to happen instead of directing them. While Keiko explains the lesson in Japanese, I stare out the window. The second graders are running laps around the empty swimming pool. I can see the tops of the kids' heads, and the top of Kobayashi-sensei's head too. He has a bald spot the size of a sand dollar and his scalp is bright red. It looks vulnerable, and cold.

This makes me think of my dad, whose own hair was already thinning by the time I was born. For a long time this didn't take away from his good looks. People said he resembled a young Marlon Brando. He had hooded eyes that could change from green to gray or blue as rapidly as his moods, and full, almost feminine lips, in contrast to his strong jaw. When I was little, he used to make me laugh by preening in the mirror and saying, "Who is that handsome devil?" as if he truly couldn't recognize himself. I'd say, "You, Daddy!" and he'd say, "Damn, I'm good-looking." Even after he lost most of his hair, he was still very handsome, right up until the last year of his life, when his skin took on the hue of wet clay and he started wearing a sad comb-over.

The last summer I spent at home, the summer before he killed himself, my mom took an extra job as a camp counselor, leaving my dad and me alone together for a month. He had changed more than physically. He didn't laugh anymore, or stay up sketching new inventions. He didn't want to be left alone, but he was unable to keep up a conversation. He followed me around the house and tagged along when I ran errands. He even wanted to come when I went out with friends. When I was short with him, hoping he'd take the hint and back off, he only clung harder. My friends asked what was wrong with him. I said that he was having some kind of midlife crisis and they nodded, rolling their eyes knowingly. I wished he was having a midlife crisis like the ones their fathers had, that he'd do something—gamble the mortgage, buy a sports car, and take off with a girl younger than me—anything besides follow me around. All my life I'd been in awe of him. I didn't want my new power.

The week before he killed himself, he got a haircut. I didn't actually see it—not while he was alive anyhow—but he described it to me over the phone. This was to be our last conversation, although I didn't know it at the time. He always went to Supercuts, to the same girl, but his usual hairdresser was on vacation that week so he'd gotten a trainee who butchered it. That was the word he used. He said that he looked like a marine, that he'd been scalped, that he couldn't even recognize himself in the mirror. He sounded devastated, ridiculously upset over something so trivial, and I felt claustrophobic listening to him complain, the same way I'd felt all summer when he trailed after me.

"It's just a haircut," I said impatiently. "It'll grow back."

"I don't know," he said. "I look bald."

"Dad," I said, "you are bald."

For a moment he didn't speak. Then he said, "I guess you're right. I'm not a handsome devil anymore." He didn't sound like he was angling for a compliment, just stating a fact, and I didn't contradict him. Of course later, thinking back on that conversation, I wished I'd told him that he was wrong, that he was still handsome. I wish I'd said a lot of things. I also wondered why he got a haircut right before he committed suicide. It seemed like such a waste, especially for a man who hated to waste a dollar. It seemed like a sign that he had wavered in his decision until the very end, that something or someone could have changed his mind.

"Marina-sensei," Keiko interrupts my reverie. "Could you please come up here?"

I turn away from the window to see that the students have already passed baskets of charcoal and acrylics and they all have sheets of paper in front of them. When I reach the front of the room, I assume she's going to give me a sheet of paper of my own, and translate the directions into English. Instead she backs away, leaving me alone.

Now the students pick up their sticks of charcoal.

Now I realize what I'm here for.

The art teacher stands with her back to the window, chin in hand, appraising me along with them. "How about . . . relaxing?" she says at last, making a Vanna White sweep of her arm across the surface of the table.

"Relaxing?" I repeat weakly.

She opens an art book to a painting of a plump white woman lying on her side, wearing only a black ribbon tied around her throat. She tells me not to worry; I don't have to take off my clothes. The kids laugh. An eerie feeling comes over me as I climb up onto the table, which hammocks under my weight. My scalp prickles and I feel like I'm floating outside of myself. My mom has a story she likes to tell about the day of my birth. There were complications, she had to have an emergency C-section, and in the middle of it she started to regain feeling. The doctors administered a shot of anesthesia that went to her heart, stopping it for a full minute, in which she was technically dead. She swears that she remembers rising above herself and seeing the heads of the doctors and my own head being lifted out of her, and fighting to get back into her body. She says that it felt like trying to swim down to the bottom of a pool.

Slowly, in bits and pieces, I watch my portrait take shape on paper. One little boy draws only my hair, a floating yellow wig. Another starts with my feet, which take up two-thirds of the page. But most begin with my nose. By all accounts, I'm overdue for a nose job. It could hold up a heavy winter coat.

"Draw what you see," Keiko keeps telling them. "Don't make a *karakuta*."

As she passes by the table where I'm reclining, I notice scratch marks rising out of the collar of her shirt, ascending her neck to the base of her earlobe. It looks like she was attacked by a cat or something. "I don't like to teach sixth-grade art," she says. "I prefer younger children. They still see something new. By twelve years, they only copy."

"But I don't look like that," I say. "At least I hope I don't!"

"They copy idea of you," she explains. "They know Western face has tall nose, folded eyelid, so they draw tall nose, folded eyelid. They can't really see you."

At the end of the period, after the students file out of the room, I stand beside her as she leafs through the stack and I see what she means. In picture after picture, I've been turned into a cartoon version of myself, my eyes two hooded balloons, my nose a big 7, with no mouth to speak of—or through—just like Kitty-chan. Keiko sighs, shuts the classroom door and turns the bolt. Then she raises the window, rummages in her Vuitton shoulder bag and pulls out a pack of Dunhill's. When she holds it out, eyebrows lifted, I nod and she sticks two cigarettes in her mouth, lighting them off the same match. I remember how Miyoshi-sensei once told me that women teachers here never smoke. I'm glad to meet another exception to the rule.

"Secret from principal," she says, handing me one. "Secret from husband too."

"Shhh," I whisper and she laughs, curved lines like parentheses cupping her mouth. "I don't smoke often," she says. "But when Koji runs away I feel so frighten. Kobayashi-sensei gives me cigarettes, to help relax."

"I'm so sorry you were scared," I say, "but Koji didn't run away. He just wanted to show me the rabbits. I was with him the whole time."

"Mmm," she says. "This time yes. He's with you. But last week he runs away after school and we can't find him until morning."

"Shit," I say. "Are you serious? He was missing all night?"

"Mmm." She takes a drag, the ember lengthening from her deep inhalation. I ask where the boy was and she says that he was down by the sea. "Shit," I say again. The cliffs in this part of town are so steep that I get vertigo just thinking about the edge. "Children have no idea how vulnerable they are," I pronounce. This is something my mom used to say when I was little and did something stupid, like jumping from roof to roof on our block.

"Vulnerable means what?" Keiko asks me.

"They don't know how easily they can get hurt."

"He knows," she says. "He wants to."

"He wants to get hurt?" I repeat, certain there's a language gap here.

"Mmm." She nods again. "It's how to get my attention."

When the bell rings to signal the start of the next period, Keiko says that I can return to the faculty room if I'd like, or I can stay and pose for a third-grade class. I opt to stay with her. The kerosene heater is right behind me, bathing me in waves of oily heat, and the fumes go to my head in a not unpleasant way. I stretch out my arm for a moment, rest my cheek on my shoulder, and Keiko tells me to go ahead and shut my eyes, telling me that my eyes are hard to draw and it will be easier for the kids this way.

Before long, I feel myself drifting into a shallow dream. I know that I'm dreaming, but this doesn't justify the fact that I can't think of the words for the most basic things, like the pronged metal instrument that carries food from plate to mouth, or the numbered grid of paper where people write their schedules. My father is there with me, testing me in a laboratory that looks a lot like the elementary school art room. He holds up one object after another while I tell him to wait, just wait a minute, to give me time to think. "Umhmm," he says, jotting something down. "And my name is?" I try to bargain my way out of this one. "Why do I need to know that anymore?" I ask, and when he says, "What do you mean?" I realize that he has no idea he's dead. I don't want to break the news, good or bad.

I wake to the feeling of fingers running through my hair. My teeth ache from grinding them in my sleep. Koji Ishii is standing beside me, studying me with his wide-set gray eyes. I want to grab the little boy and hold him tight like a teddy bear. Instead I grip his hand and he flinches. I sit up and find that the art room is almost empty. The sky outside is skim-milk white with a cast of blue, and already it's dark enough that shapes are becoming blurry, indistinct. Kim is the only other child in the room, drawing by herself at a table. Keiko stands facing the window, hanging pictures from a clothesline while gazing outside.

"I'm sorry I fell asleep," I say, standing beside her. "It's so late!"

"It's fine," she says. "I have to clean up. Kim and Koji make your portrait."

"You drew me?" I ask the little boy, placing a hand on his silky head.

"Not draw," his mother says. "He won't draw. Only *koraji*."

Koraji must mean what it sounds like, collage, because the boy has assembled my portrait from scraps. The body is a triangle of paper torn from my own self-introduction worksheet, the face that of a Japanese model cut from a magazine, with green construction paper circles glued over her eyes. For hair he used a few sprigs of hay that must have lined the rabbits' hutch, and I've got two American flag stickers—pilfered from my own box of props—for feet. "*Kawaii*," I say, wishing I knew a better word than "cute" to let him know how much I like this piece of art. I feel like that, I want to tell him: piecing together an identity, cobbling a self from scraps. Then I remember the word Keiko taught me after I attended her *ikebana* club that one time.

"It's very *wabi-sabi*," I say. Perfectly imperfect.

"You're right," Keiko says, smiling. "You have good memory too."

I tell him that I will hang it in my kitchen and think of him whenever I look at it.

"Ah, you want it?" his mom says. "I had better ask." She crouches and addresses her son in Japanese. He brings his gloved fingertips to the bridge of his nose, then shakes his head slowly. "Koji wants to keep portrait of Miss Marina," she explains. "I think he likes you so much," she says. "Usually he resists a teacher."

"Maybe that's because I'm not really his teacher," I point out.

"*So desu ne*," she agrees.

Kim gets up and hands me her drawing. She has given me a stick-figure body and a smiley face, devoting her artistic energy to sketching the school's two rabbits on either side of me, scaled big as dogs, discernible by their tall ears and cotton-ball tails, and by the fact that one is fat and smiling while the other looks like a bunny skeleton with fangs.

"*Kurai*," Keiko says. Dark.

"Someone should really help that poor rabbit," I say.

"What can we do?" she asks me. "When vice-principal buys him, he is cute baby. Since then his teeth don't stop growing. He becomes rabbit monster."

"Maybe he should be put to sleep," I suggest.

"I think he sleeps at night," she says.

"No," I say. "*Put* to sleep . . . Like . . . Forever?"

"*Kurai*," she repeats. "In Japan this is forbidden."

"Even for rabbits?" I ask.

"What if you are rabbit next time?"

"But if he's suffering," I say. "If he's going to die . . . "

"This is part of life," she says with a shrug.

"Are we taking Kim home?" Koji asks, interrupting.

"Of course," Keiko says. "We take her home every day. You know that."

"But which home are we taking her to?"

"What do you mean, which home?"

"Kim has two homes," he says, looking at me. "No one lives in the other one."

"That's not true," his mother says. "She has only one home."

"Too bad." The little boy sighs. "I thought I could go live in the empty one."

"That's not very nice," Keiko says. "I'd be lonely, you know."

"You could visit," he says. "But *only* you. And Miss Marina."

"Arigato," I say, allowing my hand to fall on his silky head once more.

Keiko tells the kids to get their stuff and meet her in the parking lot. I try to give Kim back her drawing but she won't take it. *"Dozo,"* she says in her gravelly little voice.

"For me?" I say, to make sure, and she nods. *"Arigato."*

"Arigato."

The kids have barely closed the door before Keiko turns, seizing my shoulders. "Kim can speak Japanese! She says *dozo* and *arigato*! You are good teacher, Marina-sensei!"

"I didn't teach her those words," I protest. "I hardly speak Japanese myself!"

"Maybe that's why," Keiko muses. "You can't speak much Japanese, so she must try harder to speak with you." I laugh, once more impressed by her willingness to say it like it is. She peers at me with gray eyes as focused and hypnotizing as her son's. "Marina-sensei," she says, "do you have any free time?"

"Sure," I say. "I have lots of free time."

"How about coming to my home one evening after school?"

"I'd love to," I say, not bothering to conceal my eagerness. After six months here, I still don't know where Miyoshi-sensei lives, or which apartment behind the grocery store Noriko rents. Back at our teacher training seminar in Tokyo, we were warned that the Japanese seldom entertain at home, that only a person who wants to be your close friend will invite you over for dinner. This has yet to happen, to Carolyn or me.

"How about Thursday?" she says. "Five to seven okay?"

"Thank you so much," I say, thinking it funny, charming, and very Japanese that she is already setting a cap on our time together.

"Thank *you* so much," she repeats, bowing deeply.

CHAPTER TEN

kamoshirenai: (EXP.) *maybe; perhaps; possibly*

On the drive home, I feel happier than I have in a long time. I love the big, dilapidated houses, the steamed kitchen windows with their tempered glass to prevent people from seeing inside, the fox-shaped dogs that howl and chase after my car. I love the road, the way it bends around the cliffs and follows ancient property lines, the magnificence of the sea absorbing the swirls of falling snow. I turn on the tape deck and listen to the mix Carolyn made for me after we got here. One side is labeled, "Way to school," the other side, "Way back home." Wistfully I listen to side two. Between songs, she speaks. "Hurry home," she says. "I'll be waiting for you."

I am looking down, hitting Rewind just to hear her say this again, when my seat belt snaps taut. I slam on the brakes and sit up as an avalanche of giant orange hail pelts my car. It takes a moment before I realize they're sweet potatoes.

Stopped on the road ahead of me, the speaker bolted to the yam truck keeps repeating the same line over and over. "*Oishii o-imo. Oishii kamoshirenai.*" When Carolyn and I first heard this, sung by an old man with a warbling tremolo, we thought we were listening to the chanting of a monk from the temple down the block. But the truck kept passing our house at the same time every evening, its speaker blaring the same two lines on a loop, and one day I found myself suddenly able to decipher the words.

"Delicious potatoes. Delicious, perhaps . . . "

The song cuts off and the driver steps out of the truck. He is an old man and he's wearing a neck brace, a big, stiff, plastic cone that rises from the collar of his shirt and pushes at the underside of his chin. I climb out of the car window, slipping on a sweet potato that squishes under my foot.

"*Gomen nasai*," I say. I'm sorry. "*Shitsureishimashita*." But I've committed more than a rude this time. Without speaking, he walks around the back of his truck, surveying the damage. To my relief, his vehicle looks more or less intact. It was protected from the collision by the heavy metal staircase welded to its back, leading up to the bed where a charcoal grill was roasting the sweet potatoes now covering the road. But the front of my car is crumpled, pushed in like a bulldog's snout.

"*Itai?*" I ask the man. Are you hurt?

"I . . . can't . . . speak . . . Englishverywell," he manages.

In Japanese I ask if he's okay and again he tells me in English that he can't speak English. I wonder if he can't understand my Japanese. Maybe my accent is that bad, or maybe he's so flustered to find himself in a fender-bender with a Westerner that he can't even register the fact that I'm trying to communicate in his language.

"How are you?" I try.

"I'mfinethankyou," he says, "and you?"

"I'm fine," I say. "How is your neck?"

"Your neck," he repeats.

"Your neck," I say, pointing to his brace. "Fine? Not fine?"

"Not fine," he says, shaking his head and then wincing. "Not fine!"

"I'm so sorry," I say. "It was all my fault." I don't know how to say this in Japanese, though it's another line I should have mastered. He squats to pick up the yams. He bends from the knees and keeps his torso perfectly erect and still, like someone trying to balance a pot of boiling water on top of his head. The sappy skins of the yams are coated with grit from the road. He tries to polish one with his flannel shirttail, tearing the skin. "Your car not fine," he says, and Miyoshi-sensei's words come back to me. *Temporary people probably shouldn't own a car here. The rules are different, the roads are narrow, and what would you do in case of accident?* I don't know the numbers of any tow companies. There's no AAA. And if I call the police, they will call my supervisor. I can't bear the thought of seeing him again, for the first time in months, at the scene of an accident I caused. So I'm thankful when I lean into the window, turn the key in the ignition and the engine starts.

"It's fine," I say brightly. "*Daijoubu.*"

Then he says something in Japanese that I don't understand. I think he's telling me that without filing an accident report, I won't be able to collect insurance. "*Daijoubu,*" I say once more. He frowns as he takes one of the yams and throws it back onto the grill. Not knowing what else to do, I follow his example, throwing yam after yam into the back of the truck until we have cleaned the mess off the road.

"Delicious potatoes. Delicious, perhaps . . . "

When I get home, I hear Carolyn upstairs in the bedroom doing the Tae-Bo videotape my mom sent us. She is stomping overhead, practicing high kicks as Billy Blanks calls out, "repeater, repeater, repeater," over a pornolike soundtrack of synthesizer music and studio audience groans. I wonder if the noise bothers the neighbors, what they think we're doing in our windowless home. Not what it sounds like.

There's a new care package in the entryway, the padded envelope covered with bright red apples. My mom buys these envelopes in bulk from the teaching supply company where she gets her festive bulletin board trimmings and WAY TO GO! stickers. She has been an elementary school teacher since before I was born. She's a natural. She knows how to talk to children so that they listen, and how to listen to them so that they feel heard, how to cultivate their strengths and make them feel unique and loved, each and every one. She has been teaching for so long that her voice, trained to project over the din of children, can't be turned down. And her entire wardrobe was chosen to appeal to kids, from her seasonal sweaters to the zoo that is her jewelry box.

I tear the envelope open and riffle through the contents, pulling out two packs of gold star stickers, two ballpoint pens, two boxes of Annie's organic mac-and-cheese, and two tubes of Tom's natural toothpaste. There is also a copy of *Prevention* magazine, dog-eared to an article on the fertility-damaging properties of cigarettes. I open a card with a picture of Virginia Woolf looking down her own tall nose. "*Share the goodies with Carolyn,*" she wrote in her perfect penmanship, each letter made to be copied by kids. "*Hugs, Mom.*"

Over the phone last spring, I broke the news to my mom that I had a girlfriend and that we were moving to Japan together to teach English. I hoped that this second piece of news would soften the blow of the first. She'd told me many times that she hoped that I would become a teacher too, that the job had brought her so much joy. "Is this forever?" she asked in a voice that was small and brittle, unfamiliar and awful. I told her that it was only for a year, pretending not to know what she was really asking, holding the phone away from my ear so that I wouldn't have to listen to her cry. When I was little,

I used to give her love tests. Would she still love me if I cheated? Robbed a bank? If I murdered someone? She always said yes without missing a beat. "I'd be very sad and disappointed, but I'll always love you." I suddenly realized that I'd given her one of these love tests, and that I was feeling the sting of her disappointment for the first time.

"I'm sorry," she cried, "but I wanted to see you get married and have children."

"I can still have those things," I said. I felt like I had swallowed broken glass and was trying to talk around it. "Lots of gay people have kids," I managed.

"Have you always known?" she asked. "Because I thought you were in love with Luke. I still don't understand what happened between you two."

Luke was my high school boyfriend. We went to college in different states, but we always got back together in the summers. He had four brothers and two sisters, and I liked the chaos of his family, the way I could get lost in the shuffle. He liked my home for the opposite reason, because it was quiet and he was taken seriously, and because he liked my father. Luke wanted to be an engineer, and the two of them would spend hours talking about their ideas, sitting hip to hip on the couch, sketching on graph paper. Luke was one of the people who noticed that something was seriously wrong with my dad. That's how he put it when he refused to come over anymore. "It's too depressing," he said. "You might be able to pretend like nothing's wrong, but I can't." At the time, I was glad to spend more time at Luke's, to have somewhere else to go, to get away. But after my dad killed himself, I couldn't be in the same room as Luke anymore. When he came to my father's memorial service, I refused to talk to him. Later, when he flew out to New York, I wouldn't even let him upstairs. I finally told him that I had a girlfriend, that I'd never really been attracted to him. He left me alone after that.

"Is this about your dad?" my mom asked on the phone. "Are you so angry with him for killing himself that you're turning your back on all men?" I lashed out and told her that this was the one thing in my life that wasn't about my dad, the one thing that was just mine. I said that I wished she could be happy for me, happy that I'd found someone to love, and who loved me too. "I'm sorry if you're disappointed in me," I said, "but I'm just trying to get on with my life. I hope you can get on with yours eventually too." The next time I flew out to San Francisco, there was a Gay Pride bumper sticker on the back of her car. She was wearing a rainbow-striped pin on her denim vest, and she had a key chain to match. She looked more like a lesbian than I did, and I felt a little uneasy. "You know, this might not be forever," I said.

"So it's a choice?" my mom asked me.

"I guess," I said. "I don't know."

"Because if it's a choice, if you're not gay"—in spite of her props, the word was obviously hard for her to say—"then why would you choose to make your life harder than it already is?"

"Hi," Carolyn says, appearing at the bottom of the stairs. "What did your mom send us this time?" She takes the envelope from me, reaches inside and pulls out a red fleece garment that looks like a giant version of the footie pajamas that I wore as a kid, except that instead of having two legs, it's just one big tube with arm holes.

"It's a sleep sack," I say. "Does my mom think I'm still two?"

"Your mom sends the best stuff," Carolyn says.

"Are you kidding?" I say. "I've never seen anything less sexy in my life."

"Who cares?" she says. "It looks warm."

"You can have it," I say.

"Thanks." She takes it from me and heads back upstairs, closing the bedroom door behind her.

Ever since the cat died, things between us have been even more strained. After we buried Amana's body at the edge of the river, we went back home and she collapsed on the futon in our bedroom, crying as she stroked the pillow—still matted with Amana's fur—while I stroked her arm. I asked what would make her feel better. "We could go for a walk on the beach," I suggested. "We could take a drive or go to the baths . . . "

"I don't want to take a bath," she said. "I don't want to *do* anything."

"Sorry," I said. "I just want to help you feel better."

"I don't want to feel better," she sobbed. "I'm sad, and I want to be sad, if that's okay with you."

"Of course not," I said, lying down beside her. She cried like a small child—openly, unembarrassed, snot streaming from her nose—and I thought of how young she'd been when her mom died, how a part of her had been forced to grow up right then and a part of her probably never would. She rolled over and I spooned her, tucking my knees into the backs of hers and holding her close. "That boy killed our cat," she kept saying, "and we're going to have to keep seeing him every single fucking day." Looking out our window, at the drawn blinds covering Haruki's, I wondered if he was inside. "I'll bet that's the last time Ogawa-san returns our trash," I said. "If I'm right, it's almost worth it."

"Almost worth it?" she choked.

"Of course not," I said. "I was just joking . . . "

She flipped over and I noticed that her breath smelled funny, like the rotten water in a vase holding the slimy stems of an old bouquet, or the stale mouthpiece of a telephone.

"Why aren't you sad?" she asked me.

"I am sad," I said. "Of course I'm sad."

"You don't seem sad."

"Just because I show my feelings differently—"

"I used to think that you were afraid of them," she said. "I used to think you held them in so tightly because they were so intense. I thought you'd buried your sadness deep inside of you where you wouldn't have to feel it all the time. I got that. But now I'm starting to wonder if you have any feelings. Maybe you're just cold."

"If you think that," I said, "then you don't know me at all."

I left her in the bedroom and went downstairs where I lay on the brown vinyl couch, hoping that she'd come down after me, but she didn't. "Our cat is dead," I said in a soft voice, trying to trigger the appropriate response, the wave of grief, the cathartic collapse. I was reminded of the hours and days and weeks after my dad died. Over and over I had to remind myself that he had committed suicide, that he was dead, and over and over I'd forget, and remembering was a shock every time. I had a hard time crying, even at the memorial service, where my mom cried enough for both of us, accepting comfort from anyone who wanted to give it, weeping on the shoulders of near strangers. Like Carolyn, she kept asking if I was sad. Wasn't I sad? Of course, I said then too. I could tell that she wanted me to be sadder, or more transparent in my sadness, to share it with her, split the pain. But "sad" was a pathetic little word, too small to contain what I felt. I was a shattered windshield: one tap and I'd collapse. The whole world had been pulled out from under me and I was still waiting to fall. I had wasted tears on so many silly things. How could I cry for this too?

It was starting to get dark when I heard the beep-beep-beep from in front of our house. I opened the front door and saw Haruki's bulky frame bathed in the red glow of a miniature forklift's taillights. Its steel jaws were clamped around our refrigerator, holding it suspended in midair like the time machine in *New Horizons*. "What are you doing?" I asked, but the boy ignored me as usual. I tapped him on the shoulder and repeated my question in Japanese, but he still didn't answer, so I punched his arm, my knuckles sinking into his doughy flesh. "Are you crazy?" I asked, punching him again. "Go away!" But he just stood there while his grandfather lowered the refrigerator until it was level with our entryway. Mister Ogawa got out of the cab and he and Haruki proceeded to move the Amana back into our *genkan*, pushing and shoving until the refrigerator stood right where it had before, on the darker blue square of carpet. Haruki got on his knees and reached behind the machine to plug it in, Ogawa-san opened the door and the ceiling light flickered on. Inside, it was spotless and odorless. Not only had they fixed it, they'd cleaned it. There was no sign of the dead cat, not a single hair. That was the last time Ogawa-san brought our *gomi* back.

It's snowing out, and so cold that we eat dinner in the bedroom, sitting at the *kotatsu*, our thighs roasting under the electric coil while our upper bodies freeze.

"I can't even remember what warm feels like," Carolyn says, hugging her bowl of soup. "I had to cook in mittens. I almost lost a finger when the knife slipped."

"I'm so sick of the cold," I agree. "It's all anyone talks about."

"Sorry to bore you," she says, setting her soup down. Lately she's so sensitive.

"You're not," I say. "I keep having the same conversation with the vice-principal. It's cold. It *is* cold. Isn't it cold?"

"Well it is," Carolyn says. "It's hard to talk about anything else."

When I asked Miyoshi-sensei once why Japanese houses aren't insulated, he said that gas is very expensive here. I pointed out that insulation—*like sweaters for the walls?*—is relatively cheap. He told me that Japan is an ancient country, that people had been living with the cold for so long that it had become a source of pride to endure it. But everyone here spends a fortune on electric blankets, carpets, and tables, none of which do the job; kerosene is messy, and to prevent headaches you have to leave the windows open, which defeats the whole point; and everyone talks constantly about how cold they are. Maybe that's the point, I think as Carolyn and I face each other in silence, our breath hovering in the air like empty cartoon talk bubbles. Maybe they'd rather be cold than warm, and have a guaranteed conversational standby.

I pick up my soup, take a sip, and accidentally bite down on a piece of hard carrot.

"You don't like it," Carolyn says flatly.

"I do," I say. "It's delicious, but my teeth are killing me."

"You have to go to the dentist," she says, reprising another conversation we've had many times. "Ignoring the problem won't make it go away."

"I don't know where the dentist is."

"Just ask Miyoshi-sensei."

"Okay," I say. "Can you pass me the soy sauce?"

"You never talk about him anymore."

"I never see him anymore." I didn't tell Carolyn what happened with Hiro. She was the one who wanted an open relationship, and I figured that if it didn't lead to anything, there was no reason for her to know. Besides, it was just a kiss. To change the subject, I tell her about Keiko, how she invited me to her art class, how I thought I was going to be drawing with the kids but instead I had to pose for them. "At first I was horrified," I say, "but it turned out to be really fun."

"Big surprise," Carolyn says with a snort.

"What do you mean?" I ask.

"Admit it," she says. "You weren't horrified. You loved being the center of attention, having those kids draw your picture. It's how I got you in my bed, remember?"

"Of course I remember," I say, trying to take her teasing in good fun. "Anyways, Keiko's great. She's a little messy, not into rules, with this weird, dark sense of humor. We even snuck cigarettes together in her classroom, smoking out the window like teenagers."

"Sounds like your perfect match."

"I don't know about that," I said, "but I do like her a lot. She invited me for dinner one evening this week."

"Really?" Carolyn jabs at her rice. "Did you ask if I could come?"

"Um, no," I say. "I mean, she doesn't know about us."

"Of course she doesn't."

"How about if we invite her over here next time?"

"So that I can cook for both of you once you're already best friends? Pretend to be your roommate? Sounds fun."

"Come on," I say, reaching for her foot under the table. She lets me massage it for a moment, closing her eyes. "I wouldn't expect you to bring me along the first time you went to a new friend's house for dinner."

"Fine," she says, pulling her foot back. "I'll remember that, if I ever make a friend of my own this year."

"You will," I say. "It just takes time."

She gets up and clears the barely eaten food off the table. I follow her downstairs and watch her dump her grilled eggplant with sweet miso glaze into the trash. She tells me that she's going to get the kerosene from the car. Only now do I remember that I was supposed to stop at the gas station to refill the jug on my way home from work. She slams the door as she returns to the living room with the empty container.

"I'm so sorry," I say. "I completely forgot."

"Yeah," she says. "You also forgot to tell me that you wrecked our car again."

"It's not really our car," I say, and the look on her face makes me wish I could suck the words back in. "I mean of course it's our car, but since you don't have a driver's license, and I paid for it . . . "

"I paid the key money for this place," she says, "so I guess it's not really our home."

"Yes it is," I say. "Come on, Caro."

"Is it?" she says. "Because it doesn't really feel like it."

She goes upstairs and I sit on the front stoop, smoking in the snow, my ashes blending in with the falling flakes. Carolyn was right when she said that moving together to Japan, living together for the first time here, would put too much pressure on our relationship. I thought that by crossing the Pacific together, our lives would broaden, but instead, they shrank. Here we have only each other for comfort, for consolation, for conversation, for sex, for everything. And sometimes being lonely together is worse than being lonely alone. Still, I can't imagine being here without her, and I worry that when we go our separate ways, I will feel halved.

Upstairs, she is lying facing the wall, her back to me. The covers feel icy when I crawl under them, but I don't pull her to me. There is a large gap between us. She is wearing the red fleece sack that my mom sent me, with her arms tucked inside. She looks warm.

daijoubu: (ADJ./ADV./N.) *safe; all right; okay*

When I wake up, the whole world has been transformed. The roofs are buried, each shingle capped with a white copy of itself. The road is a white river, while the river has been narrowed between stacked white banks. I listen to the soft fizz of the snowflakes pelting the river, the water rushing toward the ocean, the wind whistling through the branches of the trees, knocking clumps of snow to the ground. Mrs. Ogawa is outside as usual, wearing a high collared flannel nightgown under a down vest, emptying a kettle of steaming water into her koi pond. I imagine the carp frozen in place, tails beginning to flicker as the ice thaws. She catches me watching her and I raise my hand in a greeting. She holds up her own and we stand there for a moment like good neighbors.

Earlier this morning, I had just gotten out of the shower when Miyoshi-sensei called. Hearing his voice on the other end of the phone made my own tangle up in my throat. He said that he had a letter for me, that I should stop by the high school to pick it up on my way home from the elementary school. "It's not *gomi* letter," he stressed. "It's something else." *He could have faxed it to me at the elementary school*, I thought, but didn't point it out. I thought maybe he was just looking for an excuse to see me in person. Maybe the letter was a pretext, or he was finally going to address in writing what he couldn't say in person. I wanted the day to be over with already, so I could see him and find out.

The highway has been plowed. The road is scraped clean, a narrow chute between banks pushed to either side of the rice fields, which are buried in snow, the glittering white peaks shifting like dunes as the wind blows. Every time I pass a driver coming from the opposite direction, we each glide to a stop and squeeze against the banks, bobbing our heads at each other. *You first. No, you.* It takes forty minutes to cover ten kilometers, and I'm late by the time I coast into the elementary school parking lot, where Koji is standing all alone, wearing his yellow hat.

When I jump out of my car window, he laughs. "What are you doing out here?" I ask, afraid that he's running away again. He tells me that first period was suspended so that the kids could play in the snow. When I say that I don't see anyone, he explains that they're all on the playing field. "Come on," he says, as he takes my hand and pulls me past the staircase leading to the front doors, past the ducks and the rabbits in their hutch, around to the back of the school, where I'm relieved to find that the playground is in fact swarming with kids. In the swimming pool, an assembly line of children is building an assembly line of snowmen, screwing limp carrot noses—clearly the rabbits' leftovers—into round white faces. Other children grab sleds from a rapidly shrinking pile, throwing themselves down the snowy banks. Their bare legs look sunburned, they're so red from the cold. I don't understand why an exception to the rule can't be made on a day this snowy.

"Let's go, Marina," Koji says, picking up a sled with his free hand. Kim is sitting by herself on the edge of the pool, eyeing us wistfully, and I suggest to the little boy that he ask her instead.

"She's too scared," he says dismissively. "She won't do it."

"Just ask her," I insist.

"Kim-san," he says dutifully, "Do you want to go with me?"

She hesitates for a moment, then shakes her head, an almost imperceptible no.

"I told you," he said. "She's too scared. I need you."

None of the other teachers are sledding. I don't know if I'm even allowed to be out here, or if there's something I should be doing inside. I glance up at the faculty room and see the vice-principal staring out the window, his breath fogging the glass. He seems to be waving at me, probably waiting for me to come inside for yet another conversation about the weather. *It is very snowy day!* There are no other teachers playing with the children. But then again, that's what I'm supposedly here for. He says so all the time.

"I *need* you," Koji repeats with an earnestness that melts the ice of my heart.

"Okay," I say to the little boy. "Let's go."

Koji places the sled right at the cusp of the slope, jutting over the edge. He sits down, turns around, and pats the remaining couple of inches behind him. I straddle his body, cupping his frame with my knees, my arms wrapped around his shoulders, trying not to squeeze him too tightly, aware in a new way of how very small he is as he lifts his feet and we begin our rapid descent. The slope is steep and as the snow unzips beneath us I hold my breath until the ground levels out and we bounce and jolt to a halt. "*Mo ichi do!*" he cries out immediately. Lungs burning, I push myself to my feet and follow him back up the hill, slipping back half a step for every step forward. By the time we reach the top I'm winded, my core burning, my extremities freezing. This time I sit in front while he sits behind me, his arms wrapped around my waist, his cheek pressed to my back. At the bottom of the hill, the sled tilts to one side and tips us into the snow and I lie there for a moment, just catching my breath and taking in the blank hugeness of the sky. The same shade of white as the falling snow, it looks like it's all coming down. Koji climbs on top of me and places his hands on my face. He leans close, his expression almost ardent as he gazes into my eyes.

"*Mo ichi do*," he repeats.

Exhausted, I tell him to go by himself, saying that I don't want to slow him down. "You don't slow me down," he says. "You're very heavy. Together we go much faster!" I laugh and he says, "I need you," and then again, "I need you!" So I follow him back up the hill and down again, up and down, again and again. After a while, the repetitive slow climb followed by the repetitive rapid descent makes me think of Sisyphus and his rock. Sure, pushing it up the mountain over and over must've been a drag, but maybe, on a good day, he derived some pleasure from watching it roll back down, feeling his own body give in to gravity's pull as he followed.

Koji is getting frustrated, impatient. The more times we sled down the hill, the faster he wants to go but the less fun he seems to be having. The other kids are laughing, throwing snowballs at each other, making snow angels and Hello Kitties, but he is weirdly single-minded, almost obsessive, a sledding machine. Every time I suggest that we call it quits, he begs me to go one more time, with an intensity that makes it hard to say no. Finally he plants the sled at the top of a swath that's been traveled many times before, the snow worn down to a slick chute of ice. He waits for me to climb aboard, then sits on my lap and hugs his knees. He's so skinny that I can feel the point of his tailbone, although he barely weighs more than a big cat. As we careen down the slope, he stands up abruptly, leaning forward like the masthead of a ship while I grab the back of his uniform jacket.

"Sit down!" I cry, just as the sled catches on a clump of grass or submerged rock and catapults our bodies into the air. In the moment before we hit, it's not that time stands still, only that my mind empties and my senses take over. I hear the jangling of a school bell, I see children scatter, trying to get out of our way, I see the knobs at the top of Koji's spine, the bones like a strand of pearls, so small and close to the surface, his skin as thin as tissue. I clutch his body to mine and lean backward, and when we crash my body cushions his and his head slams into my mouth. Luckily, he is wearing his yellow hat. I am not so lucky. A spike of pain shoots through my mouth. I spit blood in the snow, cover the spot with my hand so he won't see it.

"*Daijoubu?*" I say to the little boy. Are you okay? He is crying, crying quietly like a grown-up. When he doesn't answer I answer for him. "*Daijoubu. Daijoubu.*" You're okay. You're okay. I don't even realize that I keep repeating this until he tells me to stop, wiping his eyes with the back of his glove.

"It didn't work," he says.

"What didn't work?" I ask, not sure that I understood him.

"We're here," he says.

"We need to go inside," I say, noticing a line of faces pressed to the inside of the faculty room window, all peering out at us. I wave and smile. I could've crushed him.

"*Mo ichi do,*" Koji says, as he gets up and begins to drag the sled back up the hill.

"No," I say, grabbing the sled and trying to take his hand. He wrenches free, so that I'm left holding just his glove, and then he runs away from me, into the school.

Inside the faculty room, his mother and the second-grade teacher are crouching before him, examining his hand. As I approach I can see that his fingertips are spotted with gray dots, as if he'd somehow wedged pencil tips under his fingernails. Feeling queasy, I ask what happened—afraid he got hurt when we fell—and Keiko tells me that he has frostbite.

"He has frostbite?" I repeat. "How is that possible?"

"I already tell you. He runs away. He is outside all night. *Samui desu ne?*" It's cold, isn't it? Suddenly, the greeting is less banal.

"You were going too fast," Kobayashi-sensei says, standing to his full height and looking down at me. "You were going too fast and then you—"

"*Jampu,*" Koji cuts him off.

We jumped. I jumped. He jumped. Pronouns get dropped in Japanese. This is exactly how I described my father's suicide to the little boy. I remember what Keiko told me yesterday, after I said that children don't know how easily they can get hurt. *He knows. He wants to. It's how to get my attention.* But surely he didn't want to . . . I can't even finish the thought. No child seeks pain.

"Are you okay?" the teacher asks the little boy, and Koji nods.

"I told you," Keiko says. "*Daijoubu.*" He's fine. "Miss Marina loves children."

"Marina-sensei," the vice-principal says. "Ishii-sensei said her students enjoyed drawing you so much. They experienced 3-D profile! How about returning to art class *mo ichi do?*" I look at Keiko, who smiles hopefully, and I'm so glad that she's not upset with me, and that Koji isn't hurt, that I say yes, sure, of course.

"It's so cold," she says in the art room, rubbing her hands together briskly. She ignites the kerosene heater and then opens the window an inch to let out the toxic fumes. The wind blows flakes into the room, which melt and vanish in midair. I lie across the table as another group of children draws my portrait. I try to ignore the pain in my mouth, to keep my expression pleasant, but I must not be doing a very convincing job because Keiko keeps pausing by the table, asking if I'm okay. Once again I see the scratch marks rising out of her shirt collar, darker and more obvious now as they're healing.

She tells me to go ahead and close my eyes again, but when I do I feel the thud of Koji's head. I can't drift off; the pain in my teeth is too omnipresent. In the break between periods, Keiko locks the classroom door and gets out her pack of cigarettes. It's snowing much harder now, the air a blur of snow being blown in every direction. In the swimming pool below, a tide is rising, burying the snowmen from both ends at once.

"I am so tired," she says.

"Do you still want me to come over?" I ask, hoping she'll suggest that we reschedule. When I probe my teeth with my tongue, they all seem to shift, like a row of apartment buildings after an earthquake. They all sting too. I didn't know teeth could sting. All I want to do is go home, curl up in front of the heater and drink something stiff to numb the pain.

"Ah," she says. "You are too busy?"

"I just thought, if you're tired . . . "

"I am always tired," she says. "I don't remember not feeling tired. I don't even know a word for this condition."

"Awake?" I suggest. "Alert?"

"But I am awake," she says. "I must always be alert. This is the problem."

As fifth-graders trickle in and settle into their seats, I hear one girl say to another, "I told you. Now we all have to draw her." I excuse myself for a moment and go to the bathroom to rinse out my mouth. The art room shares a hallway with the kindergarten and everything in this bathroom is tiny. The stalls are so short that I can see right over them, at little toilets that look almost cute. Less cute is my face. My skin is the color of Vaseline, my tongue scalloped with bite marks. When I spit into the sink, my saliva is threaded with blood. I push on my teeth and they wiggle. I imagine spitting them into my palm, liberated molars and bicuspids that I could shake and throw like dice, casting myself some new fate.

I swallow two aspirin and chew on a third, a trick I learned from my father, who liked to boast that he never once took a sick day from kindergarten through medical school. "There's nothing a doctor can tell me that I don't already know," he'd say before staggering off to work with a 104-degree fever. He put off visits to the dentist as well, although his own teeth were porous and prone to decay, my unfortunate inheritance. When he did go, he refused Novocain, saying that he couldn't stand the numb feeling. "He hated to give up control," my mom said. "He could never be weak." That was his greatest weakness.

I splash water on my face and return to the art room, where I have to pose for two more classes before lunch. I keep my eyes closed but I can't fall asleep. I keep thinking about my father. I think about the note he left in the glove compartment of his car, a note so short that I memorized it without trying, without wanting to. *I am sorry for the pain that this will cause you, but I am in a black hole of despair and I can't find my way out. I forfeit the right to give you any advice. Please try not to be too sad and move on with your lives.* Try not to be too sad? Move on with your lives? I've been following this advice like a dare. Maybe Carolyn is right, I think. Maybe I have no feelings; only this pain in my mouth.

Lunch today is curry rice. Usually this is my favorite school lunch, but today I can't manage to chew the mush. When two boys come to clear our trays, Kobayashi-sensei gestures at my untouched bowl and asks if I'm okay, sounding genuinely concerned.

"Usually you have big appetite," he says. "Like me."

"I'm fine," I say. "I'm just saving room."

"Saving room?"

"I'm going to Keiko's house for dinner this evening."

"*Honto-ni?*" He turns to face her. Really?

"Dinner?" she repeats. "Maybe not dinner but . . . tea and fruits okay?"

"Of course. Anything is fine," I say, feeling embarrassed. I try to remember how she phrased her invitation to come over. Didn't she mention a meal?

"I am very bad cook," she says. "My husband always say so."

"*Daijoubu*," I say. "That's fine. I'm just looking forward to hanging out."

"Hanging out?" she echoes uncertainly.

The vice-principal emerges from behind his desk and stands before us. He's wearing a bolero tie, but it looks proportionate on him. "Ishii-sensei," he says, "Did I just hear that you invited Miss Marina over for dinner to thank her for posing for you? How nice." Keiko glances at Kobayashi-sensei before nodding. "What are you making?" he presses. "Japanese food? Something from *oosa*, to remind her of New York?"

"You really don't need to make dinner for me," I say under my breath.

"Do you like steak?" she asks.

"*Suteki*," the vice-principal says, laughing and clapping his hands. For once, I get the Japanese joke. *Suteki* is the word for steak, also slang for great.

Keiko tells me that she has to pick up her older son from junior high, take Kim-san back home and stop at the grocery store before I come over. She draws a map showing the way to her house and tells me to meet her there at five.

Even though he called me this morning and told me to stop by, Miyoshi-sensei looks surprised to see me. But not as surprised as I am to see Joe Pope, sitting in my desk chair in the high school faculty room, engrossed in conversation with Ritsuko Ueno. They don't even notice as I walk past them. I finger the tasseled ends of the scarf my mom knit for me. It's made of bright yellow wool, the same Day-Glo shade as the elementary school uniform caps, and so long that I can wrap it around my neck a dozen times, until it puffs out like an inner tube, and still the ends dangle to the ground. As Miyoshi-sensei gets up to greet me, I feel as stiff and immobilized as the yam truck driver in his neck brace.

"*Ohisashiburidesune*," he says. It's been a long time.

"Yeah," I say.

"I ran into Joe at Mister Donuts this morning," Miyoshi-sensei says, burying his hands in his pockets. "Our students have been studying so hard. I thought they could use some break. It was kind of . . . spur of the moment." I nod, hoping that I don't look hurt. I suspected that he shipped me off to the elementary school so that he wouldn't have to deal with me, but this confirms it. If Carolyn knows that Joe is in town, she hasn't said a word. Last I heard, he was living at a *gaijin* residence in Osaka, the city where most Japanese television shows are filmed. Miyoshi-sensei asks if I'd like a cup of tea and I nod, trailing after him to the social corner.

He hands me my tea, as well as a piece of paper, folded into a tight little square. Apparently the letter wasn't just a pretext to see me. He sits on one end of the couch and I sit on the other as I read it, as conscious of the wide space between us as I once was of our hips touching.

Dear Miss Marina,

How are you? I'm so busy thank you and you? I hope you could enjoy playing with elementary school students every day. Maybe you feel like after a long vacation. So relaxed. Maybe too relaxed?

Reason for this letter is: some car "accident" you had with Mister Uyesugi. He is Shika's Yam Truck driver, you know? Of course you know. You crashed Yam Truck. You did not tell Uyesugi-san your name, but he knows. He knows you are Marina-sensei and he knows I am your supervisor. Everyone knows this. It's unfortunate for you in this case, and also for me as well.

Maybe you did not know that accident must be reported in Japan. I tell Uyesugi-san that this is the case. You do not know better, I say to him. So let me explain now. To collect an insurance, you need crime scene police report. Even if you do not want to collect an insurance (for example, in such case where cost of fixing car is greater than cost of car) you should file accident report. Accident entails two people. Yam Truck driver needs compensation for so many ruined yams. If you do not file police report, if you flee the scene of the crime, then it's not called accident. In this case, it's called hit-and-run. You know what I mean?

Maybe you think it's joke or it's "no big deal" because it's only yams? Maybe you didn't know one roasted yam costs 500 yen. It's kind of a splurge food for us. Uyesugi-san counted more than two hundred ruined yams on road. It's not insignificant damages.

Mari-chan I really don't want to breathe on your neck. So if such a situation occurs once more (I hope not!) let me be clear. If you stay on scene, it's not crime. It's only accident. If you flee, it's hit-and-run. Lucky for you, Uyesugi-san decided not to file a charge. So, this time you can walk. I mean this in two senses. You will not become prosecuted. Also, maybe you had better walk from now on.

> *Ganbatte, Marina-san. Please do your best. Maybe even*
> *better.*
>
> > Yours truly,
> > *Hiroshi Miyoshi*

"It wasn't a hit-and-run," I say, the words on the page sliding beneath my eyes.

"*Daijoubu,*" he says, but it's obviously not okay and he obviously doesn't believe me.

At the culture shock panel in Tokyo, we were told that it is never, under any circumstances, acceptable to cry at work here. Apparently it rips the *wa*, the social fabric, beyond repair. I can never seem to cry at the right times: when it's expected of me, when it would actually put people at ease. But now it's like a cork has been popped, a lid unscrewed, and the tears are pouring out too fast for me to get the lid back on. I am giant Alice. I could flood a room. He looks around as if for an escape hatch, a way away from this crazy foreigner, this fresh mess I've put us in.

"I'd never do that." I manage to squeeze the words out between sobs. "I would never flee the scene of a crime."

"You don't like to follow rules," he says quietly. "You've admitted so often."

"The truck looked okay. I asked the driver if he needed to go to the hospital, and he said no. I offered to pay for the yams. I really did!"

"*Daijoubu,*" he says.

"Just tell me where Uyesugi-san lives, so that I can pay him back," I say.

"*Daijoubu,*" he says one more time. "The debt is paid."

"No!" The word comes out louder and more passionately than

I intended. "I don't want you to pay for them. You already hate me."

"I do not hate you," he says.

"Then why won't you talk to me?"

"I am your supervisor," he says, but as he meets my eyes for a moment, I get a flash of the man I used to know, not my supervisor, but my friend. He bites his lip, and again I remember the feeling of his mouth pressing back against mine. *Nothing happened*, he said when I tried to talk to him about it. But then why did he send me away? Why did he jerk his hand back when he gave me this letter and our fingers brushed? Why is it so hard for him to look at me? I can tell that this attraction annoys him, that he wants it to go away, that it isn't "convenient" for him. Well, it isn't convenient for me either. But just because it isn't convenient, that doesn't make it untrue.

I get out my wallet, pull out all of the bills without counting them and hold them out to him. He glances around again, refusing to take my money. The Japanese teachers are all going about their business, ignoring the B-movie screening in the corner. Only Joe is openly staring, leaning back in his—my—desk chair, smirking. It's this that makes me stop crying. In the rock-paper-scissors of emotion, anger still beats sorrow.

mo ichi do: (EXP.) *once more; again; repeat after me*

Trying to follow Keiko's smudged charcoal map is like trying to locate myself on a landscape painting. Without labeling anything, she rendered the landmarks in three-dimensional detail. But the snow has blotted out the real landscape, the road has not been plowed again, and I can hardly see the edge of the cliffs as I drive. I concentrate on the fuzzy tire tracks in front of me, holding my breath as the car glides around the curves.

On her map, a picture of a UFO matches the one on the sign leading to the UFO museum in Hakui. Carolyn and I visited this museum last summer, shortly after we got here. It's a small building near the beach, the walls covered with drawings of almond-eyed aliens, the tables painted to look like flying saucers. According to the brochure, the first local extraterrestrial sighting was just a brilliant flash of light, witnessed by different people all across the Noto peninsula. Then a mother reported watching a shimmering vessel materialize over the waves where her children were swimming, beaming them up before blinking out. Although she was arrested for negligence, her children's bodies were never found, and every year crowds visit the site on the day of the alleged alien abduction, driving onto the beach and parking their cars facing the sea. Watching this spectacle last summer, Carolyn and I agreed that it looked like the people hoped not just to see a UFO, but to be carried away themselves, beamed up into the sky.

Halfway to the UFO museum, what looks like a real fox on Keiko's sketch is actually the stone fox guarding the entrance to a Shinto shrine. In front of the shrine stands a tree ornamented with skinny strips of paper that flutter in the wind. These are letters to the dead. According to Miyoshi-sensei, when rain or snow melts the ink and the paper turns to pulp, the messages seep into the ground and reach their intended recipients. A lot of dead people are getting mail today.

Keiko's house is the next building after this shrine, surrounded by a high fence. I pull a rope hanging from a bell, and several minutes later she appears at the gate to open it, drying her hands on her jeans before reaching out to shake mine.

"Shake okay?" she says.

"Usually you only shake hands when you meet someone," I say.

"No," she says. "Is my shake too hard? Too soft? Too quick or slow?"

"It's great," I say. "You shake very well."

"Next month, maybe my family will visit your home," she tells me.

"San Francisco?" I ask.

"New York," she says, looking confused. This is the answer on my self-introduction quiz. She tells me that her husband has to go to New York to learn more about different treatments for cancer. Her delivery is so matter-of-fact that I'm not sure what to say. Sensing my apprehension, she laughs. "Husband is a doctor," she says. "He works for nuclear power station. They send him to New York to learn more about radiation treatment." While I'm relieved that her husband isn't sick, I find her explanation equally disturbing.

I follow her up the path to an A-frame house that looks like a small ski lodge with a thatched roof, the bottom half made of stone,

the top half of dark wood. They are rich, I realize. Inside the entryway, a lamp with a paper shade hangs from the ceiling, illuminating
brick red walls covered in framed woodblock prints of a weeping
willow, a snow-capped Mount Fuji, a breaking wave. I haven't seen
such deliberately Japanese décor outside of the United States. Keiko
offers me a pair of plaid slippers, still joined by a price tag.

"It's for you," she says. "To use every time you come here."

"Thank you," I say. "I hope you'll come over to our house soon
too." I stress the word *our*. I've decided to tell Keiko the truth, to be
open with her, so that we can have a real friendship. But before I go
on, she holds up a palm and says, "What's that sound?"

"Running water?" I guess.

"Fumiya!" she cries out. "*Mo ichi do?*"

In the kitchen, two boys are standing at the sink, both dressed in
school uniforms with their backs to us. The air is thick with steam
and the sink is overflowing. The taller boy has his arms plunged up
to the elbows in the water, which he keeps scooping onto his own
plaid slippers. "*Yamero!*" says the smaller boy. Stop it! Keiko rushes
to turn the faucet off, drawing a sharp intake of breath as she pulls a
dripping, shrink-wrapped package of steak out of the sink. The meat
is gray. She slams the package on the counter and rakes her hands
through her short hair, obviously trying to calm down. Although the
water is no longer flowing, the taller boy continues to mimic the
sound it made rushing, striking the steel basin, splashing on the lino-
leum. I don't know how he's doing it, but it sounds remarkably close
to the real thing. As the real water churns down the drain and gargles
in the pipes, he begins imitating that sound to perfection too.

Keiko seizes him by the shoulders and turns him to face her. She
unbuttons his jacket and he recoils from her touch, whimpering and
giggling at the same time.

"*Daijoubu*," she says.

"It's okay," he repeats, somehow mimicking not only her words, but also her strained solicitude. After wrestling the boy out of his wet jacket, she turns him to face me. He is wearing a V-necked undershirt, his arms are long and noodle thin, and he wiggles his fingers as if practicing piano scales in the air.

"*Go aisatsu shinasai*," Keiko prompts him. "Say 'hello' to Marina-sensei."

"Hello," I say.

The boy giggles and does a manic little dance on the tips of his toes. Then he burrows his chin into his chest and hoots like an owl.

"His name is Fumiya," Keiko says.

"Hi Fumiya," I say. "Nice to meet you."

"Hifumiyanicetomeetyou," he says in a falsetto parody.

"Good job!" Keiko says. "Fumiya speaks English very well, don't you think?"

"Very well," I agree.

"His junior high English teacher says that maybe, with practice, he could be fluid."

She pulls him close and tries to kiss his cheek, but he shrinks from her touch. When she releases him, he puckers and kisses the air, touching his lips as he blows little bubbles of spit, then resumes imitating the gargling sound of draining water.

"*Yamero*," Koji says again. Stop it!

Fumiya's face both does and doesn't look like Koji's. He has a stronger chin and a longer, sharper nose that ends in a cleft. But like his little brother he is so pale that I can see the veins at his temples, and his eyes are equally wide-set, of that same lovely shade of gray. Amazing, then, just how different these eyes can be. Whereas Koji's gray gaze is generous, curious and inviting, his brother's eyes look hard and shellacked. It's impossible to find a way in. He pinches the tip of his tongue between his teeth and hisses at me.

Keiko places her hands on Fumiya's shoulders and pushes him into a chair at the kitchen table. She tells Koji to sit down too, and when he begins to lower himself into a chair at the opposite end from his brother, she says, "No, sit next to Fumiya." The little boy stands up, dragging his body like a sandbag. He sinks into the chair with a deep sigh that Fumiya copies. Keiko tells me to have a seat, pulling out the chair across from the two little boys. In the middle of the table is a plate of sliced apple pears, every slice peeled halfway, the peel lifted from the apple and cut to look like rabbit ears.

"Marina-sensei," Keiko says, "How about starting with animals?"

"Starting with animals?"

"I made some cards," she says. She holds up a stack and flips through drawings of a cow, a dog, a cat, a horse, and a bird. "For warm-up, you could begin by teaching animal names and noises." She slides the cards across the table to me. "Or something else. You are English teacher. Please teach Fumiya and Koji."

"Please teach Fumiya," Fumiya says. "FumiyaFumiyaFumiya."

Repeating his own name seems to excite him, and he sways like a rocking horse until his head almost knocks against the tabletop, but Keiko slides her palm between his head and the wood and for a moment he stops rocking, resting it like an egg in a nest.

My stomach twists in a knot as the real reason why I am here dawns on me. It is only because I speak English. Keiko didn't want a new friend. The kitchen is silent save the sound of a wall clock, a ticktock that Fumiya imitates a hair too late. If she had asked me to tutor her kids, I would have said yes. But I can't help but feel that she sensed my loneliness and took advantage of it, that she wasn't direct with me on purpose, and what I thought I liked so much about her was her directness.

"Stop it!" Koji says again. I look over, then away, but too late. I see Fumiya's legs spread, fly open, hand on his penis, rubbing so hard it looks more like stain-removal than pleasure. "*Yamero*," Fumiya repeats, eyelids fluttering. It's hard to see a twelve-year-old face contorted with lust, but the look on Koji's face is worse: shame in miniature. Koji grabs his brother by the wrist and yanks his hand away from his crotch. Fumiya makes a fist and lashes out, clipping Koji in the chin. The little boy starts to cry, bringing his hands to his eyes. "Wah, wah!" Fumiya imitates, "Wah, wah!" When Koji gulps for air, Fumiya pauses too, waiting to join back in like a dutiful choir member.

"Cow," I say in one of the brief pauses between Koji's sobs. "Moo!"

"Cow," Keiko repeats, trying to wrap her arms around both of her sons, both of whom shrink from her touch.

"Cow," I try again. "Moo!"

"Cowmoo," Fumiya says. "Moocowmoo."

Koji's crying is tapering off now that he's no longer being imitated, and as I pick the next card off the pile, Keiko sneaks away so that I can teach her boys animal sounds.

"Cat," I say. "Meow!"

"Meowmeowow . . . " Fumiya sounds like a real cat in heat. "Owmeowowmeow."

Koji won't even look at the cards I'm holding up. "You like animals," I say to encourage him.

"Not those animals," he whispers.

"Really?" I say, "You don't like cats?" He shakes his head. "How about birds?"

"I hate birds," he says.

"You do?" I ask. "Why?"

"Because they repeat," he says, picking up an apple slice. "I only like rabbits."

At six o'clock on the dot, Keiko places a plate in front of me. A thick slab of meat floats in a puddle of bloody juice, next to a potato that looks as hard as a rock.

"Aren't you eating?" I ask as she collapses beside me, looking exhausted.

"I must wait for Yuji," she says. "He comes home at seven."

"You cooked all of this just for me?" I try to sound appreciative rather than horrified.

"It's good meat," she says. "Fresh frozen."

"It looks wonderful," I lie.

"Go ahead," she says. "*Itadakimasu.*"

"*Itadakimasu,*" Fumiya repeats. He reaches across the table, but Keiko grabs his hand right before he swipes the steak off my plate. I wish I could slip it to him, but his mother pushes him back into his seat and the three of them watch as I saw off a tiny bite, swallowing it whole with difficulty.

"Are you okay?" Keiko asks. "It's no good, *ne?*" I tell her that it's great, but she looks skeptical, and I finally admit that I have a toothache.

"Toothache," Fumiya repeats. "Toothtoothtoothache."

"Why don't you fix it?" she asks me.

"I don't have a dentist."

She tells me that her husband's brother is a dentist, that he has an office in Jade Plaza. She asks if I'd like her to make an appointment for me, and when I say yes, she makes a quick phone call. It's amazing how fast this all happens, after weeks of putting it off. She gets off the phone and lets me know that the dentist will expect me the next morning at seven, that he's going to come in to see me early so that I can get to school on time. I thank her profusely, but Fumiya is rubbing his crotch again. She grabs his hand and clutches it while he writhes in his seat.

"Recently Fumiya discovers his body," she says. "I think it's normal for twelve-year-old boy. But girls complain. They feel uneasy. So his teachers put him in a room alone. Then he is bored, so he touches his body more. It's big problem."

"Is he in a special class?" I ask.

"Special class?" she repeats. "He does not need special class. Shika Junior High has no special class."

"Oh," I say. "Sorry. Of course."

"Fumiya has talent in many subjects. Especially English. He has gift for repeating. It's useful skill to learn a new language, *ne?*"

"It can be," I say, although it's painfully obvious that this boy has no idea what he's repeating, that every new sound is a tunnel down which he falls, further from everyone else in the room.

"Marina-sensei," Keiko says, "could you come back again, *mo ichi do?*"

"Sure," I say, setting down my fork.

"How about every Thursday from six to eight?"

"Every Thursday?" I echo.

"Every Thursday," Fumiya chimes in. "Every Thursday! Every Thursday!"

"The thing is," I stall, "I don't have my calendar with me. And I'm not sure what I'm doing every Thursday . . . "

"Ah," she says.

"But I could come once in a while."

"Fine," she says, but the light behind her face has flipped off. She's not even a daytime lamp. She is dark. She takes my plate and scrapes the food into the trash, while I sit at the table, feeling dismissed, but not sure if I should get up and leave.

When Carolyn returns home from the faculty party that she had to attend tonight, I am lying on our bedroom floor, curled up in front of the chugging kerosene heater, sucking on an aspirin and clutching my jaw.

"Are you okay?" she asks, standing over me. "You don't look good."

"I've been better," I say.

"How was dinner with your new friend?"

"She's not. She only asked me over to tutor her kids." I feel embarrassed admitting this to Carolyn, after the big deal I made over my dinner invitation. "One of them is autistic. At least I think he is. His mom wanted to pretend that he was normal, but he kept repeating every word I said and then he started masturbating. It was awful."

"Really? Sounds like a model pupil, if you can overlook the masturbation part."

I laugh in spite of myself, and when I do my teeth accidentally come together and the pain is so bad that I feel dizzy. I curl into a tighter ball. "I had no idea that teeth could hurt this bad," I whimper. "I'm afraid they're like Christmas lights. One blows out and the whole strand dies." As if on cue, the heater wheezes to a stop. Carolyn asks if I remembered to stop for kerosene on my way home, and I shake my head, looking up at her. There are freckles on the underside of her chin, and her hair is turning a darker shade of red, her winter coat, flipping up at the ends where it now brushes the tops of her shoulders. She doesn't say a single word, and as she heads downstairs I think that maybe this is it, it's over, I've pushed her too far and she's leaving me here and now, alone in the cold. But she returns a minute later carrying the television set and a bottle of Suntory whiskey. She pops a bootleg *ER* video into the TV, and says, "I thought watching some serious trauma victims would put your toothache into perspective, or at least distract you from the pain. And this should help you sleep." She pours whiskey into a mug, hands it to me, and then turns her back, stepping into the red fleece sack before taking off her clothes.

"You don't have to do that," I say.

"What?" she says.

"Change with your back to me. I know you want more privacy. I'm not watching."

I close my eyes and press my hands between my knees. A moment later I feel the warmth of her body behind mine, filling my hollows, her breath against the back of my neck.

"Hurry up," she says. "Get in."

"What?" I say. "Where?"

"Get in the sack," she says, and I twist around to see that she has left the front of the garment unzipped and she's naked.

"There's no room," I protest.

"Of course there is," she says. "I'll make room."

And there is, and she does, and I lie with my back to her chest, skin on skin, no gaps between us, both of us warm for once, nothing to discuss. I listen to her breathing grow regular as she falls asleep, curled around me, while I watch four episodes of *ER* until the credits roll and static fills the screen. My dad and I used to watch *ER* together. He loved pointing out the mistakes the doctors made in surgery. "Dead," he'd say gleefully. "That maneuver would've killed him, if he wasn't going to die already!" I don't know how long I've been staring at the swarm of blue and white dots on the TV screen before they rearrange themselves into my father's face, only that I'm not surprised when it happens. It's like I've been waiting for this. "How did you find me?" I whisper, and the image flickers, disappears, then reappears. "What are you doing here?" I try. "Why did you come back?" But he doesn't answer any of these questions. "How are you?" I finally ask, and at last he speaks. "I'm fine," he says. "That's what I came here to tell you. I'm fine now." *Fine. Fine.* I can tell that this word is supposed to have a magical effect, lifting the fog of my guilt, absolving me or him or both of us. "Well I'm not," I say, angrier because he didn't even ask. "I'm not fine all. Do you even care? Did you even think about me once before you jumped?" Again he doesn't answer, which makes me want to throw the remote control at the screen. But I don't want to wake Carolyn, so instead I press the power button and the blue light shrinks to a point. As he disappears, I'm seized with regret. He came all this way to find me, and once again I shut him out? But no matter how many times I turn the TV off and on, switching from channel to channel, he doesn't reappear. I'm still pushing buttons, trying desperately to get him to come back, when Vivaldi's *The Four Seasons*, wakes me up, the music so familiar by now that I can't even hear it anymore.

CHAPTER THIRTEEN

kawaisou: (ADJ.) *poor; pitiable; pathetic*

The dentist's office is inside the Jade Plaza shopping center, tucked between the 100-Yen store and a kiosk that sells cell phone cozies and charms. I don't know how I missed the door, painted with a cartoon tooth face, the paint chipping so that one eye seems to be winking at me. At seven on the dot, a hygienist wearing a pale pink uniform that fits her like couture unlocks this door. I'm wearing an old pair of gray sweats, my hair is corralled in a greasy ponytail, and I can smell the whiskey on my breath. She backs away, justifiably alarmed by the half-drunk *gaijin* moaning at the door.

"*Kinkyu desu,*" I declare. It's an emergency.

"The dentist will be with you in just a moment," she chirps, showing me to a small room with a chair covered in a narrow band of paper that rips when I take a seat. There are posters on the ceiling, photos of the Japanese countryside in every season, and one of a kitten up a tree. I wonder if the Japanese characters spell, "Hang in there."

"Hello," says a man upon entering the room. "I am dentist."

"Hello," I reply as he looms over me. He's wearing a white plastic face mask with a perforated mouthpiece and his eyes are hidden behind dark goggles. Standing beside him, the hygienist is also wearing a face mask.

"I am dentist," he says again. "You are . . . "

"I am Marina," I say, and because he seems to be waiting for me to introduce myself in greater detail I add, "I teach English at Shika *Koko*."

"Miss Marina English teacher," he repeats. "Nice to meet you. How are you?"

"Not so hot," I say. "My teeth are killing me."

"Killing me," he echoes. "Like . . . murder?"

"Exactly."

He asks me which tooth hurts, and when I explain that I can't tell anymore, that they all hurt, he says something in Japanese to his hygienist, and she hands him a delicate metal hammer. He snaps on a pair of rubber gloves, layering a second pair over the first. I wonder if all patients require this much protection, or if they are taking extra precautions with me. Prying open my jaw, he hammers on one of my front teeth and my head clangs like a bell.

"Howdy?" he says.

"What?" I whimper.

"When you feel pain, please say 'howdy.' I like Western movie."

"Howdy!" I say as he hammers the next tooth. *Clink*. "Howdy!" *Clink*. "Howdy!" *Clink*. "Howdy!" As he plays my mouth like a xylophone, tears slide down my face, soaking the paper beneath me. I ask for a painkiller, but he says that if I can't feel any pain, he won't be able to catch the bad guy. He asks me where I'm from and I tell him San Francisco. It's hard to squeeze out the word with my mouth open, his fingers all bunched up in it.

"I thought New York." I can hear the frown in his voice. I explain that this is where I went to college. "I don't like big city," he says. "I like . . . how do I say . . . *inaka?*"

"Nature," I translate.

"No," he says, banging the next tooth harder as if to punish me for a wrong answer. "A small town. Like Shika. Do you like Shika?" I can't nod because he is prying my jaw open, reaching deep inside my mouth to hammer on my molars.

"Ow!" I shriek.

"Howdy?" he says.

"Howdy!" I repeat after him, bawling in public for the second time in as many days.

For once I welcome the pinch of the needle that slides into my gums, followed by the sweet spread of numbness, blessed paralysis. As the drill whirs and the bit burrows into my tooth and enamel shrapnel fills my mouth, I close my eyes and visualize not a dentist but a locksmith, letting me back into my home. When I open them again the dentist is holding his tweezers close to my face. Something bloody dangles from their tips.

"The loot," he says. "Root. Loot. Which is correct?"

"Root."

"Root," he repeats. "Root. Root." It's like he's cheering on a sports team.

I explore my molar with the tip of my fat, numb tongue, and find that it has been hollowed out like a drinking straw, excavated to my gums.

"Pain gone?" the dentist asks me.

"Pain gone," I say. "Thank you."

"Please come back *mo ichi do* at five o'clock," he says, "so I can fill it."

I was in too much pain and too tipsy to drive to the dentist this morning, so I walked. Now I have to walk home again, to get the car to drive to the elementary school. The pain in my tooth is gone, but its absence feels like the stillness following an earthquake. Something has shifted. Things aren't what they were. Plus, I'm headed for a bad hangover. In front of the trash bin outside Mister Donuts—patrolled, as usual, by a pair of aproned old women—I bend over and gag. The alcohol burns the back of my throat, and I spit out the tiny cotton ball that was plugging the hole in my tooth. The bright red dot, stark against the white snow, reminds me of the Japanese flag. I feel the eyes of the *gomi* police bore into me. I pick up the bloody cotton ball, squeezing it in my fist as I carry on.

I walk back home on the side of the highway, just inches from the rocky overhang, planting one foot in front of the other, soaking my sweatpants' cuffs in the deep slush. The sun is out this morning and the snow is melting quickly, falling in wet clumps from the boughs of the trees, dripping down the cliff, trickling into the swollen sea. The huge waves crash against the rocks, sending up a salty mist. I kick pebbles from the path ahead of me, listening to each one tumble over the edge, followed by silence as they sail through the air. The cliffs are so high that I can't hear them hit.

At home I call the high school. The secretary transfers me to the faculty room, and Miyoshi-sensei picks up after just one ring.

"Mari-chan," he says. "Are you in trouble?"

"I'm fine," I say, wishing he didn't assume the worst. "Well, not fine. I need to take a sick day and I was hoping you could call the elementary school to let them know."

"Sick day?" he repeats as if he'd never heard of such a thing.

"I think I just had a root canal," I explain.

"*Nani?*" he asks. "What's that?"

"A dental procedure. You know, for tooth pain?"

"Miss Marina," he says, "here in Japan, most teachers don't use a rare and kind of precious sick day for tooth pain. We have no substitute teachers here."

"I'm exhausted," I tell him, clutching the phone. "I couldn't sleep at all last night, my head is pounding and I just threw up."

"You should stay home," he says quickly, no doubt worried that I'm going to fall apart on him again. "I will tell Ooka-sensei that you are not well. But tomorrow you had better return *mo ichi do* to give your special English lesson."

"What special English lesson?" I ask.

"I don't know," he says, "but Ooka-sensei told me you started something new, and now you should give it to every class in the school. It's Japanese way."

"But it's not really an English lesson," I protest.

"Not really an English lesson?"

"I think the vice-principal is trying to keep me there for English conversation." I hold my breath, wait for him to say that I've crossed yet another line with this accusation, but instead he laughs heartily.

"Probably so," he says. "Ooka-sensei loves speaking English too much. He tries to practice with me too, but he only wants to talk about the weather. It's kind of boring."

"More than kind of," I say, laughing too.

"So, Mari-chan, what is lesson that is not really an English lesson?"

"I go to the art class and lie on a table while the kids draw my portrait and talk about how tall my nose is."

"I like your tall nose," he says. "It's charm point."

"Charm point?"

"Like . . . ears that stick out, or chubby cheeks, or interesting scar."

"You mean a flaw."

"It fits you."

"Because I'm so huge?"

"Because you are strong," he says.

"Hiro," I say, "I miss our classes. I miss teaching with you. I miss—"

"I will call Ooka-sensei," he cuts me off. "Today you could stay home, but tomorrow you had better go back to the elementary school *mo ichi do*."

"Fine," I say.

"Then you can come back here."

"What?" I say. "Really? When?"

"Monday," he says. "You belong here, *ne?*"

"Thank you so much," I say. "I've missed—"

"Fine," he says. "Fine."

I am almost never home alone in the daytime, and it feels strange, like I'm getting away with something illicit. I lie on our bedroom floor in a patch of sunlight, bundled in covers, listening to the dripping patter of melting icicles, the slide and thump of snow sliding off roof shingles, the crack of the ice that coated the river in a thin skin now breaking apart, drifting like continents. I fall asleep for a while, waking up to another, closer thump—the sound of a package hitting the *genkan* floor. We only lock our front door at night. Miyoshi-sensei told us that there was no reason to, that theft is virtually unheard of in rural Japan. We never even made a copy of the key.

At the sight of my mom's handwriting, printed on the side of a large box, I feel a pang of homesickness, sharper because I'm actually home sick. I sit on the brown vinyl couch in the living room and tear open the box flaps, expecting to find the usual assortment of books, treats, and stickers.

Instead, my mom has sent a pile of things that belonged to my dad.

On top of the pile is his old suede jacket, the one he had since college, caramel colored and lined with fleece. On our family road trips every summer, driving across desert states in the middle of the night to beat the daytime heat, he used to spread it across my lap like a blanket. Now I put it on and bury my hands in the pockets. One holds a book of matches and the chewed cap of a pen, the other a smashed peppermint, still in its wrapper. These seem like clues, but to what?

Next I pull out his orange velour sweatshirt. It's the one he's wearing in most of the pictures from when I was a brand new baby. My mom says that he went out and bought it right after I was born, the softest thing he could find. She says that for months, every evening when he came home from work, he'd put on this velour sweatshirt, lie down on the couch, and place me on his chest, dressed only in a diaper, so I could luxuriate in the softness. In every picture, his big hand is always spanning my tiny back, holding me close, making sure that I don't roll off. The shirt is twenty-two years old, the exact same age as me. The orange velour is worn thin in patches that let the light through when I hold it up to my face, breathe it in. It doesn't smell like him, it just smells like the detergent my mom uses. I guess this makes sense. He has been dead for over a year now. His smell should be gone.

Under the shirt is his old camera, a manual Nikon surrounded by lenses of various lengths, each encased in a tube sock with orange and blue rings around the ankles. These are the only socks he ever wore, hiked up over his muscular shins, with cutoff jean shorts when he was working outside in the yard, even with the suits he wore only when he absolutely had to. The orange and blue rings would peek out from beneath the black cuffs of his suit pants and he'd joke, "It's my own personal fashion statement. It says, 'I don't care what other people think.'" He used to take my picture with this camera. He'd take shot after shot of me doing ordinary things: eating strawberries in a high chair, reading a book on the grass, drifting in an inner tube on a lake, my hair fanning behind me. My mom liked the posed pictures better—the ones where I was smiling—but I loved his candid shots. He managed to capture what I really looked like, or at least how I saw myself, the way that no one else ever has.

Next I pull out his big dictionary, its black leather binding cracked, the thin pages edged with gold. He had this dictionary since he was a little boy. Whenever I asked him the definition of a word, instead of telling me the answer, he'd send me to the dictionary to look it up. Then, for the rest of the day, we'd both keep using that word in sentences. The margin beside every word that either of us ever looked up is starred.

imponderable: (ADJ.) incapable of being weighed or evaluated with exactness.

One by one, I pull the rest of the things out of the box: his titanium diver's watch; that fiberglass Cheshire cat mask we made when I was in elementary school; a Ziploc bag full of tawny silt that clings to the inside of the plastic, fogging it like breath.

I know what this is, but not what it's doing here, or what I'm supposed to do with it.

Just a few weeks before moving to Japan, I went to San Francisco to visit my mom. I hadn't been back since the memorial service, and I was shocked to find this visit unexpectedly harder than the one before. My father's absence rang through the whole city, the neighborhood, through my body. There was no street corner where we hadn't stood together, no little restaurant where we hadn't grabbed a bite, no used bookstore where we hadn't stopped to scan the stacks, no ice cream shop where we hadn't sampled too many flavors before making our selections. I expected him to pop out from behind every corner and yell, "Surprise!" his darkest joke ever. I kept thinking that I saw him—holding hands with a little boy in a monkey backpack; sitting on a park bench eating a peach; riding the bus, his face half hidden behind a newspaper—and it almost seemed possible that he'd staged the whole thing, that he wanted to get out of *his* life, sure, but not out of life altogether. But of course this wasn't the case. The men looked nothing like him up close.

After a year, my mom seemed sad but also resigned, already moving toward acceptance at a clip that made me feel scared and left behind. When my dad was alive, she often served as our go-between, telling the two of us what to say to each other, when we needed to say thank you or apologize for something. "Your dad planted those sunflowers for you," she told me after I brought home a bad Van Gogh imitation from a college painting class and he planted a whole bed of sunflowers that grew tall against our apartment's back wall. "He's so proud of you. He's terrible at expressing his feelings, but he loves you so much. You need to know that." With him gone, we were unsure what to talk about. Where there had always been a triangle, symmetrical and balanced, now there was just a line. She kept refer- ring to him as "my husband," which seemed strange and proprietary, like she was staking her personal claim. But of course he had been her husband. That's what she had lost, just as I had lost my father. We'd been a family once, but now that he was dead we couldn't share him anymore. We had each lost something very different, and we had no idea how to comfort each other.

My mom and I were like a new couple, awkward and shy, and so we did what all new couples do: We went on dates, seeking out distractions. We went to the museum and the movies and the mall, to the park and the aquarium. We were tourists in our own city. It was almost fun. On my last day at home, we went to a miniature golf range, which was my idea. Everything that we did felt inappropriate and weird, so I figured we should take it to the limit. I thought that neither of us wanted to upset the delicate balance we were just starting to find, so I was confused that evening when she drove into the parking lot of a white building fronted with pillars and a mortuary sign.

"Where are we?" I asked, remembering the place in the vague way of a dream.

"We're here to pick up your father's ashes," she said.

My father's suicide note made no mention of what he wanted us to do with his remains. By choosing to jump off the bridge, he had probably hoped to drift out to sea, to spare us a mess. But a coast guard witnessed his fall and brought his body in, and later that same evening my mom had to identify him by herself while I caught a red eye from New York. By the time I got home, she had made the necessary decisions without me. He was to be cremated, his ashes divided in half, so that part of him could be interred in his parents' plot, the other part buried in a cemetery close to the city where she could visit and bring flowers. She delayed the cremation until I got home, so that I could see him one last time. She also asked them to reserve a baggie of ashes for us to scatter on the one-year anniversary of his death, although this was the first I'd heard of it.

"I really don't want to," I said.

"Please," she said, putting her hand on mine. "We need to say good-bye."

As we entered the mortuary, I remembered being there a year before. In my memory the day stood out like a slide show, flashes of vivid illumination juxtaposed against deep pockets of darkness. I remembered being shown down the narrow hallway and into a small room where I was left alone with him. My father was the only thing in that room—his body laid out on a gurney—and it seemed impossible to take it all in at once. I couldn't bring myself to look at his face, so I started with his feet. I stared at his black dress socks, his feet pointing stiffly upward, and I wondered why they'd bothered dressing him in socks but not shoes. I wondered if he hit the water feet first, if the bones of his feet were shattered, the skin bruised. Even his feet weren't safe. As I walked around the gurney, I gave the body—his body—a wide berth, as if it were an artifact on display at a museum behind a security wire. But there was no security wire to trip, no glass case, nothing separating me from the deceptive stillness of his death, deceptive because he was already settling, sinking into it, I could tell. His skin looked waxy and porous like citrus rind, his lips thin and pale, parted slightly over his front teeth, which seemed translucent and dry. Of course they were dry. He wasn't salivating. He was a husk. I wondered if the same person who'd applied the pancake makeup to his face had also massaged the emotion out of it. I imagined they wouldn't want him to look pained, or worse— relieved. But this neutrality was the deadest thing about him. I had known him exuberant and grim, ecstatic and enraged, and desperately sad, but never blank. He didn't live there anymore.

Still, I wanted to touch him. I knew that this was the last time I'd be able to. I wanted to make a big messy display of it, to fling myself down on the gurney beside him, wrap my arms around him, pepper his face with kisses, and whisper into his ear that I loved him, my daddy, my daddy. But I knew that it was too late for these words I should have spoken much sooner, much more freely, and much more often. No one would hear them but me, and I didn't want to perform for myself. I didn't want to perform at all. And I was scared to touch him. I couldn't bring myself to feel his waxy skin. But I had to touch him. It was the last time I'd be able to. I finally decided that I would touch his hair. His poor, butchered hair. It was so short.

His scalp showed pink through the stubble. But he didn't look like a marine. He didn't look tough or aggressive. He looked like he'd been sick.

Standing in the mortuary a year later, a place I thought I'd never have to return to, I suddenly heard my mother wail. "More? I don't understand! How could you have made this mistake? How can there be more?"

The woman behind the front reception desk was holding out a box. She was trying to get my mother to take it, and my mother was shaking her head and crying as the woman insisted that my mom's instructions had been followed to the letter. She had them written down on a sheet of paper my mom had signed, clearly indicating that the ashes were to be divided into thirds, with a portion reserved for scattering. This was the final third. The receptionist offered to dispose of this last box for us, if we signed a release, and my mom sobbed, "No! You can't just throw him away!"

"It's not her fault, Mom," I said, and my mom turned to look at me like I was betraying her by taking the receptionist's side. I was reminded of the time that we went to an appointment with a grief counselor, just a couple of days after the memorial service, and on the way out we came upon a cop ticketing my mom's car. She started to cry then too, explaining to the officer—a young guy on a bicycle with a leather fanny pack—exactly where we'd been and why, until he ended up not only canceling the ticket, but also giving her a big hug. In the car afterward, when I asked why she had to tell a perfect stranger what had happened, she said, "Should I be ashamed? Is it my fault?" Unlike my father and me, my mom has never had any trouble showing her emotions. Nothing used to scare me more than seeing her cry.

Because someone had to, I reached out and took the box, which was terribly heavy, and not nearly heavy enough for what it contained: a third of my six foot two, two-hundred-pound father's remains. I was afraid of dropping it. I wanted to drop it. The receptionist mouthed, "Thank you," looking at my weeping mother like she was insane, and I wanted to throw it at her smug face. Instead, I shifted it to the crook of my arm and led my mom outside. We were almost to our car when the receptionist caught up with us, a plastic baggie dangling from her fingertips.

"You asked for this," she reminded us, her tone defensive. "For scattering."

"More," my mom cried again. "There's always more."

And whose fault is that? I thought.

That evening, my mom and I buried the box in the backyard, which was in its late summer glory, the flower beds full of dahlias that looked like exploding red and purple firecrackers, the sunflowers that my father allegedly planted for me growing tall, their heads angling toward the apartment windows as if they were trying to see inside. As we lowered it into the ground and covered it with dirt, I felt like we were trying to dispose of evidence. I wondered if any of our neighbors were looking down on us. My mom said a prayer, asking for him to find peace and for us to find the strength to forgive him and ourselves for not having been able to save him. Then she looked at me, waiting for me to add something.

"Well," I said, "I guess that's it."

But of course that's not it. There is always more. I'd forgotten all about the baggie until now, holding it in my hand, such a filmy, flimsy divider separating me from what remains of him. From his remains.

"Honey? Is something wrong?" My mom's voice is groggy, thick with sleep. I didn't calculate the time difference before calling. I don't apologize for waking her up.

"What did you just send me?" As usual, the international connection is terrible, and I hear a click after I speak, followed by the echo of my own question.

"You keep complaining about how cold it is in Japan," she says. "I was cleaning out the apartment and I found Dad's old jacket, the suede one you always like to wear when you come home, so I decided to send it to you, with a few other things of his that I thought you might like to have."

"Like his ashes?" I say. *Like his ashes!*

"Only half of them," she says. "I scattered most of them in the park, in front of the Conservatory of Flowers, where we used to go for picnics when you were a little girl. It helped me to say good-bye. I thought it might help you to do the same."

"I've said good-bye!" I explode. "I'm not going to scatter his ashes in Japan. This isn't my home."

"It's where you are," she says.

"Is this your way of getting even with me?" I hold the phone at a distance to avoid the echo. But when I return the receiver to my ear, she echoes the question instead.

"Getting even with you? What do you mean?"

"Because I left and you can't."

"Sweetheart," she says, "I am not mad at you for leaving. I want you to be happy. I want you to live your life as fully as possible. And I'm okay. This is my home. I don't want to leave. I do want to move on with my life though, and that means forgiving him, and forgiving myself for not having been able to save him." She pauses, waits for me to speak, but I don't. I can't. She sounds wide-awake now, resolute and maternal. She wants to be my mom. She wants me to let her. "Scattering the ashes helped me," she says.

"Stop saying that word!"

"What word?"

"Scatter," I say. *Scatterscatterscatter.* It sounds like something to do with birdseed. Again I think of Hansel and Gretel, leaving crumbs to mark their trail out of the forest, a trail that vanished long before they could find their way home. After hanging up the phone I flip open my dad's old dictionary.

scatter: (VB.) 1. to fling away heedlessly 2. to separate and go in various directions 3. to fall irregularly or at random 4. to cause to vanish.

All definitions apply.

I put everything back in the box, bring the box into the storage area behind the kitchen, and shelve it among identical boxes of things belonging to people I've never met, former inhabitants of this house, people who are probably dead themselves by now, survived only by the junk they left behind.

Later that day, when I return to the dentist to have my tooth filled, he barely examines my mouth before saying, "Your gum still mending. I think you mend slowly."

"I think you're right," I say.

"How is the weather today?" he inquires.

"The weather?" There is no window in his office. Maybe he has no idea what it's like outside. "It's sunny," I say.

"Sunny," he echoes. "It is sunny today. Tomorrow it will be sunny again." He removes his rubber gloves and drops them into a recycling bin, but he doesn't take off his goggles or face mask. I have no idea what he looks like, couldn't pick him out of a lineup. "I like sunny weather," he says. "Sorry my English is so bad."

"Your English is fine," I say, feeling the thump of my pulse. "You speak English very well."

"I am going to New York soon," he says. "With my brother, Yuji."

"Keiko's husband?" I ask, and he nods. "Are you all going to New York?"

"You all?" he repeats.

"Keiko told me that she was going too."

"Ah," he says. "Well, Keiko wanted to go. Unfortunately, I think it's not possible because of children. They are difficult boys. They need much supervision. Yuji will be too busy . . . So he invited me. Now I had better prepare for my trip, *ne*? My English is so bad. I'm afraid no one could understand me!" I nod, distracted, wondering if Keiko knows that she has been replaced on this trip, which she was so looking forward to. "You may go now," he says, clicking off the light and elevating the chair beneath me.

"But my tooth," I say, probing the hole with my tongue. "You didn't do anything. It's still empty."

"If you are free, please return *mo ichi do* tomorrow," he says. "Maybe we could practice asking the way."

"Asking the way?" I repeat.

"You know," he says, "Like when you are lost, and you need help to find your path. I think this happens so often in a new country."

Over dinner at 8-ban ramen, I let Carolyn in on my suspicion that the dentist is delaying filling my tooth because he wants free English conversation. "Not free," she points out. "You're actually paying him." I admit that I haven't been billed for any of his services. "I guess it's a fair trade," she says. "Dental work for *eikaiwa*."

"Oh my God," I say. "I just want him to fill my tooth!"

"Then you'd better make that clear," she says, "if you don't want to spend the rest of the year sitting in a dentist's chair."

After dinner we drive to *hottorando*, or "hot land," a bathhouse near the nuclear power plant with dozens of hot tubs filled with brightly colored herbal infusions. There's even a tub with an electric current running through it, like the grocery store shock booth. This seems like a bad idea to me, and I never see anyone soaking in it.

The men who work at the plant come in their red jumpsuits, carrying plastic tubs holding soap and razors and folded pajamas, so that they can return to the dorm where they live and slip straight into bed. Grandparents come carrying toddlers, and teenaged girls come in pairs. Carolyn and I follow the example of the most self-conscious teenaged girls, covering our bodies with towels as we get into the hot water, tucking them under our armpits and between our legs. An old woman with a stooped spine tells us not to be shy, but when my towel floats free for a moment, she points at my breasts and says how "*ookii*," or big they are. Carolyn and I exchange a glance. A young woman walks to the bath holding hands with a long-haired little girl. The woman slips into the tub, the child sits on its edge, her hair forming a shawl around her, the ends dangling in the water.

"Hello, Miss Marina," the woman says. I smile. I have no idea who she is. "I teach sixth grade," she says in Japanese.

"Of course," I say. Once more I have failed to recognize this pretty young woman, although people do look different when they're naked, and it's not polite to stare. I allow myself the quickest of glances, which is all it takes to see that her body is as perfect as I would've guessed: perfect perky breasts, perfectly flat belly, thighs that don't touch. No flaws or charm points here. "Hello," I say.

"Hello," echoes the little girl seated next to her in a deep voice.

"Kim-san?" I say, and the child looks up from under her curtain of hair and grins. "How are you?"

"Mmm . . . ," she thinks for a moment and then replies, "hot."

I applaud, amazed that she remembered this word, which I only taught her class in passing. The sixth-grade teacher seems equally impressed. She grips the child's foot and says something in Japanese. I catch the words "*hajimete*," the first time, and "*hanshimashita,*" spoke. In Japanese, she tells me that Kim and her father rent the apartment next to hers, that she brings Kim with her to the baths once a week, but that the girl refuses to soak. She tugs on the girl's foot, trying to coax her in, but Kim shakes her head and says "hot" again, clearly making her point.

"She has no mother," the teacher says. "*Kawaisou no ko.*" Poor child.

"*Kawaisou usagi,*" Kim says. Poor rabbit.

I remember Kim repeating this same phrase after Koji first said it, and I remember how he snapped at her, telling her not to copy him. Someone really needs to tell the little boy that she is not like his brother, that the way she imitates him is a sign not that something is wrong, but that something is right. She is already learning how to do more than just copy words. She's learning how to combine them in new and interesting ways, to make her meaning clear, her self known.

mukou: (N.) *the other side; beyond; far away; the future (starting now)*

The sun is not just out this morning, it's actually rather warm. Slush covers the elementary school parking lot, stained with rainbows of oil. The kids wear rubber boots as they wade into the school, the slush reaching up to the knees of the littlest ones. Jumping out of my car window, I soak my shoes and splatter my pants. I'm bending over, rolling up my cuffs, when I see the two children disappear around the corner.

The top of the rabbit hutch is covered in planks of plywood but there are gaps between these planks and snow has drifted into the animals' shelter, covering the hay and melting into an icy pool. The fat white rabbit is fine. The metal trough that holds their food has been overturned and the rabbit is reclining on this dry oasis, stretched in a strip of sunlight, hind legs extended. But the skinny gray rabbit is soaked to the bone, shaking in Kim's arms as she attempts to dry it off with her uniform jacket. It looks truly monstrous with its wet fur plastered to its skeleton, teeth carving into its lower lip.

"This rabbit will die soon," Koji says, just as matter-of-factly as before.

Kim clutches the animal closer to her chest and it scratches at

her, kicking wildly until she's forced to set it down next to the white
rabbit on the overturned trough. She picks up a carrot, breaks off a
piece and tries to push it into the rabbit's mouth, but it turns its head
away and slips off the edge of the trough, sinking into slush so deep
that only its ears rise above the surface. Kim picks it up again, once
more trying to dry its fur before setting it next to the other rabbit,
but again it jumps off, this time swimming through the slush to get
away from her. She looks like she might cry.

"*Mukoo e ikitai*," the boy says. It wants to get out.

"*Mukoo e ikitai*," Kim repeats after him.

"*Yamero*," he says, stop it, in the exact same tone he spoke to his
brother.

"Come on," I say. "Let's go."

"Where?" he asks me.

"To school," I say, and he tries to jerk his hand free but I don't let
go this time, pulling him with me into the facility.

During first period, yet another sixth-grade class draws my portrait.
Again the kids all turn me into a cartoon version of myself, but this
time Keiko doesn't say to look at me more closely, to try and draw my
eyes as they really are, to give me a mouth. Her own face is as inexpressive as the cartoon faces on the students' drawings. The scratches
on her throat are healing now, fainter than before. Fumiya must have
lashed out against her attempts to calm him down, contain his wild
energy. She leaves class in the break between periods, returning with
a group of third-graders to stand at the back of the room.

During recess she goes out onto the playground, where she
sneaks puffs from Kobayashi-sensei's cigarette, the two of them leaning against the swimming pool, passing the cigarette back and forth.
As I look down from the second-story window, I wonder if she's tell-

ing him about our disastrous dinner, how I refused to tutor her sons. I feel terrible when I think of how I behaved at her house. Maybe she was using me, but she obviously needs help. I don't know what it's like to have an autistic child, but I do know what it's like to try to pretend that everything is normal when it isn't.

Today's lunch is a tuna fish sandwich on white bread, which packs into my hollowed molar. I am trying to write an email to my mom. I want to apologize for calling her in the middle of the night, getting so upset. But thinking about that conversation, and what she sent in her latest care package, makes me upset all over again. I didn't tell Carolyn about the package. I don't know what to do with it. I don't want it around. A shadow falls across my blank page, and I look up to see snow falling outside the window.

"*Mo ichi do,*" I mutter.

"*Nani?*" the vice-principal says. This morning, he barely greeted me. I hope Miyoshi-sensei didn't tell him about my suspicions that he's been keeping me here for free English lessons. Ooka-sensei is a kind man, and Shika is a small town.

"It's snowing again," I say.

"And again and again," he speaks up from behind his freshly polished desk. "This is snow country, Miss Marina. What did you expect?"

In the last period of the day, Koji and Kim are among the students who file into the art room to draw my portrait. Koji sinks onto a stool at the back of the room, while Kim hurries to claim the stool next to his. Her long hair is loose today, falling around her shoulders like it did at the bath last night. She swivels to look at Koji but he ignores her. He teeters on the back legs of his stool, staring out the window where snow is falling densely now, in such thick flakes, that the air looks as white as the sheets of paper that Keiko places in front of each child. They've been sketching for about fifteen minutes when Keiko squats beside Koji.

"You're supposed to draw Miss Marina," she says.

"I don't like to draw," he replies. "You know that."

"Okay," she says. "How about making another collage?"

"I already made one," he says. "I don't like copying. I'm not like Kim."

"Kim's not copying you," Keiko says. "She's drawing her own picture."

"I know," Koji says. "She's copying herself."

I prop onto my elbow so that I can see. At first I think he's right, that Kim is drawing the exact same picture, but then I notice something new about this drawing. The girl has two long braids and a school uniform, and she is only standing beside one rabbit: the one with the fangs. This is not a picture of me but a self-portrait, a plea for the *kawaisou*, a request for help, I think.

As the bell rings, I linger on top of the table, hoping for a chance to talk to Keiko, when a burst of static erupts from the loudspeaker, followed by the vice-principal's voice. "Because of the storm, everyone is excused early. Please return home promptly and safely!" The announcement is barely finished before Keiko dashes out of the room, leaving me behind.

I slide off the table and rush after her, reaching the top of the stairs just as she reaches the bottom. By the time I get to the bottom, she is pushing through the door to the playground, still wearing her uniform slippers. I'm about to follow her outside when what I see through the window stops me. Kobayashi-sensei is stacking sleds in a pile when she approaches him from behind and touches his back. Their forms are softened by the falling snow. All she does is place her hand between his shoulders. All he does is not move away from her touch. He seems to lean back against her palm, as if that were all it took to keep his huge body propped upright. Maybe this is why she wanted me to come over for a few hours each week, not just to tutor her sons, but to give her some time alone. Or not alone. With him. I wish she had confided in me. She might have, eventually, if I'd given her the chance. If we had actually become friends. I'm backing away when I hear Kobayashi-sensei call out, "*Dame!*" Stop! He's looking up at the building, his expression terrified. I push through the door, stumble into the snow.

Kobayashi-sensei and Keiko are both holding their hands up, flakes falling through their splayed fingers. I walk across the yard, plunging to my knees in the slush, which is now freezing over, covered with an eggshell crust of ice. When I turn to look up at the school, I see the two children sitting on the ledge of the window, bare legs dangling outside. It's only the second floor of the building, but they are so small that the distance seems enormous.

"Why are you here?" Koji yells.

"Why are you here?" Kim repeats after him.

"This is my home," he says.

"This is my home," she says.

"Go away!" he says. "I want to be alone!"

"But I want to be with you," she says.

"She can speak," Kobayashi-sensei says to Keiko.

"*Yappari,*" Keiko replies. Naturally. She cups her hands around her mouth and calls, "Koji! Go back inside! I'm going to come up-stairs now. Mama is coming!"

As he shakes his head, one of his slippers falls off, sailing through the air before landing on the soft mound of snow, which rises higher than the lip of the swimming pool.

"*Mukoo e ikitai!*" he says. I want to go . . .

"No!" I yell, but too late. The boy doesn't jump so much as drop from the ledge, holding his arms close to his body as he falls through the air with Kim, as always, just a second behind, her hair lifting above her in a black streak. As they land in the pool, first one child and then the other, the white mass seems to swallow them whole. The slush beneath the snow acts like water, yielding too easily, closing over their heads, as if they were never there at all. Keiko staggers toward the pool with me right behind her, but Kobayashi-sensei is faster than us both, diving into the slush and disappearing too. "*Mukoo e ikitai*," the boy said before jumping. I want to go . . . Abroad. Far away. To the other side. This is the word his teacher used to describe where Kim and I come from. It's also the word I used to describe where my dad ended up. *Jampu shimashita.* He jumped. I jumped. There are no pronouns in Japanese. The boy wanted to get out.

I don't know how much time passes before Kobayashi-sensei finally resurfaces. Twenty seconds? Five? An eternity and a blink. But when he does, he is holding one child in each arm. They are wet and shivering and gasping for air, but alive. Alive. Keiko takes Koji in her arms. The little boy wraps his legs around his mom's waist and she wraps her sweater around his body, pressing her forehead to his.

"I'm still here," he cries.

"You're still here," she cries. She uses her thumb to wipe the snow out of his eyes, his nostrils, his ears, as if he were a newborn just entering into this world, still bearing the traces of the last. Kobayashi-sensei holds Kim like a baby too, on her back in his arms, rocking from side to side.

"*Daijoubu?*" he says.

"*Daijoubu*," she replies, and the two teachers huddle closer together, each holding a child, oblivious to me as I slip away.

New snow covers every surface in the hutch. At first, looking through the wire mesh without seeing either animal, I assume that someone must have thought to get them out before this storm hit. Then I spot a vibrating mound. I let myself into the cage, and reach under the snow to scoop up the gray rabbit. His body feels almost too hot yet he shivers as I brush off his back, his head and paws. I tuck him into my shirt, under my jacket, close to my heart. I'm glad when he kicks me, relieved that he has a little fight left in him. He's going to need it. His heart is pumping fast, an electric current that spurs me on. I climb into my car and turn on the heater, saying, "*Gambatte, usagi-chan.*"

Fight, little rabbit. Do your best for me.

At the dentist's office, the hygienist shows me into the private room where I close the door before unbuttoning my jacket, reaching into my shirt and setting the rabbit down on the reclining seat. The animal scratches at the paper lining and I keep a hand on his back to keep him from jumping off. He trembles violently and tries to kick me again.

"*Nani?*" the dentist says. "What's this?"

"His front teeth won't stop growing," I say. "He can't eat."

"Is it yours?" he asks.

"No," I say. "He belongs to the elementary school. Koji's school."

"I am not animal dentist," he says, reaching for the doorknob. "I can't do."

"Koji loves this rabbit very much," I say in my slowest, clearest English. "He needs help, or he's going to die."

"*Wakaranai . . . ,*" he stammers.

"You don't have to understand," I say. "I can pay you. I'll give you free English lessons. I'll do whatever you want. Just please help."

"Wakaranai . . . ," he says again, but he is filling a needle with clear liquid. "You have to hold him," he says. "Hold him tight." And so I press the rabbit to my chest, gripping both sides of his jaw to steady it as the dentist slides the needle into his mouth. His mouth softens, opens at last, and he relaxes in my arms.

PART III
Rabu~Rabu

SPRING

First day of spring—
I keep thinking about
the end of autumn.

kieru: (v.) *to disappear; to vanish; to go out; to be extinguished*

As usual, the senior technical boys are practically naked when we enter their classroom this afternoon. Often at the start of the period we find a few boys still changing out of their red nuclear power plant jumpsuits and into their school uniforms. But today all thirty are wearing nothing but saggy boxers or dingy briefs. It's a rainy April day and their skin is puckered with gooseflesh, nipples hard and pursed. They sit at their desks in a parody of model pupils, smirking. "Please get ready for English class," Miyoshi-sensei says, his voice shaky. He spins around to write the target sentence on the board, but he can't hide the blush staining the backs of his ears or steady the tremble in his handwriting.

The factory foreman gets around: by *car,* on *foot,* in *an airplane.*

Once his back is turned, the boys resume doing whatever they were doing before we arrived: texting each other on their cell phones, playing video games, leafing through catalogues of sports cars, hairstyle magazines, and pornographic comic books. The comic book splayed in front of a kid named Nakajima shows a naked woman dangling from a meat hook, her legs spread and cuffed, about to be penetrated by an advancing subway car. "*Mazui,*" I say, that's disgusting! I grab the book and clap it shut, but the boy just opens it again, calmly flipping the page.

Nakajima is the senior technical class ringleader. While the other boys' bodies are awkward works-in-progress, still puffy with baby fat or gawky, stretched out but not yet filled in, he alone looks finished, hard. He has no excess flesh, but oddly he's the reigning high school sumo champion of Ishikawa. He looks like the figure on the gold trophy he won in last year's competition—the lone trophy in the lobby display case—his skin tinted an orangey shade of brown from tanning lotion. Nakajima is also the reigning class *ganguro*, or "blackface," with a perm the size of a football helmet and a gold medallion that nestles between his pecs, spelling out his "blackface" name in zirconium-studded pyrite: *MCNakaG*. His bolder classmates like to copy him, especially his habit of lingering in his underwear to delay class. I'm sure today's prank was his idea.

"Please put on your uniforms," Miyoshi-sensei says. "There's a woman here, *ne?*"

"We can't," says a bulky kid named Sumio, one of Nakajima's minions, who has Band-Aids covering his crusty nipple piercings.

"Why can't you?" Miyoshi-sensei asks.

"Kieta," says Nakajima without looking up from his comic book. They vanished.

Lots of things have been "vanishing," ever since Miyoshi-sensei and I started team-teaching the senior technical boys in late February.

The boys aren't supposed to be coming to the high school anymore. After taking their prefectural exams, they were scheduled to spend the last two months before graduation putting their technical training to use at Shika's nuclear power station. Then the prefectural exams were scored and the scores averaged for each class. In English, Shika's technical class averaged 4 percent, an all-time low for

Ishikawa, according to the front-page headlines of the local paper. In her article, the reporter happened to mention that the senior technical boys were the only students at Shika High School never to have studied English with the native speaker. They alone had no idea how fun and useful English could be.

Those were the same words the principal used when he summoned Miyoshi-sensei and me into his office. Parents had been calling, and he had to placate them. So up until graduation, the boys would be returning from the plant every day after lunch, for a special English class with the two of us. We could teach them whatever we wanted, but our lessons had to be fun and useful. Miyoshi-sensei looked pale as he translated these terms in the hallway. "I thought I was through with them," he said. "I have no fun or useful ideas. What will I do?" His dread was palpable, but I was almost glad for it. I still sensed a distance between us. He was perfectly polite, but that was the problem. This was the first time we'd spoken candidly in months. I told him not to worry, that I could bring in all of the fun worksheets and games I'd made for our other classes. "These boys are like wild animals," he scoffed. "Would you expect a tiger to fill in some worksheet? A gorilla to perform your skit?" I laughed and he groaned. "I *wish* they were tigers," he said. "Tigers can jump through hoops. Gorillas can sign, *ne?* These boys are like fish. Cold and slippery. Impossible to hook."

Before our first class, I couldn't stop thinking about how the boys had sexually harassed their last female teacher, something the newspaper article failed to mention. I imagined them leering at me, making innuendos, maybe even groping me as I maneuvered between their desks. But the boys barely looked up when I entered their classroom. They didn't stand or return my greeting. Not one of them filled out my self-introduction worksheet. They acted like I was invisible, ignoring Miyoshi-sensei too.

We're still invisible. This doesn't seem to bother Miyoshi. He simply ignores the fact that they are ignoring him, reading from the textbook for no one's benefit but his own. I can't stand it. An almost existential case of futility overtakes me every time we recite a dialogue from *English for Busy People* ("busy people" being a euphemism for laborers), our voices drowned out by their digital din. I keep thinking about those movies where an intrepid teacher transforms the difficult kids from apathetic thugs into model citizens, using spoken word poetry or ballroom dance or math. Of course I know that this is a Hollywood fantasy, but those movies always claim to be based on a true story. Maybe if I could find the thing that interests these boys, something they like doing and are good at, I could break through the wall and reach them. But every time I suggest that we try something different, from bringing in rap music to baking chocolate chip cookies in the school kitchen, Miyoshi-sensei shuts me down. "These students are eighteen years," he reminds me. "Almost men. Probably we should stick to the textbook. Discourage any kind of . . . risky behavior." Those words, "risky behavior," are the same words he used in reference to the night we kissed. I always let the subject drop.

"Are they ready?" Miyoshi-sensei asks me, still facing the board. For some reason, the one thing that gets under his skin is when we find the boys undressed.

"No," I say. "They're still naked."

I walk up and down the aisles, peering into the backs of their desks to see if any uniforms might be wadded up inside. Inside Naka-jijma's desk I see something square and silvery, something that looks a lot like my Marina bank.

The boys actually paid attention the day I brought in this bento box, filled with photocopied "Marina dollars," my grinning face collaged over George Washington's. I gave out freebies while Miyoshi-sensei reluctantly translated my explanation for how they could earn more: by saying hello, making eye contact, asking or answering questions. Basic politeness. "What can we buy with these Marina dollars?" one boy wanted to know. It was the first question any of them had ever asked me, and I peeled off several bills, telling him there would be an auction before graduation. "What will you auction off?" another boy said. "Cool things," I replied vaguely. "Like what?" he pressed, earning more Marina money instead of an answer. The truth was, I hadn't thought this far ahead, and it didn't take them long to figure out that I had nothing to offer them, nothing fun or useful, because they stopped asking questions, stopped answering mine, even stopped accepting the Marina dollars I doled out as obviously empty bribes. I stopped bringing it to class. I hadn't even realized that it was missing until now.

As I reach into Nakajima's desk, my arm brushes his hot torso.

"Look what I found in Nakajima's desk," I say to Miyoshi-sensei.

"His uniform?" he asks hopefully.

"No," I say. "My Marina bank."

He turns around and scrutinizes the object in my hands, tilting his head to one side.

"This is the most common bento box," he says, "available at 100-Yen stores everywhere. How can you be certain it is yours?"

"Because mine is missing," I say, frustrated by his reluctance to take my side.

"Nakajima will graduate soon," he says. "Probably he would not risk expulsion, stealing something he has no real use for. He has no real use for Marina money, *ne?*"

Instead of answering, I pry open the lid and turn the box upside down. If this were a movie, Marina dollars would flutter in an incriminating pile at our feet. Instead it spills a half-eaten rice ball, a banana, and a sparkly lavender cell phone. Without a word, Miyoshi-sensei crouches to retrieve these things, returning them to the box and the box to Nakajima.

"Did your uniform really disappear?" he asks the boy in Japanese.

"Obviously," Nakajima snaps at him.

"Then why don't you put your plant uniform back on?" he suggests.

"No way," the boy says. "It's soaking wet."

"Please," Miyoshi-sensei says. "There is a woman here. *Hazukashii desu.*"

"If Miss Marina is so shy," Nakajima says, "then why does she always stare at us?" Miyoshi-sensei glances at me and bites his lip. If I refuse to look away when the boys are changing, it's only because I don't want them to think that they can intimidate me as easily as they intimidated their last female teacher. I wait for him to come to my defense. "She's always staring at us," the boy continues. "It's perverted. Make her turn around. Then we'll do her stupid English lesson." His friends laugh and Miyoshi-sensei clears his throat.

"Miss Marina . . . ," he hesitates. "Maybe . . . do you think . . . could you please turn to look at the board?"

"Are you serious?" I say, feeling my own face heat up, my own hands begin to shake.

"I think Nakajima feels kind of shy to have his uniform off in front of a woman."

"Really?" I say. "Then why doesn't he put it on?"

"*Kieta,*" he replies. It vanished.

"Why do you let them get away with it?" I say.

"Get away with it?" he repeats.

"We let them walk all over us! I'm not the one who gets embarrassed every time they show a little skin. Who cares if they're undressed?"

"I'm sorry," he says. "You are kind of frantic. I can't catch much of this. Why don't you read today's target sentences? Then you will appear to have some purpose here."

I spin around, crossing my arms. The boys hate to be made examples of, so I insert Nakajima's name into the target sentence.

"Nakajima gets around," I bellow. "*By* bus, *on* foot, *in* a plane."

"*Mo ichi do*," Miyoshi-sensei says.

"NAKAJIMA GETS AROUND!" I yell, so loud that my words echo off the portable classroom walls. When I start to laugh, Miyoshi-sensei asks me what's so funny. In Japan, it's considered rude to have a private joke. Someone might think you were laughing at him. I explain that "gets around" means "sleeps around."

"It means he is sleepy?"

"It means he has sex. A lot of sex. With a lot of different people."

"Ah," he says. "It's American joke. I should share with the class, *ne?*"

To my surprise, the boys actually laugh, all except for Nakajima, who is scowling at his cell phone, studying the screen as it registers an incoming call, the ring tone a digital rendition of Roberta Flack's *Killing Me Softly*.

I heard he sang a sweet song. . .

"Nakajima sleeps around!" I yell even louder.

"Nakajima sleeps around," Miyoshi-sensei alone repeats after me.

"Shut up homo," the boy mutters.

"What did you say?" I ask, leaning over his desk. We're close enough that I can see the dandruff salting his Afro-perm, the black-heads studding his nostrils, the sleep encrusted in the corners of his eyes.

"Shut up homo," he repeats, maddeningly calm.

When I raise my hand, he doesn't duck, doesn't raise his own hand or call out to Miyoshi-sensei, who has his back to us now as he erases the sentence on the board. He just looks right at me, his eyes like two black holes, daring me to go ahead and hit him, knowing that I won't. I'm not that brave or that dumb. I'm not going to hit a student. But I can't do nothing, either. To do nothing would be like going into a bank, waving a gun around and then making a withdrawal from an ATM machine. On his desk, the cell phone starts to ring again. I grab it and drop it into my pocket.

Miyoshi-sensei and I walk in silence around the red rubber track back to the high school. He is carrying his slippers in a plastic bag. I'm wearing mine, in flagrant violation of school rules. My socks wick up moisture from the puddles. He doesn't say a word. He never corrects me anymore. He's given up, decided that I'm a lost cause. He opens the door to the faculty locker room and lines his own slippers at the threshold, then bends down to take off his Converse, stepping out of them and into his hoof slippers. I wonder when the soles of his feet last touched the ground. I wonder if he showers with his eyes closed, gets ready for bed in the dark.

"Did you hear what Nakajima-san said?" I ask at last, when I can't stand it anymore.

"Nakajima is very athletic," he says, sliding the door shut behind us.

"So what?" I say. "He's an athlete, so he can say whatever he wants?"

"What I mean is, Nakajima's talent is not English. Speaking in English, he can't understand the meaning of his words."

"Bullshit," I say as we walk up the school stairs. Each one dips down in the middle, a smooth stone trough. Miyoshi-sensei went to school here. I wonder how many times he has walked up and down this flight of stairs.

"Bullshit is bad word, *ne?*"

"Sorry," I say.

"That's fine. For me, 'bullshit' has no meaning."

"It's what you say when someone's not telling the truth."

"Of course," he says. "I know usage of the word bullshit, but I can't feel it. It's same when students speak English. Words have no power. They are just . . . having fun."

"Making fun," I correct him. He sinks into the faculty room couch and I sit next to him, careful to leave a foot of distance between us. He offers me a cigarette and I accept, lighting it for myself. "How do you say 'homo' in Japanese?" I ask, trying to sound casual.

"Homo," he repeats.

"Yeah," I say. "In Japanese."

"It's same," he says.

"I think Nakajima knew what he was saying when he called me a homo." I recall the many times I've seen Nakajima bike past our house on the river path, how he slowed down to watch me and Carolyn hanging up our bras and underwear to dry from the clothesline.

"He was talking to me," Miyoshi-sensei says.

"What?" I say. "Why?"

"He calls me this often. It's his favorite way to get . . . under my skin?"

"We shouldn't let them get away with it," I say.

"I told you before, these boys are like fish. Can fish even see us, with their small, cold eyes? I don't think so."

"But they're not fish," I say, my frustration boiling to a hot, thick stew. "They're our students, and we don't even try to discipline them. We're not really trying to teach them anything either. We're just killing time, and it's driving me crazy. I mean honestly, look at that textbook." He glances down at the cover of *English for Busy People*, at a row of cartoon figures wearing hard hats. "If I were them,

I wouldn't pay attention either. We're certainly not making our English lessons fun or useful." He takes a drag off his cigarette, holding the smoke in as long as he can before exhaling. "Fine," he says at last, rolling up the textbook and sailing it across the faculty room, where it lands in the recycling bin. "I give out."

"What do you mean?" I laugh nervously at what I'm sure must be a joke.

"For three years I taught these boys," he says. "Do you think I didn't try every method to hook their attention? I brought pop music. I played Hollywood video. I took them to MosBurger. My treat! Nothing succeeded." He looks at me directly. "When I think about these boys, even when I am home alone in my bed, I feel sick. If you think you can do better, I hope so too. From now on, I leave everything up to you."

"Miyoshi-sensei," I say, "you're a great teacher. I wasn't trying to—"

"*Gambatte*," he cuts me off. Good luck.

CHAPTER SIXTEEN

gokiburi: (N.) *cockroach*

Carolyn is sorting things into three piles: hers, mine, and discards. I am pretending not to watch as I eat a bowl of noodles, perched on the edge of the *gokiburi* couch, its vinyl the same glossy brown as the shells of the roaches who camouflage themselves against it. Now that it's spring, the *gokiburi* have returned in droves. Amana used to hunt for them in the middle of the night, scampering over our bodies to drop her twitching prey between us, expecting praise. It was a horrible way to wake up, but at least the roaches were sufficiently stunned that we could wrap them in toilet paper and flush them away. Now we have no alarm system, and it's like they know it. They are brazen, these *gokiburi*. They are huge, glutted on our waste. They can fly.

"Stop it," Carolyn says, as I jump up from the couch to inspect the cracks in the vinyl where the roaches like to hide in the foam. "You're making me paranoid." I tell her that I was sure I felt the brush of feelers against my arm and she reminds me that cockroaches aren't dangerous. "They might not bite," I say, "but when my dad was working in the ER, he had to remove one from a little girl's ear." She grimaces and I continue. "The girl could hear it in there, burrowing deeper and deeper. Did you know that cockroaches can't move in reverse? They can only move forward. So once it got in there, it was stuck. It couldn't get out even if it wanted to."

"Stop it," she says again, sealing a box with tape.

Even though it's only April, Carolyn has started a countdown of the number of days we have left in Japan. When I ask what she wants to do next, she always says that she doesn't know yet, we still have X days to go. She never loses track of that number. She crosses it off in the morning.

"We should get away for the weekend," I say. "Let's go to Kyoto."

"We just went there last month," Carolyn reminds me. I suggest that we go back to Tokyo, where we haven't been since our orientation, and she tells me that it takes eleven hours by bus and we'd just have to turn around as soon as we got there. "I wish I could get away from myself," she says. "Be someone else for a weekend. Wouldn't that be great? To be someone else for a change?"

"Would you know that you were someone else?" I ask.

"No," she says. "You'd be able to forget all about yourself."

"Then wouldn't that other person's problems just feel like your own?"

"At least they'd be different problems."

"I'd like to be you for a weekend," I say.

"That's creepy." She shudders. "It's like you want to spy on my thoughts."

"No I don't," I defend myself, stung. "But what's wrong with wanting to know what you're thinking? We hardly talk anymore."

"What do you mean?" she says. "That's all we do. You're the only person I talk to."

"You talk to Joe," I say.

"Have you been reading my journal?" she asks.

"Of course not," I say. Not that I could, I might add. Carolyn has started sealing the pages of her journal with tape. I only know this because the notebook happened to be lying there one day when I needed to take a phone message from her dad. I held it up to the light, but the writing was too faint to make out. "Are we breaking up?" I ask, pushing out the words. "Because if that's what's happening, I wish you'd let me know."

"I just need some space," she says. "We're buried under so much junk here. I want to send some boxes home so that I can enjoy my last four months."

"Well you can't take all the pickle dishes," I say. "We bought those together."

"At the hundred-yen store," she reminds me. "I'll give you the money to buy your own set if you want."

"That's not the point," I say.

"What is the point? Making this as hard as possible?"

"It should be hard," I say. "If we're breaking up." This time she doesn't answer. She just picks up another pickle dish. "What if I want to eat pickles?" I say, and without looking up she sails the dish through the air. I manage—barely—to catch it.

"You almost hit me!" I say.

"That was the point," she says. "Haven't you ever hit someone?" Before I can answer, she rolls her eyes and says, "Of course not. You never lose control. You're always standing back, watching yourself. You're like an understudy in your own life."

I want to protest, to say how wrong she is, that I lose control all the time, but I know she wouldn't believe me, even if I told her that I almost hit a boy in class today. Almost doesn't count. Almost just proves her point. So I take the pickle dish, hold it overhead and throw. She ducks and it crashes into one of the windows looking out onto the storage area. Rain blows through a hole in the rusted aluminum siding, streaking the *tatami*. For a moment, we just look at each other. Then the doorbell rings and she jumps to her feet. "Ogawa-san must have heard the glass break and sent the cat murderer to investigate," she says. "I can't deal with him tonight. You made this mess, you clean it up."

Every month or so, Haruki Ogawa delivers a peace offering. At least I think they're peace offerings. He has brought us a tin of roasted tea, a tray of grilled *mochi*, a bag of sweet bean cakes wrapped in moist cherry blossom leaves. His grandfather always watches from the yard across the street to make sure that he returns empty-handed, which is impossible when Carolyn answers the door. She refuses to touch any of it, even the fruit, convinced the boy might have injected the rind with poison. She shuts the door in his face and he has to come back again to complete the transaction with me.

But tonight I open the door to find not Haruki but Miyoshi-sensei. It takes me a moment to recognize him, dressed in a sweatshirt and jeans, his hair damp from the rain and falling in his eyes. He apologizes for disturbing me at home in the evening, saying that he has something important to discuss, something that couldn't wait. I invite him in with a heavy heart, wondering what I did wrong this time. As he steps out of his Converse, he surveys the garbage bags filled with Carolyn's discards crowding the entryway.

"Now I understand why you don't have any *gomi* troubles recently," he ruminates. "Maybe it's because you aren't throwing anything away."

"That's not garbage," I say. "It's stuff that Carolyn is sending home."

"She is moving out?" he asks.

"No," I say. "Just clearing some space."

"Ah," he says, eyeing the countdown on the refrigerator. As I lead him to the living room, we pass the kitchen where one bag that actually contains garbage is lying tipped on its side, exposing an empty carton of aloe juice and an eggshell filled with coffee grounds. At least he can see that we're sorting our burnables. He sinks into the *gokiburi* couch and I bring him a cup of tea in a ridiculous Mickey Mouse beer stein—the only cup I can find. He hands me a letter and sips his tea in silence while I read.

Dear Miss Marina,

Please don't be frighten. It's true, a previous letter usually meant you committed some error. But now it's not so. Fact of matter is, Ogawa-san reports that you became "number one neighbor." He says, "Please tell Marina-teacher I appreciate her effort with gomi, including Haruki." I should thank you too. Ogawa-san does not call my home early in the morning to inform about you. I am more rested.

I'm sorry we didn't talk so much recently. I'm sorry if you thought I was "avoiding" you. Truly I was so busy preparing students for exams that I set aside another obligation, like our friendship. All for nothing, ne? You know Japanese idiom, "to lose face"? I wish this truly happened to me. After technical boys received 4% on final English exam, I wish I had no eyes to see everyone's displeasure, no ears to hear everyone's criticism, no mouth to make a speech in English, to welcome Mayor of California to Shika.

So many times I have tried to write on theme: "Why English is useful for me." But after writing five words, "because I am English teacher," I have nothing to say. I am not good English teacher. Even five word speech is untrue. Reason for this letter is not begging for pity. Reason is asking for help. You are often reading a book or writing something. You have intellectual atmosphere. Could you help

*me write this speech? Do you have any ideas? I don't know what to
do. I am at the end of my wit.*

 That's all for now.

See you,
Hiroshi Miyoshi

At the end of the month, the mayor of Eureka, California, is coming
to Shika to sign a sister-city contract. There is going to be a festival to
welcome him, and I've been asked to run the English speech contest,
for which no one so far has volunteered.

"Your English has been very useful to me," I say. "You've explained
so much about Japanese life and culture. If not for you, I wouldn't
even have known where to throw my garbage away." He raises one
eyebrow, then looks over at the trash bag tipped on its side. "Okay," I
concede, laughing. "Maybe that's not such a great example."

"You should see my own *gomi* bin," he says. "Filled with paper
balls. When I try to write my speech, my pen becomes my enemy."

"I love the way you speak English," I say.

"The way *I* speak English?" He raises his eyebrows. "Is it so different?"

"No," I say. "It's just that you have a unique way of putting things."

"I'm happy you think so," he says, sounding miserable, "but I
can't write this speech. I can't write in English. It's too difficult."

"Of course you can," I say, holding up the letter he's just given
me as proof.

"That's different," he says, waving a dismissive hand. "When I
write to you, I picture your face. It's like talking with you. So easy
and natural." *It is?* I think, but don't say. Instead, I suggest that perhaps he could write a draft of his speech as a letter to me, describing

different times in his life that English has been useful. I offer to help him turn it into a speech once he gets out a rough draft.

"I don't know," he says. "*Maybe* I could write a letter to you . . . "

"*Maybe* you could," I agree, laughing again as I wave his letter in the air. It takes a moment, but finally he starts to laugh too, and soon we're both clutching our sides, doubled over, and I don't even realize that Carolyn is standing in the doorway until she clears her throat. She is dressed in sushi pajamas, her arms crossed over her chest.

"Hey," I say. "Hiro just stopped by to talk about something important."

"Hiro?" she says.

"Hiroshi," he says, standing up and sticking out his hand, nodding like a bobble-headed dashboard doll. "Nice to meet you."

"We've met," she says. "It's kind of late, isn't it?"

"It's like nine," I say.

"What's so funny?" she asks, and it's not that I want to exclude her from the joke, but I'm not sure how to explain. I ask if she wants to join us for a cup of tea, but she shakes her head and says that she's heading to bed. Lately she goes to bed earlier and earlier, as if in her haste to get through that countdown.

"I'm sorry to loiter," Hiro says. "I should go."

"You can finish your tea," I say.

"Right," Carolyn says. "I'm the one who should apologize for interrupting."

After she heads back upstairs I want to say something, to explain why the good feeling has been zapped from the room, but Miyoshi-sensei claps his knees and stands up. Where he was seated, a huge cockroach slides into a rip in the vinyl couch.

"Sorry," I say, disgusted and embarrassed. "I guess we should throw out that trash."

"Mari-chan," he says, "it must be kind of nice, living as a temporary person here."

"No it's not," I say. "And I hate when you call me a temporary person."

"This was not criticism." He begins walking down the hallway, stepping over the overstuffed garbage bags. "Of course I know it's difficult to be a foreigner here in Japan. There are so many rules to follow. So many people watching all the time to see if you fail. But you can choose to follow our rules or not. When you leave Japan, you will leave everything behind, including reputation. It's a kind of freedom, *ne*?"

He opens the front door and the light from the entryway illuminates my car. With both sides crushed, it looks like it went through a trash compactor, or like it was squeezed by a giant pair of tongs. He doesn't say anything, but I know that what he sees confirms what he just said. I am a temporary person, leading a disposable life.

ayashii: (ADJ.) *suspicious; strange; perverted; charming; bewitching*

There is a hundred yen coin in my favorite bathroom stall in the fourth floor girls' room. This coin sits on top of the device bolted to the inside of the stall door, a device that mimics the sound of a toilet flushing, to prevent girls from flushing the toilet over and over—wasting water and money—to drown out the humiliating sounds of bodily voiding. Over the last eight months, this coin has not moved a millimeter, even though other girls must have noticed it too, bringing their fingers within an inch of it every time they push the button to activate that flushing sound.

In other words, nothing just vanishes around here.

Today I don't have to push the button to activate the flushing sound as I pee, since Nakajima's cell phone keeps ringing from my pocket. *I heard he sang a sweet song . . .*

Nakajima is not hard to find. I don't even have to leave the safety of the girls' room. I can see him from the bathroom window, squatting on the grass. As usual he's almost naked, dressed only in a *mawashi*, the sumo wrestler's trademark loincloth. I watch as he knocks shoulders with Kobayashi-sensei. Since the start of spring quarter, the second-grade teacher has been coming to the high school every afternoon to coach sumo practice. He pushes Nakajima to the edge of the circle of dirt, but the boy ducks and the big man loses his balance, stepping out of the ring. Nakajima pumps a victorious brown fist and Kobayashi-sensei clips his ear. Grinning sheepishly, the boy bows to his sensei.

Every day after sumo practice, Kobayashi-sensei stops by the faculty room to smoke a cigarette with the other male teachers. I try not to be there. I spend a lot of time in this bathroom stall. I haven't seen Koji or Kim since he saved their lives. I want to know how the two children are doing, but I'm afraid to ask. I'm afraid he suspects that I had something to do with their jump, that he blames me, that he should.

"Do you enjoy watching a man?"

I whirl around, feeling like a voyeur, to find Noriko. As the librarian's wedding date nears, she has traded her tomboy clothes for matronly ones that bag around her skinny body, making her look like a little girl playing dress-up in her mother's closet. Today she's wearing a belted dress covered in cabbage roses and a velvet headband.

"I've never watched sumo before," I say.

"Not sumo," she says. "The rice farmers are here."

Outside the high school, girls are throwing rice at the two tractors moving slow as tanks down the road. Hanging from strings trailing behind the tractors, Sapporo cans skim and bounce across flooded potholes, spitting water at the girls' bare legs. Their wet hands are coated in pearly grains of rice, so from a distance it looks like they're wearing prim white gloves. It also looks like they're aiming not for the tractors but at the men driving them, the two farmers descending the peninsula in search of brides.

According to a recent newspaper article, these farmers grow

the finest and most expensive rice in all of Japan, in a town called Monzen at the tip of the peninsula. But the young people in Monzen are all taking off for bigger cities down south, leaving the farmers with few prospects. On this odyssey, they hope to meet two young women willing to return home with them and settle down. They also hope that when the Japanese people see how lonely they are, how much they sacrifice to farm that land, they will buy expensive Japanese rice instead of the cheaper California import. It seems unlikely that these guys will find brides, but I like the fairy-tale aspect to this quest. I like imagining the happy ending where the farmer hoists the girl into his John Deere and they roll off into the sunset together.

Ritsuko Ueno is the only girl who isn't throwing rice at the farmers. Instead she hangs back under the overhang of the school roof, shivering in her red pea coat, its hood drawn. I ask why she's not with her friends and she shrugs.

"I don't want some old husband," she says in Japanese. "I want to get out of here." I glance at Noriko, whose wedding invitation I just received. Sakura, Ritsuko's mother, made the match between the librarian and the dentist, the one who performed my root canal, who made me say "Howdy" when he banged my teeth. I imagine him and Noriko cuddling on a couch, watching Western movies on TV together.

"You're leaving in a month," Noriko says. Ritsuko is going to be the first Shika High School student to do a homestay in Eureka. "Are you excited?"

"I can't wait," Ritsuko says, but she sounds almost angry. "I want to escape Shika."

"Won't you miss Nakajima?" the librarian asks her.

"Not really," says Ritsuko with a shrug.

I have seen the two of them riding one bicycle, Nakajima pumping the pedals while Ritsuko sat with her arms around his waist, her cheek to his back. I've seen them hanging out at the grocery store, ducking into the photo booth to avoid me. He looks embarrassed to be caught happy, while she looks embarrassed to be caught with him.

"Is he your boyfriend?" I ask.

"I want to escape this too," she says.

"Good idea," I say.

Miyoshi-sensei has come outside to join us. He shakes his head as the two farmers stand up in their tractors and bow at the girls. "It's kind of *ayashii*," he says, meaning suspicious, perverted, "flirting with high school girls at their age."

"How old are they?" I ask.

"Thirty-two," he replies. "Same as me."

"That's not that old," I say.

"Thanks," he says. "I'm glad you think so. But it's too old for a high school girl."

I ask why the girls are throwing rice at the farmers, and he explains that the farmers planned this as a PR stunt, shipping bags of rice to every town through which they were going to pass for just this purpose, to guarantee an audience. "Also," he says, "they want to show that they are fun, globalized guys. For instance, they know international custom like throwing rice for a wedding."

"Usually rice gets thrown after a wedding," I point out.

"Well," he says, "they are optimistic."

A white news van pulls up behind the two tractors and a cluster of men spills out. One holds a clear umbrella over the head of another, who has a video camera perched on his shoulder, but it's the third that catches my eye with his pink and black pinstriped suit, pink cowboy boots, and bleached hair styled in Statue of Liberty spikes.

"Who is that?" I ask.

"You don't know Lone Wolf?" Ritsuko says, sounding incredulous.

"He is famous comedian," Noriko manages, one hand clasped over her mouth.

"*Very* famous," Ritsuko adds. "Number one success of Shika."

"He hosts a kind of minor variety show," Miyoshi-sensei says. "His program is on TV so late at night. Not prime time." He falls silent as a sedan parks behind the news van and Mayor Miyoshi emerges. I say hello and the mayor nods. Even though I know that his silence is the product of surgery, it gives him a regal quality. He pulls a small notepad from his breast pocket and writes something down for Hiro to read out loud.

"Miss Marina, could you please explain about *supa singuru* night?"

"About what?" I ask.

"Supermarket singles night," he enunciates more slowly. "Where your mother tried to find love, and instead bought so many groceries?"

Recently, the reporter who was writing an article about these farmers called to interview me about how people in the United States go about finding a wife or a husband. When I said that bars and parties were popular pickup spots, she said, "But how about an older woman who doesn't like bars? Or a man who is too shy to talk to strangers at a party?" So I shared a story that mom told me over the phone recently, about how she ended up at Safeway on Singles' Night, her first foray into the dating world since my dad's death.

She swore it was an accident, that she had no idea such a thing even existed. She said it was an unusually warm evening, she'd had a half day at school, and was feeling restless and lonely, so she decided to walk to the store to get some ice cream and a magazine. After seeing the banner hanging over the front doors declaring that it was

Singles' Night, she turned around and walked several blocks before stopping herself. "I don't know if I'm ready to date," she said, "but I was *lonely*." She stressed the word in a way that made me sad and uneasy. "I figured that I shouldn't be such a chicken, right? I should at least get the ice cream and the magazine that I came for, right?" Then, before I could answer, she told me that in the hour she spent at the supermarket, three different men made passes at her. When I asked why it took an hour to buy some ice cream and a magazine, she explained that she had to fill her cart. "I didn't want to look desperate," she said. "Like the only reason I was there was to meet someone. Which wasn't even true! But I didn't have my grocery list, so I started shopping with the men in mind."

"What men?" I asked, increasingly nervous.

"The ones who made passes at me," she said.

She told me that the first guy looked like he'd just gone for a run, so she picked out Gatorade for him and a box of Powerbars, "the kind you used to like to eat after runs," she added, and peanut butter and whole grain bread, energy foods. "But I'm not that athletic," she said, "so it wouldn't have worked out, even though I was flattered by his attention." The second man who made a pass at her was a dad with a little girl sitting in the top part of his grocery cart who was really too big to fit there. "He didn't have a ring," she said, "and he seemed sad, so I assumed that he was divorced or maybe even a widower." She paused, and I remembered how she had called me once and said, "I'm a widow now. I hate that word," and I'd felt jealous that at least there was a word for what she was. She picked out applesauce and pickles for the little girl, and for the dad turkey sausages and cous-cous and a bottle of white wine. "Then I realized that I was buying the things I would've bought for you and your father," she said. I had already realized this myself. The last guy who made a pass at her was an older gentleman wearing a suit and pushing a cart that contained only a pint of ice cream and a magazine, a coincidence she noted. She imagined that he was recently retired and didn't know how to fill his time, that he still dressed like he had a job to go to. She was getting up the nerve to say something to him when she noticed that his head trembled slightly, like he had Parkinson's disease.

"I don't want to be a caretaker," she said. "I just can't."

"No," I said, thinking that I didn't blame her, that she had already been one.

"Your birthday's coming up," she reminded me, asking what I wanted her to send.

"More books would be nice," I said, still unsettled.

"I could also send you those PowerBars," she offered.

"You actually bought all that stuff?" I asked.

"I spent a long time filling my cart," she said. "I couldn't just put it back."

I had no idea that my story had ended up in the newspaper. Now Miyoshi-sensei tells me that when the manager of the local super-market read the article, he decided to make a *supa singuru* night here in Shika, to help the rice farmers meet women.

"What's your *taipu*?" Lone Wolf asks, thrusting his microphone at me.

"My type?" I repeat, feigning ignorance to buy time.

"Do you like *hansamuboi*? *Romansugurei*?"

"Romance gray," Miyoshi-sensei translates. "This means an older man."

"I don't really have a type," I say, but Lone Wolf shakes his head and presses on. "How about farmers? Or maybe you prefer teach-ers?" The camera pans to Miyoshi-sensei, who looks down at his Converse, a blush creeping up his neck. "Same old Hiro," Lone Wolf laughs, punching him in the shoulder too hard to qualify as playful.

"Do you two know each other?" I ask.

"Lone Wolf went to school here too," Miyoshi-sensei says.

"Were you friends?"

"Not exactly."

The mayor scribbles something in his notebook, passing it to Miyoshi-sensei again. He clears his throat and then asks if I would like to throw some rice at the farmers, so that Lone Wolf's cameraman can capture it on film. Before I can answer, the mayor presents me with my own five-kilo burlap bag, which feels as heavy as a baby in my arms. Followed by the man with the camera, I walk into the street and take my place in the line of girls, sinking my hand into the cold grains. The rice farmers look older up close, their skin ruddy, hairlines receding. They look scared. Especially after they see me.

When the phone starts to ring in my pocket, I set the bag down and answer it so that the cameraman will finally walk away and leave me alone.

"Hello?" I say.

"Uh . . . sorry," says a male voice with a British accent. "Must've misdialed."

"Joe?" I guess, recognizing his voice. "Is that you? Where are you?"

"Right here at your local Mister Donuts, enjoying a curry old-fashioned. Very old-fashioned. Haven't had one of these classics in ages." I laugh and ask whether he's here to teach with us, and he says that he's in town for the festival. "Hang on," I say, as I catch sight of Nakajima trudging to school in his red power plant uniform. With his Afro-perm shrunken in the rain, he looks like a drenched cat: something that has lost its power. Joe says that he thought he was dialing Ritsuko Ueno. He usually stays with the Ueno family when he's in Shika, tutoring Ritsuko in English for room and board. I tell him that I'll be seeing her at the SMILE meeting this evening and offer to pass on a message.

"Smile?" he repeats.

"Shika Machi-ites for International Language Exchange." *Machi* means town, but I don't know who came up with the term "*machi-ite*." Probably Miyoshi-sensei. Joe snickers and I tell him that the name wasn't my idea. "I didn't think so," he says. "Did I ever tell you about how the folks from the Nanao City Hall once called to ask my opinion on the name they were tossing around for their new shopping mall? They wanted to name it 'Nappy,' a fusion of Nanao and happy. They asked if I saw anything wrong with that particular moniker. So I told them that yes, in fact, I saw several problems, explaining that in America, 'nappy' is a racist term for kinky hair, and in Britain that's how we refer to diapers. They thanked me very much for my time and opinion. The next time I happened to be in Nanao, I drove past the new mall. Guess what it's called?"

"Nappy," I say, laughing again.

"Roight you are." He laughs too. "Maybe I'll come to SMILE," he says. "If you'll have me, that is." I tell him that it won't be that much fun, since it's the last meeting before the festival and everyone will be practicing their speeches. He offers to help coach them, reminding me that he's an actor.

"Creamy talent," I say. "How could I forget?"

The first rule of SMILE is: in English please. The second rule of SMILE is: be direct. The third rule of SMILE is: first names only. And the fourth rule of SMILE is: smile! I didn't make these rules, Miyoshi-sensei did, and I don't enforce them, but the group members follow them like the law, and police each other assiduously too.

I throw a tennis ball into the air, aiming for the back of the tiny theater. Naturally, it lands in the lap of SMILE's worst English speaker. "*Eh?*" the yam truck driver says, holding the tennis ball up to his eyes as if the lime green fuzz might turn into crystal, revealing not his future but a simple English question. "How are . . . " he begins, then stops. As per my one and only rule, "How are you?" is strictly off-limits in a chat volley. He pauses to think, sticking his fingers inside his neck brace to scratch his throat, making a sandpapery rasp.

Uyesugi-san is recovering from surgery to defuse his vertebrae. Before acquiring his yam truck, he used to drive an eighteen-wheeler for Shika's nuclear power plant, ferrying supplies into town and waste back out. His CV radio received signals from as far as Australia, which is how he learned what little English he knows. "How about rice farmer?" he says, lobbing the tennis ball back at me. "Over and out!"

I'm not sure how to answer his question, so I ask another one instead. "Do you think the rice farmers will be able to meet women here in Shika?" I toss the ball to the left side of the theater, where the Ishii brothers are seated next to each other, both dressed in short-sleeved plaid shirts, wire-rimmed eyeglasses peeking from their pockets, even their hair parted on the same side. The dentist catches the ball.

"If so," he says, "I offer free tooth whitening for wedding gift."

"Free?" echoes the doctor.

"It's advertisement," the dentist says. "To lure new patients."

The dentist's own teeth are the color of lightly seeped tea, certainly no advertisement for his business. I never saw them when I was his patient, since he never once took off his goggles and face mask, not even when he pulled the rabbit's two front teeth, which looked like bloody knitting needles. He wrapped them in a paper towel, dropped them in the garbage can and then backed away, not answering when I asked whether he still wanted those free *eikaiwa* or "English conversation" classes I'd offered in exchange for his veterinary services. I figured I'd scared him off. I assumed that was the last I'd see of him. But there he was at the first SMILE club meeting, sitting next to his brother. Keiko was there too, in the row behind them, Fumiya to her left and Koji to her right. Behind them sat Ooka-sensei, the elementary school vice-principal, Sakura and Ritsuko Ueno, and Noriko, the high school librarian. Facing me, they looked like a jury. Keiko tried to calm Fumiya as the boy rocked in his seat, mimicking its squeak perfectly.

At that meeting, Miyoshi-sensei explained that the mayor had initiated SMILE so that the English speakers of Shika could get speeches ready for the upcoming festival to celebrate the signing of the sister-city contract. I was there to coach them. Anyone who didn't feel capable of writing a speech, but who still wanted to participate—children in particular—could recite a poem. That was a month ago. Every week I ask who wants to practice their speech and no one volunteers. But they all come without fail. They are already in their seats when I arrive. There's a reason why I know everyone in this room. These are Shika's English hobbyists, the people who have sought me out.

"Do you like my plan?" the dentist asks, handing the ball to his brother.

"Hmm," the doctor says, "I think your plan is *chotto* . . . "

"In English," the dentist scolds him.

"I think your plan is 'a little' . . . "

"'A little' what?" I prod him.

"Just . . . 'a little' . . . ," he repeats, still smiling. In Japanese, you can say that something is *chotto* . . . without making a direct criticism. It's like Mad Libs. Your listener supplies the missing word. I tell him that this doesn't work in English. "Be direct," I remind him. "You could say, 'I think your plan is a little silly,' or explain why you think it won't work."

"Okay Taichi," he says, his smile blossoming into a grin. "I think it's a little impossible. I don't see how whitening farmer's tooth for free will lure patients to you."

"Simple, Yuji," the dentist says, rubbing his hands gleefully. "Rice farmer in search of bride will be on TV. Everyone will see his white tooth. It's so unusual for farmer. Everyone will wonder, how did this happen? It's amazing! Then they will seek my services too." He throws the tennis ball over his head, and Noriko catches it.

"How about whitening my tooth for wedding gift?" she asks him.

It wasn't until I started coaching SMILE that I realized that since there was only one dentist in town, Taichi Ishii had to be the man she was marrying. The local matchmaker, Sakura Ueno, also comes to SMILE, trailing after her daughter Ritsuko. During her self-introduction, when Sakura announced, "My hobby is making marriage," the dentist cleared his throat and said, "I think hobby means for fun, *ne*? Not for profit . . ." Sakura responded, "It's hobby because I enjoy." I assumed that everyone in the room knew that she had brought the librarian and the dentist together, but no one mentioned it. And Noriko and Taichi never sit next to each other, even though they're engaged to be married next month.

"I don't think so," the dentist says to his fiancée.

"Why not?" Noriko asks.

"You won't be on TV," he says. "Also, your teeth are white enough. But maybe you could use . . . how to say . . . like a railroad track? To make straighter?"

"Braces," I offer.

"I like your teeth the way they are," Joe says, and Noriko covers her mouth, hiding a smile or a frown. Joe is seated between Noriko and Ritsuko, his arms draped across the backs of their seats. "I've missed you lot," he says. "I can't remember the last time I was in Shika."

"Eight weeks ago," says Ritsuko.

"You remember so well . . . ," Noriko says.

"He stayed at our home," Sakura says. "I made tempura. His favorite."

I remember Joe's last visit too, since it coincided with Valentine's Day. I had just returned from the elementary school and he was bumming around Shika that week. He attended all of our secretarial classes, and in each one Miyoshi-sensei asked the girls to write him valentines. In the *New Horizons* textbook, Yumi, Ken, and Pablo were all writing persuasive letters to their local papers, urging people not to litter so that the earth wouldn't turn into a trashscape. The chapter stressed the idea that persuasive language is specific. "Probably you love Mister Joe so much," Miyoshi-sensei told our classes. "It's easy to find reasons why you love him. But why should he love you? Be specific, and persuade him to choose you!"

At the end of each class, Joe chose his favorite valentine to read aloud and the girls guessed who had written it. I remember quite clearly the valentine that won first place in the freshman secretarial homeroom. "You are cool boy," Joe read. "I don't want to be near you. It's only close. I don't want to be with you. It's not close enough. I want to be you." He turned the card over but didn't speak. He looked distinctly uncomfortable. I took the card from him. On the back was written, "Ogawa, Haruki," in pencil letters so faint I could barely make them out. For a moment I hesitated too, not wanting to reward the boy who trapped our cat in the refrigerator. But as I looked at him hunkered down in his chair, willing me not to call his name, I realized that ignoring him was exactly what he wanted. So I picked up the heart-shaped box of chocolates we'd decided to give as a prize, which had come in a care package from my mom, and I held it over his head. "Good job, Haruki!" I said. "You really love Mister Joe!" Joe told me to knock it off, to stop "recruiting for the team," obviously mortified.

"I want to talk about homophobia," I say.

"Homosexuals?" asks the doctor.

"Homophobia," I repeat. "The prejudice against homosexuals."

"Oh bollocks," Joe says. "Here we go . . ."

"We often use SMILE to talk about cultural differences," I inform him. "That's what it's for." Actually, that is not what SMILE is for. But I love having the chance to find out what people here really think about difficult subjects, urging them to be direct, to speak from their hearts. "Yesterday, a boy in the technical class called Miyoshi-sensei a homo," I begin.

"Miyoshi-sensei is a homo?" Noriko asks.

"No," I say. "I mean, I don't know about Miyoshi-sensei's personal life."

"He is not married . . ." the dentist says.

"Neither am I," I say.

"It's true," Sakura says. "You are not married . . ."

"That's not the point," I say. "Why is being gay considered bad?"

"Because of AIDS," says Yuji Ishii.

"AIDS isn't just a homosexual disease," I say. "You're a doctor. You know that."

"Of course," he says, "but in 1985, first case of AIDS in Japan was a homosexual man. It's documented fact. Not . . . homophobia. After that, many people believed only homosexuals could spread AIDS."

"That's terrible," I say.

"It's crisis," he agrees. "Men won't use condom. They don't want to seem *ayashii*."

"Perverted," I translate.

"Gay," he says.

"Don't kids learn the truth in sex-ed?"

"Sexed," Fumiya repeats, turning it into one word and then laughing, wriggling in his seat as Keiko tries unsuccessfully to calm him down. Fumiya has an almost uncanny gift for latching on to the most inappropriate words, which doesn't really matter since he can't understand a thing he says. I'm not sure why Keiko brings the boys to SMILE. The conversations are over their heads and she has to spend most of her time taking care of them. She probably can't get a babysitter.

"What is sex-ed?" Yuji Ishii asks. As usual, he doesn't even look over his shoulder, as if the woman behind him weren't his wife and the boys weren't his sons, or as if not seeing the problem meant he didn't have to help.

"Sexual education," I say. "Every student in America has to take it."

"You need class to learn how to have sex?" asks Sakura. "Isn't it . . . organic-u?" I suspect she's yanking my chain. She loves to play the provocateur, the cat to everyone else's mouse. She is a flirt and a tease and a constant embarrassment to her daughter, batting her eyelashes and twirling her long hair around her heavily jeweled finger and asking questions just to get people to say outrageous things.

"Sex-ed teaches kids how to avoid getting pregnant or catching diseases."

"But how?" she asks.

"Well," I say, thinking back, "in my sex-ed class, we learned about different kinds of birth control and how to use them. We practiced putting condoms on bananas."

"*Ayashii,*" she says.

"It's not perverted," I say. "The point is to show kids that sex is normal, not something to be ashamed of, so they'll make smart choices and stay safe."

"In another prefecture," Doctor Ishii says, "some teachers tried to teach sex-ed using anatomically correct dolls. But many parents protested. They say sex is private, not suitable subject for school. We shouldn't talk about it so directly."

This strikes me as absurd in a place where condoms and dildos and boxed sets of panties (allegedly worn by the pubescent girls pictured on the boxes) are sold in vending machines alongside soda and tea, beer and cigarettes. Then again, maybe the whole point of the condom and sex toy vending machine is anonymity, to spare the customer that humiliating moment at the counter. Solutions here are often chillingly pragmatic. Recently the police broke up a high school prostitution ring. Teenaged girls were performing services for middle-aged men, who'd call their cell phones to arrange meetings at love hotels. The solution? Ban cell phones for female students.

"If guys won't use condoms then why isn't there more teen pregnancy?" I ask, realizing that I've never seen a pregnant girl here.

"There is," Yuji says. "Japan has high rate of pregnancy termination."

"Abortion?" I say. "Are they easy to get?"

"*Hai*," he says. "I mean, yes."

Ritsuko stands up and pulls up the hood of her coat, which she never took off. She apologizes for leaving early, explaining that she doesn't feel well. As her mother starts to put on her coat too, Ritsuko tells her that she wants to walk.

"But it's raining," Sakura says.

"*Daijoubu*," Ritsuko says. I'll be fine.

"I can give her a ride," Joe offers, already standing up.

"No," Ritsuko says. "I don't want to be a bother."

"It's no bother," Joe says, rushing to open the door for her. She hesitates, then steps through, out into the night. As it closes behind them, I ask who wants to practice their English speeches. No one raises a hand. "Don't be shy," I say, as they all avoid my eyes and shift in their seats. "Yuji?" I say. "*Eh* . . . " The doctor stalls. "I am so busy with so many patients . . . "

"So many patients," the dentist echoes.

"Keiko?" I try. "Why don't you make a speech?"

"English is not useful in my life," she says, looking right at me.

"I'm sorry," I say.

"My wife is upset because she can't come to New York," Yuji says. "It's not a vacation, *ne*?"

"So I guess you won't take golf clubs?" she asks.

"*Chotto . . .* " he begins, "I mean, you're being a little . . . "

"A little what?" she digs. "A little disappointed? A little fed up?" Listening to her vent, I believe I understand why these people come to SMILE. They don't need much urging to be direct.

I remind the group that they don't have to write an original speech. They can recite a poem or the lyrics of a song. I tell them to stop by my house any evening this week if they want to practice with me in private. "It won't be a contest if no one competes," I say. It will be a disaster.

Sakura gives me a ride home, so I get back a little early. Carolyn obviously didn't expect me. She is lying on the futons in our bedroom; she is naked and she is touching herself. I freeze with my hand on the doorknob as she freezes with her hand between her legs. She fumbles for the covers while I go to the window, open it wide and stick my head out, feeling like a dog in a car, wishing I were on my way somewhere else, anywhere but here. For the first time, I can smell spring in the air. For the first time in ages, I can smell the sex in our bedroom. Lately, whenever I reach for Carolyn, she says that she's frozen, that she can't feel anything, there must be something wrong with her. I always end up reassuring her that there's nothing wrong with her, that lulls are normal in any relationship, that she'll thaw. And I guess there is nothing wrong with her after all.

"I should have knocked," I say. "Sorry."

"You're mad," she says, joining me at the window, cocooned in blankets. "Don't be upset. It's not about you."

"Obviously," I say.

We both face the street, neither of us speaking for a while.

There were three futons in the closet when we first moved in. At first we slept with them in a stack, our limbs intertwined, anchoring each other on that narrow raft. Then we started placing two of them side by side with the third in the middle, a cushioned hump that allowed us to be close but sprawl a little. Lately, however, Carolyn has started moving the third futon back and forth, transferring it between the other two, which are separated by a widening gap on the *tatami*. She's so fair it's almost stingy. One night she gets the extra padding. The next, I come upstairs and find that I'm the lucky one.

"If you're not attracted to me anymore, I wish you'd just admit it," I say.

"Are you still attracted to me?" she says. "Because it really doesn't seem like it."

"Don't turn this around," I say. "At least I'm still trying."

"But that's what it feels like," she says, her voice cracking. "Like I'm homework, something to check off in a to-do list. It's not sexy."

"So this is my fault too?" I say.

"Just answer my question, and be honest for once. Don't say what you think I want to hear. Are you still attracted to me?"

"No," I say. The word is out before I can think about it, the verbal equivalent of a door slamming. "Not lately," I add, slipping my foot in the door. "But that doesn't mean—"

"Just stop," she cuts me off. "You want this to be over too, but you don't want to be the one to call it quits. You want it to be my fault. That's why you keep pushing me to say that we're breaking up." She takes my hand. "It's no one's fault. Relationships change. Most of them end. Maybe we should just feel good that we made it this long."

Her words are harsh but her tone is gentle, and part of me knows that she's right. That part of me wants to soften. It would be a relief to stop fighting, to give up. To give in. But her fingers are sticky and I pull away. When I climbed the stairs to our bedroom, my heart didn't pound in anticipation. When I saw her masturbating, I didn't feel turned on. I can't remember the last time I felt that tug in my belly, the insistent tug of desire. No—I'm lying. It was the night I kissed Miyoshi-sensei.

"My supervisor has a spare room," she says. "She offered to let me live there for the rest of the year. I think I'd like that, being part of the community where I'm teaching. She wouldn't charge me anything, so I could keep paying my half of the rent here."

"Great," I say. "It sounds like everything's all worked out. Nice timing."

I'm turning twenty-three this week. If Carolyn remembers that my birthday is coming up, she hasn't mentioned it.

"I've been waiting for months," she says. "She offered to let me move in after I told her that Haruki killed our cat. You have no idea how hard it's been for me to have to see him every day. I know you weren't as upset as I was, but—"

"Stop telling me how I feel!" I explode. "You think you know everything, but you don't. I killed the cat."

"What are you talking about?" she says, smiling uncertainly. "No you didn't."

"The day before she died, I brought home flowers and she ate them and got sick."

"That was the night she didn't come home," Carolyn says. "You said not to worry. You told me she'd be home when she got hungry."

"Because," I say, "something was wrong, and it was my fault, and I didn't want you to know."

Nakajima's cell phone starts to ring from my pocket. *I heard he sang a sweet song* . . . I push what looks like the Off button, but this just makes it ring louder so I take it downstairs and into the storage area, glad to leave the bedroom, this discussion, Carolyn and her narrow, accusatory eyes. I shove the phone into a box, slam the door behind me and curl up on the cockroach couch.

CHAPTER EIGHTEEN

samishii: (ADJ.) *lonely; solitary; desolate*

During first period, I stand at the faculty room windows and watch the freshman secretarial girls swim laps in the newly filled pool. They look like synchronized swimmers in their matching pink bathing suits and caps, kicking and lifting their arms in unison. Only Haruki Ogawa is not among his classmates. When he claimed that his swimming trunks had "vanished" from his locker, Miyoshi-sensei asked me to supervise him in the faculty room during my free period. Now he is sitting at Miyoshi-sensei's desk, doing the same nothing he always does: just taking up space.

"Why did you kill our cat?" I ask, standing over him with a cup of hot tea. I don't know if he understands or not. His face remains as inexpressive as a pudding, his hands lumps of dough. I imagine these hands scooping up our cat, thrusting her into the fridge and slamming the door. I imagine him pressing his bulk against the door, listening to her cries get fainter and then stop. Up close, his body emits a sour, moldy smell, like laundry that has been left in wet piles. I've seen the technical boys following him around, flapping their hands in the air and saying, *kusou*, "you reek." He really does.

Recently, another Japanese *hikikomori* or "shut-in" made the papers after a young girl he kidnapped escaped from his room. She was seven when she was kidnapped, seventeen when she escaped. For ten years he kept her hostage in the house he shared with his mother, who claims never to have known that this child was under her roof, sharing the meals she left outside her son's bedroom door. The girl wasn't interviewed, to protect her confidentiality, but I wish I knew her side of the story, why it took her so long to run, and what it's like to come back to life now, if it's possible. Haruki spent four years shut in his room. He might be able to answer this question. But he's not speaking. At least not to me.

Once again, the technical boys are wearing only their underpants when I enter their portable classroom. But today Miyoshi-sensei is not standing with his back to the room. He is sitting in the desk next to Nakajima, his head on his arms, apparently napping. I apologize for being late, explaining that there was a line for the photocopier.

"It's okay," he says, sitting up, but not getting up.

"I made a worksheet," I say. "Should we hand it out?"

"If you'd like," he says with a shrug.

When the stack of worksheets reaches his desk, he takes one as if he were a student. He's acting like them too, aloof and disinterested, though for once they are looking at him, waiting to see what he'll do—or fail to do—next.

"You are almost finished with high school," I say, standing alone at the front of the room, holding up a worksheet that Carolyn decorated with drawings of people at work: a woman in a white jacket with a stethoscope; a boy in a McDonald's uniform holding a box of fries; a guy waving a conductor's baton. I explain to the students that they should each circle a hobby, then follow a line to its logical career. "I like making bread," I say, following a line with my finger, "so in the future I will become a . . . baker." The boys stare blankly. "I like playing guitar, so in the future I will become a . . . rock star." I ask if there are any questions. No one raises a hand. Miyoshi-sensei pulls a rice ball from his pocket and unwraps it. The sound of crinkling cellophane fills the room, along with a vinegared whiff of pickled plum.

"Can you please translate what I just said?" I ask him.

"Sorry but I was not listening." While I repeat myself, he finishes his snack, removes the plum pit from his mouth and examines its glistening strands, then wipes his hands on his pants, making the boys laugh.

"What's the matter with you?" I say.

"Nothing?"

"Then why won't you translate?"

"Because it is not realistic," he says with a sigh.

"You mean it's too hard for them? I can simplify the sentences."

"Sentences are not problem," he says. "Problem is, these boys could not become architect or symphony conductor. These are dream jobs for best students from top universities. Not for technical students of Shika High School." He uncaps a bottle of Coke and sucks the tan foam that spurts from its mouth. "Maybe one or two who are very lucky will get jobs at Shika's nuclear power station. Most will work at gasoline stand or convenience store. I'm sorry but it's fact."

I scan the room, wondering if the boys understood his grim prediction, if they're resigned to these dead-end futures or pissed off. I notice that one kid has vertical stripes shaved into eyebrows and rubber plugs stretching out both earlobes. Another has somehow managed to bleach just the roots of his spiky hair, so he looks like a porcupine. Then there's Nakajima, whose Afro-perm, growing out, resembles an exploding mushroom cloud. "Just ask what they like to do for fun," I say, inspired by an idea of what might reach them. "If they say they like to style their hair, that's great. They can be hairdressers!" Miyoshi-sensei finally translates the question into Japanese. In response, Nakajima mutters something that makes the boys around him hoot.

"What did he say?" I ask.

"Blow job."

"What?"

"It's Nakajima-san's hobby." He shrugs again. "It's fun for him."

Back in the faculty room, Miyoshi-sensei flips through the worksheets while I stand beside him. "They all wrote blow job!" he exclaims. "Every one!" In fact, they all filled in the worksheet the exact same way: I like <u>BLOW JOB</u>, so I will become a <u>GIGOLO</u> when I grow up. Gigolo was my contribution. I couldn't think of another career to go with that particular hobby. The boys found the notion of a male prostitute hilarious. "Great job!" they kept saying. "I want!"

"Well," I say, "since that was the only thing you wrote on the board . . ."

"No," he says, "I mean, I can't believe they all wrote! I didn't know some of these boys could make alphabet shapes. But look! It's good English, *ne?*" He glances around before opening the bottom drawer of his desk, which is slung with files. "I think I have something that could be quite useful for you," he says, riffling through the drawer. From the back he pulls out a cardboard tube, uncaps it, and slides out a roll of posters, smoothing them on his desk. At first I think he's showing me his stash of porn as I take in a poster showing a naked white man leaning into a naked black man's arms. Both look like they were cast from the same Chippendale mold, their hairless torsos glistening. *I thought you loved me enough to tell me everything* reads the caption. The next poster shows a woman lying with her head on another woman's lap. *With you, I thought I was safe*. In the final poster, an Asian woman straddles a John Lennon look-alike, offering him a condom. *Avoid risky behavior!*

"Do you recognize?" Miyoshi-sensei says.

"It's what you told me after the *enkai*."

"No," he says, blushing. "I mean posters. I got them on my first trip to California. I was exchange student in Eureka. I rescued them from high school trash bin. I couldn't understand my eyes." As teachers start to fill the faculty room, he slides the posters back into their tube and hands it to me. "How about using these to teach sex-ed?" he asks in a quiet voice.

"Are you serious?"

"It was your idea," he says. "You told SMILE club that Japanese students should learn sex-ed in school."

"Who told you that?"

"Yuji Ishii," he says. "He has only medical practice of Shika, so he sees patients with all kinds of condition, including STD or unwelcome pregnancy. He thinks sex-ed would benefit Shika's students too. Especially technical boys. But how can we hook students' attention without hooking parents' attention?"

"I don't know," I say, because he seems to be waiting for an answer.

"By teaching in English," he replies with a grin. "Maybe we found the one subject to interest these boys!"

"But they won't understand a word," I protest.

"Neither will parents," he says. "It's good idea, *ne*?"

"I don't know," I stall. "What if we got caught?"

"Be sure to include a grammar point in your worksheet," he says. "So it looks like English lesson and not sex-ed."

"What kind of grammar point?"

"How about prepositions," he says. "In, out, next to . . . But make it sexy." He laughs when I say that the whole point of sex-ed is usually to make sex seem unpleasant, so that kids won't want to have it without protection. "Technical students are eighteen," he says. "They know well, sex is not unpleasant." He bites his lip and again I find myself staring at his mouth, remembering the feel of it. He riffles through his drawer, handing me one last "curiosity object," an English pamphlet describing every conceivable sexual act, beginning with *frottage* and ending with *anal penetration*. I imagine standing at the front of the room, asking the boys to repeat the word "Rimming!" after me.

Then he hands me a piece of paper covered in his cursive.

Dear Miss Marina,

How are you? I'm kind of tired. As you suggested, I brainstormed about times in my life when English was useful. During this storm, here are some memories that fell like rain from my brain.

First I remembered going to school as small boy and hearing English for the first time.

When I was small boy, every day my mother went to work at the bank, my father went to work at Shika's Town Hall, my older sister went to school, and I stayed home with my grandparents. Every day was like every other day. Time flowed like a river. I would make a picture or play in the garden or go to pick mushroom or wild mountain yam with my grandmother. Often my mother said, "Hiroshi wa samishii desune . . ." I knew "samishii" means "lonesome," but I did not feel it. Still, when she said, "Soon you will go to school and make good friends," I felt excitement. Before first day of school, my mother taught me to shout, "HAI!" after teacher called my name, and "GENKI!" for how are you. I was worried to do it correctly, and I practiced so much. I did not realize that I couldn't really make a mistake. If I made a mistake, no one would notice. All children shouted together. My voice became erased. For first time ever, I felt lonesome. I wondered if other children felt the same. They seemed GENKI, but maybe they were also hiding behind the group. One day we had a visit from an English teacher. He was a Japanese. This was before so many English teachers became imported. It was kind of confusing. This man's face was like ours, but he made funny sounds. He taught us to say, "This is a pen." Another children felt foolish, but I didn't mind. It was relief to hear my own voice again. He said I spoke very well. I experienced pride, but also something else. I realized that I was different. This was first time I used English, but I don't think it shows how English is useful in my life.

Next I thought about attending high school class trip to Fuji-san. Of course Fuji-san is Japan's mountain, but this was the first time I used English with a native speaker.

Before bus departed, all teachers said, "Make a memory!" and "Take a picture so you couldn't forget anything!" and "Have the trip of a lifetime!" Bus drove all night, and I didn't sleep after another boy took my pillow as a joke. Finally morning arrived. There was Fuji-san, poking through clouds. (Should I say "between"? What is correct preposition for position of mountain in sky?) After many long hours hiking to tip of Fuji-san, we all agreed we had a "wafu." This means a Japanese wind blowing in our spirits. Really I was "winded."

Naturally, everyone wanted to take group picture. Italians enjoy eating spaghetti. French enjoy making love. Japanese enjoy posing in front of some monument or scenic wonder. Rule for group picture is: whole group must be there. Usually there is some tree or garbage can to put a camera on, or someone from outside group to perform this favor. But Fuji-san's tip was bald, and only other tourist was foreign girl. She had golden hair and pale eyes like you.

"Hiroshi," one boy said to me, "You take our group picture." Teacher agrees: this is good solution. There were twenty students in

our class, and twenty cameras, so I became busy. Then the pale eyed
girl suddenly appeared in my frame.

"Excuse me," she said.

"That's okay," I said. It was first time I used English with native
speaker, so of course I felt nervous, but also excited. I loved English
class, even if we only said, "This is a pen. Is that a pen? It is a pen!"

"Do you want me to take picture for you?" she asked.

"That's okay," I said again.

"But you aren't going to be in it," she said.

"That's okay," I said again. Then I worried she thought I couldn't
understand because I said the same thing every time. So I joked,
"Maybe I am not handsome boy. So they don't want me in picture."
She laughed and said, "You are too cute. You make them look bad."
And I felt great. I could share English joke! Other students couldn't
understand, so I laughed harder to make them jealous of me.

On return bus ride to Shika, all classmates agreed: "That was
the trip of a lifetime!" Over and over they said those words. Also, "We
made so many memories. We will never forget this trip!" I thought,
trip of a lifetime? Memories of Fuji-san? Sorry but I wanted to see
more than Japan's mountain. I wanted to travel the world. So I went
to university and studied English, etc . . . Then I returned to Shika
to take this teaching job. Maybe my father influenced the board of
education to hire me. It's good job. I know I should be grateful. But
sometimes I feel confusion. English should be my passport. Why am
I still here?

Of course I have taken many trips. On my trips, I always take
many pictures. But I travel alone. This is why my photo albums
are full of school bathroom or cafeteria trays. Using English, I
could ask another person to take my picture. But I guess I am too
Japanese after all. I still think photo should show a group, or friends
laughing, or lovers holding hands.

Again, I don't think this proves usefulness of English in my life.

Finally, I thought about how English is useful when I sing karaoke. I should begin by saying that singing is not truly my "hobby." "Hobby" means for fun I think. But karaoke is how I speak my truth. If I use speaking voice to say to someone, "I am lonesome," especially if I say in Japanese, they will find me kind of pathetic and probably run away. In any case, I would never say this. But if I sing, "I feel so all alone," in style of Elvis Presley, maybe they will not run away. Maybe they will come closer, to enjoy great song, and lonesome feeling will go away.

Problem is, life is not karaoke booth. This strategy does not work in real world. So even if singing English songs at karaoke is my passion, it's not really useful.

Now you can see why I could not make this speech. Thank you for listening to me.

That's all.

See you,
Hiro

"I love it," I say, and I mean it.

"It's too dark," he says.

"It's honest and open."

"Too honest and open. If I made this speech, I would feel kind of naked. I could only share such private thoughts with you."

The other teachers are returning from their classes to the faculty room and I can feel them looking at us, wondering what we're up to, huddled together like this.

"You found these sex-ed posters at a high school in Eureka?" I ask, and he nods. "The town this American mayor just happens to come from?"

"My host-sister is married to the mayor. It's how I could invite them."

"So why don't you write about what it was like to live in an American family."

"But she was there," he says. "Maybe it's boring for her to hear stories she knows."

"No way," I say. "She'll love to hear your memories of that summer. And I'm sure your English was useful to you then."

"Okay," he says. "I will try once more. But this becomes final attempt."

kirei: (ADJ.) *beautiful; lovely; clean; tidy*

This morning when I wake up Carolyn is in the kitchen, standing over a pot of boiling water, wearing boxer shorts and a gray T-shirt with the sleeves cut off, her skin flushed and damp. I watch her use chopsticks to pull steaming rings of dough from the pot and deposit them on the toaster oven tray.

"Hey," she says, startling at the sight of me in the door frame. "Happy birthday."

"You remembered," I say. "Thank you."

"Of course," she says. "You only turn twenty-three once."

She reaches out to tuck a strand of hair behind my ear, then kisses the corner of my mouth, a compromise between lips and cheek. We haven't talked about our fight, or the fact that I've been sleeping on the couch downstairs.

"I can't believe you made bagels," I say. "My favorite breakfast."

"They're no H&H," she says.

"They look amazing. You really didn't have to go to so much trouble."

"I know," she says. "I wanted to. It's your birthday."

I feel a pang of sadness, remembering that we had an exchange almost identical to this one on the first night that we slept together. Every ending is written in its beginning, but you can't see it until you look back.

"I wish it wasn't my birthday," I say. "Twenty-three is such a nothing number."

"At least you've got two years before you become a Christmas cake."

For some reason, lovers in Japan get together to eat sponge cake on Christmas Eve. These sponge cakes go half off on December 25, when no one wants them anymore. At twenty-five, an unmarried woman is referred to as a Christmas cake.

We set the coffee table in the living room with a makeshift tablecloth and Carolyn carries in a platter of bagels and cream cheese. I thank her again as she hands me a mug of coffee, the milk whisked to a froth so it looks like a cappuccino. She sits across from me on the floor and watches while I cut a bagel in half, spread it with cream cheese and take a bite.

"It's really good," I say. "Aren't you eating?"

"I'm not hungry," she says. "I couldn't stop picking."

She tells me to open my present, handing me a large flat object wrapped in the front page of the *Daily Yomiuri*. I peel the tape back carefully from the newspaper, unwrapping a book with a green Lucite cover and rice paper pages. "Did you make this?" I ask and she nods. "It's beautiful." On the first page, she has written the word *mukou*—abroad, the other side—over a drawing of our house. On the next page is a drawing of Amana, lying with her chin tucked between her paws. I turn this page fast, swallowing hard. On the third page she has glued the photograph of our digital daughter, half her, half me, posed between us on a park bench, looking so much like a real child that it hurts. There's nothing else after this, just page after blank page.

"Thanks," I say.

"I didn't get lazy," she says. "I left the rest for you to fill."

"With what?" I ask.

"Photos, drawings, whatever you want. It's a scrapbook. I know you like to get rid of things, but this way you have a place for your memories."

"I can't imagine my life here without you," I say.

"I know," she says. "Me neither."

AVOID RISKY BEHAVIOR!

Fill in each sentence with a preposition from the following list:
around, inside, next to, against, with

    Then decide if you SHOULD or SHOULDN'T do this (if it's safe, or risky)

---

1. "I want to lie down _____ you."   You should/shouldn't do this.

2. "I want to wrap my arms _____ you."   You should/shouldn't do this.

3. "I want to press my lips _____ your lips."   You should/shouldn't do this.

4. "I want to have unprotected sex _____ you."
   You should/shouldn't do this.

5. "I want to come _____ you."   You should/shouldn't do this.

The secretarial students don't seem shocked by my "Risky Behavior" worksheet, which has no illustrations decorating its borders, nothing to give its content away. I was surprised when Miyoshi-sensei suggested that we try the sex-ed lesson on them before giving it to the boys. "I want to see if they can catch the meaning," he said. The first three girls manage to answer the questions correctly with no translation assistance. I read the fourth question and he calls on Ritsuko Ueno.

"I want to have unprotected sex . . . you," she says.

"Can you fill in the blank?" I ask, but she only shrugs. "With," I say. "I want to have unprotected sex *with* you."

"Okay," she says flatly.

"Do you understand the word 'unprotected'?" I ask, and no one answers. I look to Miyoshi-sensei for help, but he is squinting at the worksheet again. I ask if they remember the lesson in *New Horizons*, when Yumi, Ken, and Paolo had "to protect" the earth from litter. They nod and I say, "So what does 'to protect' mean?"

"To keep safe," replies Haruki in his raspy whisper.

"That's right," I say. "Good job!" My praise has the effect of a finger poking a snail. His chin folds into his neck and his shoulders hunch around his ears. "What's the opposite of protected?"

"Basshimasu," he mutters.

"I'm sorry," I say. "I don't understand that word."

"To punish," Miyoshi-sensei translates.

"Hmm . . . " I stall. "That's an interesting guess, but the word I was looking for was *unsafe*. Unprotected sex is unsafe." I write this on the board and then I read the final question, "I want to come . . . you."

"I am confused," Miyoshi-sensei says. "I think correct answer is, 'I want to come *with* you.' But you wrote that correct answer is, 'I want to come *inside* you.'"

"Both sentences work grammatically," I say.

"But meaning is different?"

"Sort of." I hope he won't press for clarification.

"Prepositions are so difficult," he says. "I want to come near you. I want to come next to you. I want to come beside you. I want to come close to you. . . . To me, it's so many ways to say the same thing. Can you hear something I don't?"

What I can hear, for the first time, is the way these little words—words distinguishing the relationship between one thing and another, one person and another—also keep them apart. No matter how close you get, you are still separate, still stuck in your own skin.

Carolyn and I are at Sakura Ueno's home. She is dressing us up in kimonos to wear to the festival to welcome the mayor from California. Before we got here, she laid her entire collection on the floor of an otherwise empty room at the back of her house. The tatami was covered in a patchwork of folded silk in every hue and pattern imaginable.

Through the sliding glass doors at the back of the room, a cherry tree is in full bloom. The blossoms look like popcorn against the branches, which have no leaves yet. It's the first blossoming cherry tree that I've seen in Japan.

"*Totemo kiree desu*," I say to Sakura. It's so beautiful. In Japanese, she explains that her tree blooms early because it's in the courtyard, protected from the elements.

"It's not time yet," she says. "The flowers will fall fast."

She tells me to undress and then she walks in a tight circle around me, taking the measure of my curves, no doubt figuring out how to say—in the politest way possible—that none of her kimonos will fit my Western body. But finally she picks up a white cotton kimono that hits me mid-shin. I'm disappointed by the plainness of her choice, but it turns out that this is just kimono underwear. Over it she layers a coral kimono covered in giant purple morning glories that look like old-fashioned phonograph heads. The sleeves hang like pillowcases, so long that they almost brush the tatami.

"Furisode," she tells me these sleeves are called. "Like a butterfly wing. Only unmarried girl wears this style. It means you're available." She stands behind me and pulls the kimono tight around my body, folding the cloth at the waist so that the hem just grazes the tops of my feet. She loops a cord around my rib cage, so tight that I feel like I'm being squeezed by a boa constrictor. Over this cord she wraps an obi covered in psychedelic swirls of purple, green, blue, and gold, slipping a foam bustle into the back.

"Kiree desune?" Sakura says to Carolyn.

"Beautiful," Carolyn agrees. "But the obi doesn't match the kimono."

"That's right," Sakura says in Japanese, explaining that the obi and the kimono shouldn't match perfectly, that a too close match is boring, that some difference creates interest. I wonder if this is the same formula she uses when she matches two people. For Carolyn she chooses a pale blue kimono with a cherry blossom print, the center of each flower dusted with gold pollen. Then we stand side by side in front of the mirror, taking in our transformed selves. "You look so Japanese," Sakura says, but this is not true. We look more Western than ever, the way a man in drag can look like more of a man through the makeup and the gown. But the kimonos have erased the nip of our waists, flattened our breasts, given us new silhouettes, and Carolyn likes the effect. I can tell. Sakura calls to her daughter, asking her to come and see, and a minute later Ritsuko appears in the hallway, dressed in pajamas and frog slippers, her face puffy.

"Daijoubu Ri-chan?" Sakura asks her.

"I'm fine," she says in English.

"Kiree desune?" she prompts her too.

"So beautiful," Ritsuko says, barely glancing at us.

"Shall we all have some tea?" her mother suggests.

"I have homework," the girl answers. "Sorry." She shuffles back to her room and Sakura frowns. "I don't know what's wrong with her," she says softly. "Lately she's so moody." She shrugs and returns her attention to us. "At the festival," she tells me in Japanese, "you will have to wear this kimono all day. You should practice walking and sitting in it." I nod, turning around so that she can unwrap my obi. Instead she suggests that we take a trip to the supermarket, as a kind of dress rehearsal.

"Right now?" I ask. In the mirror, Carolyn and I lock eyes. She looks frankly horrified, silently pleading with me to get us out of this. But Sakura is already squatting at our feet, dressing us in ankle socks and wooden-soled slippers, telling us how much fun it will be, how everyone should see how beautiful we look. Not knowing what else to do, we follow her down the hall to the front door. I'm glad when she drives away without waiting to make sure that we follow. It's hard to climb into a car window wearing a kimono.

Slung across the front doors to Jade Plaza, a sign reads, Supa Singuru Naito!—Supermarket Singles' Night. Inside the front doors, the two farmers sit on folding chairs in front of a table covered in a pyramid display of burlap bags, each one stamped with the promise that the rice was grown locally, perhaps by these very guys. Next to them stands Lone Wolf, dressed in a three-piece suit of contrasting plaids seamed with safety pins. As we walk in, his cameraman captures our entrance on film, the red light blinking.

"You need rice," Sakura says, steering a cart toward their display.

She applied lipstick in the car and styled her hair in a French twist. She is camera ready.

"We have rice at home," I say. "Lots of it."

"You can always use more," she chirps. "It's my present."

"What's going on?" Carolyn whispers.

"I don't know," I say, although I can guess. Sakura is the town matchmaker. Tonight is Supermarket Singles' Night, a chance for these farmers to meet eligible girls. Maybe that's why she dolled us up in kimonos: to try to make us seem more familiar, less intimidating to these two hayseeds. Rice seeds. If so, her plan seems to be failing miserably. At the sight of us, they trade looks that I recognize from my most reluctant English pupils. One doesn't hand me a bag of rice so much as shove it at me.

"*Arigato*," I say.

"No English," he replies, crossing his forearms in a big X.

Sakura takes the rice from me and places it in a grocery basket, then leads us away from the two farmers. Maybe I was wrong in my suspicions, I think as we begin shopping for the ingredients to make sukiyaki. Everyone is staring at us. They seem bemused, but also oddly approving. An old woman strokes my sleeve as I pass and whispers, "*kiree*." Men nod and children grin. Lone Wolf and his crew continue to trail after us, filming everything as she picks out a tray of meat sliced ribbon thin, a basket of mushrooms and another of sugar snap peas, bottles of sake and soy sauce and dashi, and a bag of sugar. At the checkout counter, Sakura insists on paying for the groceries, a birthday present to me.

"Thanks," I say. "How did you know it was my birthday?"

"Miyoshi-sensei told me," she says, beaming. "Let's enjoy birthday donuts together, okay?"

"Okay," I say with a shrug.

As soon as we enter Mister Donuts, I see Joe sitting at a booth across from a black-haired man whose back is to us. Two coffees and a plate of crullers sit on the table between them, alongside an ashtray in which a cigarette is burning unattended, sending a finger of smoke into the fluorescent light. When Sakura stops by their table and clears her throat, Joe looks up and presses a fist to his mouth. The man across from him turns and startles. Sakura places her hand on my back, gently pushing me onto the seat next to Miyoshi-sensei. Carolyn sits next to Joe.

"What's this?" Joe says. "Is there some costume party I wasn't invited to?"

"You are invited," Sakura says brightly. "Tonight Miss Marina will make sukiyaki."

"*This* is why you wanted us to meet you here?" Miyoshi-sensei says to Sakura in Japanese. "You said you had something you wanted to talk about in person. Something you couldn't discuss over the phone, that it was too important."

"I wanted to surprise you," Sakura says.

Miyoshi-sensei's body is stiff next to mine. His hand shakes as he reaches for his cigarette, then reconsiders and puts it back in the ashtray.

"I don't get it," Carolyn says.

But I do. I was right about the setup, just not about who we'd been set up with.

"So," Sakura says, "are you free tonight, Mister Joe?"

"Sure," Joe says. "I'd love to have dinner with the two of you."

"Three," Sakura corrects him.

"*Nani?*" Miyoshi-sensei says. What?

"Love connection!" Lone Wolf howls. I hadn't realized that he followed us in here too, along with his cameraman. He traces a heart in the air with his fingertip, then pretends to shoot a bow and arrow first at Miyoshi-sensei and then at me. He sits down next to me, shoving me up against Miyoshi-sensei. "So, Hiro-kun," he says, "you still like foreign girls, *ne*?" He wiggles an eyebrow and yowls, "mrow!"

"*Yamero*," Hiro mutters. Cut it out.

"Don't be so shy," Lone Wolf chides him. "It's not sexy."

Miyoshi-sensei peels the lid off a plastic thimble of cream. "Tonight is not so convenient for me, Miss Marina." He dumps the cream into his coffee, watching the undulating pattern unfold. "But I'm sorry to miss your birthday celebration."

"That's fine," I say. "Really, don't worry about it."

"*Kowai*?" Lone Wolf goads him. Are you scared? He reaches an arm behind me to muss Miyoshi-sensei's hair. Miyoshi-sensei slaps his hand away, then stands up abruptly. There is an awkward shuffle as both Lone Wolf and I stand up to let him out. "*Faito!*" Lone Wolf cries as Miyoshi-sensei strides across Mister Donuts, leaning forward, both hands deep in his pockets. "*Faito! Faito!*" In the ashtray, his unsmoked cigarette burns out, leaving behind a long column of ash that holds its shape for a second and then disintegrates.

While Joe and I sit on the *gokiburi* couch, Carolyn kneels on the floor and fills three Mickey Mouse beer steins with sake. We're both wearing the sheer white robes that went under our kimonos. As she leans forward, she exposes the swell of her breasts, the freckles smattered between them. I see Joe pry his eyes away.

"You swear you didn't know that was a setup?" I ask him once more.

"Give me a modicum of credit," he says. "I wouldn't try to come between the two of you. Not that I wouldn't enjoy doing just that." I roll my eyes, but I can't bring myself to really care about the innuendo, which he made almost dutifully, as if he had to play to our expectations. I wait for Carolyn to tell him that there is no "two of us" anymore, but she stays quiet, drinking her sake as if it was water and she was parched.

"Poor Hiro," Joe says as he pulls from his pocket a tin containing the first joint I've seen since leaving the States, fat and fragrant. Carolyn tells him that we can't smoke pot in the house, that the neighbors might smell it. This is just an excuse. She never wants to smoke pot. She says that it has no effect on her, that she hates the way it turns people into philosophers of the obvious. I used to enjoy it for that very reason. My boyfriend Luke and I got stoned all the time. I think of what she said in our fight, how I never lose control. When Joe suggests that we go to the beach and smoke the joint there, I jump at the chance.

It's foggy out, humid and pleasantly warm, a true spring night. Moonlight filters through the haze, casting its silvery glow across the sand. We all take off our shoes and walk to the edge of the water, letting the waves play over our toes. The water is no longer bone-chillingly cold. It holds the memory and promise of summer. Ahead of us a group of sandpipers runs to keep their distance, gathering in a huddle, each perching on one leg. Joe offers Carolyn the joint and she doesn't say no. She doesn't like to be the prude, the goody-goody. As he lights it for her, he stands closer than necessary, shielding her from a nonexistent wind. She barely inhales.

"You won't feel anything like that," Joe says. "Have you never smoked before?"

"Of course I have," she says. "Lots of times."

"You've got to do it like this," he says, sucking so hard that the rolling paper crackles and the cherry comets toward his fingers. He hands the joint back to her and she takes another shallow hit before thrusting it at me. I inhale deeply, enjoying the searing sensation at the back of my throat, the immediate light-headedness as I bend over, hacking. "That's more like it," Joe says, thumping my back. "If you don't cough, you won't get off." I try to give the joint back to Carolyn but she shakes her head. As we walk down the beach, chasing the sandpipers, Joe and I pass the joint back and forth, trailed by a pungent cloud of smoke.

"Why 'Poor Hiro'?" I say.

"What?" he says.

"You said 'Poor Hiro.' Like being set up with me would be so awful."

"That's not what I meant," he says. "It's just a lot of pressure, innit? Being the mayor's son, trying to live up to the legend. His dad was a local hero, bringing the plant to Shika, making jobs so that people had a reason to stay here. But now that there's a petition to shut it down and he's got cancer, no one knows how to treat him anymore. I think everyone's embarrassed. They wish he'd just disappear, which he will do soon enough."

"There's a petition to shut the plant down?" I ask, wondering how Joe knows so much more than I do when he doesn't even live here anymore. Then I remember that he stays with the Ueno family whenever he visits. He has never had to cook a meal for himself.

"Haven't you seen those women with the clipboards outside Mister Donuts?"

"I thought they were *gomi* police."

"Mothers against nuclear power. They've got a lot of local support and national attention. That's why it's so important to Hiro that this American mayor is coming to Shika, and why he asked Lone Wolf to come with his camera crew. He wants Shika to get on TV for something good, so that his father can be a hero one more time."

"That's sweet," I say.

"Do you really think his dad wanted to set the two of them up?" Carolyn asks, sounding deeply skeptical.

"He'd have to be pretty desperate," I say sarcastically.

"I only meant that you're not Japanese."

"But everyone knows how much Hiro likes you," Joe says.

"He does?" Carolyn and I both say at once.

"Sure," Joe shrugs. "But it's irrelevant, isn't it? He knows he doesn't stand a chance."

"What I want to know," I say, feeling the heat of Carolyn's stare even in the darkness, "is why Sakura wanted to set the two of you up."

"I guess she wants me out of the way," Joe says.

"Out of whose way?" Carolyn asks.

"Noriko's," I guess.

"The librarian?" Carolyn says. "I forgot you used to date."

"Very casually." Joe takes another drag of the joint, then passes it to Carolyn who only pretends to smoke before handing it to me. "Still, you're probably right," he says. "Sakura must be worried that I'll try to interfere, ruin her match with the dentist. I really should try to keep her from making the biggest mistake of her life."

"You're such a player," I tell him. "If Noriko wasn't getting married, you wouldn't even be thinking about her right now."

"What makes you such an expert on me?" he says.

"Because you're a typical guy," I say. "You only want what you can't have, and once you've got it you don't want it anymore."

"What do I have?" he says.

"Whatever you want," I say.

"You don't know everything," he says, suddenly dead serious in a way I've never heard him before. "You don't know the half of it."

"I know that when you sneeze, someone gets a Kleenex out to wipe your nose." I have actually seen Sakura Ueno do this. Joe closed his eyes like a little child and let her wipe his face. "When you make a mess, it's cute," I say. "When you throw a bag of trash in the wrong can, the whole town doesn't talk about it for months. You have no idea how easy you have it here, just because you're a guy."

"Maybe," he concedes. "But I didn't always have it so easy."

"Well then," I say, "if I were you then, I'd never leave Japan."

"I know," he says. "I'm not planning to."

"Really?" Carolyn stops walking. "Never?"

"Look," he says, "I'll spare you the sad story of my childhood, how when my parents split up, they fought over which one had to keep me, how most of the kids in the town where I grew up never make it to London for a weekend, let alone foreign shores. Let me just say that you don't know how hard it was to get out of there, how many people said I never would, or what I'm willing to do so I don't have to go back. I will go from school to school teaching English like a traveling salesman. I'll dress like a banana in a pudding ad and say 'yum yum' a thousand times if that pays the rent. I haven't got much, but I do want to keep what I've got. And I do know how good I have it here."

"Sorry," I say sheepishly, looking at Carolyn. She picks up a huge strand of kelp, holds the bulbous end and whips it against the sand. Joe offers her the joint and she refuses. "Why did you say that Hiro knows he doesn't stand a chance?" I ask Joe, at last, to change the subject and fill the silence.

"Because of you and Carolyn, of course."

"But he doesn't know about me and Carolyn."

"Well I'm sure he has his suspicions."

"Maybe, but the only way he could know for sure is if you told him."

"Roight . . . " Joe makes his sorry-looking face. "It's somewhat possible that I might conceivably have let the information slip a while back."

"You asshole!" I say. "I can't believe you did that!"

"I was only trying to spare him the humiliation of asking you out."

"What?" I say. "When?"

"Over the holidays. We went out for a cheery Christmas pint, and he asked, ever so casual like, whether you were available, if you had a '*raba.*' The way he put it, 'lover,' not 'boyfriend,' I figured he knew. But he seemed quite shocked when I told him about you and Caro. Shocked and a bit dejected."

"I can't believe you told him," I say again. I feel the water suck back under my feet, the wet sand sliding beneath me.

"I can't believe you care so much," Carolyn says. "Unless you like him and you're pissed that Joe ruined your chances."

"That's not the point," I say.

"Oh my God," she says. "You do like him. Well what's stopping you? You're a free woman. You can do whatever you want."

"What?" Joe says. "What do you mean?"

"There is no two of us anymore," I say. "We broke up."

"Oh," he says, after a moment. "I'm sorry." He actually does sound sorry, which for some reason makes me angry. I don't know why he gets to me, or why I always want to provoke him. It's like an itch where the more you scratch it the worse it gets. It's like he's every guy who has ever let me down. I know this isn't fair, but I can't help it. Joe pulls a second joint from a tin and hands it to Carolyn, who shakes her head, so he passes it to me instead.

"Do you want to go home?" I ask.

"No," she says.

"Are you upset?"

"No," she says again. "Why should I be?"

"Come on." I try to give her the joint. "It's my birthday. Let's try to have fun."

"You two have fun," she says. "I hate smoking pot. I never feel anything."

"You just have to hold it in," I say.

"You're the expert," she says drily.

"I can show you how it's done."

"Oh please," she says. "May I have a lesson?"

And suddenly I feel pissed at her too. I'm not the one who wanted an open relationship, the one who said that real desire shouldn't be pinned down, attached to only one person. I want to prove something—I'm not sure what—so I take another drag, sucking as much smoke in as I can before I grab the back of her head, press my lips to hers and exhale into her mouth. When she tries to pull away I grip the whorl of hair at the nape of her neck and hold on tight, keeping my lips mashed to hers when she coughs. She struggles, her teeth banging against mine, her tongue muscular and sharp. It's the dark side of our first kiss, fueled not by passion but resentment. But apparently we put on a good show because when we break apart Joe says, "I've never seen you two kiss before. That was lovely." His voice sounds weird, choked and husky.

"That wasn't a kiss," Carolyn says, wiping her mouth with the back of her hand.

"Sorry," he says. "I shouldn't have watched."

"I can show you a real kiss," Carolyn says, reaching for his hand.

There is an odd relief in seeing the thing you dreaded made real. Dread is almost always worse than the thing itself, and then it's over. As I watch her kiss him, wedge her leg between his, bite his lower lip, then pull back to trace it with the tip of her tongue, I'm not sure what to do. She kisses me the same way—her signature move, apparently. I'm standing there frozen when she reaches for my hand and pulls me closer. She stops kissing Joe and begins kissing me. It's the most ardent kiss we've exchanged in months, but it feels like acting. As she slides her hands inside my robe, over my waist and up the sides of my breasts, I feel like the girls in a porno, making out for the benefit of some guy. Joe's expression is at once lusty and sheepish. He looks like he's watching a porno. Adding to the effect, a wave crashes over us, soaking our kimono underclothes and sticking them to our bodies. We gasp and break apart, drenched and panting. Then Carolyn reaches for Joe's hand, pulls him to me and backs away. It's like musical chairs. Musical lips. There are so few ways to do this, so few combinations for just two pairs of lips, two tongues, two sets of hands. To keep it interesting, you have to keep switching partners I guess.

He is willing to play. He places his hands on my shoulders, closes his eyes and parts his lips. I don't know why I kiss him back. Curiosity maybe, or so that Carolyn doesn't one-up me, or the urge that you feel, when holding something fragile, to squeeze. His lips are thinner than hers, edged with stubble, and his tongue feels cold and thick and gummy. At first I can't stop feeling the separate components of the kiss, and then I get caught up in it. My breath snags and I want to push him down in the sand, climb on top of him and stub him out. But then another wave hits us, a big one, and as it sucks back into the ocean, we are toppled and dragged under by its force.

Carolyn dives under and starts swimming and I follow. Joe falls backward, kicking his long legs behind him. The farther out we get from the shore, the smoother the surface of the water, so the stars reflect in its mirror and it's almost like being in outer space. But it's the ocean, and the thing about the ocean is that it's never still, not for one second. It's like a human body that way, moving, cycling, churning, changing. I think about how every movement we make we initiate by sending messages through our brains, but this happens so fast that we don't even realize that what we think are involuntary actions are actually millions upon millions of choices. I choose to dive under and open my eyes, to feel the sting of the salt, to see the blackness stretching below. I choose to let antigravity or whatever force it is push me back to the surface, where I find Carolyn treading water, kissing Joe again. Then she stops and kisses me once more, and I swear I can taste him on her mouth. The ocean is still moving, of course, doing its own pulling and pushing, a fourth to round out our number. It pushes us into the sand and we stumble out in our waterlogged clothes, heavier and clumsier than before, like astronauts returning to earth. Carolyn stands behind Joe, wraps her arms around his waist and sucks on his earlobe. When she starts to slide her hand down the front of his pants, he groans and turns to face her. Watching them kiss again, the relief goes away. But I am not angry anymore either. I'm not even jealous, not really. It's over. We can stop trying. I am free. I turn around and walk away.

They don't even notice I'm gone.

omoshiroi: (ADJ.) *interesting; funny*

In books, when a mystery is solved, it's like a bow slipping off a present to reveal the gift inside: case cracked, case closed. But in life, when one piece of the puzzle fits, it often seems as if that piece had simply been lifted from somewhere else on the board, creating a new gap. I have no idea who would have stuffed the technical boys' high school uniforms into boxes in our storage area, where I was sure to find them. The first one I find is in the electric sukiyaki pot. There are yellow stains on the underarms of the shirt, and the balled up jacket and pants smell of mold. As I keep opening other boxes, I find more and more of these uniforms hidden in plain sight, a clue to a mystery I hadn't even realized existed.

I had just returned home from school when someone knocked on the door. I assumed it would be Carolyn, coming to collect the stuff she left behind. The last time I saw her was at the beach a week ago. She stayed out all night, and the next day, while I was at work, she packed up her suitcases and moved down to Hakui. When I came home that day, I thought we'd been robbed when I saw that half of the shoes were missing from the *genkan*. But since very few women here could fit into either of our big shoes, that didn't make sense. Then I saw the note on the refrigerator.

M: I'm sorry for leaving without saying good-bye, but this isn't really good-bye. I'll be back soon to get the rest of my things, and so that we can talk. I'd say that we should stay friends, but we're not friends, are we? We're more like family, in the ways that we drive each other crazy, can't live together to save our lives, and love each other deeply. I don't want to lose you. I hope you feel the same way.

C.

I had my speech ready. I was going to say that family doesn't leave without saying good-bye. But when I opened the door, Carolyn wasn't standing on the other side. Instead, I found myself drowning in a pair of gray eyes.

Keiko was holding Koji in her arms. He was straddling her hip and she was holding him tight, the way she did after he jumped out of the window. Fumiya stood beside her, muttering something, his head jerking around like a bird.

"Say 'hello' to Marina," Keiko prompted Fumiya. The older boy didn't respond, but Koji said, "Hello," and then grinned at me.

"You have a new tooth," I said, pointing to his mouth, my hand shaking.

"Big tooth," Keiko added, kissing his cheek.

"Big tooth," Fumiya repeated. "Big, big, big tooth."

"I look like the rabbit," Koji said in Japanese.

"How is that rabbit?" I asked, my stomach lurching. The rabbit spent a night recovering from dental surgery in our bathtub before I brought it back to the elementary school, sneaking it into the hutch at dawn. It was bedraggled and wobbly, its fate far from secure, but I wanted it to be there when the kids arrived.

"*Futotta*," Koji declared happily. It got fat.

"The children love this rabbit," Keiko said. "So thank you."

"Thank your brother-in-law," I said. "He saved its life."

"It's okay," she said. "He needs new patients." It took me a moment to realize that she'd cracked a joke. When I laughed, she grinned and I felt my eyes well up. Keiko looked alarmed. I lied and said that I'd been chopping onions before they arrived, but it was obviously just a story. "Maybe now is not a good time," she said, explaining that she'd come to practice for the English speech contest.

"It's a fine time," I said, stepping aside. I asked if they'd like to join me for dinner, explaining that I had all of the ingredients for sukiyaki and no idea how to cook it. Keiko said that they didn't want to bother me. "I know you are so busy," she said, and I assured her that I wasn't busy at all. Finally she nodded and set Koji down. As I led them down the hall, he slid his hand into mine.

The gloves were off.

It was then that I ducked into the storage area to search for the electric sukiyaki pot, and discovered the boys' school uniforms, stuffed into every nook and cranny that could hold and hide them. Someone must have broken in when we weren't here and left the uniforms behind as a message or a warning. But of what, I don't know. It's creepy, but nothing I can deal with at the moment.

In the kitchen, Keiko has turned on the rice cooker and is chopping vegetables. When I tell her to stop and relax she says, "You don't trust my cooking?"

"You're my guest," I say. "I can chop while you practice your speech."

"Oh no," she says. "I will not compete in English speech contest."

"You're not?" I ask, confused. "I thought that was why you came over."

"No," she says, looking at me head-on. "Fumiya will compete."

My stomach lurches again. From across the counter separating the kitchen and the living room I can see him bouncing on the couch. He is dressed in running shorts, his legs shockingly white. As the backs of his thighs smack the vinyl, he smacks his lips in an echo.

"Fumiya-kun," Keiko says, "*Jyabauokki taimu!*"

Fumiya shoves his hands under his butt, sucks in a deep breath, and then rambles through a long phrase of gibberish: "Twasbrillig andtheslithytoves didgyreand gimbleinthewabe allmimsymimsymimsy . . . " Keiko claps her hands and he stops abruptly. She and Koji both look at me with twin expressions of pride.

"That was . . . " I begin.

"It's *Jyabauokki*," Koji says. "Don't you know? From *Arisu?*"

Of course. From *Alice in Wonderland*. "The Jabberwocky." I vaguely remember having read this poem as a kid and seeing it inexplicably printed on a brochure at Shika's museum of nuclear power. Keiko explains that this is how Fumiya learned it. After she took the two boys to the museum, she brought home the English brochure and read it to them for fun. Fumiya insisted on hearing it every night before bed, and soon he had learned the whole poem by heart, without trying.

"Mimsymimsymimsymimsy," Fumiya says again, grinning at me.

Keiko brings the electric sukiyaki pot into the living room and sets it on the coffee table. The cutting board is arranged with slices of meat, squares of tofu, sugar snap peas and mushrooms. Using chopsticks, she dips a piece of raw meat into the hot broth, swirls it around for a minute until it turns from deep red to light pink, and then passes it to me.

"It's delicious," I say, and it is, sweet and rich and soft, almost creamy.

"More delicious than the steak I cook for you at my house?"

"Your steak wasn't bad," I lie. "I just had a toothache."

"It's very bad," she says. "At that time I'm so stress. I'm sorry."

"Do you feel less stressed now?"

"Not one hundred percent," she says, "but better." She dips another slice of meat into the pot and then holds it up to Koji, who opens his mouth like a baby bird. Fumiya opens his own mouth and chews in time with his brother. He's sitting with his feet up on the couch and his knees spread, hands cupping his groin. I'm afraid he's going to start masturbating again, but Keiko asks in Japanese if he's hungry and he considers the question, or at least the morsel caught between her chopsticks. She places it on a bowl of rice and waits for him to plant his feet on the ground before sliding the bowl to him.

"Fumiya is artistic," Keiko says. Then I realize that she actually said, "Fumiya is autistic." I am not sure if I should act surprised, or what I should say, so I just keep quiet and listen. "Before, we don't want to admit it. His teacher makes suggestions for treatment, but we resist, hoping he will improve. This does not happen. In fact he gets worse. So now we try new strategy. Goal is to reward appropriate behavior. For example, Fumiya has echo tendency. To repeat is so stimulating. We can't make him stop this, so we must find appropriate context and reward. Maybe speech contest is appropriate context for repeating. And he loves a clap sound. If he recites this poem during Shika's festival, maybe people will clap . . . " She trails off, dipping a mushroom into the broth, and then chewing slowly. "But probably California's mayor expects to hear perfect speech by fluid English speaker, not recitation by autistic child."

"No one else is participating," I say. "If Fumiya enjoys reciting this poem and you think it would be good for him, then I think he should do it. As long as you think he's up for it, getting onstage with all those people watching him."

"All of those people," she echoes. "Am I up for it? For so long I am *hazukashii* . . . "

"Ashamed," I translate, knowing she doesn't mean shy or foolish.

"But lately I just . . . don't care so much. He is my son. Maybe I can't make him perfect son like everyone else. But I can try to help him, *ne*? Little by little."

And so for the next hour I coach Fumiya. At first sounds cartwheel out of his mouth, but I can get him to break up the lines by clapping whenever he should stop, and before long he is slowing down, separating every phrase, pausing between words. As he anticipates my applause, he actually looks at me, picks up on my cues, mostly manages to follow them. It's dark and Koji has fallen asleep on the couch, his head on his mother's lap, when she glances at her watch.

"I'm sorry it's so late," she says, stroking Koji's hair. "Isn't your friend coming home?"

"My girlfriend," I say. "No. She moved out."

"Good friend?"

"Girlfriend," I repeat. "You know . . . my *ra-ba*?" I've always hated this word. It sounds so cheesy, so show-offy. But Keiko looks confused or uncertain and I want to finish what I started so I say, "*shi-ko-re-tto ra-ba*?" Secret lover. And suddenly I get why there are so many *eikaiwa* or English conversation enthusiasts among people who have no plans to go abroad. I get why the members of SMILE come so regularly even when they never intended to make a speech at the festival. When you want to say something difficult, when you want to get something off your chest, it's so much easier to do it in another language. It's like a costume for your words.

"Oh," Keiko says. "*Omoshiroi*."

"Funny?"

"Interesting," she says. "It must be nice. No *gokiburi* husband to expect dinner on a tray while he watches baseball . . . always someone to talk to you."

"Well," I say, "my relationship with Carolyn had its own problems."

"Had?"

"We broke up," I say. "Hey, I thought you didn't know the past tense. You always use the present."

"Really?" she says. "Eh. I do not realize this. I guess it's because of Fumiya."

"What do you mean?"

"Fumi only uses present. For him, there is no difference between yesterday, today, and tomorrow."

He really lives in the moment, I think, remembering Einstein's definition of insanity as doing the same thing over and over but expecting new results. Only Fumiya probably doesn't have these expectations. He probably finds the predictability comforting.

"What kind of problems did you have with your *ra-ba*?" Keiko asks me.

"I think we were too similar," I say. "Not our personalities, but our circumstances, at least here. There wasn't enough difference to keep things interesting, and it made us competitive. Also, it was difficult to have to hide all the time. We were pretending so hard not to be lovers that after a while we really weren't lovers anymore." I think about this, how we started by living a lie, and soon the lie turned into the truth.

"I understand," she says. "I have . . . I had . . . *shi-ko-re-tto ra-ba,* too. We also shared similar circumstances, and we also had to hide." She looks down at Koji as she says this. His lashes look long and luxurious against his pale cheeks. His eyes flutter beneath his lids. I wonder what he's dreaming about.

"Kobayashi-sensei?" I guess.

"You know?" she says. "I try to be so careful! I try to hide my feelings so well!" She sounds shocked, but not upset. Actually, she seems glad. Secrets are lonely. The fun part of hide-and-seek—the whole point of the game—is getting found.

"Is it over?" I ask.

"Mmm," she says. "My life is difficult enough, *ne*?" I wonder who decided this, who called it off. She sighs and says that they should probably leave, that her husband is going to expect dinner when he gets home from work and Koji needs to go to bed. At the door, she thanks me for helping Fumiya and then gives me a quick, fierce hug.

"Good-bye," I call out as they get into their car.

"Good-bye," Fumiya repeats and Koji grins, flashing his big new teeth.

I'm washing the sukiyaki dishes when I hear another knock at the door. This time I open it to find Miyoshi-sensei, his arms filled with blooming cherry branches. Tucked between the stems is an envelope. "Happy birthday Mari-chan," he says, handing me the knobby bouquet. "I know it's late. I have an important thing to tell you. I'm sorry to disturb you and Carolyn."

"That's okay," I say. "She moved out."

"Really?" he says. "Where?"

"She's living in Hakui," I say. "She wanted to be closer to her school."

"Ah," he says. "I see."

He follows me down the hall and accepts my offer of tea. I can feel him mustering the nerve to say something and I force myself to keep quiet for once instead of filling in the blank space with my nervous chatter.

"You have big hands," he says at last.

"Thanks a lot," I say, wanting to sit on them.

"I meant it as compliment," he says. "Your hands look strong. Like you. Mari-chan, I must ask a favor." He is still looking at my big hands. "I know it's a burden, but could you teach our classes alone tomorrow?"

"Of course," I say, although his request surprises me, since he's the one who told me that teachers here never take sick days. "Are you okay?"

"I'm fine," he says. "I have to take someone to the hospital in Nanao."

"Is it your father?" I ask.

"No," he says, pausing to sip his tea. "Can you keep my confidence?"

"Of course," I say. "Who could I tell?" For the first time, I notice that there are honey-colored rings around his irises. His face is dangerously close. It would be so easy to make the same mistake twice. "It's Ritsuko," he says. "She is in a kind of trouble. Maybe she was . . . unprotected. With huge consequence. Do you catch my meaning?"

"She's pregnant?" I guess, hoping that I'm wrong.

"Mmm," he says. "Tomorrow she will have procedure to terminate."

I think back to the way Ritsuko left SMILE club early this week, claiming not to feel well. Then I remember what we were discussing right before she left. I've been told that abortion isn't stigmatized in Japan, that it's not considered a big deal. But I've also seen countless roadside shrines filled with row after row of *mizuko* or "water babies," faceless granite dolls that look like chess pieces, dressed in pastel rompers and hand-knit bonnets, toys and candy arrayed at their feet. These *mizuko* are available for purchase by women who've miscarried or had abortions, to serve as vessels for the frustrated spirits of their unborn children. It's the stuff that makes me sad, the clothing piled behind the statues in larger and larger sizes, all that guilt.

"Again, I must ask you to keep my confidence," Miyoshi-sensei says. "If anyone discovered that I took her to the hospital for this reason, I could get in huge trouble. But it's my responsibility, so . . . "

"What do you mean, your responsibility?" I ask.

"Ritsuko is my student," he says. "My best English student. I encouraged her to go abroad to study English this summer in California. I helped arrange homestay. Ri-chan's dream is becoming tour guide. It's not impossible. She is very determined. But she is only sixteen years. Sixteen is so young. She shouldn't be alone tomorrow."

"What about the father?" I ask. "Shouldn't he go with her?"

"She won't tell."

"You mean she won't tell you who he is, or she won't tell him she's pregnant?"

"She wants to keep private."

"Nakajima is her boyfriend," I say.

"My responsibility is to help Ri-chan," he says, "not to force confession."

"You keep talking about responsibility, but shouldn't he at least help her pay for the abortion? He got her into this mess. It shouldn't be your job to clean it up."

"My job is to take care of my student," he says. "I am doing my job."

"You are very kind," I say. "Most teachers wouldn't do what you're doing."

"Most teachers are probably smart," he says.

"I'd like to help," I add. "If there's anything I can do, please let me know."

He places his stein of tea on the table and circles the rim with his fingertip. "Maybe there is something you could do for Ritsuko . . . " I nod, and he clears his throat. "Following procedure, she will feel discomfort. If she goes home, she will have difficulty hiding this from Sakura. Maybe, if you don't mind, she could stay here for one night? She could say you are helping her with English. You will speak English together, *ne*? So it's kind of true."

"Sure," I say.

He thanks me and stands up and I follow him to the *genkan*, where he bends down to put on his shoes and finds them still on his feet. "I forgot to take off my shoes!" he says, sounding as upset as if he'd discovered that he weren't wearing any pants. I tell him not to worry about it, that I wear my shoes indoors all the time. "You do?" he asks. "Really?"

"I'm a temporary person," I remind him.

"I wish you were not," he says before slipping outside.

After he leaves, I go to the kitchen to put the flowers that he brought me in water. As I arrange the cherry branches in a Mickey Mouse stein, his envelope tumbles out. I take the letter upstairs to read in bed.

Dear Miss Marina,

This is final attempt to write speech on why English is useful for me. You said before, "Why not make speech on memory from homestay in Eureka, California?" Now I will show you why not.

I was eighteen years when I went to California to participate in immersion-style English program. According to dictionary, "immersion" means sinking in, like drowning in water. Immersion also means living in a host family. To my surprise, I arrived in Eureka and learned that my "family" was just one man, divorced DEA officer. Do you know DEA meaning? It's "Drug Enforcement Agent." He told me to call him "Dad." Then he laughed when I said "Dad" in front of other DEA officers. He called me "Son" and they laughed more.

"Dad" had a big moustache and he always wore mirror

sunglasses, like police from a TV show called Cops that he enjoyed watching so much. His refrigerator only had beer and milk. Other host parents took foreign students to the movies or Disneyland, but "Dad" only drank beer or milk and watched Cops show. I think he was kind of depressed because of divorce, and because his children hated his guts. This is what he said so often, after drinking many beers. "My kids don't get me. Only you get me," he said and I nodded and said, "Mmm."

One day he brought me on "drug bust" to secret garden filled with marijuana plants. Together with DEA team, "Dad" seized criminal property. It was like Cops show, only nobody was beat up. "Dad" said to me, "I'll bet you don't see much weed back in Japan," and I agreed. "I'm giving you a real American experience," he said. "Fuck Disneyland." After that, I never mentioned my desire to attend Disneyland again.

To tell the truth, this "immersion" experience was kind of lonesome. So I was happy when "Dad's" daughter came to visit at the end of the summer, even if she took guest bedroom and I had to sleep on bumpy couch in family room. Sliding glass door of family room went to backyard. Every night, Kathy left through this door, and every morning she came back again before sunrise. I don't know where she went. I pretended to be sleeping. In the morning, "Dad" would say to me, "I thought I heard you go out last night, Son," and then Kathy would say, "Me too!" and I would feel panic. If I don't tell truth, I betray him. If I tell truth, I betray her. I decided to keep her confidence. One time, she took me to the beach with her friends. Listening to their conversation, I could enjoy learning slang and idiom. "Beats me," she said when her friends asked who I was. "Some dude my dad's milking for child support money. He's supposed to be learning English, but he's like mute." I had to look up this word.

One night I am lying on bumpy couch, pretending to sleep, when Kathy comes and sits next to my body.

"Dad's working tonight," she says.

"Oh," I say, sitting up.

"Have you ever smoked dope?" she asks.

I say, "What's dope meaning?"

She says, "The weed you helped my father to harvest."

I say, "This is confiscated police property!"

She says, "You are kidding, right?"

I say, "I am man, not kid, and I can speak!" She laughs and so I laugh too. After smoking dope, I become hungry, but of course only beer and milk live in the refrigerator. Kathy orders a pizza with ham and also pineapple, which is delicious or not, I can't decide, so I have to keep biting it again and again to check.

"You are stone," Kathy says.

"I am not stone," I say.

Suddenly she says, "Remind me what your name is." I say, "What?" She says, "Your name, I forget what it is. I asked my dad, but he doesn't know."

WHAT?!?

After <u>two months</u>, "Dad" does not remember my name? Then I realize: maybe he never knew. Maybe this is why he calls me "son." I feel humiliation. I try to speak, to answer the question, but nothing comes. Why? Because I can't remember my name! Probably you think it's impossible. But it is truth! My own name is like an English vocabulary word I learned and then forgot. I am standing in a flooding river and I can't swim. I am immersed.

"I don't know!" I say.

"I guess you really are stone," Kathy says.

"I am not stone!" I say. "I am man. But it's true that I often feel like stone."

Then she lies down with (next to? beside? on?) me and admits that she also feels like stone so often. But not that night. After that happens, we never talk about it. Maybe she feels regret. I don't know. Once more, English was not so useful for me.

After I returned to Japan, every year I send New Year card to "Dad," and after he remarries, I begin to receive Christmas newsletter. Like such, I learned that Kathy got married to the mayor of Eureka. So I had idea to form sister-city relationship. Shika rhymes with Eureka. Also, both towns are close to the sea. I think it's good match.

In my official proposal, I said that Shika's town hall would pay their airplane tickets. First Kathy wrote to say thank you, that they felt so excited for this trip and opportunity. But after I sent travel itinerary, she wrote again. In American newspaper, they read about power plant accident in Tokaimura. Article mentioned other plants in Japan, including Shika. So she learned about the campaign to close our plant. She tells me her husband feels nervous to form relationship with nuclear power town. Maybe people of Eureka don't want it. "We're still coming," she said, "but we can't promise to sign a contract until we see Shika and talk to people." I have not admitted this to my father. I told him, "It's a done deal." I told him, "You will be on TV, and everyone will feel so happy and remember what a good mayor you were."

So why do I admit all of this to you now? Two reasons. Reason one: to explain why this festival is so important to me, and also why I can't make a speech. When I first came back to Shika after my summer in Eureka, everybody asked "what was best experience of your trip?" I couldn't admit truth. Best experience was forgetting my own name. This is effect of immersion. This freedom comes from new language. But also, I think, from "dope." This is reason number two for sharing my story with you.

I know you smoked some "dope" at Shika's beach, together with

Carolyn and Joe. I am not judging. The black pot shouldn't judge the black kettle, ne? But I should warn you to be more private when you practice risky behavior. One male student spotted you, and he reported your transgression to me. We are lucky. If he reported to principal, I could not protect you, no matter how much I want to. You would be sent home, or even to prison. I really don't want this. So please take more care.

Yours,

Hiroshi Miyoshi

abunai: (ADJ.) *dangerous; risky; close*

Please rank the following on a RISKY BEHAVIOR
scale from 1–10.
1 means SAFE SEX (*anzen na sekkusu*).
10 means DANGEROUS SEX (*abunai na sekkusu*).

1. French kissing (a tongue goes *inside* another person's
mouth): ____

2. Masturbation or "jacking off" (a person touches his or her
own genitals):____

3. Frottage (two bodies rub all *over* each other, without penetration):____

4. Making out (kissing, touching fingers *to* breasts or genitals):____

5. Fellatio or "blow job" (a penis goes *inside* someone's
mouth):____

6. Cunnilingus or "eating out" (a tongue goes *inside* someone's vagina):____

7. Protected vaginal intercourse or "fucking" (penis, *inside* condom, goes *inside* vagina):____

8. Unprotected vaginal intercourse (penis, *without* condom, comes *inside* vagina):____

9. Anal intercourse or "ass sex" (penis comes *inside* anus):____

10. Rimming (a tongue goes *around* anus):____

I leave the faculty room ten minutes before the boys return from the nuclear power plant, to hang the posters around their classroom. Today's worksheet was easy to make. I just pictured Nakajima's face. All night long, I couldn't stop thinking about the things that Miyoshi-sensei has told me recently: that it's against the law to teach sex-ed here; that boys won't wear condoms for fear of seeming gay. I kept thinking about fifteen-year-old Ritsuko at the abortion clinic, and about Nakajima sneaking into our house with his classmates' school uniforms. He must have been there when we went to the beach. He must have followed us, and reported everything back to Miyoshi-sensei.

The boys enter the shed still dressed in their red nuclear power plant jumpsuits. They circle the room like sharks in an aquarium tank, taking in the posters I taped to the walls. They stare at the two naked men holding each other, the woman lying with her head on another woman's lap, the Asian girl offering the white guy a condom.

"*Nani wo kore?*"—what the hell?—mutters Nakajima.

"Avoid risky behavior," I read the caption. "Do you understand?"

He ignores me as usual, unzipping his jumpsuit and peeling it off.

"Dame!" I say. That's forbidden. "Keep your clothes on!"

"Atsui yo," it's hot, he says, and he's right. The windowless portable classroom feels like a sauna, rank with the mingled smells of B.O., hairspray, and the dried guppies that the boys like to snack on. As usual, Nakajima's classmates follow his example, stripping to their underwear, sprawling in their seats, fanning themselves with the worksheets I placed on each desk before they got here.

"Today we are studying safe sex," I say in Japanese, hoping that I got the phrase right. When I looked up "intercourse" in the dictionary, I found *sekkusu,* a word imported from the English. I understand why *sekkuhara* or "sexual harassment" had to be brought over from English, but *sekkusu?* What did they call sex before?

"Where's Miyoshi?" asks Sumio, picking at his infected nipple piercing.

"He couldn't be here today," I say. "He has some important business to take care of." I stare at Nakajima, wondering if he has any idea what his girlfriend is doing. He takes a plastic pick out of his pocket and begins fluffing out his Afro-perm. His hair, bleached a coppery shade of orange, looks like a dandelion gone to seed.

"We scared him off," he jeers.

"You are not scary," I say. "But you are dangerous."

"Dangerous-o!" the boys repeat after me. This is the one English word they all know, their equivalent of the girls' favorite word: "cute-o."

"Sumio," I say. "On a scale from one to ten, if one is very safe, and ten is very dangerous, how risky is French kissing?" I approximate this in Japanese.

"Dangerous-o," he says. "Ten!"

"Come on," I say. "Kissing is not that dangerous. You could catch a cold, or maybe herpes, but it's a lot less risky than other sexual acts."

"Dangerous-o," he says again. "After you kiss a girl, she sticks to you like rice."

All of the boys crack up, Nakajima the hardest of all.

"Let's skip to number eight," I say, standing beside him. His skin looks even darker than usual, tanned from daily sumo practice. "Unprotected vaginal intercourse," I say. "What does that mean, Nakajima?"

"Penis *without* condom comes *inside* vagina," he reads in a monotone.

"Do you know what a penis is, Nakajima?"

"Yes," he says, spreading his legs ever so slowly, making the boys laugh again.

I lean forward, careful not to touch him as I reach into his desk. The banana is still in the bento box, more black than yellow now. From my pocket I pull out a condom that I bought from the vending machine behind the grocery store this morning, while every passing car slowed down to watch. "Please put this on your banana," I say. He crosses his arms and glowers. "Maybe you can't," I push him. "Maybe you don't know how. Let me show you."

I rip open the wrapper, pull out the condom, which is slimy with lube, and try to shove it in his hand. He resists, but I am stronger, forcing his fingers around the condom and the condom over the banana, squeezing so hard that the banana spurts out of its jacket, splattering white goo all over our fingers, my shirt, his Afro-perm. It's such a stupid moment, the punch line to such a dumb joke, but the boys have laughed at dumber ones, and I'm surprised when they remain silent. Then I realize that they're looking behind us, where a square of sunlight is spreading across the floor. The classroom door is open, and people are standing there.

"Miss Marina," an oddly uninflected male voice says. "We. Have. Visitors. Today. From. America."

I turn around to see the Japanese mayor—Miyoshi-sensei's dad—standing beside a petite blond woman with a baby strapped to her chest, facing out. The baby has her mom's sharply bowed lips, round face, and blue eyes, but her skin is nut brown and her hair is a wild tangle of coppery curls. Standing next to them is a trim, light-skinned African-American man with a bald, shiny head. He blots his face with a handkerchief as he enters the classroom, followed by a scrawny boy of eleven or twelve wearing pants so baggy that it seems like he could walk right out of them.

"What's going on here?" the man asks, looking at the posters with a frown.

"Nothing," I say. "We were just in the middle of an English lesson."

"What. Are. You. Teaching." Mayor Miyoshi says. His voice box doesn't allow for subtleties of tone, but his expression is appalled. The school principal, by contrast, is smiling hysterically.

"Prepositions?" I say.

"You've got a funny way of teaching English," the American mayor says.

"We're trying to make it useful," I say. "Useful and fun." I hope the principal catches these words.

"I think they used these same posters in my sex-ed class," says the woman.

"Sex. Ed." the Japanese mayor repeats. "You. Teach. Sex. Ed."

"I think Hiro got these posters in California," I explain nervously. "He said that he pulled them out of a trash can at a school in Eureka."

"That sounds like Hiro," she says. "He was always collecting weird souvenirs from the trash, asking me what it all 'signified.' What did he used to call them?"

"Curiosity objects?" I guess.

"That's right!" she says. As she laughs again, the baby laughs too, kicking her feet against her mother's belly. "I'm Kathy," she introduces herself, "and that's my husband, Benedict, and Ben Junior, and this little person attached to me is Phoebe." I introduce myself and she asks where Hiro is. "I can't wait to see him," she says.

"He had to run an errand today," I say.

"That's too bad," she says. "Can you believe it's been fifteen years? I wonder if he'll even recognize me without my big bangs." She laughs again, glancing at her husband, who is stroking the narrow band of hair encircling his upper lip and chin as he scrutinizes the boys. No, not the boys. Nakajima. I watch him take it all in: the giant Afro-perm, the synthetically darkened skin, the gangsta medallion and the notebook scrawled with the words *BLACK FACE* over a drawing of a clenched brown fist.

"I think I've seen enough here," he says.

When Miyoshi-sensei arrives at my house, he is wearing a small pink gingham backpack and I smile before remembering why he's here, whose backpack he must be carrying. It takes five minutes for Ritsuko to cover the distance from the car to the door. She is walking like a very old person, but she looks terribly young in her gym suit and pigtails. She bows and says, "*Ojamashimasu.*" The formal greeting upon entering someone else's house translates literally: "I'm in your way." Miyoshi-sensei crouches to untie her sneakers, easing them off her feet, then stashing them in the shoe rack next to his own.

"How are you?" I say.

"I'm fine, thank you," she says.

But she doesn't look fine, and I'm scared by the thought of the long night ahead, the two of us alone. I know so few words of comfort in Japanese. Or in English, for that matter. She winces as she sits on the couch.

"Do you want another blanket?" I ask. "Some tea? A magazine?"

"I'm fine, thank you," she insists, tucking her legs beneath her.

Miyoshi-sensei beckons me into the kitchen. "I brought sushi," he says, holding up a plastic bag. "So you won't have to cook. Also, for us, sushi is a kind of comfort food." He begins to divide the sushi between two plates.

"Won't you stay and eat with us?" I ask, not wanting him to leave.

"I can't," he says. "I must dine with my father and the visiting mayor." I note that he doesn't mention Kathy. "How was class today?"

"Well . . . " I hesitate, "the mayor and his family stopped by for a surprise visit."

"I know," he says, squeezing soy sauce into a saucer.

"You do?" I ask, assuming that his father must have told him what happened, and relieved that he's not more upset.

"I arranged for this visit. I knew the boys wouldn't be rude in front of them."

"Thanks," I say. "I wish you'd told me." Warned me, I mean.

"Sorry," he says. "I had many things on my mind."

"Kathy was sad to miss you."

"Mmm," he nods.

"She said she's changed a lot. What was she like before?"

"Kind of *itazurako*," he says. "Like a bad girl. Wild and rebelling. I felt surprised to learn she married a town mayor." He hands me the soy sauce and leads the way into the living room, carrying the sushi. Then he kneels beside Ritsuko, telling her that she should really try to eat something. She sits up and reaches for a piece of tuna sushi, chewing slowly as if even her teeth hurt.

"Can I have cup of water?" she says in a small voice. "Is that okay?"

"Of course," I say quickly. "You can have anything you want."

"No," she says. "I mean, is 'can I have cup of water' okay English?"

"You don't have to speak English," I say. "Just relax. Speak Japanese." For the first time since she got here, her eyes fill with tears. Miyoshi-sensei presents her with his handkerchief, its corner monogrammed with the characters for his name. I wonder who made it for him. His mom? "You should say, '*May I* have a glass of water,'" he tells her.

"*May* I have a glass of water," she repeats.

"Good," he says. "That's correct. Very good pronunciation, *ne?*"

And this is how he comforts her. He is her teacher, and she is his responsibility, and he takes care of her simply by sitting next to her—beside her, with her—while I slip into the kitchen to get that glass of water she asked for correctly. Only there are no glasses in the cupboard, and none in the sink either. I remember seeing more Mickey Mouse beer steins in the box in storage. But while the box is still there, it's now filled with uniforms. I call out to Miyoshi-sensei, who joins me in the storage area, and I open one box after another to show him my find. He takes it all in, then pushes aside two boxes and presses his face to a rusted out patch in the aluminum siding.

"He can see you coming and going," he says. "He knows when you're home and when you're gone, so he can enter without detection . . ."

"Nakajima?" I ask, shuddering.

"No," he says, shifting the box to block the hole. "Haruki."

"Is he still upset because we got him in trouble about the cat?"

"What cat?" Miyoshi-sensei says.

"The one he trapped in the broken refrigerator."

"Your refrigerator was never broken," he says. "That is why Haruki got in trouble. For doing this same thing many times. Entering your house. Sometimes unplugging your refrigerator. He wanted to sabotage you."

"But why did he take the technical boys' uniforms?" I ask.

"Maybe you guessed correctly that those boys bullied Haruki. Maybe he felt relief when they stopped coming to school. Maybe, when they returned every afternoon for your special English class, he blamed you. He hoped that without uniform, they couldn't come to school anymore. Or you would feel frighten and refuse to teach them. Then they would go away, and he could be a stone again."

"They must have treated him terribly, to make him like this."

"They did not make him like this," he says. "When I was a boy, I also received *ijime*. Bullying. But I am not like this, *ne*? I am not stone."

We are standing side by side, both facing the wall of boxes, when I feel the back of his hand brush against the back of mine. For just a moment we are closer than next to, closer than near. There is a call and response between my body and his body, a language beneath the skin. Then he pulls away. He buries his hands in his pockets, opens the door, and I follow him out of the storage area. In the living room, Ritsuko is already asleep on the couch. He pulls the blanket up over her, tucking her in.

The sun wakes me up before *The Four Seasons*. Downstairs, Ritsuko is sitting up on the couch, watching a videotaped *ER* episode. "Call it," a nurse yells at a doctor, who is slamming his electrified paddles against a patient's exposed chest. "He's gone! Call it!"

"Good morning," I say. "Did you sleep well?" Immediately I regret the question. But she nods and flicks the TV off, standing up as if we were in class and I had just called on her. I ask what she'd like for breakfast, offering to make rice and miso soup, hoping she won't mind that it's from a package, but she says that she'd like to try American breakfast.

"Sure," I say. "I'll make you some pancakes."

"I love *hottokeki*," she says. "Can you show me how?"

So I guide her through the steps, measuring flour into a bowl, cracking eggs, adding milk and melted butter, ladling the batter into a pan and telling her to watch for tiny bubbles that break without filling in. It's fun to cook with her, a relief to have something to do together. Again I almost forget why she's here. The first *hottokeki* is sizzling in a pan, turning golden at the edges, when I hear the cell phone start to ring from inside the storage area. *I heard he sang a sweet song* . . . I can't believe that it still has power. Ritsuko freezes at the sound, holding her spatula in midair like a flyswatter.

"I know this phone," she says.

"It's Nakajima's," I say. "I took it from him in English class."

"He took it from me," she says.

"It's yours?" I ask, and she nods. "Why did Nakajima have it?"

"He wants to know who calls me. He is very jealous boy."

I go into the storage area and bring her the ringing phone. Next to the number flashing on the digital display are the letters: JYO. I hold it out to Ritsuko, who shakes her head after glimpsing the caller ID. "I don't want to talk to him," she says adamantly. Not sure what to do, I return the phone to the box in the storage area. She ladles another circle of batter into the pan and watches it cook. At the back of the refrigerator I find an old bottle of maple syrup, just a crystallized inch remaining, hard as amber. I place this on the table next to a crumb-studded stick of butter and two pairs of disposable chopsticks in their paper sleeves.

"Is this how to eat *hottokeki* in America?" Ritsuko asks.

"Sorry," I say. "I couldn't find any forks."

She nods, then uses the tip of a chopstick to perforate a bite-sized wedge. "Thank you," she says, looking down as she swirls the bite in syrup.

"You made them," I say.

"I mean for taking me," she says. "I could not go home."

"It's nothing," I say. "I wanted to. I'm glad I could help. And I'm sorry."

"Why you are sorry?"

"I'm sorry for what you had to go through."

"Go through?"

"I'm sorry for what you lost," I try. "I'm sorry that you had to be alone."

"But I wanted to be alone," she says. "I want to be alone."

"Good," I say. "That's good." She is chewing her first bite when I ask the question that's none of my business. "Was Joe the father?" She finishes chewing, swallows, then takes a long drink of milk.

"Maybe," she says at last.

"Does that mean yes?" I press. "Because if he was, then you should really tell someone. It's wrong. You're sixteen years old. And he was your teacher."

"Does maybe mean yes in English?" she asks me.

"No," I say.

"Maybe means no?"

"Maybe means maybe. It's an expression of uncertainty. Like 'I don't know.'"

"This is what I mean too. Maybe Nakajima was father. Maybe Joe. I don't know."

"Oh," I say. "I'm sorry. It's none of my business."

"Boyfriend was Nakajima," she says with a sigh. "In December, I tried to end it. But he was so sad. He begged to try again. He said he loves me. If he loses me he will have nothing. He will hurt himself. So I say we can get back together. I don't want him to be so sad. I think it's easier to end it when I go to California. But he doesn't want me to go. He tells me he will die without me." She stabs at a pancake with the tip of her chopstick. "So I cheated. I did what I wanted. I am very selfish girl. Now I only want to be alone."

"You are not selfish," I say. "You're young and smart and your life is just beginning. There's nothing wrong with wanting to be alone. You shouldn't feel guilty."

"Maybe," she says. "But I feel sad."

"I know," I say. "Of course you do. But you did the right thing."

"I know," she says. "Why are you crying?"

faito: (N.) *fight*

On the lawn in front of the museum of nuclear power, a makeshift wooden stage faces tarps spread across the grass in lines neat as ruled notebook paper. High school girls wearing aprons over their school uniforms carry trays of beer and tea, squid threaded onto skewers, and lurid, glistening red wieners. Keiko and her boys are sitting on a tarp toward the back. When I wave, Keiko beckons me to join their little group.

"You look . . . " she says.

"Ridiculous," I say. Sakura insisted that many women would come to the festival dressed in kimono, but the only other person wearing one is the heavily made-up old lady singing twangy *enka* ballads on stage. I sit with my legs stretched in front of me, peeling back the kimono hem to show Keiko the shorts I have on underneath. I tell her that I couldn't put on the obi by myself, and she admits that she doesn't know how to tie one either. Koji scoots onto my lap, plants his feet on either side of me and leans back. I press my chin against the top of his head and wrap my arms around his solid, warm little body. Fumiya sits cross-legged, clucking his tongue like a metronome, tilting his face to the sun, blinking against the glare.

"Where's Yuji?" I ask.

"New York," Keiko says.

"At his medical conference?"

"Probably playing golf."

"I don't think there's much golf in New York City," I say.

"Don't worry," she says. "He will find it."

"Hello," Miyoshi-sensei says, squatting beside us. He is wearing his suit and a celadon green tie and he looks upset, his eye twitching, his face pale, and his body tense.

"What's the matter?" I ask.

"Maybe American mayor won't sign sister-city contract."

"Are you serious?" I ask, and he nods. "Because of the power plant?"

"*Ano ne* . . . " he stalls. "After visiting the high school, he expressed some reservations to send American students to study abroad at Shika High School. He is afraid we do not celebrate diversity here."

"What diversity?" I say. "Everyone here is Japanese."

"I know," he says. "I try to explain we have no diversity to celebrate, but he is not convinced."

"I'm sorry," I say. "Have you told your father?"

"Not yet," he says. "My father is upset about something else. He said that when they entered the technical boys' classroom, you were forcing a condom into Nakajima's hand. He could not understand his eyes."

"I was trying to teach him how to put it on a banana," I say sheepishly. "It was part of my sex-ed lesson. I'm sorry. I shouldn't have tried to teach it without you."

"Probably not," he agrees.

"Is there anything I can do?" I ask.

"I think you have done enough," he says. He tells me that it's time for the festival to begin and I should come up front to the judges' table. There is going to be a short sumo demonstration before the speech contest. I take a seat at the table beneath the stage along-side the local dignitaries: gray-haired men in gray suits under a gray cloud of cigarette smoke. Across from me sits the American mayor, who is trying to help his wife with their fussing baby. Her cries are so loud that it's hard to hear Miyoshi-sensei when he gets up on stage and speaks into a microphone, explaining the rules of sumo for the Americans. "There are three ways to lose in sumo," he says. "Number one, if you step outside the ring. Number two, if you touch the ground with anything but a foot. Number three, if you try such cowardly fighting practices as pulling hair, kicking or punching."

The American mayor isn't listening. Their baby is arching her back and crying, her wails growing louder and more insistent. "I think it's all the cigarette smoke," Kathy says. "I'll take her for a walk and see if I can get her to fall asleep in the pouch."

"Should we wait for you?" Miyoshi-sensei asks, covering the microphone.

"Don't bother," she says. "I've never been a big wrestling fan, but Ben Junior loves it. He's on his middle school team. This should be a real treat for him."

Two high school girls rush onto the stage and spread a round, black rubber mat across the floor. Then they retreat and Miyoshi-sensei calls the wrestlers to come on out, but the stage remains empty. He shifts his weight from foot to foot, his microphone from hand to hand, glancing at his watch, scanning the crowd, looking everywhere except at Lone Wolf, who is narrating into his own microphone while his cameraman films the empty mat. "Where are the wrestlers?" His amplified voice fills the air. "The crowd grows restless. Everyone is bored. Will there be no sumo match today?"

"We're here," says Nakajima, panting as he runs up the stairs, dressed in a black sweatshirt and baggy jeans, his Afro-perm puffed out bigger than ever. He is trailed by Haruki Ogawa, who is wearing his school uniform.

"You're late," says Miyoshi-sensei. "Why aren't you in your *mawashi*?"

"*Kieta*," Nakajima replies. They vanished.

"Really," Miyoshi-sensei says, looking at Haruki.

"*Honto ni!*" Nakajima insists. "Right out of our bags!"

"Fine," Miyoshi-sensei says. "You can wrestle in your clothes."

"No way," says Nakajima. "That's no fun. Sumo is about bodies." His pants are so huge that he can pull them down without undoing his fly. Then he yanks his sweatshirt over his head so that he's wearing just his boxer shorts, which are green with bright yellow frogs. The crowd goes wild. Girls giggle and shield their eyes. Boys whistle and clap each other on the backs. Old men chuckle and old women shake their heads. For a moment their reactions puzzle me. The *mawashi* is far more revealing than this, a narrow strip of white cloth cutting a swath between the butt cheeks. But it's a uniform. The crowd hoots and calls for Ogawa-san to take his clothes off too, and when it's clear that they're not going to relent, Haruki moves in his usual slow motion, stripping as if there were a gun to his head. Dressed only in a sad pair of tight briefs, he looks like the real sumo wrestler, meaning he looks like a giant baby. His upper body is so fat that his arms seem to float, buoyed by the rings of his chest. His thighs are so big that he has to keep his legs spread.

"Those are the two boys that are going to wrestle each other?" the mayor asks me.

"Yeah," I say.

"That doesn't look like a fair contest."

"You're right," I say. "It won't be."

Miyoshi-sensei puts the whistle in his mouth, nods at each boy, and then blows. Nakajima squats, lifting one leg in the air and then the other while Haruki remains frozen. Only when Nakajima lunges does Haruki bolt, running downstairs, and through the crowd.

"What's going on?" the American mayor asks me. "Why won't he fight the kid?"

"He's scared of him," I say.

"That's crazy." He sounds furious. "I can't just sit here and watch the boy get ostracized. Go on, Ben." He nudges his son. "Wrestle with the brother."

The brother?

Before I can speak, correct this mistake, the boy is already walking onto the stage, taking off his own sweatshirt. The crowd applauds. The boy grins and waves at his mom, who has returned with the sleeping baby. He still has the chest of a little boy, sunken and sweet, with tiny nipples the pale pink of pencil erasers. His brown skin is just a shade darker than Nakajima's, his curls just a little less tightly coiled.

They could in fact be brothers.

"I got the rules," he says to Miyoshi-sensei, who looks nervous as he backs slowly away. Nakajima shows the boy how to do the squatting and leg lifting thing. They lock eyes, and when Miyoshi-sensei blows the whistle, they charge at each other and the littler boy wraps his arms around the bigger one.

Nakajima doesn't let the boy win, but he does allow himself to be pushed around the circle a few times before he nudges him out of it. When they bow at each other again, both wear grins as wide as bananas. Nakajima offers to wrestle anyone else in the crowd, and a bunch of junior high school boys take him up on his offer, all stripping to their underwear before climbing up onstage. I've never seen Nakajima look this happy. Like the rest of us, he just wants to be good at something, left to do this thing.

When I climb up onstage, his smile wavers.

When I begin to unwrap my obi, he looks downright uncomfortable.

"Sumo not for girl," he says, but I only smile, stretch out the moment, slowly opening the kimono, easing it off one shoulder and then the other.

"Dangerous-o!" Lone Wolf howls into the microphone.

The crowd is silent.

Catching sight of Miyoshi-sensei, who is covering his mouth with one hand and shaking his head with perceptible horror, I quickly slide the kimono off to reveal my tank top and shorts. Everyone claps and laughs, even Nakajima. "Teach me," I say, so he shows me how to warm up. Then we lean into each other, shoulder to shoulder. As I push against him, he matches my force exactly. This is just what my dad used to do when I was little and we'd arm wrestle. It drove me crazy, the way he could hold his arm steady while I exhausted myself, pushing without progress. It was his way of showing love. He wouldn't let me win, but he didn't want to crush me either.

Nakajima shifts, trying to throw me off balance. I manage to stay within the ring, bending down to grab hold of his ankle. He twists easily out of my grasp. "Nakajima gets around," he whispers. When I start to giggle, he seizes my own leg and holds it in the air while I hop backward, laughing even as he pushes me out.

"Okay," Miyoshi-sensei says. "I am sorry, Miss Marina, but Nakajima is still undefeated sumo champion!" Everyone claps and whistles and calls his name, "Nakajima! Nakajima! Nakajima!" But suddenly the chant shifts. "Ogawa?" yells one of the senior technical boys. "Ogawa! Ogawa! Ogawa!" It's more jeer than cheer.

As Haruki climbs the stairs and takes his place in the ring, members of the audience place bets over which boy will win. The one with the sumo title, or the one with the sumo body. Once more Miyoshi-sensei raises the whistle to his lips, and this time both charge, ramming bodies like big animals battling for a small territory. Haruki bears down on Nakajima, using his chest to push him to the far side of the ring. But then, at the last moment, Nakajima swivels out from under Haruki, throws him off balance and seizes his ankle, uprooting his massive leg. Haruki freezes as Nakajima starts shoving him toward the edge of the ring, moving him like something inanimate, a piano or a refrigerator. I can't help but feel disappointed. If this were a Hollywood movie, Haruki would have to win. He's the underdog. He has the physical advantage and the motivation to beat his former bully. And what a thrill it would be to defeat Nakajima at his own sport, in front of an audience, and on TV.

"Unbelievable!" Lone Wolf intones. "The fat one appears to be losing!"

Haruki breaks the first rule of sumo, kneeing Nakajima in the groin. As Nakajima doubles over, Haruki throws his whole weight on top of him, clamping his hand around his throat. They roll over each other and off the edge of the stage, and even after they hit the ground Haruki doesn't stop punching and kicking, as if he'd been saving up all of that stillness, storing all his wild energy for just this moment, just this chance.

A couple runs through the crowd, prying the boy off Nakajima. The woman is wearing the jade green uniform of the grocery store, and she takes off the jacket, using it to soak up the blood streaming from his nose. These must be Nakajima's parents. I recognize the man from behind the window of Shika's one barbershop, which serves a clientele of plant workers. He has a perm too. They guide their limping son through the crowd, propping him up with their arms, ignoring Haruki who is sitting with his forehead pressed to his knees. Miyoshi-sensei takes off his own suit jacket and sets it on the boy's shaking back.

"Is he okay?" I ask.

"I should probably take him home," Miyoshi-sensei says.

"It looked like he wanted to kill Nakajima."

"He wanted to win," he says. "Of course it's not the right way. He should not have broken rules. But for once he was not a stone, *ne*? Maybe next time he takes a better risk."

"Is he going to be suspended from school?" I ask.

"This would not be punishment for Haruki."

"No," I agree. "I guess it would be a reward."

"It would be giving up," he says.

He helps Haruki to his feet. His suit jacket flaps like a tiny cape on Haruki's huge body. With snot streaming down his face and eyes of glass, the boy looks like a refugee, someone who has lost his home and has no idea where to go.

Lone Wolf and his camera crew position themselves in front of the stage as I take the microphone and announce that it's time for the English speech contest. I wish I were still wearing the kimono instead of this tank top and shorts. "If any of you would like to make a speech in English, now's the time!" I repeat once more, but again no one steps forward. The SMILE members scattered throughout the crowd avoid my eyes.

"*Tsumaranai*," I hear Lone Wolf mutter to his cameraman. This is boring.

"*Wakaranai*?" I ask the crowd. Do you understand me?

"*Wakaranai*?" a familiar voice echoes.

From the back of the lawn, I see Keiko and her boys making their slow way toward the stage. Fumiya is rubber-kneed, trying to wriggle away from his mom, who is holding him by the elbow, dragging him forward while Koji pushes him from the back. When the three of them finally straggle up onstage, I try to give Fumiya the microphone but he swats at my hand, so I place it in the stand and step aside.

"It's *Jyabauokki* time," Keiko says to Fumiya, who just looks at her and giggles.

" 'Twas brillig," I prompt him, clapping once.

"Witttthhhhhh," Fumiya blows into the microphone. The sound crackles through the PA system and he widens his eyes and jumps, frightened by the echo of his echo.

"Twas brillig," I try again.

"Witttthhhhhh," he says again before scratching his chin with the microphone, then lowering his hand to his crotch. He laughs but no one laughs with him. Even Lone Wolf is silent, his cameraman standing beside him, capturing everything on film.

" 'Twas brillig," Koji speaks suddenly in a loud, clear little voice.

"Mo ichi do," Keiko urges her younger son, who moves forward to stand next to Fumiya, reaching for his hand. For once the older boy doesn't recoil from touch. He looks down at his little brother and beams. You can tell how much he loves him. " 'Twas brillig," Koji says again, "and the slithy toves, did gyre and gimble in the wabe." This time, when he pauses, a voice repeats after him, a uninflected voice from the crowd. At the dignitaries' table, the mayor, Miyoshi-sensei's father, is standing up. As he repeats after the little boy, the sound coming out of his voice box is slightly robotic but clear and easy to follow.

"All mimsy," Koji starts the next line.

"All mimsy!" Fumiya yells, and everyone laughs.

"Were the borogoves, and the mome raths outgrabe," the mayor finishes.

And this is the segment that ends up on Lone Wolf's variety show, not the story of two mayors signing a sister-city contract—which they do, later that same day—not the story of two rice farmers driving tractors across the Noto Peninsula in search of brides, not even the story of two boys using sumo wrestling to settle an old grudge, but the story of two real brothers, neither of whom can answer the question "How are you?" in English, who nonetheless managed to memorize Lewis Carroll's *Jabberwocky* and recite it in front of everyone in town, with the help of a man whose own voice had all but vanished.

chiru: (v.) *to fall; to scatter; to dissolve; to break up; to die a noble death*

On the Monday morning after the festival, I arrive in the faculty room and find Miyoshi-sensei waiting for me at my desk. He has a cup of tea in each hand. "Thank you for yesterday," he says, handing me a cup.

"You're welcome," I say, "but I didn't do much. I'm glad it wasn't a disaster."

"Me too," he says.

"Did your father have fun?"

"I think so. All night, he continued repeating this poem, over and over. I don't know why he likes it so much. Maybe it's memory lane trip for him. But memory of what?" I laugh, then stop as the principal enters the faculty room, addressing Miyoshi-sensei in formal Japanese. "Principal has some important thing to discuss," he translates, "concerning Miss Marina's special methods for teaching English."

"Okay," I say, braced for the worst. No doubt he wants to discuss the class he walked into on Friday, the posters on the wall, the condom I shoved into Nakajima's hand. The air in the principal's private office is already dense with smoke, as acrid as an airport smoking lounge, but he lights up another cigarette before sitting down. He pulls a piece of paper from his desk drawer. I can't see through the haze, but I'm sure it must be my sex-ed worksheet. I'll bet that he's going to ask me to explain my own risky behavior before he sends me packing.

"Last year in August," Miyoshi-sensei says, "I became your supervisor. This means I am responsible for you. Also, this means that if you do something, bad or good, then it reflects on me and I look bad or good as well. It's Japanese way. This is why I feel so nervous when you don't follow rules, like breaking a *gomi* law. Do you understand?" I nod, looking at his hands, which remain steady as he takes the sheet of paper from the principal, then presents it to me. But it's not my sex-ed worksheet, or a letter detailing my latest errors. Instead it's an official-looking document on thick and creamy card stock, covered in vertical lines of Japanese characters, with a bloodred seal at the bottom. "Principal and I agree. Here at Shika Koko, you have found many ways to make English useful. Useful and fun." The principal nods, although I suspect he has no idea what's being said. "This is a contract. Principal would like to invite you to renew, to teach for one more year here."

"Really?" I say. "Even after the sex-ed lesson?"

"Yes," he says. "I explained usefulness of this lesson, without naming a name, and principal came to understand why you taught such a thing. But he would rather you did not repeat this lesson."

"Wow," I say, thinking how brave he was to come to my defense. "Still, I'm surprised he wants me to keep teaching here."

"To be truthful," Miyoshi-sensei says, "probably he would offer contract renewal to anyone. It's kind of routine procedure. It's so tiring to explain the rules to a new foreigner over and over, always answering the same questions. Like having a new baby every year. But he sincerely hopes that you will accept this offer."

"Do you?" I ask, trying to catch his gaze through the smoke.

"My desire is not relevant to this matter," he says, accepting a cigarette from the principal. "Would you like one?" he asks me.

"Thanks," I say, "but I think I finally quit. At least I'm trying."

"Good for you," he says. "It's very difficult, I know well. I've tried many times."

"I can help you," I offer. "My mom sent me another huge box of Nicorette. Whenever you have a craving, just ask me for a piece and I'll give you one."

"Ah," he says. "Well, this would be difficult too."

"Why?"

"Because," he says, "I have been transferred to a new high school. Nanao Koko, on other side of peninsula."

"You're switching schools in September?" I ask.

"Not September," he says. "Japanese school year starts in April."

"But that's this month!" I exclaim, and he nods. "Who will be my supervisor?"

"Her name is Takeuchi-sensei," he says. "She is from Monzen, same town as rice farmers. She was transferred from Monzen agricultural high school. Probably Shika will seem huge to her, like Paris or Milano. She may be your supervisor, but you should be her guide." The principal says something in Japanese and Miyoshi-sensei continues. "So how about contract renewal? Could you make a decision now, or do you need some time to think about what you want to do next?"

"I can't believe you got transferred," I say.

"Actually," he says, "I requested this transfer. Nanao High School is high academic. It's kind of a promotion for me. I won't have to supervise foreign English teacher. Instead, I will run English literary journal. Can you imagine such a thing here?" He shakes his head and laughs. "It's good thing I had so much practice writing letters to you."

"Yeah," I say. "Good thing I was so difficult to supervise."

"This is not what I meant," he says quietly.

The ceiling in this office is low, pressing down on me, reminding me of the low ceilings in interstate motels, the kind of motel where you stay as you drive from one place to another, not bothering to note the name of the stopover town. Shika is a stopover town. Why would I stay here for another year, teaching English to students for whom it has no real use or purpose, only serving to remind them of how stuck they are?

"I can't imagine being here without you," I say, and when the principal asks for a translation, Miyoshi-sensei says, "She's considering your offer."

As usual, the technical boys are nearly naked. Fingerprints encircle Nakajima's neck and he has a split lip in a shade of purple that matches Haruki's bruised and swollen eye.

"*Shitsureishimashita*," Haruki says, bowing deeply. I have committed a rude.

"In English," Miyoshi-sensei says. "This is English class. And be direct!"

"I . . . " Haruki begins.

"Stole," Miyoshi-sensei prompts him.

"I . . . stole . . . *seifuku*."

"Uniforms," Miyoshi-sensei translates. "You stole their uniforms."

"Who cares?" lisps Nakajima in Japanese. "We don't need them. We're almost out of here."

"Actually, I want mine," says Sumio, looking down at his pierced nipple. "I'm cold."

"I want mine too," another boy chimes in. "It's going to rain today, and I'm supposed to go to the city. I don't want to wear my plant uniform. I look like a hick in that thing."

"I'm supposed to give mine to my little brother," says a third. "My mom's been threatening to make me pay for the missing one. Those things are expensive."

"Miss Marina," Miyoshi-sensei says, turning to face me. "Could you please accompany Haruki to your house? I think there are too many uniforms for him to carry alone, and he should not enter without you."

Haruki rushes out of the building ahead of me, and I'm glad that we don't have to walk side by side, that I won't have to try to talk to him. My skin still crawls when I think of him sneaking into my house over and over, trying to "sabotage" me by unplugging the refrigerator so that our groceries would go bad, following us to the beach and spying on us there. I know he saw us smoke the joint, but I wonder if he watched us kiss. I wonder how much he reported back to Miyoshi-sensei. Probably everything.

When I get home, Joe's truck is parked in the driveway, windows rolled down. From the entryway, I hear a rhythmic thumping sound in the bedroom. I run upstairs and fling open the door, where I find Joe seated on the floor, drumming his fingers on the back of his guitar while Carolyn stuffs T-shirts into a duffel bag. She looks up and smiles.

"Hey M," she says. "I'm happy to see you."

"Sure," I say. "That's why you came over when you thought I'd be at work."

"There was an assembly this morning so I got off early," she says. "Joe was teaching in Hakui so he offered to help me move the rest of my stuff."

"How sweet," I say. "That Joe is a real gentleman. Just ask his sixteen-year-old girlfriend, Ritsuko."

"She's not my girlfriend," Joe says, towering over me. "You don't know what you're talking about."

"Does Carolyn?" I ask, trying to push him out of the way.

"No," Carolyn says, calmly folding more T-shirts and putting them in her bag, "and I don't care."

"You don't care that Joe fucked a student? That he took advantage of a freshman?"

"I lost my virginity when I was fifteen," she says, "to a thirty-year-old guy who worked at the same firm as my father."

"So that makes it okay?" I cut her off. "Because you were taken advantage of too?"

"I seduced him," she says, zipping her bag shut. "He treated me like an adult, and he taught me a lot of things, and it wasn't a bad choice."

"But you were just a kid." I say, "He had the power."

"In a way," she says, "but in a way I did. I could've told someone. And I wasn't being held against my will. I'm the one who ended it."

"Well, I don't think Ritsuko had a lot of power," I say, "and I think sixteen is pretty young." I almost add, *to have an abortion without any support*, but I don't know if she told Joe that she was pregnant, and it's not my secret to divulge.

"I think I love her," he says, standing with his back to us, looking out the window. "Not that it matters. She won't even return my calls."

"Really?" Carolyn says. "I thought you wanted a partner. Someone who can speak her mind."

"I know she's young," he says without turning around, "but she's amazing."

"It's true," I say. "She can speak her mind." I can't even hate him anymore. Nothing is ever simple. "Why did you come back here?" I ask Carolyn.

"To get the stuff I left behind," she says.

"That junk?" I laugh. "You never get rid of anything."

She slings her bag over her shoulder. "I miss you," she says.

"You didn't even say good-bye."

"I'm here, aren't I?"

This line sounds oddly familiar, but I can't remember when I heard it before. Then suddenly I do. It was in our dorm lounge, late at night, right after I told her that I was afraid that the wave of grief might wash me away. She held me while I sobbed, and I barely even knew her. She took me to her room. She took care of me. She got me out of there.

"Is someone downstairs?" Joe asks.

"Haruki," I say.

"What the fuck is the cat killer doing here?" Carolyn says.

"I don't know," Joe says, "but I think he's taking off with your things."

Downstairs, the door to the storage area is still open and all of the boxes on the shelves are empty. I notice the address written on the side of one of these empty boxes, written in my mother's handwriting. This is the box that used to contain my father's things.

The box that held his remains.

I fly out the door, down the street, catching up with Haruki as he rounds the corner, carrying a bulging black garbage bag over one shoulder. I grab the garbage bag and dump it out on the street, but all I can see are uniforms.

"Where are the things that were in the boxes?" I ask in Japanese.

"*Gomi ni narimashita*," he says. It became garbage.

"When did you throw it away?"

"Earlier this week," he says.

"What day?" I ask. "What kind of garbage did it become?"

"Moeru gomi."

Burnable garbage.

I know the rules. Burnable garbage gets collected only on Tuesdays in this neighborhood, from the bin in front of Mister Donuts. It must be thrown in clear plastic trash bags, so everyone can see what you're throwing away. Today is Monday, and the bin in front of Mister Donuts is not just filled with plastic trash bags, it's also surrounded by them, literally buried under them. It looks like a mountain of trash. Mount Garbage. *Gomi-san.*

"Maybe it's for the best," I say to Carolyn, who insisted on coming along after I told her what Haruki threw away. "I didn't know what to do with his stuff. Now I guess I can just forget about it. Move on." But she won't accept my defeat. She never gets rid of anything, and she won't let me either. I watch her scale the mountain of trash, stepping from bag to bag in her heavy combat boots. With her shredded tights and miniskirt, she looks like a superhero. Garbage Girl. She looks as fierce and androgynous and lovely as ever. Carolyn is not afraid of the ugly parts of life. She doesn't look away, or even want to. Having reached the summit of *Gomi-san*, she calls down to me, asking me to tell her everything that was in the box. I close my eyes and try to remember. "A suede jacket," I begin, "a camera and some lenses wrapped in tube socks, a dictionary and an orange velour sweatshirt . . . " The one he bought when I was a baby, because it was the softest thing he could find. My chest hurts like I've been breathing smog.

"Anything else?" she prompts me to go on.

"Just some ashes," I say, sitting on the curb and burying my face in my hands.

"Ashes?"

"My mom thought I might want to scatter them here. To say good-bye. I couldn't even bring myself to open the baggie. I guess Haruki scattered them for me."

"Don't worry, we'll get them back," she says, picking up another bag, examining its contents and pitching it down the side of the mountain. "I'm looking for the orange velour sweatshirt. That should be bright enough to show through the plastic. I doubt the kid threw away a camera."

"It was really old," I say. "It probably didn't even work anymore."

"But it's not burnable," she says. "He probably put it in the bin by the river."

"I'll go look," Joe offers.

"That's a good idea," Carolyn says to Joe, "but hurry back, so that you can help me look through all of these bags. This could take a while."

A Mister Donuts employee stands in the open door to his shop, nervously fingering his visor while he watches Carolyn move the mountain. "Um, excuse me," he calls out in Japanese, "but what are you doing in the trash?" Carolyn ignores him and continues tossing bags over the side of the bin, where they land with soft plops at my feet. He looks at me, the tears streaking my face, the tendrils of snot I keep wiping with my sleeve, and he goes back inside, no doubt to call the police about the crazy *gaijin* falling apart in front of his store. If throwing the wrong trash away is a minor violation, then this must be a major crime. With every bag that Carolyn discards, I find myself increasingly disappointed. And disappointed in my disappointment. My dad walked away from this junk. He had no more use for any of it. Why should I be its keeper and treasure what he trashed? Carolyn is so driven and efficient that it doesn't take her long to empty the entire bin. She hoists herself out of the Dumpster like someone climbing out of a pool and tells me not to lose heart, that there are still tons of bags surrounding the bin. "Don't worry," she says, sitting beside me and taking my hand. "I won't let your dad's things get thrown away."

"Burned," I choke. "Can ashes burn? What do you think happens to them?"

"They probably disappear," she says.

"Dust to dust," I say. "The perfect ending."

"No it's not," she says, squeezing my hand. "It's a terrible ending."

"What difference does it make?" I sob. "I had to do something with them."

"But you didn't," she says. "Someone else did. If you want to throw them away or burn them, then fine. That's your choice. But you have to make it."

"My mom was right," I cry. "There's always more. It's been almost two years since my dad killed himself, and we're still dealing with the mess he left behind. It will never be over. There will always be something else to get rid of."

"You're wrong," she says, standing up and looking down at me. "Someday you'll go home and find that nothing belongs to him anymore. Mail with his name will stop coming. People will stop asking if you miss him. And maybe you won't. Or you will, but only in an abstract way. You won't be able to picture his face anymore. You won't remember what his voice sounded like, or his laugh, and you'll wish you had something to hold on to, to remind you of him. You'll wish you had all of it, every single thing, because no matter what you held on to, it won't be enough." She is crying too now, and I wrap my arms around her and hug her close, the way she taught me.

"Now tell me everything that was in the box again," she says, still holding me.

"I told you," I say. "There was a suede jacket, a camera, a dictionary, an orange velour sweatshirt, a baggie of ashes. Oh, and a cell
phone."

"Your dad had some special cell phone?"

"No," I say. "It was Ritsuko's."

Joe has returned victorious, camera slung around his neck.

"Call the bags," I order him.

"What?" he says.

"Ritsuko's cell phone is in there. It's probably out of batteries,
but you never know."

While Joe dials, Carolyn and I circle the mountain of garbage,
crouching low and pressing our ears to the plastic, listening to the
trash. People walking toward the donut store stare at us and keep
their distance. A woman carrying her own bag of trash turns around
and walks away. Suddenly Carolyn dives into the pile, pulling out a
ringing trash bag.

It's all there.

Alone in the bedroom, I lay it on the tatami: jacket over shirt,
dictionary where a hand would have been, camera for a missing face.
As if I could build him from scraps. Fill in the blanks. Fill in my
blanks.

Once, when I was in the second grade, my father pulled me out
of school for a week and the two of us took a trip, driving from California to Arizona, to visit his younger brother who was working as
an engineer in a copper mine. My dad had a week off before starting
his residency. He'd entered medical school when I was in preschool,
which meant that he came home after dinner most nights, was gone
again before I woke up the next morning, and when he was around
he was bone tired. On his rare days off, we'd go to the beach as a

family. My mom and I would walk on the sandy path beside the road while he drove in the bike lane, keeping pace with us. He wanted to spend time as a family, but he was too tired to walk. More than once I saw him start to fall asleep standing up, sway, and then catch himself. The trip to Arizona was my mom's idea. On one of those walks, she told me that my dad and I should spend more time together, just the two of us. She told me that we should make an effort to know each other, before I was grown up and we both regretted the time we'd missed.

I barely knew my uncle, who was shorter and more compactly muscled than my dad; he had less hair, a sharper nose, and thinner lips; yet they still looked so much alike that I was confused when I saw them together, standing side by side like a man and his funhouse mirror image. My uncle explained that children weren't allowed down in the mine, where it got up to four hundred degrees. "You'd burn right up," my father teased me, messing my hair, which was his way of showing affection. I believed him. I worried that after descending into the copper mine, my own father might end up shrunken. He took a tour while I waited in the car with the windows down. It was one hundred degrees out, and I had enough math in me to understand that it was four times hotter down there. The longer it took for my father to reappear, the more certain I became that he had burned up, that I'd never see him again. But he came out intact, bewildered to find me sobbing in the hot car.

"I'm fine," he said, messing up my hair again. "I'm tougher than that, kiddo. You don't have to worry about me."

I don't remember many details from the rest of the trip, but the drive back home stands out clearly in my memory. As he drove, I lay on my side with my head on his lap, reading the stack of books I'd brought along. "You should look out the window," he said. "You never know when you'll be back in this part of the country. You might

never get the chance to see this again." But I didn't care. I loved reading while the warm wind blew into the car; I loved the soft, grainy
feel of his cut-off jeans under my cheek, and the way he kept a palm
on my forehead to protect me from the steering wheel. Sometimes
I read aloud to him. We took our time getting back. He turned off
for every scenic vista, every state park. As usual, whenever a plant
caught his eye, he'd pull over and have me stake a lookout while he
dug it up and placed it in a bag to replant in our garden. His hatch-
back had no trunk, only a rear cavity with a sloped back window,
and by the end of our road trip we'd filled it with so many liberated
natives that the headlights of the cars behind us were softly filtered
by their foliage.

The very last night of our trip was also the night that Halley's
Comet returned to earth. He must have been planning for us to pull
into the observatory on the night it burned a path through the sky
for the first time in seventy-five years, but the coincidence seemed
miraculous at the time. As we drove up to the planetarium, he explained that a comet was really just a chunk of dust and ice left over
from when the world was made. "Every seventy-five years," he told
me, "this particular chunk of ice and dust orbits close enough to the
sun that the gasses catch on fire. What you see, the tail of the comet,
is really just dust in flame. But what's special about Halley's Comet
is that even though we can't see it coming, we always know exactly
when it will return."

"But how do we know it's the same chunk of ice and dust?" I
asked. "What if it's different? How do we know?" I was used to repeating myself over and over, asking questions he didn't answer, not
because he couldn't answer them, but because he couldn't hear me.
When he got started talking about science, he lost all sense of his
audience. He was fascinated by the way things worked. He had to
take things apart in order to understand them. "How do we know?"

he repeated my question. "Thanks to the astronomer who figured it out, the man it's named for, Edmund Halley. The tragic part is, no one believed him at the time, and he didn't live to see his prediction come true."

In the planetarium parking lot, we sat on the hood of his car, our tailbones making two lasting dimples in the thin sheet metal. I saw the fuzzy tails of light arcing behind what looked like a falling star, but was really cosmic dust. It was cool out, a shock after the desert heat, and he took off his orange velour sweatshirt and gave it to me. I pulled the sleeves over my bare legs, wearing it like pants, and nestled against him, burrowing under his arm. "Keep your eyes open, kiddo," he said, squeezing me gently. "This is one thing you won't see again in your lifetime, guaranteed. At least not with me." I looked at him, but he was staring up at the comet.

The last summer I spent at home, when my mom went to work as a camp counselor, my dad and I were left alone together for the first time since that trip to Arizona. I was selling popcorn and candy at a movie theater, which earned me a free pair of tickets to any movie playing. Even at his most depressed, my dad still liked getting away with something, getting something for free, and on the nights I had off sometimes we'd go to the movies together, sitting through screwball comedies and summer action flicks with absurd chase scenes and explosions that lit up the screen like fireworks. It was a relief to sit in the darkness without having to talk. We'd stop at Burger King on the way and get 99-cent Whoppers—no drinks or fries because that's where they ripped you off—and sneak them in.

The last night we spent together was at the end of one of those Indian summer days when San Francisco almost stops functioning because of the heat. I was wearing a sundress, and the air-conditioned theater felt refreshingly cool when we first entered it, but quickly became too cold. I remember that he laid his suede jacket across my lap to keep me warm, just like he used to at night on our road trips. We ate our burgers and we both relaxed, laughing obligingly at the silly comedy on-screen. I don't remember much about the movie, only that when it ended and the credits started rolling, we kept sitting there even after the lights in the theater came on and a team started cleaning the trash off the floor.

"I'm really going to miss this, kiddo," my dad said, putting his hand on the back of my hair and leaving it there. "I hope you know that." The summer was almost over. My mom was coming back home and I was headed back to school. I was twenty-one, about to begin my adult life. I thought I knew what he was talking about. "I guess it's time to go," he said, but his hand was still on my hair and he made no move to get up, and neither did I.

PART IV

O~Bon

SUMMER

It's not like anything
they compare it to—
the summer moon.

Although it must have been this hot when we first arrived in Shika, I feel unprepared for the humidity of July, assaulted by the sun that is up before Vivaldi's *The Four Seasons* blasts from the loudspeakers. So every morning, before brushing my teeth, I put on my bathing suit, then the *yukata* I bought on a weekend trip to Kyoto—a last trip with Carolyn before she returned to New York to start culinary school—and walk the five blocks to the sea, a path I could follow with my eyes closed by now.

No one else is ever at the beach this early. It's all mine, as far as the eye can see. I slip out of my *yukata* and wade into the water, which gets warmer day by day. There's no shock of entry. I swim out as far as I can, as far as I dare, until I am out of breath from swimming and from the awareness of myself as I would look from up above, a speck in the blue sea. Then I turn around, hold my knees in my arms to keep my feet out of the darker, colder water below, and look back at Shika.

From the sea I can see it all: the scalloped coastline, the tire-tracks perforating the sand, the wind-bent pines that look like old people hunched over canes, the smokestacks of the nuclear power plant up on the hill, the school. From the sea, it looks like a postcard, if there were postcards of Shika. I roll over onto my back and let the current carry me where it wants to, where it will, closing my eyes, always surprised to find myself closer to the shore when I open them again.

This daily ritual is something I keep private, so I am taken aback when, in the middle of July, Hiro says to me out of the blue, "You had better stop swimming in the sea, *ne*? Maybe it's not such a good idea anymore." Since he is no longer my supervisor, I call him by his first name and he no longer calls me "Miss" Marina. This took a little getting used to. But now, three months after his transfer to Nanao High School, I almost never slip up and call him "Miyoshi-sensei."

It's after dark and we are sitting at a table at the local bar, a joint that caters mainly to plant workers, almost exclusively to men. This bar is the only place in town that serves food past nine, which is when Hiro gets back to Shika from Nanao most nights. The first time he asked me to meet him here, he wanted my help reading through the stack of submissions he'd received for the English literary journal. We disagreed on our favorites. He preferred the sentimental poems cluttered with strange metaphors. I liked the funny stories about daily life. The next time he didn't bring any student writing. I was happy that he didn't have to invent an excuse to hang out with me, but I sort of missed reading the submissions together.

The mama-san at this bar has gotten used to our strange pairing and ways. Without needing to be asked, she brings us a large Sapporo to share and a dish of *oden*—tofu—two boiled eggs, and a hockey puck of simmered daikon radish for me; fish sausages and a skewer of chicken skins for Hiro.

"Who told you that I've been swimming in the sea?" I ask, piercing an egg with the tip of a chopstick. The crumbly yolk turns the broth creamy.

"No one," he replies. "I can smell it on you." He blushes.

"The surf is very calm," I say, struggling to stay calm myself. "And I'm a strong swimmer. I'll be sure to wash off better, so I don't smell so fishy."

"Smell isn't problem," he says, his eye twitching. "Smell is not unpleasant, only salty. Your swimming ability is not problem either."

"Then what is the problem? Are women not supposed to swim in the sea? Is that it? Or is it because I'm a teacher? Is there a rule against teachers swimming in the sea?"

"Have you noticed anyone else swimming in the sea lately?" he asks, his fingertip tracing a path down the condensation of the beer bottle.

"No," I say, "but I thought that was because I go so early."

"It's because it's not safe."

"Oh my God." My skin suddenly feels hot and itchy. I take a long swill of beer. "Is the water contaminated? Is it the nuclear power plant?"

"Water is fine," he says quickly, refilling my glass. "Problem is jellyfish."

"Jellyfish?" I repeat. "I haven't seen any jellyfish."

"Not yet," he says. "Maybe they will return on July twenty-eighth."

"Maybe?" I tease him.

"Mmm," he nods. "They will return on July twenty-eighth."

"Return from where?" I ask and he shrugs, picks up his bowl, and slurps the broth. "The jellyfish follow our calendar?" I press. "They're punctual, Type-A jellyfish?"

"Yeah," he says. Lately he has begun using my expressions. *No way. Oh please. Give me a break.* I don't know if he's aware of this or not, and I don't want to point it out because it's so endearing that I don't want to make him self-conscious and stop.

"Do the jellyfish have a very important date to keep? An appointment with a squid perhaps?"

"I don't know," he says, frowning. "I only know that's when they will return."

"How convenient," I say, borrowing one of his own favorite words.

"I'm only trying to help you, Mari-chan," he says, "so you won't get hurt."

"You're trying to supervise me."

"Yeah," he says again. "Sorry. Old habits are difficult to shake."

Nakajima is also at the bar, sitting at a corner table under the big TV bolted to the ceiling, watching a sumo match. Next to him sits Ogawa-san: the *gomi* police himself. Both men are wearing red power plant uniforms, and white hand towels tied around their foreheads, Rambo-style. According to Hiro, shortly after Haruki beat Nakajima up in front of the whole town, Nakajima was given a job at the plant, directly under Haruki's grandfather. I don't know if the old man had any say in this, but I assume it was a lucky break for Nakajima, who buzzed off his Afro-perm and stopped tinting his skin brown. He looks more vulnerable now that he's not hiding behind a costume. I wonder if he knows that he actually fooled someone into thinking that his disguise was for real. I'm sure he'd be thrilled.

As Hiro and I step up to the cash register, Nakajima looks back and forth between us. He wiggles one eyebrow suggestively and says, "Hello Miss Marina. Hello Miyoshi-sensei."

"Hello Nakajima," I say. "How are you?"

"You owe me," he says.

"What?"

"I say hello. I get Marina dollar."

"You're right," I say. "I do owe you." When I tell the mama-san to add his drink to my tab, Nakajima seems flustered, but also pleased. He offers me an edamame from the dish on their table and I accept, popping the soybean into my mouth and thanking him.

"Avoid risky behavior," he says.

"What does that mean?" Ogawa-san asks him in Japanese.

"Have fun," Nakajima translates. "At least I think that's what it means."

"Avoid risky behavior," Ogawa-san repeats after him slurrily, lifting his glass.

Once we're safely outside, Hiro and I both double over, laughing so hard that we can't speak. We are still laughing even when he drops me off at home. I get out quickly, wave good-bye. He waits until I'm safely inside before driving off.

With the landlord's blessing, Hiro helped me to empty the rest of the boxes from the storage area, and then we took down the corrugated tin siding. Now the windows look out on the street. From the living room, I watch Mrs. Ogawa gardening by moonlight on this warm summer night, singing a lullabye to her fish as she feeds them.

Every Saturday, Hiro drives down to Kanazawa City, to the convalescent hospital where his father is receiving an aggressive round of chemotherapy, which will probably be his last. One Saturday morning, he calls to ask if I'd like to keep him company on the trip. I am honored and touched, misunderstanding the invitation, which he means literally. He wants company for the two-hour drive, but has no intention of bringing me to the hospital to see his father. Instead he drops me off at the Daiwa department store, where I spend two hours working my way from the bottom up. I wander around the basement, filled with stalls of food almost too pretty to eat, then take the escalator up to each floor, where I covet women's clothing and shoes I could never fit into and buy a few cards with funny English written on them. One says, "Let's Trip!" over a picture of a plane; the other says, "Breast wishes." At the planned time, I meet up with Hiro at an art gallery on the top floor.

The exhibit on display is the work of a recently deceased outsider artist. Like seven-year-old Koji Ishii, this man liked to tear things apart, newspapers and photographs, money, stamps, ripping these images into snowflake-sized pieces, then reassembling them into pointillist collages of crowd scenes. Always crowd scenes. Hiro and I walk around the gallery, moving from picture to picture in silence. When I finally ask what he thinks of the art, he says, "Eh . . . I only came for you. I don't really like art."

"What do you mean?" I say. "How can you not like art?"

"I prefer music," he says.

"That's ridiculous," I say. "You don't have to pick. You can like both."

"You're wrong. There is not enough time," he says, taking off his glasses and cleaning them with his shirttail. "You do have to pick."

In his car, the stereo starts up when he turns the key in the ignition. He's been listening to an English language tutorial, a chapter called, "at the hospital." These words scroll across the digital display. "I am short of breath," narrates a woman in a proper British accent. "I can't sleep. My head aches. My heart is pounding. I am irregular."

Hiro stops in the middle of the parking lot off-ramp, gripping the steering wheel. "All of this applies to me," he says. "I am irregular."

"How was your dad today?" I ask.

"Same," he says. "Not good. Lately I am always waiting for bad news. When my phone rings, I feel afraid to answer. But also I am tired of waiting. Sometimes I want the bad news to happen already."

"Your dad has cancer," I say gently. "He's been in a lot of pain for a long time, and you've had to watch him suffer. Of course you're tired of waiting."

"What about you?" he says. "Did you feel the same way?"

"It's different," I say. "My dad killed himself." This is the first time I've spoken these words in a year. "*Jisatsu*," I say, in case he didn't get it.

"I know," he says.

"You do?" I ask, and he nods. "How could you know? Who told you?"

"No one had to tell me," he says. "When you mention your father, you never say how he died." Hands still on the steering wheel, he turns to look at me, ignoring the honking car behind us, even though we're blocking the ramp out of the parking lot. "In Japan, we know well what this means." I look down at my own hands, my big hands, which are so much like my father's.

"When my mom called to tell me that he killed himself," I say, "I heard her crying and I knew what she was going to say before she said it. I knew, and I hadn't done anything about it. I didn't even tell him that I loved him the last time we spoke."

"I think he knew," Hiro says.

"He'd been depressed for so long," I say. "By the end, I think I wanted something to happen too, even if it was something bad."

"Your father was also in pain," Hiro says. "It's not so different."

"But I didn't help him," I say. "He was depressed, I know, but he didn't have to die. He could've gotten better. Maybe I could have stopped him."

"Maybe," Hiro says, and for some reason this is what I need to hear. It doesn't mean yes or no. It means maybe. It means we'll never know. I curl up in my seat facing him, holding my knees, pressing my face to my arms, crying and crying and crying, and he comforts me in the same way he comforted Ritsuko, not by patting me or offering false promises that everything is going to be fine, simply by staying there, present, beside me, not turning away.

The afternoon of Noriko's wedding, he picks me up in an unfamiliar car. It's some kind of Japanese sports car, platinum, tricked out with a neon-framed license plate, a fin that sticks up in the back, and rimmed hubcaps that are blindingly shiny. The bucket seat is so low to the ground that it feels like I'm sitting on the pavement. The car registers bumps that aren't visible on the road.

"Fancy new car," I say.

"It's used," he says, "but it's in perfect condition."

"Pre-owned," I tell him. "New-to-you."

"It's not mine," he says. I wait for him to elaborate, and when he doesn't I assume that it must be—or must have been—his father's. Maybe it's an early inheritance. As we drive together to the Royal Hotel, I ask him to run through a brief list of what I should or shouldn't do at a Japanese wedding. At first he says not to worry, just to enjoy myself, that no one expects me to know the rules.

"Tell me anyway," I say. "I don't want to do anything rude."

"Okay. To begin, don't seem too happy," he gives in without further prodding.

"*Don't* be happy?"

He nods. "Japanese wedding is a kind of serious and formal occasion. When we enter the hotel, say "*omedeto gozaimasu*" to the person at the front desk."

"I'm supposed to congratulate the receptionist?"

He nods again. "Then you should present your gift money to the receptionist."

"Gift money?" I echo, my throat tightening as I think of the wrapped book in my bag, a thesaurus I asked my mom to send for the occasion. Granted, it isn't the most romantic wedding present, but I wanted to give Noriko something personal, something that she couldn't get here, and she's always asking for synonyms of the words she already knows. As Miyoshi-sensei brakes to a stop at a red light, he reaches across me, opens the glove compartment and pulls out a white envelope.

"This is for you to present," he says.

"I can't let you pay my gift money."

"Don't worry," he says. "I knew you would not be prepared."

"I was prepared," I say, pulling out the gift that I wrapped with pretty silver paper and a white satin bow. I tear this wrapping off, holding up the thesaurus. Hiro takes it from me, flipping through its pages.

"How useful," he says. "Probably this would come in handy at my new school, when I am helping students write poems and stories in English. Maybe I could purchase from you?"

"Don't patronize me," I say.

"Patronize . . . " he repeats, and before I can offer a definition he flips to the word in the thesaurus. "To treat like a child. To infantilize." He looks up at me. "You are not a child, and I don't want to treat you like this. You are strong woman. I know well." He's echoing the words of the gender lesson we taught together long ago, but he's not making fun of me. His sincerity makes me blush. The sports car plunges into a pothole in the road, then launches for just a split second into the air. We both gasp, and then he grins. For the duration of the ride, he continues telling me what to do and not to do at a Japanese wedding, the list going on and on, even after we're parked in the hotel parking lot. "There will be a gift for you too," he says at last. "Don't open it. Say thank you to bride and groom before you leave the reception. But don't say *sayonara*."

"Don't say good-bye."

"Don't use any words to suggest separation. It's bad luck."

I follow him through the hotel's front doors, where he congratulates the receptionist, hands her his gift envelope and steps out of the way so that I can congratulate her too, and hand her mine.

The wedding is beautiful, somber, largely incomprehensible to me. Noriko wears a white kimono, white face powder, a white Shinto headdress that looks like a boat made of paper. True to Hiro's predictions, it is not a jolly affair. No music plays as she walks down the aisle and no one gushes over how lovely she looks, although she does. Her father cries, and to my surprise so do I, just a little, as she and the dentist pledge to spend the rest of their lives together.

At the reception, Noriko changes into a meringue of a Western wedding gown. She and Taichi sit on wicker thrones on a small stage, holding court while the rest of us dine on a sticky pasta carbonara with little flecks of nori. Hiro is seated at the table right beneath the stage. I wish I were up there next to him, across from Keiko and Yuji Ishii. Instead I am at the Shika High School faculty table, next to my new supervisor, Takeuchi-sensei.

Takeuchi-sensei is a woman in her late fifties, recently divorced, as several teachers have taken it upon themselves to inform me. She dyes her hair a stark, matte black, and seldom touches up her gray roots, so that it looks like a wig that's sliding off. She has virtually no eyelashes and a voice with two volume settings: a whisper and a yell. When we teach, she stands at the back of the room, leaning against the wall with her eyes closed, keeping them closed even when she yells, "*Shizuka!*" Be quiet! The girls can't stand her. Teachers from adjacent classrooms often pop their heads in to make sure that everything is okay. "Fine," she whispers, closing her eyes again. "Everything's fine."

In the past three months, Takeuchi-sensei has made exactly one contribution to lesson planning. One day, she brought a stack of index cards to class and asked all of the girls to come up with a personal motto. "Words to live by," she explained in Japanese. "Like an advertisement for yourself." For her own motto, she was torn between "Shop 'til you drop," and "A penny saved is a penny earned." When she asked me what my motto was, I plagiarized a Beckett quote I'd memorized in college. "Try again. Fail again. Fail better." She made no comment, but later I discovered this index card—which I'd tossed into the recycling bin—displayed under her clear plastic desk cover, next to a picture of herself beside her teenaged daughter, in front of the Statue of Liberty.

"Do you like a Japanese wedding?" Noriko asks me. She is making her rounds, handing gift boxes to each guest. I nod and smile and thank her for my favor, forgetting whether I'm supposed to do that or not. "You look beautiful. Are you having fun?" I ask, remembering too late that one is not supposed to seem too happy at a Japanese wedding, that it's not meant to be a fun occasion. But she nods and says that she is having a good time. I'm also not sure whether it's rude to get up and go talk to the guests at other tables, but I decide to take to heart what Hiro said to me earlier: no one expects me to get everything right. There are some advantages to being a temporary person here.

"Hey," I say, standing between Hiro and Keiko. "What are you guys talking about?" I have had a few glasses of champagne, just enough to make me bubbly.

"Yuji and Hiro are talking about fun things to do in New York," Keiko says. "I told you Yuji could find golf. He always finds golf on his vacation."

"It was not vacation," Yuji says, smiling as he does whenever he speaks English.

Recently, Keiko and Yuji invited Hiro and me over for dinner: Japanese pizza, with corn and dollops of potato salad, unexpectedly delicious. I didn't know that Hiro had been invited too. We each went straight from work, in separate cars, but we got there at the same time and I watched him watch me climb out of my car window. He didn't mention it, but I was still ashamed. At dinner, we all traded local gossip. Another petition to shut down the plant is circulating. Lone Wolf's show is moving to prime time. One of the male teachers at the junior high got arrested for soliciting sex via cell phone from what he thought was a thirteen-year-old girl, but was actually an undercover cop. After we ran out of gossip, we played a simplified version of the game Taboo, where the goal is to get your partner to guess the word written on a card, without using that word directly. The first card I pulled had the word "gorgeous," written on it.

"Beautiful," I started the game.

"Cherry blossoms," Hiro guessed.

"Pretty," I tried again.

"You," he said, blushing when we all laughed.

"Fumiya," Fumiya broke in, breaking the tension beautifully.

Fumiya and Koji were partners, and Fumi turned out to be good at Taboo, as long as Koji gave him the same prompts and repeated those cards several times. "You" became the cue for him to say his own name. "Greeting" prompted him to say "Hello." I noticed that Koji loved to prompt him, edging as close to conversation as his brother can get for now. We had a good time, all six of us. Keiko seemed relaxed around Yuji. I would've said that they had a happy marriage. But tonight at the wedding the air between them is tense.

"You should give your wife a break," I say impulsively. "She needs a vacation too."

"Hear, hear," Keiko agrees, raising her own glass of champagne.

"She is mother," Yuji says. "You know our situation . . . maybe there is no vacation from this."

"It's not our situation," Keiko says. "It's our son." She looks at me as if for encouragement, and I want to cheer her on, but I also don't want to overstep my bounds, or to make things worse for her. "I think you could take care of them," she says, carefully cutting into her strawberry chiffon cake. "Just for one night . . ."

"Where would you go?" he asks. He's still smiling, but now it looks like the pasted on smile of a gymnast trying to execute a tricky landing.

"I don't know," she says. "Maybe to *onsen* hotel." There are hot spring hotels all up and down the coast, all-inclusive places where people go during the summer to relax, get pampered, have their every need anticipated.

"Who would you go with?" he asks, looking at her a little sadly.

"I don't know," she says again. "Maybe with Marina?"

"I'd love to go," I say. "I've never been to a Japanese *onsen*, and I'd be too nervous to go by myself. What if I did the wrong thing?"

"It's true, there are many rules at Japanese *onsen*," Hiro says, with a glint in his eye.

"What rules?" Yuji grumbles. "It's just a bath." But then he says, "Okay."

"What?" Keiko says, fork frozen in midair.

"I can take care of the boys for one night, *ne*? It's not that difficult."

"Thank you," Keiko says. He doesn't speak, but when she offers him the bite of her cake, he opens his mouth and lets her feed him, just like the newlyweds onstage.

Afterward, in the parking lot, Hiro asks me whether I like the car.

"It's really nice," I say.

"It is really nice," he agrees. "Probably nicer than a temporary person should have."

"What?" I say.

"I'm not patronizing. I did not buy for you. It's . . . *loaner*. On a test drive. Situation is, this car has only nine months left of *shakken*." *Shakken* is the Japanese equivalent of insurance. "Your contract has nine more months. And the car you are driving is not safe. If you had an accident, you might not have time to climb out window. I think you had better buy this car. If you like it, I mean. I can negotiate a very good deal for you."

"I love it," I say, accepting the keys. 'Thank you so much, Miyoshi-sensei."

"Hiro," he reminds me.

Tonight, Hiro and I are taking turns soloing. We are at Big Echo, in a karaoke box that is truly just a box, a booth facing a screen that displays song lyrics and plays videos that are hopelessly out of sync with the words. On the drive back into town from Noriko's wedding, I mentioned that I wasn't really tired, and he suggested that we could maybe sing some karaoke. This is the first time we've done this since the night we kissed, all those months ago.

Now he is singing The Beatles' "Nowhere Man." His eyes are closed, which means he knows the words by heart, and also that I can look at him without his knowledge. His skin is pale and smooth, except for the faint laugh lines fanning from the corners of his eyes. There's a tiny nick in his earlobe—the trace of an old piercing? A remnant of a wilder youth? One of his sideburns is a few millimeters shorter than the other, and his upper lip is fuller than his lower lip. He is all charm points. His forehead and cheekbones are shining, damp from singing in this hot box of a room. The speed is off— this beat of the slow song is galloping forward—and it's his doing. Between verses he keeps reaching for the dials of the control panel, accelerating the rhythm so that he can barely catch his breath. On-screen, a frustrated dolphin repeatedly leaps out of its Marine World tank and belly flops.

"That was great," I say when he finishes and the room is once again silent.

"I don't think so," he says. "Please do not give me a compliment I did not earn. Then I worry that you are not honest with me."

"Okay," I say. "Your voice sounded good, but it was a little fast."

"Yeah," he says. "I wanted to finish this song quickly. I wanted it to end."

"Then why did you choose it?"

"Sometimes I come here alone to sing," he says. "I sang this song alone before, but I never paid attention to words. *He's a real nowhere man. Sitting in his nowhere land.* Tonight I realized that this could be me. A nowhere man."

"You are not a nowhere man," I say. "You're here with me."

"Yeah," he says again, placing the microphone in my hand. Our fingers touch briefly before he pulls away. I flip through the catalogue, wishing the songs were listed not just by title, but also cross-referenced by meaning or purpose. There are songs about love in so many mutations and guises, love offered and rejected, accepted and betrayed, remembered and missed and sparking, sparkling, new, but somehow none of them are quite right. I'm about to pick an ABBA song—"Supertrooper," which as far as I can tell means absolutely nothing at all and is therefore totally safe—when I find it. The risky but almost perfect song to say what I haven't been able to say without the cushion of a melody, the aid of a rhyme, the cheat-sheet of someone else's phrasing.

The words, "in the style of Patsy Cline," flash on the screen, where for once the video almost makes sense as a backdrop for the music. A Japanese girl in a Country Western dress and cowboy boots square dances with a Clint Eastwood look-alike.

I fall to pieces. . .

Like Miyoshi-sensei, I sing with my eyes closed. I launch my whole heart into the song, trying to outpace my nerves, to remember what he told me once, that we only forget how to sing when we learn to be afraid.

You want me to act like we've never kissed. . .

Under the table, I feel his knee against mine. I shift slightly, just to make sure he knows that we're touching, that he's not mistaking my leg for the table.

You walk by, and I fall to pieces.

"It's so sad," he says when the song ends.

His knee is still there.

"All of the best songs are sad," I say.

"It's true," he agrees. "Why is this?"

"I think it's because they help us feel things that are hard to feel. It's like you wrote in one of your letters, if you say to someone, 'I'm lonely,' you just sound needy, but if you sing it, you turn it into something beautiful, and you give them a way to share the experience. Then you become less lonely."

"You remembered what I wrote," he says, sounding amazed.

"Of course," I say. "I love your writing."

"I also don't want to be just your friend," he says. "I also don't want to pretend we never kissed." I want to say, "What?" I want to ask him to repeat himself, to make sure I heard him correctly the first time. But instead I stay quiet. "Mari-chan," he says, "how about your friend, the one you lived with before? May I ask what happened?"

"She moved back to New York," I say.

"But before, I think you had some kind of . . . special friendship."

"She was my girlfriend." Now he's the one who doesn't speak. It would be easy to offer a partial version of the truth, but I don't want to lie to him about something this important, or anything. "I met her right after my dad killed himself," I say. "I think she brought me back to life. I know that sounds dramatic, but that's what it felt like. I was in shock. I was numb, and she made me feel things again. She made me do things I never would have done on my own, like come to Japan. If not for her, I have no idea where I would be right now, but I wouldn't be here."

"Then I am glad you met her too," he says. "You must be sad that she left."

"Yeah," I say. "I am sad. I loved her. I still love her, and I miss her, but our relationship didn't work. It wasn't right, especially after we moved here."

"Because you are both a woman?"

"I don't think that's why," I say slowly. "I think I can love a woman or a man. I really don't have a type."

"You don't have to pick," he says. "You have so many options."

"I guess it might seem like that," I say, "but love is rare."

"*Sodesune*," he agrees.

"What about you?" I ask, my heart migrating into my throat. "Is there anyone special in your life?"

"Maybe," he says.

"Oh," I say. "Anyone I know?"

"I am private person," he says.

"Of course," I say. "I'm sorry."

"Last fall, when you kissed me, I felt sort of shocked. I was your supervisor, *ne*? To have workplace romance is very . . . frowned over?"

"Frowned upon."

"Frowned upon," he repeats.

"I'm sorry," I say again.

"But now I am not your supervisor. For many reasons, I am happy about this."

"I made a lot of extra work for you."

"Yeah," he says, leaning closer. "This is one reason."

Under the table, we clamp our legs together to steady their trembling. I lean in too, he shuts his eyes, and the distance between us collapses. Right before we kiss, I wonder what this means, what will happen next, whether I'm making a mistake. Will we have to keep this relationship a secret? Will it become a relationship? Will people disapprove?

Then I stop thinking.

I stop thinking and just give in.

It is the lot of the dead to wander.

These words come from a guidebook entry on O-Bon, the Japanese festival of the dead. Next to New Year, O-Bon is the most important holiday in Japan. At O-Bon people return to their *furusato*, their hometowns, to visit shrines and pay tribute to their departed family members, and to talk with them. Apparently, the dead are wandering all the time. That's their lot. But only at O-Bon does the invisible barrier separating the dead from the living lift. We can't see the spirits, but they can see us, and hear us, and hear our prayers. To celebrate O-Bon, all faculty and students get the week off. But everyone I know, including Hiro, is busy with familial obligations, so I spend most of my time swimming, and reading books my mother still sends in regular care packages.

My mom is seeing someone now: the cabdriver who brought her home with all of the groceries she couldn't carry back from Supermarket Singles' Night. He helped her carry them inside, and then he said that she must be feeding a crowd, and when she admitted that she lived alone and had no idea what to do with all that food, he offered to fix her a meal. She'd bought salmon and potatoes, he could see them in the bag, and he said, "When I look at these ingredients, it makes me want to cook a fish curry for you, the kind that cooks slowly, for a long time over a gentle flame, until the potatoes almost melt in your mouth." And she asked if he meant it, and he said that he did, and within twenty minutes the curry was simmering softly on the stove, while he went out and finished his shift, and by the time he came back later that night it was exactly the way he'd described it.

"Mom," I said, when she told me the story, "was that safe?"

"I guess not," she said, "but it was wonderful. Scary, but wonderful."

I had told her that I wanted her to move on with her life. I know that I want her to be happy. She is a hot-blooded woman with love and affection to spare, who shouldn't have to be alone. Still, it's like Carolyn said. We are moving forward, further into the future, further away from my father, and in some ways this makes me miss him more. Sometimes I yearn for the raw time when his death was still so fresh that I could feel the displacement of the molecules in the air, not yet closed around the space he left behind.

One especially hot morning in the middle of O-Bon, I wake up coated in sweat. The humidity is visible, a brown veil obscuring the horizon. Just like every other day, I walk to the beach wearing my *yukata* over my bathing suit.

I've almost reached the water's edge when I see them, thousands upon thousands of jellyfish, strewn across the wet sand, turning over in the surf, floating in the water near the shore. They are not clear, unlike other jellyfish I've seen. They are blue, bluer than the sea itself. Hiro warned me that they would come—no, that they would *return*—on this very day, but somehow this makes the sight even more stunning.

I can't go swimming today. I can't float on my back, lose myself in the sea, allow the waves to push and pull me where they will. The jellyfish have returned, and they are getting in my way. My father was deeply cynical about anything spiritual. He believed that people find signs because they want to find them, see ghosts because they want to see them. He always said this dismissively, as if believers were a little dim-witted, to be pitied in their faith. But he also had a wicked sense of humor. "Is this your idea of a joke?" I ask, not expecting a reply. It may be the lot of the dead to wander, but what about the living? What's our lot? I stare at the jellyfish, borne in and out by the current, tossed onto the sand and picked up, again and again.

I tie the sash around my *yukata* and walk back home, rummaging through the storage area and finding the box with my mom's hand-writing on the label. Then I return to the sea and walk straight into the water, up to my knees in the lapping waves, not caring if my *yukata* gets wet or if a jellyfish brushes against me as I turn the baggie upside down. The ashes fall like mist, melting in the humidity, clinging to my fingers, dispersing across the water, and salting the blue forms. The jellyfish have no mouths that I can see, no faces at all. They are halfway between liquid and solid, earth and sea, above and below.

As I scatter the ashes in the waves, I don't say good-bye. Even if the barrier separating the dead from the living has lifted and he can hear me, I don't want to say a word that suggests separation or worse—closure. It's bad luck. Besides, this grief isn't over. It has barely begun. I squat and hold the baggie in the sea, watching it expand and fill with water like a little lung, watching the water clean the last dust from its clear plastic sides until it is empty. I wade into the water still wearing my *yukata*, float on my back and look up at the big gray sky, waiting to be stung. But all I can feel is the wet cotton billowing around me, holding me up when it should be pulling me down, maybe even protecting me.

ACKNOWLEDGMENTS

I would like to thank my writing teachers, beginning with my mother; Bob Bumstead; the incomparable Timea Szell; and Michael Cunningham. At Iowa, it was an honor to learn from Marilynne Robinson and Frank Conroy. Thanks to the wonderful John l'Heureux, Tobias Wolff, Elizabeth Tallent, Eavan Boland, and Mary Popek, for countless forms of support. A huge debt of gratitude to the Truman Capote fellowship and the James Michener/Copernicus award. Thank you to Meghan Quinn for more than I can list, and to Hiroshi Nishita and Chikako Ishida, who shared so much about Japan.

Thank you to readers and friends Sarah Braunstein, Robin Ekiss, Matthew Irbarne, Kaui Hart-Hemmings, Chelsey Johnson, Thisbe Nissen, Cathy Park-Hong, Eric Puchner, Curtis Sittenfeld, Nick Syrett, and Shannon Welch. A very big thanks for the special help from Sara Michas-Martin, Katharine Noel, Glori Simmons, Stephanie Reents, and Ghita Schwarz. And to Jeff O'Keefe, for the title.

Thank you to my amazing agent, Lisa Bankoff, and to the editor of my dreams, Jeanette Perez, who helped me to envision and create a better book.

Thanks to my family for your love, guidance, and enthusiasm: Merrill and Willis Watrous, Barbara and Ellen Watrous, Mary Ann and George Kalb, Deborah Johnson, Ward Schumaker, and Vivienne Flesher. And a big thanks to the littlest member, Max Watrous-Schumaker, already a creative force and inspiration.

And finally to Matt Schumaker, my best reader, my best friend, my love.

About the author

2 A Conversation with Malena Watrous

About the book

5 Malena Watrous:
Alien Encounters of the Closest Kind

Read on

13 Author's Picks: Favorite Books
Set in Japan (plus one movie)

Insights,
Interviews
& More...

A Conversation with Malena Watrous

Let's start simple—where are you from?

I was born in San Francisco, and my family moved to Eugene, Oregon, when I was in eighth grade. I went to college at Barnard, in New York, and to the University of Iowa Writers' Workshop. I returned to San Francisco six years ago.

When did you start writing?

In elementary school, my friend and I coauthored a fifty-page "novel" about her father's childhood exodus on foot from Ethiopia to Kenya. It involved a lot of wild animal encounters, illustrated in color. I also tried to write about my great-grandmother's childhood. She emigrated from Norway to Minnesota. When her father slipped under a horse's hooves and died, she ended up an indentured servant. I was drawn to tragic stories of orphans.

> ❝ This was the first love story that got under my skin, and it still does. ❞

Do you remember the first book you fell in love with and why it affected you so strongly?

It was definitely *Jane Eyre*. Another tragic orphan story. Jane has such a strong and honest voice. She's lonely and passionate, self-aware and bookish, prickly but sympathetic. And I like the brooding Rochester too, stuck with his crazy wife in the attic. He sees and loves Jane for who she is, and vice versa. This was the first love story that got under my skin, and it still does.

Who are some of your writing influences?

I get inspired by what I'm reading all the time, but I try not to stick to any particular influence, for fear of being imitative.

When you're writing, do you have an audience in mind? Are you writing for someone in particular?

Not exactly, although sometimes when I am having trouble figuring out how to tell a story, or if my voice feels muffled, I will imagine my friend Nick reading it. We've known each other since college, and not only is he a total laugh slut—he laughs so easily, it's wonderful—we also have overlapping taste in fiction. If I can write something that he would want to read, then I'm happy.

How much does your background, whether it be the city you grew up in, your family, your experiences, make its way into your writing?

I'm like a magpie. I collect bits and pieces from my present and past and tuck them into fiction. When I'm writing steadily, I feel like my powers of perception are heightened. That said, the stories are invented. Real life—mine, at least—doesn't have much plot.

You teach creative writing to students of all ages. Are there any lessons you think are essential for up-and-coming authors? ▶

66 I'm like a magpie. I collect bits and pieces from my present and past and tuck them into fiction. 99

A Conversation with Malena Watrous
(continued)

The best piece of writing advice I ever got was to try and write the book that you want to read, the one you wish was on your bookshelf. It sounds simple but it's hard. I also think that there is always room for fiction writers to break new ground by trying to describe the present—always changing—moment. My favorite authors, from Edith Wharton to Flannery O'Connor, all wrote from their particular place and time. You get to define the moment you're living in, and it's always changing so there's always new ground to cover.

After spending some time in Japan, did the language difference, or Japanese in general, affect your writing at all?

Definitely. I love the playfulness of Japanese, in particular *katakana*, the special alphabet used to colonize foreign words, and the ways that Japanese English borrows and misuses certain terms like, "Let's . . ." Let's English! Let's donut! More generally, as I wrote this novel, I both enjoyed and was frustrated by the limitations the characters faced in communicating. This is something I also experienced when I lived in Japan. How do you communicate deeply, sincerely, with humor or passion, when you have a limited number of overlapping words?

Do you feel there are differences in the way the Japanese regard novelists versus Americans?

I was surprised that the Japanese novels that I read in translation didn't seem as popular there. Not that many people that I spoke with had heard of Haruki Murakami, for instance. I was surprised by how many adults read manga, a lot of which is really graphic. Businessmen in suits would seem utterly unabashed to be reading pornographic comic books on the subway.

66 The best piece of writing advice I ever got was to try and write the book that you want to read, the one you wish was on your bookshelf. 99

4

Malena Watrous
Alien Encounters of the Closest Kind

THE DAY I RECEIVED my placement letter from the Japanese Ministry of Education, I looked up Shika in a guidebook. I was twenty-two years old, at loose ends working a string of odd jobs in New York, so I'd decided to apply to the JET program, which sends five thousand foreigners per year to teach English in every corner of Japan. Unfortunately, Shika was unlisted, and my guidebook dismissed the Noto Peninsula as one of the most remote regions of mainland Japan, a place with no sights of real interest and not worth visiting by tourists.

This did not turn out to be true. There is a lot to see and do in the area, especially for those with a taste for unusual entertainment. Sure you can go to Kyoto and do the textbook temple tour, followed by a prepackaged performance of Noh, Kabuki, and Bunraku theater, all condensed to an hour to fit the Western attention span. But if you want to see something different, but equally Japanese, here is my list of the best, you've-got-to-see-it-to-believe-it tourist destinations in and around the Noto Peninsula, none of which made my guidebook's cut.

It's generally accepted that truth is stranger than fiction, and in rural Japan this is certainly the case. Japan, a nation known for its uniformity, is also a mecca of weirdness, proof that the pressure to conform breeds eccentrics. Some like to contain their eccentricities within museums. Lucky for you, this means that for a nominal fee, you can gawk at your leisure. And since Japan is the size of California, you can get to the Noto Peninsula from Tokyo on an overnight bus, waking up by the Sea of Japan as an attendant hands you a moist towelette.

Arisu-kan

When I asked my new supervisor about the music that kept waking me up every morning, ▶

> **It's generally accepted that truth is stranger than fiction, and in rural Japan this is certainly the case. Japan, a nation known for its uniformity, is also a mecca of weirdness, proof that the pressure to conform breeds eccentrics.**

Alien Encounters of the Closest Kind
(continued)

he told me that it was broadcast from Town Hall to test the emergency evacuation system at the power plant. The privilege of choosing the morning tune rotated among the bureaucrats, whose taste ranged from baroque classical to saccharine Japanese pop music. After a few months teaching weekly adult English classes at Town Hall, I could usually guess who had chosen that morning's tune. Shika's treasurer was a big fan of The Carpenters' "Top of the World."

I arrived in Japan in July. The high school was technically on summer break, but teachers had to come to work every day in case students dropped by. None did. I was told that I was very lucky because I only had to sit at my desk from eight to two (instead of four) every day. The other teachers spent their time in the sweltering faculty room smoking cigarettes, playing a board game called Go, and commenting on how hot it was. I'd brought a stack of novels with me from the States, which I finished all too quickly. One day, the history teacher who sat beside me observed, "You are like International Man of Mystery, Austin Powers," he explained, "because you read so much." Apparently reading was mysterious. Then he informed me that Shika's library had an excellent selection of English classics.

I saved my trip to the library for the last Friday before the new semester, looking forward to sinking into a fat classic. Unfortunately, the "excellent selection" consisted of three slim volumes: *Breakfast at Tiffany's*, *The Bridges of Madison County*, and *Alice in Wonderland*. I was standing there, crestfallen, when someone tapped me on the shoulder. A silver-haired man in a business suit and rubber sandals introduced himself as *Kamono-sensei*. He told me that he was a retired teacher and offered to give me a tour of Shika. In New York, I would never have gotten into a car with some strange guy who picked me up at the public library. But this was rural Japan and he seemed harmless enough.

> " After we left the museum, [my guide] took me out for *kare raisu*—white rice drowned in silky yellow curry, topped with thin cutlets of breaded pork. . . . Then he drove me home and I never saw him again, just like the white rabbit who vanished down the hole. "

He drove me to *Arisu-kan*, Shika's *Alice in Wonderland*–themed museum of nuclear power. A 1/25 scale model of the plant functioned as a playground for toddlers, who could crawl around in a cross-section of the reactor pressure vessel. In the Garden of Radiation, kids learned "what happens to the uranium in the case of an earthquake." An English sign read, "Furthermore, don't miss the exhibitions on nuclear power station simulations, ECCS, reactor scrimmages, and others." On a map of Shika, blinking Cheshire cats showed local radiation measuring points. I had no idea what was normal or dangerously high. My guide seemed uneasy when I asked whether there had been any problems at the plant. "A few," he admitted. After we left the museum, he took me out for *kare raisu*—white rice drowned in silky yellow curry, topped with thin cutlets of breaded pork. He insisted on treating. Then he drove me home and I never saw him again, just like the white rabbit who vanished down the hole.

Cosmo Isle

In the summer months, the Noto Peninsula was blisteringly hot. I spent most of my free time at the beach, swimming in the sea and dozing on the second-longest bench in the world, where there was always plenty of space. One day at school, my supervisor took me aside and told me to be sure not to fall asleep while sunbathing, lest I get abducted by aliens. He was a savvy, cosmopolitan guy, a pillar of the community. This was my first indication that he might also be nuts. "North Koreans," he specified, voice dropping as if there might be some in the vicinity, just waiting to chloroform us and smuggle us back to their desolate motherland, which he swore was how they did it.

The line between fact, fiction, and science fiction turns out to be blurry.

North Korea is on the other side of the Sea of Japan, and there have been reports of ▶

> ❝ My supervisor took me aside and told me to be sure not to fall asleep while sunbathing, lest I get abducted by aliens. . . . 'North Koreans,' he specified, voice dropping as if there might be some in the vicinity, just waiting to chloroform us and smuggle us back to their desolate motherland, which he swore was how they did it. ❞

Alien Encounters of the Closest Kind
(continued)

Japanese people abducted from the Noto and brainwashed by their North Korean captors. In addition, the Noto's shores have been used as a dumping ground by human traffickers from China. So the possibility of bumping into an "alien" on those wind-battered beaches was indeed real, even before a woman from Hakui swore under oath that a UFO had beamed up her two missing children one summer afternoon while the family swam in the sea. Most of the people I spoke with expressed doubt over her testimony, followed by, "But you never know . . . it *is* Hakui."

Hakui, a town ten miles south of Shika, has a reputation as UFO central—Japan's own Roswell, New Mexico—and local businesses capitalize upon the town's reputation. It boasts a love hotel with pods in lieu of beds, a bathhouse with UFO-shaped tubs, a ramen restaurant where each object in the bowl of noodle soup is supposed to replicate part of the alien abduction experience, and a museum called Cosmo Isle, complete with a landing strip for alien spacecrafts.

Cosmo Isle contains a few legitimate exhibits on outer space. NASA provided a lunar module and a real spacesuit. Also displayed is the spacesuit that Tom Hanks wore in *Apollo 13*. But most people come to see documentation of human encounters with extraterrestrials. "Photographs" of almond-eyed aliens cover the walls, as well as shots of mysteriously dented crops, and of the survivors of alien abductions— the folks left behind after their loved ones were beamed up by UFOs.

I never ran into any aliens on the beaches of the Noto—not the spectral variety in any case. But I made a trip to Hakui's annual sand castle competition (the towering medieval edifices would have been more impressive had cement not been allowed in their construction), that also featured a beauty contest, where another foreign English teacher—a big-breasted blonde in a bikini—was crowned that year's queen, her satin banner decorated with UFOs.

Hanibe Gankutsuin

The title for weirdest museum in the prefecture has got to go to *Hanibe Gankutsuin*, the Museum of Hell, located outside Komatsu, at the foot of the peninsula. A sculptor-turned-priest (and leader of a sect that suggests there might be such a thing as a "fundamentalist Buddhist") molded the exhibits from the local red clay, beginning with the giant Buddha head that towers over the parking lot. Apparently the body will follow, though the priest hasn't made much progress since he started filling the caves with dioramas of demons tormenting sinners, the statues built slightly larger-than-life but otherwise as realistic as mannequins.

I was first brought to *Hanibe Gankutsuin* by my friend Chikako, a junior high school secretary who would shout, "Huge size!" whenever I entered the faculty room. This might have been offensive, but she always followed it with, "Same size!" She was probably five-ten at the most, about the same height as me, but when we walked down the hall side by side, both students and teachers would stop and exclaim, "*Takai!*" or "So big!" in awed tones, as if witnessing a real-life freak show. Chikako brought me to a store that carried "our size" clothes, baggy pastel tracksuits and voluminous T-shirts that said "blackface" and "bling-a-ling." After our shopping expedition, she made a surprise stop at the Museum of Hell. "You won't believe," she said as we climbed down a flight of stairs into the flickering caves.

Taking in the hellacious exhibits, I often couldn't tell what the sinner's crime was, or how the punishment fit it. A man with a penis as big as a log sat with his tiny hands pressed to either side of it, looking dopey. Was he guilty of excessive masturbation? Was his huge cock a punishment? A gray-haired *sarariiman* ▶

> **❝** [Chikako] was probably five-ten at the most, about the same height as me, but when we walked down the hall side by side, both students and teachers would stop and exclaim, '*Takai!*' or 'So big!' in awed tones, as if witnessing a real-life freak show. **❞**

Alien Encounters of the Closest Kind
(continued)

(salaryman) chased a girl in a junior high school sailor uniform, his tongue dangling halfway down his necktie. I assumed he was the pervert, only to find her featured in the next cave, stuffed into a giant mortar, a demon pulverizing her tantalizing (and now bloody) legs.

Some of the dioramas featured statues of real people—people still alive but obviously destined for hell—like tabloid queen Masami Hayashi, the infamous *kare onna*, or "curry lady," who poisoned the curry she brought to a neighborhood potluck and killed a half-dozen people. Hayashi enraged the nation when she refused to explain why she did it, but everyone knew that her neighbors picked on her for not doing her share of chores, and for breaking *gomi* rules. Her actions were truly monstrous. Still, I understand how the *gomi* police could push a woman to extremes.

In Shika, the list of *gomi* separation rules was truly epic. Electronic goods were especially hard to dispose of, even though many people took pride in having the newest models and replaced them often. It cost a lot of money to get rid of a car. I should know, since I crashed three, proving that temporary people probably shouldn't drive in Japan. I wouldn't have been astonished to find a statue of myself, perhaps crammed into a garbage can, at the Museum of Hell. I said so to Chikako, who laughed, having heard of my *gomi* infractions. She told me to stand next to the statue of the "curry lady" for a photo. As I did, I noticed that we were exactly the same height.

Mawaki Onsen (and others)

Being naked in public felt weird the first few times. But I quickly became addicted to the Japanese baths, especially the *onsens*, or natural hotsprings, and shed my inhibitions along with my clothes. There are baths all over Japan, from the dazzling facilities at luxury hotels like the one where the entire faculty of Shika High School spent the night (attendance mandatory) over New Year's, to the humble establishments in every neighborhood with signs depicting three plumes of steam. While I tried to sample as many as I could, as often as possible, my favorite bathhouse was undoubtedly *Mawaki Onsen*, located near the town of Wajima at the tip of the peninsula.

While the entrance fee at that time was just 300 yen, less than a convenience store sandwich, the natural setting rivaled the luxury of any hotel. Crown Princess Masako visited Mawaki Onsen on a trip to the Noto, and even though her fertility was the subject of endless media speculation at the time, she looks almost relaxed in the picture framed on the lobby wall.

Perched on the cliffs over the sea, dozens of *rotemburo*, or outdoor tubs, overflow down the jagged rocks, trickling into the raging surf below. On one side of the facility, divided by a high bamboo wall, are tubs made of a velvety cedar that leaves a lingering perfume on your skin. On the other side, the tubs are lined with smooth river rocks. The sides flip weekly between the sexes, and I could never decide which was my favorite. The bathhouse stays open until late at night, which is by far the best time to go, especially when it's snowing. Nothing beats being naked in a blizzard, your body scalding while snow catches in your lashes and melts on your tongue.

The Noto Peninsula borders "Snow Country," and it snows almost continuously from November through May. My friend Chikako taught me how to snowboard at a small resort where they blasted hip-hop onto the slopes, which I attempted to translate through crude gestures. Despite our linguistic limitations, Chikako and I soon recognized that we shared an irreverent sense of humor and that we both liked taking risks. When she informed me that on Wednesdays lift tickets at the ski resort were free for women, I introduced her to the concept of ▶

Alien Encounters of the Closest Kind
(continued)

the "sick day." I'll never forget picking up the phone one Wednesday morning to hear Chikako say, "I don't feel so good, and you?"

After a long day of surreptitious snowboarding, we enjoyed a blissful soak at *Mawaki Onsen*. Following the bath we got *akasuri*, a form of Korean exfoliation that takes place in a steamy back room where women in black bras and underwear rub you down from head to toe with scouring pads. If this sounds remotely sexy, it's not. Within minutes, your skin sloughs off in grimy piles, revealing a painfully raw undercoat. But it was fun to lie on a gurney alongside Chikako, two naked pink giants, sharing a joke that needed no translation.

The bathroom of the house that I rented in Japan was extremely unappealing. Mushrooms actually sprouted in the grout. So I usually bathed at the end of the block, at a public bathhouse that had one tub for men and one for women. Divided only by a cloth partition, you could hear chatting from the other side. In the evening, people would walk over from their houses wearing pajamas and carrying plastic tubs of shampoo and razors and soap, and towels slung over their shoulders. While my neighbors and I didn't always coexist in perfect harmony, I loved participating in this local ritual, sitting at the wall of showers alongside grandmothers giving each other shoulder rubs and mothers scrubbing down their children before bed. I felt accepted, unexceptional in my nudity. Stripped down, we're all sort of funny-looking and gorgeous, lumpy and perfect, more alike than alien. ❧

> ❝ I felt accepted, unexceptional in my nudity. Stripped down, we're all sort of funny-looking and gorgeous, lumpy and perfect, more alike than alien. ❞

Author's Picks: Favorite Books Set in Japan (plus one movie)

Out, by Natsuo Kirino

It's ridiculously hard to throw away anything unusual in Japan without attracting attention. When a woman who works the graveyard shift at a *bento* box lunch plant kills her abusive husband, she enlists the help of three female coworkers to dispose of the body. The ladies almost get away with it. This noir thriller is fascinating for its depiction of the lives of working-class women in contemporary Japan and their uneasy friendships.

The Elephant Vanishes and *Norwegian Wood,* by Haruki Murakami

Haruki Murakami never gives lengthy setting descriptions, yet Japan is clearly both backdrop and subject of his fiction. His story collection, *The Elephant Vanishes*, includes "Sleep," about a housewife who suddenly doesn't need any. At first it seems like a gift—she stays up all night reading novels—but she soon becomes robotic and disaffected. Murakami always blurs the line between the real and imagined. His novel, *Norwegian Wood*, is a moving coming-of-age story set in Tokyo at the end of the sixties. The plot is plausible, but it definitely shares the same uncanny sensibility.

Fear and Trembling and *Tokyo Fiancée,* by Amelie Nothomb

The Belgian author Amelie Nothomb spent her early childhood in Japan, then returned as a young woman. These experiences inspired several short novels. In *Fear and Trembling*, Amelie goes to work as a corporate translator in Tokyo and enters an almost sadomasochistic relationship with her female supervisor, who demotes her to bathroom janitor to humiliate her. It's an interesting window into Japanese office life and a fresh take on DeSade. The more recent *Tokyo* ▶

13

Fiancée describes a perfect yet doomed romantic relationship between Amelie and a young Japanese man.

My Year of Meats, by Ruth Ozeki

The narrator of this hilarious novel is a purple-haired, six-foot-tall Japanese American woman who works for a Japanese reality TV show sponsored by the American beef export lobby. Disgusted to discover the corruption and greed at the heart of the meat industry, she starts filming exposés instead of puff pieces. The book also follows a repressed Japanese housewife moved by the show to transform her life. Ozeki used to work on Japanese reality shows funded by corporate sponsors like Phillip Morris. She has unique insight into Japanese culture, as well as how it feels as an artist to sell out.

The Pillow Book of Lady Sei Shonagon, by Sei Shonagon

Sei Shonagon was a court lady in tenth-century Japan who allegedly received a bunch of notebooks from the empress, which she used to jot down reflections, observations, and lists. Her insights still ring true one thousand years later. Things that give an unclean feeling: the inside of a cat's ear. Annoying things: thinking of something to add to a letter after having sent it. Embarrassing things: parents cooing over an ugly child. Pleasing things: finding a large number of tales one has not read before or acquiring the second volume of a tale whose first volume one has enjoyed.

The Pearl Diver, by Jeff Talarigo

When a cut on a pearl diver's hand fails to heal, she is diagnosed with leprosy and—in keeping with the Japanese laws of the time—her name is expunged from her family registry and she is banished to an island leprosarium. This novel about being shunned manages to be tragic but not grim. Despite her constricted circumstances, the pearl diver finds beauty and creates

66 Sei Shonagon was a court lady in tenth-century Japan who allegedly received a bunch of notebooks from the empress, which she used to jot down reflections, observations, and lists. Her insights still ring true one thousand years later. 99

meaningful relationships. In spare and lovely prose, Talarigo draws a chilling parallel to the treatment in Japan of AIDS patients.

Naomi, by Junichiro Tanizaki

This is Japan's *Lolita*, at least in its setup. A man in his thirties can't stop thinking about a fifteen-year-old girl from a lower socioeconomic class. Motivated by a love of all things "modern" and Western, he persuades her to move in with him in an unconventional arrangement where she will not be subservient in any way. Like Lolita, young Naomi has depths, life experience, and powers of manipulation beyond what her older lover imagines.

Tokyo: A Certain Style, text and photographs by Kyoichi Tsuzuki

The documentary photographer Kyoichi Tsuzuki wanted to document the way people really live in one of the most magical and congested cities on earth. So he got the keys to the apartments of Tokyo-ites from all walks of life and paid surprise visits to photograph the clutter crammed into tiny spaces. Flipping through this book satisfies my curiosity to see into people's private lives, and makes me feel better about my own messiness.

Kitchen, by Banana Yoshimito

The main character in this strange and sweet novel is a young girl who is all alone in the world until she meets a boy who works at a flower shop and happens to have a transsexual father. Like Murakami, Yoshimoto writes fables set in the here and now.

After Life, a movie directed by Hirokazu Koreeda

Anyone with an interest in Japan is bound to fall in love with this moving, melancholy movie. It opens on a group of people of different ages shuffling into a facility that looks like a Japanese public school. These people have recently died, and they now have one week to choose a single ▶

Author's Picks *(continued)*

"best memory" from their lives, which the staff at this facility will then recreate on film (using B-movie props like cotton puff clouds) for them to reenter for eternity. *After Life* is poignantly understated. No one rails against death, even as they quietly grieve what they've lost. There are rules even in the afterlife, and for the most part even the dead obey them. ∾

Don't miss the next book by your favorite author. Sign up now for AuthorTracker by visiting www.AuthorTracker.com.